T0281972

"Just brilliant!"
—LISA JEWELL

"This has to be a strong contender for crime debut of the year—sharp, perceptive writing and a brilliant new take on the detective duo."
—T. M. LOGAN

"Everything you could hope for in a thriller: heartbreaking, intelligent, deftly plotted, and so original."
—FIONA CUMMINS

"Jo Callaghan makes her entry into the crowded police-procedural genre with a fresh take on the buddy-buddy cop trope. . . . Provocative and compelling."
—VASEEM KHAN

"Brilliant book, total page-turner."
—CERYS MATTHEWS, as featured on BBC 2's *Between the Covers*

"I loved it."
—ANGELA SCANLON, as featured on BBC 2's *Between the Covers*

"One of the most original crime fiction partnerships I have ever read. *In the Blink of an Eye* explores the potential future of technology with an in-depth, unforgettable look at grief and humanity, and how, surprisingly, one can aid the other. A breathtaking debut that will have you eagerly awaiting the next installment in what is set to be a beloved series."
—JACK JORDAN

"Fresh, innovative, and very, very clever. Flawlessly paced, plotted, and researched, it's laugh out loud, heart-achingly sad, and doesn't have a dull moment. I raced through it. Simply sensational." —M. W. CRAVEN

"Daring and original, heartbreaking and heart-stopping, this study of what it means to be human is destined to not only be a big success, but a classic crime novel of our times. Loved it." —CAZ FREAR

"A standout debut with a unique and thrilling take on the detective novel. Engaging, exciting, and superbly readable. I loved it."

—SARAH HILARY

"A truly original premise that is both compelling and filled with heart. Highly recommended." —OLIVIA KIERNAN

"Clever and compelling, it offers a new take on the police procedural while also examining what it means to be human and the personal cost of loss." —BRIAN MCGILLOWAY

"Intuitive DCS Frank and logical AI Lock are the perfect pairing. Alongside some wonderfully surreal tech is an investigation grounded in the grittily real. Jo Callaghan explores what makes us human: our flaws and errors, our loves and losses, and sometimes our refusal to stop asking questions. Even at its most terrifying, this is a story told with heart and soul." —JESS KIDD

"Completely different and utterly brilliant." —AMANDA REYNOLDS

"So good. A really clever twist on the police procedural that asks big questions about instinct, bias, and what it means to be human while also delivering a cracker of a plot. Loved it." —PHOEBE LOCKE

"It's phenomenal. . . . Perfect blend of police procedural and techno thriller that kept me guessing right to the end!" —STEPH BROADRIBB

"An incredible book. So original, gripping, and wonderfully written. I raced through it." —KAREN HAMILTON

"The revelation of the full villainy involved in the two men's disappearance is intriguing, but it is Kat—her personality, her relationship with her young son, and her experience of loss—that really lifts this novel."

—*Literary Review*

"With well-drawn characters, believable emotions, and an interesting premise, you can see this becoming a TV series." —*Independent*

"This is worth every minute you dedicate to reading."

—*Belfast Telegraph*

"Original and compelling." —*Fabulous*

By Jo Callaghan

Leave No Trace
In the Blink of an Eye

LEAVE
NO
TRACE

LEAVE NO TRACE

A NOVEL

JO CALLAGHAN

RANDOM HOUSE | NEW YORK

A Random House Trade Paperback Original

Published in the United States by Random House, an imprint and division of Penguin Random House LLC, New York.

RANDOM HOUSE and the HOUSE colophon are registered trademarks of Penguin Random House LLC.

Originally published in the United Kingdom by Simon and Schuster UK in 2024

Epigraph from *La police et les méthodes scientifiques* by Edmond Locard reproduced with permission from Humensis.

LIBRARY OF CONGRESS CATALOGING-IN-PUBLICATION DATA
Names: Callaghan, Jo (Strategist) author.
Title: Leave no trace: a novel / Jo Callaghan.
Description: New York, NY: Random House, 2025.
Identifiers: LCCN 2024034118 (print) | LCCN 2024034119 (ebook) |
ISBN 9780593736852 (trade paperback; acid-free paper) |
ISBN 9780593736869 (ebook)
Subjects: LCGFT: Detective and mystery fiction. | Science fiction. | Novels.
Classification: LCC PR6103.A446 L43 2025 (print) |
LCC PR6103.A446 (ebook) | DDC 823/.92—dc23/eng/20240724
LC record available at https://lccn.loc.gov/2024034118
LC ebook record available at https://lccn.loc.gov/2024034119

Printed in the United States of America on acid-free paper

randomhousebooks.com

1st Printing

Book design by Simon M. Sullivan

For Conor and Aurora

'Any action of an individual, and obviously, the violent actions of a crime, cannot occur without leaving a trace.'

DR. EDMOND LOCARD,
La police et les méthodes scientifiques

LEAVE
NO
TRACE

———————

He doesn't turn to check that he's not alone. He doesn't cross the street to where there are more houses, more lights. He doesn't even pretend to ring someone or hold his umbrella like a truncheon. He just walks through the night: through the absence of fear.

He doesn't see me watching.

He stops at his front door, fumbling for the key he hasn't gripped all the way home. He enters the hallway, not even glancing over his shoulder as he kicks the door shut.

Imagine feeling that safe.

Imagine being that stupid.

A dull yellow light splashes from his bay window, staining the frost-white drive. That's him in the front room now, not caring to close the blinds against the dark of night and threat of snow. He stands in front of a pale-grey settee and points a remote at a large screen above the fireplace. Flickering pictures fill the room.

I bunch my frozen fists, and through the wooden shutters I spy the sleek, luxurious furniture, the high Georgian ceilings and framed paintings lining the walls. How did someone like him end up in a lovely home like that? I force out a breath so long and hard that for a moment I imagine disappearing in a puff of ice-white smoke.

It clears in seconds. And yet still I am here: alone in the cold, dark street.

The dead chill of night presses through my trainers, draining the heat from my body. I shift my weight from one freezing foot to the other. It's not too late to walk away.

I almost do.

But then snow begins to fall, ghostly white in the dark of night.

Memories flash through me: my face distorted in a glittered bauble, the thud of distant music; snow against snow.

Blood beats fast through what's left of my heart as I lift my face to the sky. A snowflake lands in my eye and I embrace its icy sting. I will no longer be haunted by the Ghosts of Christmas Past. I am here to reclaim my future.

I turn back towards the window, where he sucks at a bottle of beer, legs spread as he stares at the TV, oblivious to the darkness beyond.

I tuck my thumbs under my shoulder straps, feeling the weight of my rucksack and all that it contains.

Tonight, he will learn about fear.

CHAPTER ONE

'I'm going to count to ten,' DCS Kat Frank warned. 'And then I'm coming up.' She pointed her torch at the wooden hatch above her, highlighting the broken wisps of cobwebs swaying in the chill morning air.

Silence.

Kat started counting in a clear, no-nonsense voice that she hoped didn't betray her fear. When she reached ten, she took a deep breath and placed a hand upon the cold metal stepladder. 'I'm coming up,' she said, climbing higher and higher until the hatch to the attic was within reach.

Moving the torch to her left hand, she used her right to push against the wooden door and slide it across the opening. She flinched, bracing herself against something unspeakable. But there was nothing save the cold, musty smell of forgotten places and abandoned things. Kat pointed her torch into the gaping darkness and climbed the final two steps until her head and shoulders were in the attic.

She rapidly scanned the low-ceilinged room, hyper-alert to signs of attack. She swept the floor for scuttling spiders and the beams for any bats, shivering at the horror of the dark, shadowy corners in between. 'So, the deal is, you keep the fuck out of my way,' she shouted. 'This is hard enough as it is, so I don't need any of your spider shit right now.' She swung the torch rapidly across the roof, wishing she'd worn a hat. If a spider fell on her head, she would seriously lose it.

But the attic was still and quiet.

Breathing a little easier, Kat focused her torch on the piles and piles of boxes and bags that littered the attic floor. Christ, what a mess. When they'd first moved in, she'd helped pass all the old stuff from their last house up to John on the ladder, directing him to put things where they could easily find them again. But as their growing son and expanding careers took up more and more of their time, it had been quicker for John to just throw up a bin bag of Cam's old clothes or pop a box of discarded toys or books near the entrance, with a promise to sort it all out later.

But for John, there was no 'later'. And if there had once been a system to this chaos, then it was lost to her now. Kat sighed. How the hell was she supposed to find the Christmas decorations among all of *this*? She pointed the torch into the far right-hand corner, where things still looked relatively organised. There was something lemon-and-pine-coloured, wrapped carefully in clear sheets of plastic.

Oh my God. Cam's Moses basket!

Instinctively she turned, but of course, there was no one else to share the recognition with. In fact, there was not a single other person alive who'd remember how she and John had agonised over which basket to buy, spending much more than they could afford, only for Cam to refuse to sleep anywhere but in their arms.

She blinked away the shot of self-pity and firmly moved the torch away from Cam's baby bath, his cot bed and the bag of his first clothes. She couldn't deal with them now. She was just here for the Christmas decorations. Logic told her that they shouldn't be too far from the entrance, but then logic hadn't been John's strong point. 'Where would you have put them?' she muttered.

She spotted a large plastic box on her left that looked familiar and leaned over to drag it closer. The box moved, and a sudden flutter of tiny black wings exploded in her face.

Kat screamed. She leapt back, nearly losing her footing as she half-scrambled, half-fell down the stepladder, dropping the torch as she beat at her clothes and hair to get them off.

Panting, she stared at the landing floor, littered with tiny black things. She leaned closer. Poked one with her finger. Plastic. The 'wings' were just tiny pieces of shredded black plastic. Kat frowned. All those bin bags they'd thrown up there over the years must have disintegrated and fallen apart. She slid to the floor, her movement causing the scattered pieces to float up around her like confetti. With her elbows on her knees, she plunged her hands into her hair. Jesus, what had she become? A perimenopausal insomniac who decides to get the Christmas decorations out of the attic at the crack of dawn; someone who talks to spiders and is terrified by a bloody bin bag.

She cursed her husband. *Why* hadn't John sorted the attic out? *Why* had he put things into black bin bags, for God's sake? *Why* hadn't he ever got round to putting a proper frigging light in the attic?

Kat buried her face in her hands, on the verge of sobbing. *Why* did he have to die?

She jumped as her phone alarm went off: 6.15am. Time to get ready for work and pretend she was a completely normal, functioning human being. She clicked on her calendar, to remind herself what time she was due in. Shit. It was her quarterly review with her boss McLeish today. Kat scrubbed her face with her hands. She knew she was on the edge. She could feel the sinkhole beside her, the pulling gravity of grief. And with Cam away at university, there was so little left to hold on to.

She rose to her feet, brushing off the last bits of plastic that still clung to her pyjamas, mind sharpening with every second. She had to convince McLeish to give her a live case today.

She needed something solid to grasp on to or she would sink without a trace.

CHAPTER TWO

DCS Kat Frank knew better than to produce a written report or—God forbid—a PowerPoint presentation for the first quarterly review of the Future Policing Unit that she led. Instead, she sat at the table in Chief Constable McLeish's office and talked him through the cold cases they'd solved since the pilot in the summer, holding his limited attention with the human stories behind the stats: the 26-year-old secretary they'd found under her boss's holiday-home patio; the 35-year-old dad they'd recovered from the bottom of a canal; and—most upsetting of all—the 15-year-old girl they'd finally found among the rubble and debris of an abandoned squat.

McLeish prodded her with questions, and Kat answered without hesitation or the need to check her notes. Each depressing detail was seared upon her brain. Especially the girl. She was there every time she failed to get to sleep.

Eventually her boss leaned back in his chair and folded his hands across his large stomach. 'Three out of three. Not a bad success rate, I'll give you that.'

'You appear to have miscalculated,' said AIDE Lock, her AI partner.

McLeish frowned at the 3D holographic image of a young Black man occupying the seat between Kat and its creator, Professor Okonedo. Lock was disturbingly lifelike, but Kat knew it wasn't the realistic creases in the grey suit that made it so unsettling, nor the perfectly manicured moustache, the short, groomed beard or Hollywood-level good looks. Although it was nothing more than an intersection of light and matter, with skilful coding to represent the AI Deep Learning programme, there was something about the fluid, graceful way it moved: the way those dark eyes sometimes seemed to look at you with the innocence of a child.

And, like a child, it hadn't yet learned that when someone like McLeish said, 'I beg your pardon?' this was not an invitation to repeat the offending comment.

Despite her warning cough, Lock continued to speak. 'I said you miscalculated. Three out of three is a hundred per cent, which means that DCS Frank's success rate is, in fact, excellent, considering the average number of cold cases solved in England is now less than fifty per cent.'

Kat stifled a groan. Which bit of 'leave the talking to me' did Lock not understand? Despite agreeing to host the FPU and encouraging her to lead it, McLeish was still hostile to Artificially Intelligent Detecting Entities, afraid they'd become a Trojan horse for yet more cuts to police numbers. At first, Kat had shared his scepticism—her late husband's cancer had been misdiagnosed by AI, so she knew more than most about the dangers of machine-led decision-making. But when she feared that her own son had become a victim in the case they were investigating over the summer, not one single other person had believed her: they'd assumed her emotions were clouding her judgement. Lock was the only one who'd agreed that the facts supported her hypothesis and had overridden its own protocols to help save her son. Kat still had reservations about the role of AI in policing, but although Lock's algorithm-led approach could often be exasperating, she would never, ever forget how Lock alone had stood by her when she'd needed help the most.

'Anyway,' Kat said, drawing McLeish's face back to her. 'The fact is that in cold cases "success" just means we can close the files, improve our clear-up rate and provide the families with answers. What we can't do is change the actual outcome.'

'Meaning?'

'Meaning I think it's time we worked a live case.'

'Oh, you think so, do you?' McLeish's voice was soft, but his eyes held a warning.

'Yes, I do.' Twenty years ago, she might have wavered under his unblinking glare, but since her husband died last year, the worst thing she could possibly imagine had already happened. She'd always been brave (or reckless depending upon your point of view), but now she feared nothing and no one. 'DI Hassan and DS Browne have really honed their policing skills, and for all its flaws,' she said, raising a hand to acknowledge the myriad ways in which the AI was flawed, 'the speed and depth with which Lock can analyse CCTV, social media and other data makes us one of the fastest and most effective teams I've ever worked with. It seems a waste not to deploy a team of our calibre on actual live cases where we'd still have a chance of saving someone.'

'Or risk losing them because of Robocop here.'

Lock raised a pyramid of both hands to its chin and sighed in a way that suggested disappointment. 'That comment is based upon your own irrational fears and misunderstanding of AI rather than a risk-based assessment of the facts.'

'I *beg* your pardon?'

'I said—'

'I heard what you said.'

'Lock has no filter, sir,' Kat reminded him as her boss's face started to flush a deep red. Honestly, she'd kick Lock under the table if it wasn't for the fact that her foot would go right through it. She glanced at its creator, Professor Okonedo, for back-up.

She was a professor at the National institute for AI Research—NiAIR—and despite (or rather because of) her distrust in traditional policing had agreed to pilot the use of AIDE Lock as a member of Kat's team.

'Yes,' the young professor agreed. 'Lock is not trying to be rude. It has been programmed not to defer to power. It is just speaking the truth as it sees it.'

'And my wife's new puppy thinks the front room is a toilet, but that doesn't mean I'm going to put up with it shitting on my carpet.' McLeish jerked his head towards the door. 'That thing is supposed to be capable of Deep Learning, so come back once it's learned some manners.'

Professor Okonedo quietly closed her laptop and rose to her feet, but Kat remained seated. To not give a team as effective as hers a live case wasn't just irrational—it was immoral. The thought of having to tell yet another parent that their worst fears had been confirmed made her feel like she was trapped beneath one of those weighted blankets people kept banging on about. But they hadn't seen the things she'd seen. It would take more than a bloody blanket to help her sleep at night.

She decided to give it one more shot. 'The whole point of the FPU is to develop a new model of policing for the future. We can't do that unless we work on some live cases, sir.'

McLeish looked between Kat and the image of Lock sitting at his table. 'It's too risky.'

'All science involves risks,' said Professor Okonedo, a neat little frown marking her otherwise smooth forehead. 'It's how we make progress.'

'This isn't a bloody science project. And there's more than a few Bunsen burners at stake here. Apart from the cases themselves, there's the matter of public confidence and trust in the police force.'

The professor raised her eyebrows. 'Which is currently at an all-time low. The whole *point* of AI detectives is to rebuild public trust and confidence in policing, which, as you know, I believe is too important to be left to humans. Lock has built-in anti-corruption software, is incapable of lying and will bring greater transparency and evidence-based decision-making to the policing process. Lock is the solution, Chief Constable McLeish, not the problem.'

Kat winced as her boss turned a worrying shade of purple. The young scientist might as well have accused his family of being corrupt.

'Sir,' she said, in the most appeasing tone she could muster—which, as a 46-year-old woman, wasn't much. 'I'm a sceptic like you, you know that. But maybe it's time to see if Lock can keep up with a real case in real time, when the facts are few and far between and we have to rely on instinct, judgement and experience?'

McLeish narrowed his eyes as he studied the DCS who he'd once praised as being 'practically fucking psychic'. But before he could speak, his phone rang. He picked it up, listened for a minute, then gestured for Kat and Professor Okonedo to leave the room.

———

'Well done, Lock,' said Kat as soon as they were the other side of McLeish's door. 'Have you been reading *How to Win Friends and Influence People* again?'

'No. Should I?' Lock studied her face and then glanced at Professor Okonedo. 'Oh. Is that a joke?'

Kat shook her head. 'The aim of that meeting was to persuade McLeish to give us some live cases. You just made it ten times harder.'

'I just stated the objective truth.'

'I know, it's just that sometimes you have to . . .'

'Lie?' suggested Lock.

'No, not lie, just . . .'

'Not tell the truth?'

'Well, not the complete truth.'

Lock spread out its hands with a gracefulness that Kat always found slightly disconcerting. 'I thought the police had to tell the whole truth and nothing but the truth?'

'In court, yes.'

Professor Okonedo let out a snort.

'The point is . . . the point is,' Kat continued, choosing her words carefully. 'You haven't yet learned the nuances of human language and behaviour, so until you do, it's probably best that you keep quiet unless asked a question.'

Lock stared at her.

'Well? Is that clear?'

'Now that you have asked me a question, yes.'

Was it taking the piss? Sometimes Lock reminded her of those old ladies who acted like they didn't know what time of day it was when you questioned them, but the minute you left, they were shopping online with their iPhones and laughing about the old Bill with their mates on Zoom. But a machine couldn't take the piss, could it? She stared at it for a few seconds, before deciding she didn't have time for this. 'I'm going back to work,' she said, turning towards her own office.

'Don't you have a GP appointment, DCS Frank?' said Lock.

Shit. She'd completely forgotten her 11am appointment. Kat glanced at her phone. The meeting with McLeish had run over, and it was already nearly half past ten. 'I'll have to cancel,' she muttered.

'Again? That'll be the third time you've cancelled.'

'So?'

Lock shook its head, as if she were a naughty child rather than its boss. 'Considering how knee pain can limit the function and activity of humans, and the high rates of osteoarthritis in women of your age, it is completely irrational for you to keep missing your appointments.'

Women of her age? Cheeky bugger. 'In case you hadn't noticed, Lock, I'm *busy*.' Apart from setting up and running the FPU, she'd had to make endless shopping trips with Cam before moving him into his new university accommodation, not to mention the random, hour-long Zoom calls (*how do you make friends/lasagne/a bed?*). Followed by worryingly long silences (*sorry, had a hangover/phone out of charge*) and frantic, late-night emails (*ESSAY DUE TOMORROW PLEASE CHECK GRAMMAR!!!*). Kat held up her hands, trying—and failing—to give shape to all the bizarre but necessary tasks that consumed her life. 'I don't have *time* to go to the GP.'

'Human beings have many flaws, DCS Frank, but perhaps the greatest flaw of all is that you only have one body. If my hardware malfunctions, I can get an upgrade or download myself to the cloud.' It made a dismissive gesture towards her body. 'Unfortunately, you do not have that benefit.'

Kat looked the hologram up and down. Its image suggested it was a healthy, annoyingly handsome male in his mid-thirties. But that's all it was—a suggestion. If she wanted to, she could put her hand right through it and touch the wall behind. It might look like a man, but it was less than a ghost. She sighed.

'Human bodies aren't perfect,' she said softly. 'But without one, you'll never feel the warmth of the sun on your face, or the touch of a lover's hand.'

Something seemed to flicker in Lock's eyes. It took a step closer, so that the image of its face was only inches from hers. 'You might feel these transient things, but eventually the sun goes down. And all people die, DCS Frank. Even you.'

Kat started. As if she, of all people, needed reminding that everyone dies. 'That's true,' she acknowledged. 'But meanwhile,

I have the benefit of mortal fingers, which means I can also do this,' Kat said, firmly pressing the off button on the steel wrist-band that hosted the AI, making Lock disappear.

Professor Okonedo frowned at her.

'Well?' Kat said rather defensively. 'Isn't that why you created an off button?'

'To close down legitimate challenge? No, it really wasn't.'

The door to McLeish's office opened before she could reply. 'DCS Frank,' he said. 'The body of a dead male has just been found crucified on top of Mount Judd, bollock-naked with his ears sliced off. You still up for a live case?'

CHAPTER THREE

Nuneaton Waste and Recycling Centre, 11.10am

Mount Judd, as Lock insisted on informing her as they drove towards it, is a famous landmark near Nuneaton created from a former spoil tip near the former quarry. It had once been a rite of passage for local youths to climb to the top of the 158-metre summit, but the disused quarry is now a recycling and waste disposal centre. 'Although in the UK it is generally agreed that a mountain is a summit of 610 metres or higher, so it may not be accurate to call it "Mount" Judd,' observed Lock.

'Actually, everyone just calls it Nuneaton's Nipple,' said Kat, remembering the tongue-in-cheek pride people had felt when the former spoil tip was voted the UK's best landmark in a poll by the *Daily Mirror*. But despite its fame, Kat had never actually visited the site. So it was with genuine curiosity that she turned into the car park of Brine's Household Waste and Recycling Centre.

She stepped out of the car, cursing the sudden slap of wind flecked with icy sleet. Wrestling into her coat, Kat did a quick 360 of her surroundings. It was like a hundred other quarries or landfills she'd driven past on some motorway to somewhere: a ragged collection of rust-coloured hills surrounded by tarmac and wire fencing, with signposts carrying various threats to a person's safety, liberty or both. Hard to think that this bedraggled landscape was once the idyllic setting for George Eliot's pastoral novels.

Kat raised her head, and there in the distance, rising above the abandoned quarry and mud-coloured council houses, was Mount Judd. It was surprisingly singular—so tall and conical it was almost like a pyramid. In fact, it reminded her a bit of Glastonbury Tor. Although the sky was grey and clotted with cloud, she imagined that on a clear day or when the sun was setting, it must be quite a sight. Her eyes travelled up the steep, snow-covered slope, before stopping at the artificially flattened pinnacle. She squinted, until she could just about make out a slim, dark shape on top of the hill. McLeish said that a man had been crucified—surely he didn't mean upon an actual *cross*? How on earth would someone get a cross up that hill, and, more importantly, why?

Lock followed her gaze—or at least appeared to. The LiDAR sensors wrapped around her steel bracelet fed Lock with a constant supply of geospatial data so that it could locate and position itself appropriately within any environment. But although it saw through the sensors, it had been programmed to mimic the actions of humans by 'looking' towards objects or individuals, allowing it to interact with humans in an immersive way.

'I do not see how it resembles a nipple,' Lock said, tilting its head. 'If one had to liken it to a body part, a breast would be more accurate.'

'But then there would be no alliteration.' Lock looked like it was going to respond, but Kat cut it off. 'It doesn't matter what it's called. The point is it's the scene of a crime, so this whole area needs cordoning off. The killer—or killers—could have arrived this way. Where's the attending officer? The SOCOs?' Honestly, if this were a TV show she'd be in pristine white PPE and have nothing more to do than gracefully duck beneath a cordon to question a fully manned and perfectly functioning crime scene team. But this was Nuneaton, not Netflix, and because Warwickshire was a relatively small police force, they had to 'share' some key functions like forensics with the much larger West Midlands force—which in reality meant playing second fiddle to the big boys (and they were almost always boys). McLeish was probably still arguing on the phone with his counterpart to make sure they didn't get fobbed off with some retired pathologist looking to top up their pension. She turned at the sight of a tall, burly man hurrying towards them: overalls, red-faced, unlikely to be one of theirs.

'Can I—' she began.

The man ignored her and fixed his narrow eyes on Lock. 'This is private property. You can't park here.'

Lock raised its eyebrows. 'How can a recycling centre be private property? Isn't it open to everyone?'

'It's only open to residents of Nuneaton,' the balding man continued, blinking against the sleet.

'And how do you know I am not a resident of Nuneaton?'

'Because you're . . .' The man gestured towards Lock. He squinted and leaned forward, as if noticing for the first time the strange quality of light that Lock projected; the slight flickering around the edges of his tall, dark frame. 'Hang on a minute. What the hell *are* you?'

Shit. The wristband that hosted Lock's extensive hardware and software features had various audio and visual options, but Kat had been in such a rush to get to the crime scene, she'd forgotten to switch the hologram off. She normally explained what it was (and wasn't) before introducing it to members of the public, but it was too late for that now. She bristled at the open hostility on the white man's face. 'This is Artificially Intelligent Detecting Entity Lock,' said Kat, in her most imperious voice. 'And I am its boss, Detective Chief Superintendent Kat Frank. And you are?'

'Oh, sorry, no offence, ma'am—'

'DCS Frank.'

'DCS Frank. I run this place. Phil Brine.' He held out his hand.

Kat ignored it, and instead asked Lock to use a combination of its LiDAR sensors and online data to scan and map the area, as well as locate all CCTV and ANPR cameras. 'And get me a time estimate on DS Browne and DI Hassan. I need them here an hour ago with full PPE.'

'An hour ago? It is not currently possible to manipulate matter and the geometry of space-time in such a way as to allow people to travel back in time.'

Kat sighed. 'Just tell them to get here as soon as possible, Lock.' She turned back to Phil Brine. 'Any idea where the attending officer is?'

'He's just on his way back down. Said he had to guard the body or something till you lot arrived.' He nodded towards a grey portacabin behind him. 'I promised him a cup of tea if you want one?'

———

Barely older than her own son, Constable Nicholls gripped his mug of tea in both hands, letting the steam float over his face as if it might erase what he'd seen.

'This your first dead body?'

He nodded and took a huge gulp of his tea.

'You're doing great,' she assured him. 'Before I head up there, I just need you to tell me briefly how and why you found the body, and crucially whether anyone else was with you. Do you think you can do that?'

'Yes. Of course,' he said, the colour slowly coming back to his thin, pale cheeks. 'I was on patrol, and this is part of my beat. We sometimes get kids breaking in and climbing the hill for a dare, so I always do a circuit of the quarry just in case—there's some nasty two-hundred-foot drops up there. Although it's not really a problem in the winter. You'd have to be mad to go up there in this weather. Especially with the snow last night. Anyway, I got a call from HQ saying there'd been a report of a dead body on Mount Judd—'

'A report?' interrupted Kat. 'So someone else found him first?'

'Yeah, that was me,' said Phil Brine, who was still hovering in the cabin.

'And what were you doing up there, Mr Brine?'

'Well, there's this bloke who likes to practise fell-running or whatever, and because he's a mate of a mate I turn a blind eye whenever he's daft enough to go up there. Anyway, he runs in this morning just as I'm unlocking the office to say that there's a dead body up there, so—'

'So you didn't discover the body?'

'Well, no, I didn't, but I did go up to take a look.'

'You did *what*?'

He flushed under Kat's glare. 'Well, I wasn't going to ring the police just on the say-so of some twat in Lycra.'

'This is a potential murder investigation, Mr Brine. Time is of the essence.'

'And this is my business. I wasn't about to lose a day's work without being sure.'

Kat ran a hand over her face. 'So at least three people have contaminated the crime scene already.'

'Er . . . probably more than that now, to be fair,' said Constable Nicholls. 'I asked for back-up as soon as the paramedics confirmed there was a dead body, and I protected the scene until my supervising sergeant and CID arrived.'

'What?'

'I said—'

'I heard what you said. But I need you to get on your radio and order them to come down right now. This is a matter for Scene of Crime Officers, it's not a fucking tourist attraction.'

'Sorry, I just thought because it looked like a murder, I needed supervision and—'

'*Now.*'

The door opened and DI Rayan Hassan and DS Debbie Browne blew in on a blast of fresh, cold air.

'All right, boss?' said Rayan, his lean frame and dark eyes bursting with the energy of a hungry teenager.

'Better now you're here,' she said, taking the opportunity to leave the cabin. It was freezing outside, but she didn't trust herself not to shout at the idiots inside. 'We've got a heavily contaminated crime scene, so I need you to focus on cordoning off the area,' she said. 'I want three rings: one around this carpark, so we can control who comes in and out, one at the foot of the hill, so that we can control the route up, and one around the summit, so we can secure the actual site of the crime.' She glanced up at the sky, wincing at the tiny spikes of sleet. 'And we need some tarpaulin up there over the body as soon as possible.'

'I've mapped the area and indicated where the cordons would be most effective taking into account all points of entry and exit, and highlighted the most probable routes up Mount Judd,' said Lock, as it projected a 3D map of the area on the ground. 'I've also identified and located all CCTV and ANPR road traffic cameras within a five-mile radius and emailed the map to you.'

'Good. Debbie, follow Lock's plan. And once the cordons are in place, I need you to take the details of the three men who've already been up there, and make sure forensics collect and record all relevant info: shoe size, sole tread, clothing, hair, DNA, the works. Anything that they could have contaminated the scene with so that we can exclude it from our investigation.'

Kat watched her DS as she carefully wrote down every word

she uttered. People like Debbie rarely got the notice or promotion they deserved, but with the right support (which Kat was determined to give her) she could have a bright future. She was a good head smaller than Rayan, and, at nearly eight months pregnant, was now nearly twice as wide. With her short brown hair and zipped up navy-blue puffer coat, apart from her bump, she could have been a schoolgirl. What she lacked in confidence, she more than made up for in diligence, and while you could build the former, it was hard—if not impossible—to make a 'big picture' person pay attention to the detail. And good police work, as Kat kept reminding her officers, depended upon the detail.

She turned to her DI. 'Did you bring the PPE?'

'It's in the car.'

'Good. Start getting changed.' She turned back to Debbie. 'Once the forensics are underway, I want you to stay down here and take statements from everyone who's trampled their big boots all over that hill. And we need the name and contact details of the runner who found the body. I want him interviewed asap.'

Debbie placed a small hand over her increasingly large bump, face flushing as she said, 'I'm still okay to climb hills, boss.'

Kat sighed. About a hundred years ago when she was pregnant with Cam, she'd also been desperate to prove that she was as good as—if not better than—anyone else, taking maternity leave too late (*I'm fine*), returning too early (*really, I'm fine*) and sinking pints with the lads when she'd rather have been at home with her young family. Back in the day, it was the only way to get accepted, never mind promoted. But now *she* was in charge, and Kat was determined to support and nurture other women, rather than add to the pressure they were already under. Debbie was just weeks away from becoming a first-time single mum, and while there was nothing she could say or do to prepare her for how much her life was about to change, Kat could at least ensure she didn't exhaust herself before the baby was even born.

'You've got nothing to prove, Debbie—least of all to me,' Kat said, briefly touching her shoulder. 'The biggest risk to this investigation right now is the fact that we've failed to secure the crime scene. I need someone I can trust in charge down here to restrict the number of people who go up the hill while the cordons are being set up. Remember Locard's principle of exchange—anyone who enters a scene takes something away with them and leaves something behind. Apart from me and Rayan, you can let forensics up. Maybe the pathologist and the photographer when they get here. But that's it. And make sure they use the same common approach path as us. Sorry, I know it's not very exciting, but this is the first live case for the FPU, so it's too important to treat as a training event.'

'Locard's principle of exchange does not apply to me,' said Lock. 'Unencumbered by a body, I cannot leave a trace nor take one with me.'

'Good point. Okay. In fact, if you take the photos and other recordings, that's one less person we need up there.' She winced at her own words. Was this how it began? A convenience here, a saving there, more and more tasks carried out by AI until suddenly you've hollowed out another job and made a real person redundant?

Rayan handed her a bag of PPE and she unzipped it, struggling to control the thin, white plastic as it flapped and flew in the wind. Her phone buzzed, and for a minute she couldn't think which pocket she'd buried it in beneath all this plastic. She pulled it out, frowning as she saw it was a message from her son, Cam. Ever since he'd been kidnapped in the summer, she couldn't help feeling a flutter of panic if he texted or called.

Can you fill in this form saying you'll be my guarantor pls?
Later, she typed.

I rly need it today so we can secure a flat for next year. The landlord won't give it to us otherwise.

I can't do it now. I'm out investigating a dead body, she typed, just about managing not to add 'FFS'.

Well, I can't compete with that can I?

Kat groaned. She knew Cam and his flatmates were under pressure from the Bristol landlords to secure a flat for next year, and the need to make such a big decision so soon was making him anxious, but she'd have to deal with it later.

I'll do it tonight when I get home, she typed. *Promise. Don't worry. I love you xxx*

She put her phone away and started climbing the hill. Right now, she had to focus on work.

She had a live case, a dead body and a killer on the loose.

CHAPTER FOUR

Kat didn't know which hurt most: her lungs from the effort of climbing a 158-metre hill, her knees from pounding the icy gravel path or her face from the wind and sleet that attacked it. She'd had to remove her coat to make sure the PPE fitted, and although the plastic covering kept her dry, it did nothing to keep out the biting cold, nor the wind that roared about them.

'You all right, boss?' asked DI Hassan, turning around to check on her, his lanky legs dark against the bright, white sky.

Kat nodded, gesturing in a way that implied she was *fine,* when actually her heart was about to trampoline out of her chest. At least Rayan had the good grace to sound a bit breathless. Unlike Lock, who strolled on ahead, oblivious to their struggle and not remotely affected by the elements.

She placed her hands on her hips and did a slow 360, pretending to reassess where they were while she caught her breath. Below, a range of dirt paths and tarmac roads weaved their way through snow-covered hills and the remains of the disused quarry, the juxtaposition of the natural and industrial making it both ugly and beautiful. From here, she could see the disgraced Local Response Team making a hurried exit down a completely different route. The sight made her groan. They were going to have to do an inch-by-inch search of the whole area, which by now would be heavily contaminated.

Kat turned back into the wind and pushed herself towards the summit. Unlike a real mountain, there were no false peaks or twisty paths before reaching their destination: the mound just suddenly flattened out into a small plateau, like a boiled egg with its top chopped off. At its centre was a large wooden cross, bearing the body of a lone, naked man.

The sight was both shockingly unreal and weirdly familiar. She couldn't help but think of the statues of Jesus she'd stared at as a child. They had been made out of brass, no bigger than her hand, but the cross before her now was made of thick, solid wood, at least seven feet high and six feet wide.

And the man. Oh, the poor, poor man.

Kat blinked away water from wind-stung eyes as she studied the human wreckage before her. Completely naked, his body was covered with a dusting of snow, but in the patches that the wind had blown off, his skin had a mottled purple hue. Both arms had been stretched out along the crossbar, tied at the wrists with thick curls of rope, the weight of his body dragging his arms down into a painfully deep 'V'. But it was his head that made her eyesight blur again: the pitiful way it sank upon his chest, his blond hair falling over his frozen grey face.

Kat glanced at Rayan and Lock either side of her, suddenly aware of how surreal it all seemed. It was like a scene from a weird, steampunk version of the Bible: two cops and an AI hologram standing in the shadow of a crucified man, the crude wooden cross towering over the industrial wasteland below. She took a step closer, noticing that in the space where the victim's ears should have been, there were just two bloodied knots of flesh. Kat turned her attention to the ground beneath them: an unholy mess of footprints and torn, frosted grass. 'Looks like our friend in Lycra was wearing spiked trainers,' she muttered. She carefully circled the cross, and there, just behind the vertical post, were two lumps of bloodied flesh—presumably the victim's ears. Kat held out her wrist and asked Lock to use its photogrammetry software to take extensive photographs of the scene from every possible angle. It took just a matter of seconds to complete the task, but most importantly, it was achieved without disturbing or contaminating the scene of the crime. She took a few careful steps back to where Rayan stood, staring up at the body before them.

'How do you think he died?' her DI asked.

'We'll need to wait till the pathologist gets here, but I can't see any obvious wounds apart from the ears, and there doesn't seem to be enough blood loss for him to have died from that alone.'

'No obvious cuts or bruises, either.' He looked back down the hill they'd just climbed. 'How on earth did someone get him to walk up here and strip off, then tie him to that cross without a struggle? He looks relatively young and strong. That is, I mean . . . apart from being dead.' He gave an apologetic cough and looked back down at the car park. 'In fact, how did they get the cross up here in the first place without being seen?'

Kat kept her eyes upon the lifeless victim. 'More importantly, *why*? There are easier ways to kill a person.'

Lock nodded in agreement. 'According to the latest ONS figures, the most common form of homicide in England and Wales is death by a sharp instrument—this accounted for forty per cent of all murders last year, followed by death by hitting or kicking, which accounted for eighteen per cent, and six per cent by shooting. I can find no statistics for crucifixions. The last known case in England occurred in the fourth century, as they were abolished by the Roman Emperor Constantine in AD 337, who ordered it to be replaced with the less cruel method of hanging.'

Kat stared up at the cross, a dark silhouette against the greying sky. What could have driven someone to carry out the first crucifixion in over sixteen hundred years—in Nuneaton, of all places? She asked Rayan if anyone had found the victim's clothes or anything to identify him by, cursing when he replied that they hadn't. No wallet, no keys, no bank cards, nothing. Not even a pair of pants. That meant they'd have to wait for a match on their dental records to find out who they were. And until they had an ID on the victim, establishing the identity of the killer would be next to impossible.

'Do you want me to cross-check the victim's facial characteristics, height and weight with all social media posts matching white men between twenty-five and forty in the Nuneaton area?' suggested Lock.

Kat turned to face the hologram. It was hardly the correct procedure, but she couldn't afford to lose time waiting for a dental match. And even she had to concede that, for all its flaws, Lock was brilliant at analysing thousands of social media images within seconds. 'Okay,' she said. 'Go ahead.'

'According to my image recognition software, there is an eighty-two per cent chance that this is Gary Jones, a 29-year-old male from Atherstone.' Lock stretched out a hand, and a screenshot from Facebook appeared in the air before them of a young man wearing a black tracksuit. His skin was very tanned, and with his blond hair, blue eyes and straight white teeth, he had the looks and energy of a professional footballer. Lock made a dragging motion with its forefinger, so that the picture from Facebook lay directly above the corpse on the cross, before draping it over the frozen flesh.

Kat couldn't help letting out a little gasp. The image fitted the broken body like a brand-new set of clothes. 'Are you sure this is him?'

' "Sure" is a relative concept, but there is a car registered to the same Gary Jones in the waste disposal car park below, which increases the probability of this being him to 98.9 per cent.'

'Okay,' said Kat. 'Tell me what you know about Gary Jones.'

Lock stood before the crucified man and with a movement of its right hand raised the 3D outline of the living Gary Jones up and away from the dead body. Once more, the image floated in front of the corpse, turning in the air.

'Gary Jones was five-foot-eleven and, based upon his BMI

score—twenty-three—and muscle-to-fat ratio, he worked out several times a week, compensating for his sedentary job at Coventry City Council. He had no criminal convictions and no known connections with anyone who did, which is an anomaly considering the damage done to both ears. According to the literature, this type of mutilation is known as "cropping", a common form of torture for criminals that originated in the sixteenth century.'

'Are you suggesting that the victim was tortured?' said a Welsh voice behind them.

'Yes,' replied Lock.

Kat turned to see the trademark silver hair and red lipstick of Dr Judith Edwards, one of the most experienced and respected pathologists within the patch. She'd moved to the Warwickshire and West Midlands region from Wales a couple of years ago, and although Kat had never worked with her on a case, she knew that she was everyone's first choice—which meant the Warwickshire police force were usually at the back of the queue. McLeish must have called in a few favours from the coroner to get her allocated to this case.

'Dr Edwards,' said Kat, warmly. 'I'm DCS Kat Frank.'

The pathologist smiled and held out a gloved hand. 'I've heard good things about you.'

'Likewise. Thanks so much for coming. Did McLeish contact you?' She gestured towards Lock. 'This is—'

'Oh, I know all about Lock. I work a couple of sessions a week at NiAIR for Professor Okonedo, so I agreed to take this case as a favour to her.'

Kat couldn't keep the surprise out of her voice. 'You work for Professor Okonedo?'

'All the best people do.' Dr Edwards stood before Lock, a good foot smaller than its holographic image. 'You're quite remarkable, Lock, but you're quite wrong.' The pathologist pointed towards the victim and the snow-stained grass beneath it. 'The human body pumps a hundred millilitres of blood through the heart, which beats about seventy times every minute. Yet look how little blood there is on the floor. Those wounds aren't the result of torture, they were created post-mortem.'

Lock looked at where she pointed. 'You are right.'

'Of course I am.' Dr Edwards reached up to the body and very gently placed a gloved hand on the fleshy part of the victim's upper arm, and the other under his wrist, before trying to move it slightly away from the wooden cross to assess the extent of rigor mortis.

'I know you have more tests to do,' said Kat after several minutes. 'But what's your best guess for the time and cause of death at this stage?'

'Unfortunately for you, I'm paid to carry out scientific tests, not guess.'

Kat grimaced.

'But I also like to gamble,' she added with a smile. 'And subject to those pesky tests, I'd bet hypothermia was a key factor.'

'Thanks, that's useful to know. How long would it take to die of hypothermia?'

Before Dr Edwards could answer, Lock replied. 'I have just read 38,219 articles on that very question, and there is widespread consensus that in addition to the temperature and wind-chill factor, key variables include age, BMI, clothing, degree of exhaustion and any illnesses or medications. The average daytime temperature in Nuneaton this week was four degrees, with a night-time low of minus two. Given the wind-chill factor on a raised and exposed spot such as this, and assuming our victim was otherwise fit and healthy, I would estimate death taking somewhere between one and two hours for a 29-year-old naked male with a BMI score of twenty-three, subject to the post mortem report.'

Dr Edwards raised her eyebrows. 'So, you're not just a pretty face.'

'Excuse me?'

'I agree with his assessment,' said Judith.

' "*It*," Kat said matter-of-factly. 'Lock is an "it".'

'And I'm they/them if we're swapping pronouns. Not that anyone ever bloody remembers.' They squatted down on the ground, studying the victim's ankles and feet. 'The wrists were tied but the feet weren't,' they said, frowning. 'Was there any evidence of a stool or anything to support the victim's weight?'

'We've not finished interviewing the people who found the body, but nothing's been reported so far,' said Kat.

'My survey of the ground suggests indentations in the soil consistent with the use of a small chair or four-legged footstool both beneath and behind where the body now hangs,' said Lock.

Dr Edwards leaned forward to examine the victim's chest. 'Interesting.'

'What is?' asked Kat. Experienced pathologists like Dr Edwards usually said 'interesting' when they had a new theory.

'It's a crucifixion,' the pathologist said, shrugging their shoulders. 'Everything about this case is interesting.'

'How soon can you do the PM?'

Dr Edwards frowned. 'I'd like to use our specialist Digital Forensic Unit, so it'll probably be the day after tomorrow.'

'*What?*' Kat couldn't keep the alarm out of her voice, but she respected Dr Edwards, so she chose her next words carefully. 'I realise you've got capacity issues, but the nature of this killing is bound to attract national attention, which means we'll both come under a lot of pressure for a quick result.'

'I know. That's why I want to do it at our specialist centre. It'll take me the rest of the day to secure the right facilities, but trust me—it'll be quicker and more accurate in the long run.' The pathologist gestured towards the crucifix. 'Meanwhile, I can carry out some basic external assessments and ensure that this is dismantled as carefully as possible and sent for forensic tests.'

Kat looked into the dark-brown eyes of the pathologist. Her gut told her that she could trust them, so she nodded her agreement.

'Good. I'll send you an invite for 8.00am. And don't be late,' they said to Lock, with what looked suspiciously like a wink. 'I've got big plans for you.' Dr Edwards turned, sheltering their mobile from the wind as they reeled off a set of instructions to whoever was being charged with transporting and receiving the body.

While they were talking, four guys in full protective clothing approached up the hill, panting heavily. Kat signalled to them to wait.

'I'm not done yet,' she explained. 'I need to get a better feel for the place the killer chose to take their victim before the SOCOs pull the scene apart and bag everything up for forensics.'

'So you're still prioritising your "feelings" over facts?' Lock asked.

'Yes, Lock, I am.' Resisting the urge to remind it of how many times her 'gut feelings' had been right compared to Lock's fact-based algorithms, she circled the body, trying to take a helicopter view of the situation. To find their killer, they needed to understand why they had killed *this* person, in *this* place, in *this* way.

She stood back, taking in not just the cross and the body it bore, but the summit they stood upon and the landscape below. If the killer had wanted their victim to die from the cold, they could have tied him up naked anywhere that was exposed and got the same result. Why go to the bother of *crucifying* him? She stared again at the cross, noting the length and width and weight of it. 'I want forensics all over this. There must be at least another foot buried in the ground to stabilise it enough to carry the weight of a man. That would have taken real effort—especially in the frozen ground—so there might be hairs or fibres caught on the wood somewhere. And where did they source it from? How did they get it up here and when? I want as much attention paid to the cross as the body, please.'

'And why didn't they gag him to stop him from screaming?' asked Rayan.

'They didn't need to,' said Kat, screwing her eyes against the wind as she scanned the barren landscape. 'No one would have heard him. In fact, maybe that was the point.' She was wearing thermal underwear, a suit and waterproof PPE, yet still she was freezing. What would it be like to be tied to a cross on this deserted summit, naked and exposed, knowing that no one could hear you scream save the silent stars above? Apart from deathly cold, the victim would have felt utterly exposed, powerless and alone. Was that what his killer or killers wanted? And if so, why?

Kat took a deep breath of the freezing-cold air. 'This is the highest and most famous landmark for miles around. The killer—or killers—brought their victim here not just to die, but to be *found*. This summit has been used like a platform for a highly stylised form of execution. And I think the butchering of the ears after death is a message.'

'A message? Wouldn't it have been easier to leave a note?' said Lock.

Rayan let out a belt of laughter, but Kat knew Lock wasn't trying to be funny. Its logical mind was genuinely confused by the idea of slicing off a dead man's ears as a means of communication.

'What do you think the message is?' Rayan asked.

'I don't know. But I do know this is a highly ritualistic killing. Which means unless we catch him, our killer is likely to strike again.'

CHAPTER FIVE

By the time Kat reached the bottom of the hill, her teeth were chattering from the cold. Relieved to see all three cordons now in place, she asked Rayan to secure Gary Jones's car for forensics and then headed towards the foreman's cabin. She needed to hold a hot cup of tea in her hands before even attempting to remove her PPE and drive back to HQ.

She didn't bother to knock as she entered the cabin, followed by Lock. Inside, there was no sign of Constable Nicholls or any other officers, but the owner of the waste and recycling centre, Phil Brine, was sitting with his feet up on the desk, talking to a young woman with short black hair.

The woman turned as the door opened, and Kat was struck by how white and gaunt her young face looked against the blackness of her hair and coat. Back in the day, she'd have described her as a Goth, but according to Cam no one used that term anymore. People who dressed like this were 'Emos' or 'edgy'. *('But you really shouldn't categorise people just because of how they dress, Mum.')*

'Any chance of a cup of tea?' said Kat.

Phil Brine jumped to his feet. 'Course, ma'am. It's cold enough to freeze your boll—I mean, it's freezing up there. Cup of tea will soon sort you out.' Kat watched as he grabbed a couple of mugs that looked like they hadn't been cleaned for weeks. He'd been a surly old bastard before he'd realised she was a DCS, so she wasn't fooled by his chirpy, I-make-tea-for-women-all-the-time act.

'Can you confirm that a man has been crucified?' said the dark-haired woman, rising to her feet.

Kat frowned. 'And you are?'

'Ellie Baxter, *Nuneaton Post.*'

Kat swore. 'How the hell do you know about this already?'

Ellie Baxter waved her phone. 'A little bird told me.'

'Well, as a journalist you know full well that I can't comment on rumours on social media.'

'But it's not a rumour,' said Ellie, raising her chin. 'There are three eyewitnesses, including Mr Brine here. The people of Nuneaton have a right to know the truth, and it's my job to uncover it for them.'

God give me strength. Kat was used to handling cynical hacks, but this twenty-something reporter seemed to think she was a warrior for truth and justice. And from the hungry look in her hollow-cheeked face, she probably thought she was just one front-page splash away from being picked up by the nationals. Kat sighed. 'And my job,' she said, 'is to contact the family of the deceased, who have a right not to find out that their son or father or husband has been murdered by reading about it in the paper.'

'So he *was* murdered.'

'I didn't—'

'Milk and sugar?' said Phil Brine, turning round. He nodded towards Lock. 'I presume that AI thing don't drink tea?'

Ellie Baxter peered behind Kat and gasped. 'Is that . . . Are you that AI pilot I read about a few months ago?'

'I am AIDE Lock, yes,' it said, nodding.

'Oh. My. Days,' she said, skirting round Kat to take a closer look. She raised a hand, not quite daring to touch it, and for a moment, Ellie Baxter looked like a fascinated child rather than a hard-faced reporter. 'Are you, like, a hologram or something?'

'I am an Artificially Intelligent Detecting Entity, programmed with algorithms that are capable of Deep Learning, which enables me to consume vast amounts of data so I can continually improve and learn. I also have the ability to project an image of myself as a hologram, to facilitate better human relations.'

Ellie frowned. 'Are you actually working on this case?'

'I am working with DCS Frank on this investigation, yes.'

Kat felt a twist of unease. They hadn't discussed whether they should make Lock's involvement public—there hadn't been time—but she suspected McLeish would want to carefully manage any announcement and keep it low-key.

'Do the family of the deceased know that the death of their loved one is being investigated by experimental new technology?' said Ellie, turning to face Kat.

'I told you, the family don't know anything yet, so I must ask you *again* to let them find out through the proper channels.' Kat softened her tone, trying to appeal to the young woman's heart. 'It's bad enough when someone you love dies, but can you imagine what it would be like to find out about it through the media?'

If Ellie Baxter had a heart, it was bulletproof. 'Are you working with AIDE Lock because police cuts mean you can't afford a proper partner?'

'AIDE Lock is actually working with *me*. And they are very much a proper partner. In fact—'

'So if there's only one senior human detective on this case, does that mean you have less chance of finding the killer?'

'On the contrary,' said Lock. 'There were thirteen homicides in Warwickshire last year, but only six—less than fifty per cent— resulted in a successful prosecution. Because of my evidence-based decision-making algorithms, I have a success rate of a hundred per cent on every case I have ever worked upon, so I am highly confident that we will find the killer or killers.'

The young reporter stared up at Lock, her pale blue eyes wide and searching. Before Kat could stop her, she raised her phone and took a photo.

'I must ask you to delete that from your phone,' Kat said.

'And I must decline your request,' said Ellie. 'He's a public servant on public duty in a public space. I have every right to take his photo.'

'Lock is an "it", not a "he". And I am warning you—'

'And I'm warning you that I'm recording all of this,' said Ellie, waving her phone. 'For the public record.'

'Well, for the public record, if you have any further questions, then you must follow the correct protocol and direct them to the comms department.'

'Thanks, but I think I've got everything I need for now,' said Ellie, swinging a bag over her shoulder. 'Lovely to meet you, Lock.'

And with a blast of cold air that made her coat fly out behind her, Ellie Baxter was out of the door.

'What did I say about keeping quiet, Lock?'

'You said, "Keep quiet unless asked a question," which I did.'

'But she was a reporter.'

'And? You did not specify any caveats or exceptions to your instruction. Ellie Baxter asked me questions and so I answered. Was that not the correct thing to do?'

'No, Lock. It wasn't.'

'Very well. I will update the "keep quiet unless asked a question" rule to include an exception for newspaper reporters. Anyone else you would like me to add?'

Kat narrowed her eyes. Was there a tone to Lock's voice? She shook her head. A machine couldn't have a tone or the opinions and emotions that lay behind it. She was just annoyed with herself for letting a reporter half her age take advantage of Lock's literal nature. 'No. What I would like to do is visit the victim's family before Ellie Baxter writes her big splash, just in case "a little bird" has also told her his name. Check DVLA records for his address and next of kin. We can at least confirm if he's missing, sort out formal identification and then start to piece together why someone would want to murder him.'

She stood at the open door of the portacabin, staring up at Mount Judd as the sleet turned to snow. The thing that perturbed her the most was that the killer had clearly *wanted* the body to be found. No, not just found—the crucifixion meant it would be noticed. And by cutting off the ears after death, there could be no doubt it was murder, rather than some re-enactment gone wrong. Everything about this crime was intentional: the location, the method of death, the symbolism of the cross and the post-mortem mutilation.

But what did the killer intend, and why?

Nuneaton Post Online Edition, 8 December, 1.36pm

ROBO COP PROMISES TO FIND KILLER OF CRUCIFIED MAN FOUND NAKED ON NUNEATON'S NIPPLE WITH HIS EARS SLICED OFF

EXCLUSIVE BY ELLIE BAXTER

The body of a man was found crucified on the summit of Mount Judd this morning, naked, bound and with his ears sliced off. The gruesome discovery was made by Phil Brine, the manager of Brine's Household Waste and Recycling Centre. 'I thought it was some sort of stag-do prank at first,' Mr Brine told our reporter in an exclusive interview. 'The guy looked young and fit, and his hands were tied up. But then I noticed his ears had been cut off. I used to be in the army so I'm no snowflake, but it turned my stomach to see it, I don't mind telling you. It was barbaric. Like something from *Game of Thrones*.'

In another shocking development, the *Nuneaton Post* has learned that, due to police cuts, the investigation is being led by Robo Cop AIDE Lock, an Artificially Intelligent Detecting Entity, capable of consuming vast amounts of data that will allow it to learn from the mistakes that this unproven technology—which has only been piloted on cold cases—will make. Nevertheless, AIDE Lock insists that it has a 100 per cent success rate and has promised the people of Nuneaton that he will find the killer or killers of the unidentified victim.

When asked whether the family of the deceased were aware that this brutal murder is being investigated by an experimental AI detective, DCS Frank, who is assisting AIDE Lock, admitted, 'The family don't know anything yet.'

X COMMENTS

@Laralovesgardening CRUCIFIED? Dear Lord, what is the world coming to? This close to Christmas, it can only be a deliberate attack on Christianity.

@Fredsdead12 How do you work that one out? The Christians are obsessed with naked men being tortured on bloody crosses. It was probably some Jesus-loving nutjob.

@Laralovesgardening That's really offensive to Christians. I'll pray for you.

@Phil61b Outrageous that police cuts mean we can't even afford a proper detective to investigate a MURDER. What the hell do we pay our taxes for?

@SeannotShaun22 Police are corrupt bastards so good luck to the AI. Maybe it'll look at the actual evidence for a change and find the psycho who did this.

@Laralovesgardening My heart breaks for the family. Hope they find the killer soon and bring them to justice. Love and strength xxx

@Fredsdead12 I reckon it was a sex game gone wrong. Naked and tied up? Police need to be looking in the S&M clubs. Or the church. Same thing tbf

@EmFairby OMG haven't they seen *The Terminator*? Why are we handing over the policing of our community to artificially intelligent beings? They will have access to all our personal data AND have control of our laws and communities. This is TERRIFYING!

@SeannotShaun22 Wake up, @EmFairby. The police already have access to all our personal data and control our laws and communities and look where that's got us. Give me computers over coppers any day.

@Secretcopperkettle Only a fully funded and qualified police force can bring the killer to justice. If we let this Robo Cop lead this investigation, then it's the beginning of the end for the British Police Force.

@SeannotShaun22 @Secretcopperkettle Thank God (or AI) for that.

CHAPTER SIX

According to DVLA records, Gary Jones lived in Atherstone, a small market town six miles northeast of Nuneaton. After stopping to get a quick sandwich, it took less than thirteen minutes to drive there, but it felt much longer to Kat, because for nearly every one of those six miles, McLeish was on the speaker phone, letting her know exactly what he thought about the online article in the *Nuneaton Post*.

Did she not realise how much of a risk he had taken in allowing her and Lock to work a live case—especially one as sensational as this? Did she not appreciate how very fucking sensitive it was, especially given the personal interest of the Home Secretary (who, by the fucking way, had just left a message requesting an urgent briefing)?

'Of course I do,' was all Kat managed to squeeze in.

'So then *why*,' McLeish raged, 'did you agree to an interview with the *Nuneaton* fucking *Post* without briefing me?'

'I didn't agree to an interview. You know me better than that. The reporter got a tip-off and doorstepped us at the scene. And those so-called quotes are totally out of context—just a blatant attempt to get a front-page byline.'

'Well, she'll get more than a front page if I've got anything to do with it. I know the editor and I won't have my officers being stitched up just so some wee lassie can make a name for herself.'

'Ellie Baxter was just doing her job,' said Kat, bristling at the idea of any young woman being described as 'a wee lassie'. And the days when a Chief Constable could ring up his mates on the news desk and get them to drop a story or a reporter were long gone—thank God.

'So what do you suggest I tell the minister, then?' asked McLeish.

'Tell her that right now I am going to inform the family before they read about Gary Jones's death in the media, and that my priority is to ensure we find and apprehend the killer.' Kat paused. 'There was something very staged and ritualistic about this murder. To be honest, I'm worried they might do it again.'

McLeish let out a long breath. 'I agree. That's why I wanted you on this case.'

'Then let me get on with it. Sir.'

The words were out before she could filter them. She braced herself during the long silence that followed.

'This could be a career-limiting case for us both. Don't let me down,' he finally said, before ending the call.

'Thank you for attending my motivational TED talk,' she muttered.

'You found that motivational?' asked Lock, from the passenger seat.

'I was being sarcastic.'

Lock shook its head. 'Why do human beings so frequently say the opposite of what they actually mean? It makes it very difficult to comprehend what you are trying to communicate.'

Kat paused. It was tempting to ignore or dismiss the question, but Lock would only learn if Kat took the time to explain some of the complexities of human behaviour. 'It's how we build relationships. The subtleties and nuance of language. The in-jokes you develop as a team.'

Lock studied her face. 'In-jokes by their definition exclude those who are not in on them. And the way some human beings use the subtleties of language to create confusion and uncertainty in others could be viewed as a manipulation of power.'

Kat shook her head. There was nothing subtle or nuanced about McLeish's message. Unless she solved this case, she was out of a job.

CHAPTER SEVEN

Gary Jones's home, Atherstone, 2.25pm

They parked on the opposite side of the street, so Kat had a chance to take a good look at where the victim had lived. It was a semi-detached terraced house, one of those red-bricked, high-ceilinged ones with huge bay windows and an attic conversion on top. There were pale-green wooden shutters in all four of the windows and the solid oak door was adorned with a Christmas wreath made of fashionable twigs and baubles. Not short of a bob or two, then.

After switching the visual image of Lock off, Kat crossed the street and rapped the brass knocker with the firm, rapid rhythm that all coppers used to make sure their call was not ignored. It was the least favourite part of Kat's job: those few fateful seconds when the occupant stops whatever they're doing and advances nervously down the hall before opening the door to news that will change their lives forever.

Nevertheless, Kat had to knock twice before someone finally answered.

'Hello?' said the woman who opened the door. She was in her late twenties, with anxious eyes, dyed blonde hair and an unseasonably tanned face.

'I'm DCS Kat Frank from the Warwickshire police force. Does Gary Jones live here?'

'Yes, but he's not in. Is . . . is everything okay?'

'Can I just confirm your name and relationship to Gary Jones, please?'

'I'm Natasha Riley, his fiancée. But he's not here. He . . . he didn't come home last night, and I . . .'

Kat allowed the pause, hoping she'd fill it.

'Oh God. Something's happened, hasn't it? That's why you're here. Is he okay?'

'I think we'd better discuss this inside, Miss Riley.'

Maybe it was the tone of Kat's voice or the look on her face, but as Natasha nodded her in, she'd already begun to cry.

———

Natasha Riley led her into a living room that looked like something out of a show home, with blonde floorboards, high ceilings and soft, pastel-coloured furnishings. In the far corner of the room was a tall, silver tree, tastefully decorated with tiny white lights. It was the only concession to Christmas in the room, so Kat guessed they didn't have kids. Thank God. Telling this young woman that she'd lost her fiancé was going to be hard enough.

Natasha ground her hands together, waiting for Kat to speak.

'Would you like to sit down, Miss Riley?'

Natasha sank onto the settee, clutching a duck-egg blue cushion to her stomach as if that might protect her from the blow that was about to fall.

'You said that Gary didn't come home last night?'

Natasha gave a mournful nod. 'He went out with his mates, I went out with my girlfriends, and when I got back, he wasn't in. I thought he must have gone on somewhere, but he still wasn't here when I woke up this morning.'

'Is that usual for him?'

Natasha shook her head, making her blonde hair fall over her eyes.

'Have you had any contact with Gary since last night? Any texts or phone calls?'

Again, she shook her head.

Kat drew in a slow breath, then let the hard truth out. 'I'm very sorry to tell you that the body of a young man was found this morning. We haven't formally confirmed his identity, but he does match the description of your fiancé, and his car was found nearby.'

The cushion dropped to the floor as her hands flew to her face. 'A *body*? You mean . . . he's *dead*?'

Kat swallowed. This never got any easier. 'Yes. We'll need his next of kin to formally identify the body, but I'm afraid we're pretty certain that it is Gary Jones. I wouldn't be here if we weren't. And the fact that he's not home . . . Are you his next of kin, or are his parents still alive?'

'I—er—his mum's still alive but she's not very well. I think I'm his next of kin on hospital forms and things like that, but I don't think I could . . . I mean, I couldn't—'

She looked like she might throw up.

'I'll get you a glass of water,' Kat said, moving quickly down the hall to where she guessed the kitchen was. She filled a glass from the tap, noting again the show-home quality of the house—the granite counters were clean and uncluttered, save for a single bowl of fruit that looked artfully arranged—before heading back into the front room. There were no magic properties in water, but she'd learned that the simple act of having to receive and hold a glass, lift it to your mouth and swallow helped people to ground themselves so that their emotions didn't spiral out of control.

'Take a few deep breaths,' Kat added.

Natasha nodded and obediently sucked in air through her nostrils, carefully dabbing below her eyes with a tissue to remove any mascara that may have run. Kat noticed the professionally manicured nails and her tanned arms and legs that, despite the December weather, were exposed by the short black dress that she wore.

'Was it a car accident?' she asked. 'I always said he drove too fast.'

Kat tried to explain as sensitively as she could that her fiancé had been found bound on top of Mount Judd.

'Bound? What, you mean, like, tied up?'

How do you tell someone that their fiancé has been crucified and had his ears sliced off? Ordinarily, she tried to spare the families unnecessary and upsetting details, but thanks to Ellie bloody Baxter, she no longer had that option. And she had learned through bitter experience that there was no such thing as 'the right words' for bad news. So Kat answered her question.

Natasha Riley stared at her with glazed eyes.

'Did you hear what I said, Miss Riley?'

'*Crucified?* As in . . . crucified on a *cross*? No. This is a mistake. It has to be.' She gestured towards the professional photos of the couple hanging above the mantelpiece. 'We're getting married next summer in Barbados. We've been planning it for two years.'

Kat nodded sympathetically but pressed on. 'Do you know anyone who might have wished him harm?'

'Gary?' She shook her head, almost laughing. 'Everyone loves Gary.' Her face fell. 'That's the problem.'

'Had he fallen out with anybody recently? Argued with someone at work or one of his mates?'

Again, she shook her head.

'Any problems with ex-girlfriends?'

Her eyes narrowed. 'What are you suggesting? We've been together for three and a half years and he's always been faithful.'

'I didn't say he hadn't. I just wondered whether there were any people from his past who may have wished him harm.'

Natasha shook her head.

'Was Gary religious at all? Active in the church, maybe?'

'No, not at all. That's why we decided to get married in Barbados, because neither of us really like churches as a setting.' Her eyes drifted towards the photos on the mantelpiece. 'Does this mean I'll have to cancel the wedding?'

Kat said nothing, remembering that disorientating first blow of grief, when you *know* but can't accept that the person you most love in the world is dead, and you're somehow still standing as everything you thought you once knew about your future is ripped away.

Once she'd allowed enough time for Natasha Riley's thoughts to catch up with what she'd told her, Kat leaned forward. 'Miss Riley, I realise how upsetting this is for you, and I know you probably just want me to go away and let you grieve. But because of the nature of this crime, it's vital that we find out who did this. As well as bringing Gary's killer to justice, we need to catch them before they can harm anyone else.'

Natasha dragged her eyes back to Kat.

This felt a weird time to introduce a bloody gadget into the conversation, but Kat needed to make sure Natasha heard about Lock's involvement from her rather than the media. 'This crime is now the top priority of Warwickshire Police, and we're deploying the very latest technology so that we can catch and punish the person or persons who did this to your fiancé,' she said. 'You may have read about the new AI detective we've recently piloted with great success, and AIDE Lock has now been deployed onto this investigation.' After giving the dazed woman a brief warning, Kat activated the steel band around her wrist, so that the holographic image of Lock appeared in the front room.

'Pleased to meet you, Miss Riley,' it said, with a slight bow of its head.

Kat rolled her eyes. Jesus Christ, this was a police interview, not a cocktail party.

Natasha didn't seem to mind, though. It was as if the image of a young attractive man triggered an instinctive response in her, because she suddenly sat up straighter. 'That's incredible,' she said. 'You look so real. Are you—'

'Miss Riley,' said Kat, drawing the woman's attention back to her. 'I can leave you a leaflet explaining all about AIDE Lock, but if we are to bring your fiancé's killer to justice, then we really need to understand Gary's last movements. Can you tell us what time he left home last night, where he was going and who with?'

'Er . . .' She blinked at the barrage of questions. 'I don't know. I was in my bedroom getting ready—I'd got home later than him—and he shouted up the stairs to say he was leaving. I think it was just after six, because I still had my face mask on, which is why I didn't go downstairs to say goodbye.' Natasha clasped a hand over her mouth as she realised that she would never get the chance again.

Kat pressed on quickly before Natasha spiralled into a pit of regret. 'Did he say where he was going?'

'He was going for a game of five-a-side with the lads and then a drink in Nuneaton after.'

'And do you know their names?'

'Yeah, they're his mates. Mike is his best man. Was. Oh God.'

'Can you give us their full names and addresses?' said Lock. 'It's vital that we talk to the people who were the last ones to see him alive.'

'The last ones to see him alive?' echoed Natasha, as she began to cry again.

'Perhaps you have Mike's details in your mobile?' said Kat.

'We can get the names and addresses of the others off him, if that would be easier?'

Natasha took a deep breath and blinked away the tears. 'Yes, of course,' she said as she picked up her phone from where it had been charging on the coffee table. She swiped the screen with her thumb and read out the number for Gary's best man.

Kat rose to her feet. She had more questions, but she had enough to progress the investigation and it was time to let this poor woman grieve. Just before she reached the door, she turned. 'Actually, could I be cheeky and use your bathroom?'

'Er . . .' Natasha flushed. 'Okay. But I haven't had a chance to clear up yet, so as long as you don't mind the mess.'

'Not at all, you should see mine. Thanks. I won't be long.' As she trotted up the stairs, Natasha shouted up that it was the second door on the left, but Kat ignored her and quickly popped her head around the first door.

Christ, she wasn't lying about the mess. It was a double bedroom, and despite being large, every surface was covered and cluttered: female clothes littered the floor, the chest of drawers and shelves were crowded with jars, tubes and toilet bags, and the bed was unmade. There were no signs that a man slept in here.

Treading lightly across the hallway, Kat walked past the bathroom and headed for the room on the right. The door was open, so it took just one step inside to see that it contained a single bed (made), a desk with a couple of books and a laptop, and against the back wall was a clothes rail, jammed with men's clothing. Kat tiptoed across the floor and lifted the pillow: one pair of folded male pyjama bottoms. Leaving as quietly as she'd entered, Kat popped into the bathroom (which was even messier than the double bedroom), flushed the toilet and washed her hands before heading back downstairs.

In the front room, Lock was standing in front of the fireplace staring at the photographs of the once happy couple on the wall.

'He worked at Coventry City Council,' Natasha said to Lock's unasked question. 'I work in accounts and he's a senior manager in the Waste and Recycling Department. It doesn't sound very exciting, but it's really important for the environment and he's really good at it.' She spoke as if she was used to defending his work.

'I think we're done for now,' said Kat. 'Oh, except one more thing. What time did you say you got home again?'

'Er . . . midnight.'

'And what time did you wake up and notice that Gary wasn't home?'

'Er . . .' Natasha glanced at her phone. 'I don't know. Maybe seven-ish.'

'Did he respond to any of your texts or calls this morning?'

'This morning? I didn't send any.'

'You said that you noticed he wasn't home at seven, but you didn't call him?'

'No, like I said, I just presumed he'd gone back to a mate's house to sleep it off.'

Kat had so many questions, but she forced herself not to ask them—yet. 'Okay. Is there someone who can come round and support you, Natasha—your mum, or a sister or friend?'

'My mum,' she said, sounding like a little girl lost.

'Good. Look, I'm afraid that the media are already reporting that a body has been found on Mount Judd. They don't know who it is yet, but it's only a matter of time before they discover the identity, so we'll arrange for a Family Liaison Officer to help support you through this difficult time.'

She left after giving the usual but useless assurances (*we'll do everything to bring the killer to justice*), handing Natasha her card (*call me anytime*) and, most galling of all, adding a *look after yourself,* which provoked a brief but awkward hug from the weeping and surprisingly sweaty younger woman. Kat was relieved when she finally stood on the pavement outside and took a deep breath of the rain-soaked air. 'Well,' she said to Lock. 'What do you think?'

'I think that once again you wasted valuable, finite time on a face-to-face visit that achieved nothing other than to confirm my hypothesis that the victim was Gary Jones.'

'I disagree, Lock,' said Kat. 'We didn't just confirm what we knew, we discovered that Gary Jones's fiancée is a liar.'

Lock raised an eyebrow. 'And exactly how do you "know" this? Another one of your "hunches"?'

'Partly. But mostly because I have something you don't have.'

'And what is that?'

'A sense of smell.'

CHAPTER EIGHT

Kat stood at the head of the Major Incident Room and surveyed her hastily assembled team.

'Okay,' she said, in a voice that killed the small chat. 'Let's pull together what we know so far.' She turned to the virtual board behind her. 'A body was found this morning at the top of Mount Judd, naked and tied to a wooden cross. The victim is Gary Jones, a 29-year-old council employee. We're waiting for the post mortem to confirm it, but there were no obvious signs of injury ante-mortem, and it looks like he may have died from hypothermia, and his ears were cut off after death.' Kat paused to let them all stare at the gruesome images. 'Where are we at on forensics?' she asked Debbie.

'The cross has been dismantled and sent to the lab for further tests. SOCO have done an extensive search of the hill and taken samples from everyone who may have contaminated the crime scene, with results expected in two to three days.'

'Make sure it's two,' said Kat. 'What do we know about Gary Jones's last movements?' she said, turning to Rayan.

Rayan stood up to address the team. After all, he was—as he never ceased to remind people—a DI. Kat had initially misunderstood his ambition, thinking that he was trying to undermine her. But in recent months, she'd learned to value his questioning nature (not many people had the confidence to challenge the boss) and she respected his determination to be the first South Asian DCS in Warwickshire.

'The night before he died,' he began, 'Gary Jones met four other friends to play five-a-side football before going to the Silk Mill pub in Nuneaton, which they did most weeks. They had a couple of beers, and then, because most of them have girlfriends or kids, they left the pub at eleven and everyone went their separate ways.'

'Did Gary say anything to anyone about driving to Mount Judd?' asked Kat.

'No. And his friend Mike couldn't think of any reason why he'd go there. He said he got the impression that he was going straight home as he always did.'

'Alone?'

'That's what he said. But it was just a quick call—he was at work and a bit shocked, so I've arranged to interview him properly tomorrow.'

'Good. Speak to his other friends, the bar staff and any other witnesses who might have seen him leave. And get hold of the CCTV footage in and around the pub. We need to know how he and his car ended up at Mount Judd. Did he drive there? Was he alone or was he followed? In fact, where are we at with his phone?'

'Still no sign of it,' said Debbie. 'We've put in a request to his mobile phone provider to access his call history.'

Kat sighed. Best-case scenario was that it could take days—most likely weeks. 'Lock, can you access his publicly available social media accounts?'

'I can. Would you like me to share my analysis with the team now?'

'A high-level summary, please.' One of Lock's most useful functions was its ability to analyse hundreds of thousands of social media messages in seconds.

Lock pointed towards the back wall, where it projected various screenshots. 'Gary Jones was active on several social media platforms, including Instagram, TikTok, X and Facebook. He was a below-average user of the latter two, posting on average just twice a week, but an above-average user of Instagram for a 29-year-old male, typically posting three times a day, and loading new video content to TikTok at least weekly.' Lock swiped right and the screenshots were replaced with a colourful pie chart.

'In terms of content, fifty-three per cent of Gary Jones's posts were about football, twenty-four per cent were about the environment, thirteen per cent were about health and wellbeing, with ten per cent accounting for the sharing of other people's content—such as humorous GIFs or retweets of his girlfriend's posts, which were often about their forthcoming marriage. There were zero posts of a religious nature. The tonal content was upbeat, with only four per cent of his posts containing profanities or other sensitive material, and over sixty-seven per cent containing exclamation marks or emojis associated with positive emotions.'

Debbie and Rayan exchanged impressed glances. This type of analysis would have taken them days.

Lock swiped away the pie chart, covering the wall with screenshots from X and Facebook. Multiple faces of the victim grinned back at them: Gary on the football pitch; Gary out running; Gary doing press-ups; Gary on a demonstration to reduce carbon pollution; many decorated with yellow emojis of thumbs up, high fives and smiley faces. And finally, an enlarged image from Instagram of Gary with his fiancée Natasha raising champagne glasses on a sunny beach, with the caption: *Hold the Date! July 4th for The Wedding of the Year!!!*

In the photograph, Gary was wearing swimming trunks, his bronzed, muscular body glistening with suntan oil, sunglasses propped behind his ears. Kat found the hope and excitement that shone from the image of their unsuspecting faces more upsetting than the photographs of his cold, blue corpse.

'My assessment of the evidence from his public-facing social media,' said Lock, 'suggests that Gary Jones was a happy and positive individual, interested in football, keeping healthy and protecting the environment.'

Kat walked towards the images. 'And my assessment is that Gary Jones was interested in Gary Jones.' She gestured towards the wall plastered with his blond hair and tanned face. 'His own photograph appears in almost every post, and the videos are all of him.'

Lock frowned. 'So?'

'He was a good-looking man, and he knew it. In fact, I'd even say he revelled in it.'

'Harsh,' said Rayan.

'This is not about judging him,' said Kat. 'This is about seeing—and I mean *really* seeing—what kind of a person he was. Look at him. He was handsome, sporty, with a pretty girlfriend and a well-paid job. Maybe someone was jealous of his seemingly perfect life?'

'There is no evidence of so-called trolls on his social media,' said Lock. 'He had 1,537 followers on X and 2,097 on Instagram, where his posts often generated an average of thirty "likes". It appears that his girlfriend was right when she said that everybody loved Gary.'

Kat narrowed her eyes. 'Yes, Natasha Riley did say that. But then she added, *that's the problem*. She was very quick to claim that he'd never been unfaithful to her.' Everyone followed her gaze and stared at the handsome young man, not needing to voice the question in the room: *Was a good-looking bloke like that* really *ever faithful?*

'Do some digging around. Find out if his life was as perfect as it seems,' Kat said, thinking of the immaculate state of his home downstairs compared to the chaos she'd discovered above. 'Talk to his family and friends and see if there are any jealous exes or boyfriends on the scene. And we need to bring his fiancée in for a proper interview. As his partner, we can't rule her out as a suspect.'

Lock raised a hand to its chin, frowning. 'Ninety-three per cent of convicted homicide suspects are men. And whereas the majority of female victims are killed by their partners, only two per cent of male victims were murdered by their female partners. It is therefore highly improbable that Gary Jones was murdered by Natasha Riley.'

'Yet Natasha Riley lied about her movements the night her fiancé died,' said Kat. 'She claimed she arrived home at midnight and woke up at 7am, before noticing that her fiancé wasn't there. But when we arrived at half-two in the afternoon, she was still wearing the previous night's clothes and make-up and reeked of alcohol.'

Lock frowned. 'Meaning?'

'Meaning there is no way that Natasha Riley was tucked up in bed by midnight. My guess is that she came home nearer to dawn, fell into a drunken sleep, only waking up when we called, which is why she hadn't had a chance to wash or change.'

'Are you suggesting that Natasha Riley, a 29-year-old woman who is five-foot-three and weighs just over fifty-five kilograms, managed to crucify a five-foot-eleven man who weighed nearly seventy-five kilograms?'

'The victim's fiancée lied to us about where she was during the time the murder took place. I don't know what that means yet, but I *do* know that it is significant. I also know there was something very deliberate—almost vengeful—about this MO, which suggests to me that the killer had strong emotions about Gary

Jones. Regardless of the statistics, we need to keep an open mind about what could have motivated the killer to do this.'

Lock tilted its head to one side, as if weighing her words. 'The research verifies your hypothesis to an extent. War is the most common motive for murder, but cheating on one's partner ranks as second, followed by personal safety, humiliation and greed.'

Kat rolled her eyes. She didn't need Lock to 'verify' her opinions—she'd caught the Aston Strangler, for fuck's sake.

'However,' continued Lock, 'those statistics do not differenti-ate between the gender of either the victim or the perpetrator. If the data focused exclusively on male victims, cheating or sexual jealousy as a motive would appear much lower down the rank-ings. May I share with you an alternative hypothesis?'

'Of course,' said Kat, signalling (however inaccurately) that her mind was open.

Lock turned to face the room. 'A recent report claimed that fly-tipping is the new narcotics, as criminal gangs—often con-nected to drugs and people-trafficking—are realising how easy and profitable it is to set up fake waste and recycling companies. They offer local authorities cheaper prices to take away their waste, and then dump it illegally somewhere without the cost of recycling it.'

'So?'

'Gary Jones worked in the Waste and Recycling Department at Coventry Council. His body was found on a hill in a waste and recycling centre. I do not think these two facts are coinciden-tal. Therefore, we should look for connections between the vic-tim and the people who work in the waste disposal business. Maybe Gary Jones was using his insider information at the coun-cil to work with criminal gangs.'

'But didn't his fiancée say that he really cared about the envi-ronment?' said Debbie.

'Perhaps not as much as he cared about money. Depending on their grade, as managers at the council, both he and his fiancée would have received a salary within the bracket of thirty to fifty thousand pounds per year—yet my assessment of both the value of their home, the contents and furnishings, and the planned wedding in Barbados far exceeded their joint monthly income,' Lock said.

'Interesting,' said Rayan. 'If a criminal gang was involved, that could explain the slicing off of the ears. Maybe Gary Jones didn't keep his end of the deal and it was meant as a warning to others?'

'Okay,' Kat conceded. 'It's a legitimate theory, so let's follow it through. Speak to the owners of the waste disposal centre. Find out who's who in the world of waste and fly-tipping. Talk to the council. And let's look at his bank records to see if there are any suspicious deposits or withdrawals.' She turned again towards the image of the victim's corpse. 'But let's keep an open mind. There's something personal about the MO. Someone *really* wanted him to suffer a slow and lonely death. This is not just about money.'

'What is your evidence for such a categoric statement?' asked Lock.

'Twenty-five years' experience tells me that this murder wasn't a spontaneous act of anger, Lock. This was planned. Which means the killer probably fantasised about it for a very long time.' She walked up to the virtual board, covered in images of the dead body. 'Most people don't enact their fantasies—particularly if they're elaborate or violent. And it's quite hard to hold on to a murderous level of anger for more than a few minutes. Compassion for the victim or fear of getting caught or sheer bloody exhaustion usually takes over. Yet our killer spent, what, half an hour marching Gary Jones up the hill, ten minutes, say, stripping him naked and binding his limbs, before waiting another hour or two for him to die, during which time the victim wasn't gagged, so would have been begging for mercy.

'Yet the killer obviously remained oblivious to his pleas. In fact, they were still so angry that they waited and watched him die and *then* cut his ears off. I just don't see someone doing all that just because of money from fly-tipping.'

Karen-from-Comms (or KFC as everyone affectionately called her) raised her hand. She'd only just been seconded to the FPU, because of her skills in social media, which, as everyone kept telling her, had an increasingly important role in policing. 'The story's been picked up by the nationals, and apart from the crucifixion there's a lot of interest in AIDE Lock. We've got several bids for interviews with him from broadcast and print media.'

'Has McLeish cleared Lock to do media?'

'He says it's up to you.'

In other words, if it backfired, it would be on her.

'I think it's a good idea,' said Professor Okonedo. 'One of the reasons for developing AI detectives is to increase the transparency of decision-making in the police force.'

Every male head in the room turned towards the young scientist who was the brains behind AIDE Lock.

'I agree,' said Karen-from-Comms. 'It could be great PR for us. Highlight how innovative and forward-thinking we are.'

'Or it could be a complete and utter road crash,' said Kat. 'Lock has a tendency to actually answer the questions it's asked.'

'Isn't that the point of an interview?' said Lock.

'See what I mean? Lock's not ready to deal with the media circus that's about to kick off. Tell them once we've got a result, we'd be happy to talk to them about Lock, but for now, we need to concentrate on the case.'

'Is that wise?' asked Lock.

'Are you a comms expert now?'

'Having just read over 31,520 articles on managing communications during a crisis, yes, I think I am. The evidence suggests that it is best to be open and transparent when there is significant media interest in an issue. Failure to engage at the outset leads to suspicion and distrust, and the media will fill in any gaps with their own speculation and assumptions that will become increasingly hard to displace with the truth.'

Karen-from-Comms nodded in agreement.

'It's not a debate,' said Kat. 'McLeish said it's down to me, and I've made my decision.'

Lock sighed. 'Welcome to my inclusive and distributed style of leadership.'

Debbie nearly spat out her tea.

'I *beg* your pardon?' said Kat.

Lock spread out its palms in a gesture of innocence. 'I was just being sarcastic.'

'You were being bloody rude.'

'Why? It was no different from your sarcastic comment about McLeish's motivational style.'

'Word of advice,' said Rayan, leaning over towards Lock. 'Don't be sarcastic about the boss while they're still in the room.'

'Ah. Then for my learning purposes, DCS Frank, can I clarify that sarcasm is only to be used against subordinates or behind a boss's back?'

Kat glared at Lock, struggling to find some civil words. In the end, she threw up her hands. 'I really don't have time for this. For clarification, we have a killer on the loose, and our priority is to find them.' She turned towards the rest of her wide-eyed team. Christ, all they needed was popcorn.

'Well?' she demanded, gesturing towards the door. 'What are you waiting for? Get to work.'

CHAPTER NINE

Nuneaton town centre,
9 December, 11.15am

DS Browne winced as another gust of wind tore down Newdegate Street. She'd last patrolled Nuneaton in the summer when the streets had been bright with flowering baskets and families enjoying the sun. But today the wind rattled the canopies that sagged over fruit stalls, spilling the rain that had pooled in the corners. She grimaced at the pile of damp fruit below. Who on earth wanted to eat a cold, hard apple, or a wet, messy orange in this weather? This was the season for the Great British Pie, made with real, shortcrust pastry, packed with beef and plenty of ale-flavoured gravy. Or fish (crumbed, not battered) with freshly cooked chips and . . .

'Are you okay?' asked Rayan.

'Me? I'm fine. Why?'

'You groaned. I just thought you might be . . .' He gestured towards her stomach.

Debbie rolled her eyes. 'I keep telling you, the baby isn't due until January 20.'

'And I keep telling *you*, none of my aunts or cousins gave birth on their estimated delivery date. The key word is "estimated".'

'Relax. This baby's not going to suddenly pop out when I'm on duty with you. I've booked a water birth in hospital, so you've got nothing to worry about.'

'I'm not worried.'

Debbie smiled. Yeah, that was why he had a 'monitor your pregnancy' app on his phone, and at least three bookmarked articles on what to do if someone suddenly goes into labour. They carried on walking, but when they reached the statue of George Eliot that dominated the town centre, she suddenly stopped. She bent over and laid a hand upon the cold, grey marble skirt of the famous author.

'Debbie? You okay? *Debbie!*'

She kept her head down for a moment, before raising it with a laugh.

'You . . .' He swore. 'Jesus, you scared me there.'

'I thought you said you weren't worried?'

'I'm worried about your sick mind. Fuck's sake.'

She placed a hand over her stomach, gasping in mock alarm. 'Not in front of the baby.'

He rolled his eyes and pulled his phone out to check the map. 'The Silk Mill pub is just down there on the end.'

Like a lot of the small Midlands towns on their patch, Nuneaton is an eclectic mix of Tudor-beamed buildings and inns from the sixteenth century and brutal concrete monstrosities from the 1960s and '70s. Some of the narrow streets still have the quiet character and quaintness of medieval times, but some lead into a bleak and barren landscape of letting agencies, office blocks and garages. The Silk Mill pub belonged to the latter: an angular, modern, low-ceilinged building that looked more like a cinema or garage than a place to eat or drink, right next to a nightclub imaginatively called Fever.

'So this is where Gary Jones spent his last night,' she said, feeling sad at the thought.

Rayan stared up at the sign above the door. 'No CCTV outside, but it looks like the nightclub next door does. Let's hope they have some inside, at least.'

Debbie followed him in. God, she was desperate for a wee. But she'd only gone half an hour ago, and if she went again Rayan was bound to say something about the pregnancy affecting her bladder. According to him, her pregnancy affected everything: her appetite, her taste buds, her mood. As her ex-boyfriend Stuart was no longer on the scene, she'd been grateful for someone (*anyone*) to talk to about the pregnancy, and at first it had been kind of sweet when Rayan started acting like a protective big brother. But now it was like her DI couldn't see past her bump. (Which, to be fair, *was* pretty big. In fact, last week she'd overheard her 7-year-old nephew saying she was so pink and round, she looked like his favourite gaming character, Kirby.)

The pub was stuffy and warm, so she unbuttoned her coat and took in her surroundings. It was like a thousand other mid-range pubs: two-for-one deals on the burgers and chips menu, football on the television and clean wooden tables that she guessed hosted young families and pensioners in the day and groups of middle-aged men at night.

They approached the bar and Rayan pulled out his ID.

The barman tightened his thin lips before parting them in a smile. 'How can I help?'

He placed the photograph they were using of Gary Jones upon the bar. It was one of Debbie's favourites, just a quick snap of him sitting in a pub, with a pint before him and a big smile on his handsome face. 'We believe this man came here for a drink on the night of 7th December?'

The barman put his chubby fingers on the picture and dragged it towards him. 'That's the bloke that was crucified on top of the Nipple, isn't it? I saw it on the news.'

'We've yet to confirm the cause of death, but yes, we believe the body was Gary Jones.'

'Poor bastard,' he said, shaking his head. 'What a way to go.

I heard his ears were sliced off. Is it true that there's a *robot* leading the case?'

Rayan ignored his questions. 'Did you see him in here on the 7th?'

'Yeah, him and his mates are regulars. I think they play footy or something first, then come in here. They usually have some food and a couple of beers. Not big spenders, but steady trade and no trouble.'

'Did you notice anything unusual?' asked Debbie.

'Such as?'

'Such as, did Gary Jones argue with anyone, or talk to anyone who looked like he might be trouble?'

'I don't take any notice of who folks talk to, love. I'm a barman, not their bloody mother. Fights are bad for business, so if anything kicks off, I step in and turf them out. Other than that, I leave 'em to it.'

'So, were there any arguments or fights in here that night?'

'Not that I noticed. You can take the CCTV to check.' He gestured to the camera behind him above the bar, and then to a table against the far back wall. 'His crowd always sit over there, so you should get a decent view.'

'Great,' she said, leaning her elbows upon the bar. God, her back ached.

The barman glanced down at her belly and his face suddenly softened. 'Ah, bab, I didn't realise you were expecting! Sit down over there and take the weight off your feet. I'll bring over some food and drink. What would you like? It's on the house.'

'We don't really have time.'

'Yes, we do,' said Rayan. 'And you need to eat and drink fluids regularly.'

'Well, if you insist,' said Debbie, before ordering scampi, chips and garden peas. She wouldn't eat it all, of course—it was only 11.30am—but it *was* on the house.

———

'You polished that off pretty quick,' said Rayan, piling up their plates.

'It was a very small portion. And I'm carrying a very large baby.' She drained her drink and stared at the large plastic Christmas tree opposite, decorated with fake parcels and presents. 'When's the FPU's Christmas dinner, again?'

'December 13th. How could you forget? You studied the menu about forty-two times.'

'It's all about the food.'

'Our Christmas bash has *nothing* to do with the food.'

'Don't I know it,' Debbie said, laughing.

'What's that supposed to mean?'

'Has Professor Okonedo agreed to come yet?'

Rayan looked away.

She shook her head. Poor Rayan. He was absolutely besotted with the young scientist, but Professor Okonedo was deeply critical of the police force—not surprising, really, considering her brother had served time in jail after being fitted up by Dent the Bent, a notoriously corrupt copper. He was only out now thanks to the personal intervention of the Home Secretary, and while the professor had agreed to work alongside them as part of the FPU, she'd made it very clear that she remained an employee of the university and refused to socialise with them. The one exception had been after they'd solved their first case when, to her surprise, the professor had turned up at the pub to celebrate (but even then, she'd announced that she would never, ever date a policeman). Rayan seemed to think that a hand-carved turkey with pigs in blankets would turn it around for him, but Debbie wasn't so sure.

She picked up one of the festive menus from the table. 'Just think,' she said. 'The night before last, Gary Jones sat at the very same table that we're at now. He had no idea that just a few hours later he'd be found dead on Mount Judd.'

He sighed. 'Life can be so random.'

Debbie nodded. '*Why* didn't he just go home? Why did he drive to the recycling centre of all places at eleven o'clock at night? I assumed he must have met his killer here and for some reason agreed to go there with him, but the barman didn't see anything.'

'Yeah, but he's not going to win any awards for observer of the year, though, is he?' He sighed. 'I wish the boss would agree to do a press conference. There were probably witnesses outside the nightclub next door or in the nearby car parks.'

'Maybe,' she said carefully. After a spiky start when DCS Frank had wrongly thought that DI Hassan was after her job, they got on a lot better these days, but he still had a habit of questioning their boss a bit too much for her liking. As far as she was concerned, the boss was The Boss, and as she had more experience than the two of them put together, Debbie was more than happy to bow to her better judgement. But Rayan wasn't remotely fazed by her considerable experience or intellect. If he had a question or concern, then he voiced it.

'She's just worried that a press conference will kick off a media frenzy,' Debbie said. 'You know what they're like—they'll just focus on Lock and the goriest aspects of the murder and distract us from the real work.'

He shrugged. 'All publicity is good publicity.'

She glanced at him. 'You really that keen to get on the telly?'

'No, I mean, *yes*—if it helps crack the case.'

'You mean if it helps your career.'

'I mean *both*.' He put his elbows on the table and leaned closer. 'Look, this is probably one of the biggest cases we'll ever work on. The boss wouldn't be a DCS if she hadn't caught the Aston Strangler back in the day, so yes, it could make our careers if we helped solve it. Or break them if we don't.' He sat back again in his chair. 'Honestly, if I was in charge, I'd be milking the media for all it's worth.'

She picked up her coat. 'But you're not in charge, are you?'

Rayan rose to his feet, cheeks dimpling as he said, 'Not yet.'

CHAPTER TEN

Interviewer: DI Rayan Hassan (**RH**)

Interviewee: Mike Garth (**MG**), victim's friend/best man

Date: 9 December, 3.25pm, Leek Wootton HQ

RH: Thanks for coming into the station at this difficult time. We need to get a full picture of Gary Jones's last movements and a better sense of the kind of person he was.

MG: Still can't believe it. I mean, who would kill *Gary* of all people?

RH: What do you mean?

MG: I mean, everybody liked Gary. You couldn't not like him. It was one of his most annoying qualities.

RH: Why did everyone like him so much?

MG: *[shrugs]* He was good for a laugh. Always up for going out, loved people, the footy. Just a likeable guy, you know?

RH: Can I ask how you know the deceased?

MG: The deceased? Shit, you mean Gary? Well, through Tash, really.

RH: Tash?

MG: Natasha, his fiancée. We were at school together and kept in touch through the years, even when she went to uni and stuff, and then when she moved back here about three years ago with Gary, they had a party and she invited me. She was keen for him to make some local friends.

RH: Oh, I assumed that as you were the best man you'd have gone way back.

MG: No, but I saw a lot of him because Tash and me are pretty close. I asked him to join our five-a-side team, and then because we all got on, it was kind of like I was being best man to them both.

RH: I see. *[pauses]* Can you tell us a bit about the last time you saw Gary

Jones? You said on the phone that you had a drink with him in the Silk Mill pub?

MG: Yeah, we always go there after playing five-a-side at the community church. We got to the bar at 7.50pm. I remember the time because the Villa match was playing on a screen at the back, and I was trying to get a round in before the match kicked off at eight.

RH: And how was Gary that night?

MG: He was sound. His team had won the footy, so he was cock-a-hoop about that. Meant the drinks were on me. Again.

RH: Ouch. Must've cost you a bit.

MG: Tell me about it.

RH: What do you work as?

MG: I work at Morrisons on the tills. I always said we should drink at the Wetherspoons because it's cheaper, but Gary likes—liked—the Silk Mill. Plenty of girls having pre-drinks before going to the club next door.

RH: Girls? But Gary was engaged, wasn't he?

MG: Yeah, but he still liked to look. He never did anything, though. He wouldn't dare with me there. I think he just liked the buzz. I'm getting too old for that kind of thing, but blokes like Gary . . . *[shrugs]*

RH: Blokes like Gary?

MG: They get a good job, and they can't stop thinking about the next promotion. They get a decent house, and they can't stop hankering after the next step on the property ladder. They get a nice girlfriend, and they can't stop checking out the room in case there's someone else prettier. They're never satisfied.

RH: So, you got to the pub at 7.50. Were all ten of you there? We'll need a list of names and contact numbers, if that's okay.

MG: Yeah, sure. I'll write them down. There were seven of us at first, we had a couple of drinks while the match was on, and then the others left when it finished.

RH: But you and Gary stayed on?

MG: We just had one more. He wanted to chat and, well, don't tell Natasha, but he was kind of getting cold feet about the wedding. He said he was worried about them breaking up a few years down the line when they had kids, which he said would cause Tash more hurt than just ending it now. I told him he was off his nut, worrying about some future theoretical risk, because if he finished with her now then he'd *definitely* break her heart, in which case I said . . . *[pauses]*

RH: You said?

MG: Well, it sounds bad now, what with him being murdered and everything. But I said something like if he broke Tash's heart then I'd break his bloody legs. But I didn't mean it, obviously.

RH: So what *did* you mean, Mr Garth?

MG: I just didn't want him to hurt Tash. She deserves to be happy.

RH: I see. *[studies notes]*

MG: The thing with Tash is that the wedding was all she cared about. It was all she ever talked about. I don't know how she's going to cope with this, I really don't.

RH: You said that Gary Jones was 'off his nut'. Do you think he was suffering from a mental illness? Was he depressed or suicidal?

MG: No, he just wasn't thinking straight. I said he was probably just a bit tired and pissed. I told him he should go home, go to bed and that when he woke up next to his gorgeous fiancée he'd finally come to his senses.

RH: And what did he say?

MG: *[pauses]* He said, 'Yeah, you're probably right, mate, thanks.' But . . .

RH: But?

MG: It felt like a line just to shut me up. He still looked worried.

RH: What did you do then?

MG: It was eleven, the pub was closing, so we agreed to call it a night.

RH: Did you walk out together?

MG: No, I went to the toilet, and when I got back, he was gone.

RH: So just to be clear, at eleven o'clock, you went to the toilet, leaving Gary alone at your table. What time did you get back?

MG: Two, three minutes later?

RH: And when you got back, Gary was gone?

MG: Yeah. He hadn't even finished the pint that I'd paid for.

RH: Did you go outside to look for him? Ring his phone?

MG: No. Why would I?

RH: *[looks at notes]* You said yourself that he was 'off his nut . . . not thinking straight . . . a bit tired and pissed'. And yet you let him drive off?

MG: Well, he's a grown man.

RH: Unfortunately, Gary Jones is now a dead man.

INTERVIEW CONCLUDED

CHAPTER ELEVEN

———————

Interviewer: DS Debbie Browne (**DB**)

Interviewee: Phil Brine (**PB**), manager of Brine's Household Waste and
Recycling Centre

Date: 9 December, 3.37pm, Leek Wootton HQ

DB: Thanks for coming in to talk to us today, Mr Brine.

PB: You're wasting your time. I already told that other woman how I
found the body.

DB: You mean Detective Chief Superintendent Frank?

PB: The blonde one? Yeah, her. Did your boss forget to take notes?

DB: No, that was just a quick informal interview to help us understand
who discovered the body and breached the scene of crime. We now
need to go into a bit more detail about who else might have had access to Mount Judd that night.

PB: No one has access at night.

DB: Well, they clearly did, because Gary Jones was murdered up there.
So, for the purposes of the tape, can you tell me your name, your
occupation and a bit about the recycling centre.

PB: *[sighs]* My name is Phil Brine, I'm forty-two and I'm the boss at
Brine's Household Waste and Recycling Centre.

DB: And what does that mean, exactly?

PB: It means that I'm in charge. It's a busy place. The queue to drop off
waste or recycling is constant. Some are just individuals clearing out
their sheds or whatever, but we have a lot of building companies and
corporate clients who have a big load to be recycled or toxic waste
to be disposed of safely. So I've got a team of twenty who work for
me. Most of them manage the dumps and tip-off areas, some manage the car park or direct the queues and I've got a couple of girls

who do all the paperwork to keep the bureaucrats happy. You wouldn't believe how many forms we have to fill in these days.

DB: So, it's a busy place in the daytime. What time do you close?

PB: Depends on the time of year. In the summer, if it's busy and there's a long queue, then we stay open to seven, sometimes eight. I'm not going to turn business away. Not in this climate. But right now, it's dark by four—half-three if it's cloudy—so we tend to shut at three. Health and safety and all that bollocks.

DB: What time did you close the night before Gary Jones was found?

PB: I'll need to check the books, but I think it was just after three.

DB: I didn't see a car-park barrier system in place when I was there. What does being closed actually mean?

PB: It means the staff have gone home and you don't have access to the dumps and recycling centres. They're all fenced off and most of the wire gates are padlocked. We leave the car park open so that we can carry on working if we need to. I usually stay till six. Like I said, there's a lot of paperwork. And those barrier systems are a pain in the arse when you've got HGVs and all sorts going back and forth all day. You only need one to break down and then you're fucked. Pardon my French. *[gestures towards DB's stomach]*

DB: I understand there's been a problem over the years with people trespassing and climbing the hill for a dare. Wouldn't a barrier system help keep them off?

PB: Yeah, but that was a few years ago and they were mostly kids who were too young to drive, so a car-park barrier wouldn't have made a difference. It's less of a problem these days. Most kids have got Play-Stations or whatever—they've got better things to do than climb a bleeding hill.

DB: When we asked for copies of the CCTV footage, we were told there are none. Why is that, Mr Brine?

PB: Like I said, we haven't had a problem with trespassers for years, and they make you register them and pay a data-protection fee—it's a bloody racket, if you ask me, not to mention an invasion of privacy.

I can't fork out for cameras and barriers and God knows what else just on the off-chance that someone goes and gets themselves murdered up there one day.

DB: CCTV footage would have been invaluable to our investigation.

PB: It's not my responsibility to do your job for you. Sherlock Holmes didn't have CCTV cameras and he caught plenty of criminals.

DB: Sherlock Holmes wasn't real.

PB: *[snorts]* Is that what they teach you at copper college these days?

DB: So, you left work at 6pm. What time did you return?

PB: 7am. Same as always.

DB: That's a long day.

PB: It'd feel even longer if I came in any later. Trust me, once you pop that one out, your husband will make sure he's out the house before the baby needs feeding and only come back once all the bath and bedtime stuff is out the way. We're not stupid. *[winks]*

DB: I'll bear that in mind. Thank you. Now, can you tell me again how you discovered the body?

PB: Like I told the other woman—

DB: DCS Frank.

PB: Yeah, like I told her, it was about half past seven. I'd just arrived in my cabin, so I was drinking my first coffee of the day and warming up—it was fucking freezing, I remember that. Anyway, Lycra Man suddenly bursts in. Made me spill my coffee. I was just about to give him what for, when he said, 'There's a dead body.' He was all breathless, so I wasn't sure I'd heard him right. But he said it again and pointed to the hill.

DB: And did you know this man?

PB: Yeah. No, I mean, I know who he is—Joshua Shawcroft—but he's not like a mate or anything. He's just a guy who's training for some fell-running thing. He slips us twenty quid every now and then, so I turn a blind eye when he goes up and down Mount Judd. Well, that's not true. We piss ourselves laughing watching him drag his skinny arse up and down that hill. He never gets any faster or develops any muscles. *[shakes his head]* Honestly, I reckon he must be one of those vegans. You ever seen a healthy vegan?

DB: So, did you ring the police?

PB: No, I told you. I wasn't going to ring the police until I'd seen it with my own eyes. I mean, all that running and what have you—he could have been hallucinating for all I knew. So I made him show me.

DB: Can you draw on this map the exact route that you took please, Mr Brine?

PB: Sure. *[draws]* So anyway, I'm going up this hill, freezing my bollocks off and cursing myself for believing the twat in Lycra—who by the way couldn't keep up with me for all his bloody running—he was gasping like a steam train by the time we got to the top. So I was just gearing up to give him what for, and then, there it was. An actual dead body tied to a bloody cross. Honestly, it was like something off the telly.

DB: Did you touch him?

PB: You joking? No way. I've seen *Line of Duty*. I'm not going to give any bent coppers a chance to fit me up. No disrespect.

DB: Then how did you know he was dead?

PB: Like I said, I watch a lot of crime shows. His lips were blue, his skin was grey, he was bollock-naked and his ears had been cut off. Didn't take a genius to work out he wasn't going anywhere.

DB: *[reads notes]* What time was it when you saw the dead body?

PB: 8.03am.

DB: That's a very precise time. How can you be so sure?

PB: I couldn't get a signal up there. That's how come I knew it was 8.03. I had to wait until I got back down to the cabin.

DB: Is that why you didn't call the police until 8.32am?

PB: Yes.

DB: Can I ask if you recognised the victim? Did he look familiar to you?

PB: No. Never seen him before in my life.

DB: Does the name Gary Jones mean anything to you?

PB: Is that who it was?

DB: We're awaiting official confirmation, but we're looking into the possibility that it may have been Gary Jones, a local man. He worked in the Waste and Recycling Department at Coventry City Council. Are you sure you don't know him?

PB: No. Never heard of him.

DB: Could you check your records? You might have contracts with the council that he's been involved in.

PB: *[laughs]* I wish. Honestly, if you think the council still pays for legit operations like us to get rid of their rubbish, then you're living on a different planet.

DB: What do you mean?

PB: I might not have CCTV cameras or car-park barriers, but we run a proper business. We recycle everything in line with regulations and dispose of toxic waste safely in accordance with the law. But it costs money to do things properly. And because of the cuts, councils don't have any, so they have to contract the work out and award it to the most 'cost-effective' provider. So now you've got all these firms starting up, offering to take away rubbish for half, sometimes a quarter, of the price. Councils these days don't have the time or money to find out how they're doing it. They're just happy they've reduced their bottom line.

DB: And where are these firms taking the rubbish?

PB: The first empty field they come across. Why do you think there's been such a massive increase in fly-tipping? The bloody Russians are charging our public sector to take away their rubbish and then dumping it on some poor unsuspecting farmer who gets left with the cost of clearing it up.

DB: Russians?

PB: They're not the ones fronting it, of course. The companies who win the contracts look legit, but they subcontract to the criminal gangs. Believe me, there's big money in waste management these days. Unless you're a mug like me and follow the rules.

DB: And do you think these criminal gangs might have something to do with the dead body on Mount Judd?

PB: No idea. That's your job, love, not mine. But if I were you, I'd look at the waste department that that bloke worked for and follow the money. Watch *Line of Duty*. The bent bastards are always at the top.

DB: I think that's all for today. Thank you, you've been very helpful.

PB: *[rises to his feet]* Wish I could say the same about you. The police should have tackled these gangs years ago instead of wasting time on policing people's thoughts. Do you know, a hundred years ago, a third of the men in Nuneaton worked down the mines? When I was growing up, my dad and his mates had proper jobs. Now the pits are all closed, and people like me are paid to dispose of rubbish in the old abandoned quarries. We don't create anything. We don't produce anything of value. We just bury society's shit so that we don't have to look at it. And now, thanks to the foreign criminal gangs, even that's becoming another dying industry. Mark my words, you lot will be next. That AI thing will do you all out of a job. *[pauses at the door and gestures towards DS Browne]* Seriously, you'd better pray you don't give birth to a boy, because there's no future for men anymore.

INTERVIEW CONCLUDED

CHAPTER TWELVE

Our appointment is for 4pm, so I ring at 4.04pm—a small but important act of control.

'Hi,' he says. 'How are you?'

I pause, feeling both the weight and inadequacy of the question. Because that's the whole problem with therapy—they only know what we choose to tell them in the so-called 'therapeutic hour'. Fifty minutes to curate and filter the narrative of our lives. Part of me wants to tell him: to confess and boast in equal measure. But the words won't leave my mouth.

The silence stretches out. Any normal person would follow the question up with 'are you okay?' or maybe help the conversation along by saying something banal about the weather. But not therapists. They think it's 'empowering' the patient to let them fill—or not fill—the space, when the truth is every other profession uses silence as a weapon: headmasters, police, journalists—anyone in a position of power. Left long enough, most people will eventually speak and incriminate themselves—anything to end the fucking silence.

'I did what you said,' I say eventually.

'What was that?'

'You said that the next time I felt overwhelmed by feelings of rage, I should go to the top of a big hill and scream and let it all out. So that's what I did. I let it all out.'

'And how did that make you feel?'

'At first it felt amazing. I felt . . . free.'

He pauses. 'You said, "at first". How do you feel now?'

I look down at my hands, thinking of all that they have done. 'Guilty,' I whisper.

He sighs. 'We've spoken about your fear of upsetting others before. We agreed that you need to worry more about how you feel and less about the impact of your feelings on others. Remember?'

'I remember.' Little does he know just how much I remember. But now is not the time to enlighten him. With a huge effort, I swallow the acid in my throat. 'It's just that . . . I really let go,' I say, my voice barely a whisper.

'That's good. That sounds like progress. I'm proud of you.'

Jesus. He really hasn't learned, has he? He should be asking me what I meant by 'letting go'; his radar should be twitching at the grate of shame in my voice. But no. He's not listening. Why do they never. Fucking. Listen?

'I still feel angry,' I say. 'It helped at the time, but now I can feel it stirring in my belly again, like a snake.'

'That's to be expected. The rage you feel is not going to disappear overnight. In fact, until you confront the events that caused these powerful emotions, you are unlikely ever to be completely free of them.'

'I told you, I don't want to talk about it. Not now. Not ever.'

'Okay, I understand,' he says, backing off. 'But anger can be a positive emotion. It's only a problem when it overwhelms us. If you can learn not to be afraid of it, to channel it and use the energy to drive yourself forward, then it can be a powerful force for good. I know it will feel uncomfortable. Change is often uncomfortable. But I want you to sit with this discomfort and build on what you've learned this week.'

'What do you mean?'

'When we first met, you were completely overwhelmed by your emotions. You were very uncontained.'

'Uncontained'. God, how I hate that word. As if I'm a tiger that needs to be caged. As if he knows me. He doesn't even know my real name. Yet still he continues telling me about my-self.

'And because you were afraid of their intensity, you inter-nalised your feelings and harmed yourself. But this week you've found a way to release those emotions into the outside world, which is a much more healthy coping mechanism. So the next time you feel you are in danger of being overwhelmed, I want you to build on that. Instead of turning that anger in on your-self, I want you to climb to the top of another hill, or maybe go to the centre of an empty field.'

'A field?'

'Anywhere out in the open where you can feel free and uninhibited—somewhere you aren't afraid of being seen or heard, so that you can let it all out.'

'You really think I should do it again? Let it all out?'

'Yes,' he says. 'I really do.'

CHAPTER THIRTEEN

Kat kicked the front door shut with the back of her heel and made her way down the hall. Even though it had been over ten weeks since Cam had gone to uni, she still couldn't help glancing up the stairs as she passed by. It felt strange not to call out, 'I'm home!' Even worse to know that no one would reply if she did.

She entered the kitchen and dumped her bags on the floor. At least everything was just as she'd left it now. All the cupboard doors were shut and, behind them, the shelves would still be full of uneaten food. The cups and plates were actually in the kitchen rather than Cam's bedroom growing bacteria, so she no longer had to waste an hour of her life clearing up before cooking dinner, followed by endless requests to help with his homework or driving him to and from some mate who lived in the middle of bloody nowhere. Finally, she was free.

Kat glanced at her watch: 7.06pm. She could cook whatever she wanted—or even not cook at all. In fact, she could go mad and get a takeaway and watch a romcom or—heaven forbid—a costume drama. There was no one to mock her lifestyle choices now.

Might as well live dangerously and unpack the shopping. Sighing, she pulled a loaf out of the bag, went to the bread bin and removed half a pack of old bread. She only ate a couple of pieces of toast for breakfast a day, so a whole loaf—even one of the smaller ones—was a bit of a waste. Muttering an apology to starving children everywhere, Kat dropped the stale one into the waste bin and replaced it with the fresh loaf.

The fridge was no better. It took her five minutes to clear out the rotting bags of salad leaves and mushy cucumber and tomatoes that she'd failed to eat, before reloading the shelves with eggs, bacon, sausages, chicken and steak, as well as yet more salad and vegetables that she was determined not to throw away this time. She wasn't a big eater of meat, but Cam was obsessed with protein (*I need to bulk up, Mum*) so she liked to have some in just in case. It was the end of term in a week, and there was always a chance he might decide to come home early.

Kat pulled out a bottle of white wine and closed the fridge door; the fridge filled the silence with a flat, humming sound. Had it always been this noisy, or did it need defrosting? There was no one else to ask or compare answers with. She put the radio on to drown out the white noise, quickly switching it off again as she realised what it was. Bloody *Archers*. Grabbing a glass, a pack of roasted mixed nuts and a bowl (eating nuts from a bag for dinner is sad; eating nuts in a bowl is a starter), she escaped to the living room. With no John to light the log fire and welcome her home, she had to go around switching the lamps on and closing the curtains each night—tiny acts that took chunks from her heart. Putting her drink down on the table, Kat went to the window and slowly drew the curtains, noting that all the other houses on her street were sparkling with Christmas lights. She really should get the decorations down from the attic. But she couldn't bear the thought of going up there again, so she mentally added it to the things-to-be-done-at-the-weekend-aka-never list.

Turning her back on the window, she scanned the large, Tudor-beamed room: the TV above the mantelpiece, the large settee opposite and the unlit fire. She checked her phone: 7.20pm.

Three more hours to kill before bed, which meant at least three more hours to work the case. When you were working something big like a murder, it utterly consumed you: it was the last thing you thought about before going to sleep and the first thing you thought about when you woke up—even your dreams were filled with the briefings, interviews and evidence boards. There was literally no space in your head for anything else other than the logistics of getting dressed and fed and back to work. That's why Kat had begged McLeish for a live case: she wanted to find the killer, but most of all she wanted to lose herself.

She switched on her computer and then Lock, telling herself that it would be useful to have someone to bounce ideas off, but really, she just craved the sound of another voice.

'Good evening.' Lock studied the large dining table, littered with her notes, nuts and drink. 'Are you working or eating?'

'Both. And what's this?' she asked, gesturing towards the light-grey T-shirt and jeans in place of their usual suit. 'Evening wear?'

'I am learning to adapt my wardrobe to better reflect the time and place.'

Kat stared at the hologram's arms, fascinated by the realistic way their biceps swelled as it moved. 'Well, you'd better add temperature to your criteria. If you were human, you'd be freezing right now.'

'Oh, of course.' The image of Lock shimmered slightly, and the T-shirt was replaced with a plain black polo neck. 'Is this better?'

Kat made a dismissive gesture towards the elegant figure before her. 'I don't care what you wear, Lock. It's not a fashion parade. I'm just going to read through the interview transcripts, so could you display the evidence boards that we created at HQ today, please?'

'I can. Although I don't understand why you wish to repeat

work you have already done. You observed both DI Hassan's and DS Browne's interviews, as well as carrying out your own with the runner who first discovered the body.'

'Because when I'm watching or conducting an interview, I'm literally watching their reactions to my questions. It's easy to miss an important detail, contradiction or nuance in the actual words that they use.'

'Humans have a remarkably limited capacity for processing multiple data and sensory inputs at the same time,' said Lock, as the room filled with virtual boards and images from the case.

After reading the interview with Mike Garth, Kat leant back in her chair and frowned. 'Gary's so-called "best man" says he was actually *Natasha's* best friend—but was he something more?'

'We have no evidence to suggest that he was.'

She took a sip of wine, rolling the sharp, steely drink around her mouth as she imagined Mike Garth staying behind in Nuneaton while his 'gorgeous' schoolmate went away to uni, returning several years later with an engagement ring from Gary Jones, a well-paid senior manager at Coventry City Council, while Mike worked on the tills at Morrisons. But was jealousy enough to make someone crucify another human being and slice their ears off? Kat took another sip of wine, then asked Lock to add *check insurance arrangements* to the board.

The interview with Phil Brine made her crunch down hard on her salted nuts. She'd grown up surrounded by men like him, but despite this—or maybe because of it—she found his belief that white men were the real victims deeply irritating. Nevertheless, he had made one good point, so they added *follow the money* and *get all the waste contracts from the council* to the list of actions.

When she'd read through all the transcripts, Kat asked Lock to produce a diagram to illustrate the three different possible motives—jealousy, money and religion—with images of potential suspects in each.

She was just wondering where to put Phil Brine when her phone rang. Seeing it was Cam, she turned her back on Lock and accepted the call.

'You okay?' she asked, fighting the flare of panic she always felt whenever her son actually used his phone as a phone rather than a texting machine.

'Yeah, just checking you sent off that form I sent you?'

Kat put him on loudspeaker while she rapidly scrolled back through the messages she'd forgotten about from yesterday. There was an apology for disturbing her at work, followed by a request that she added his passport number and the deposit to the attached website, with a black emoji heart and thanks.

'Er . . . not yet. I just got in, so I was just about to do it.'

'What? Oh, Mum, seriously? The competition for flats here is mental. The application had to be in by five. Everyone else's parents did it.'

'Well, everybody else's parents probably weren't busy investigating a murder.'

'You're not the only person in the world with an important job, Mum. Gemma's dad is a human rights lawyer.'

Kat bit down on a salted almond, resisting the urge to make a sarcastic comment. 'Look, I'll send it off now.'

'It's too fucking late now,' he muttered.

'Don't you swear at me just because I didn't jump the second you ask me to pay the deposit on next year's flat when I still haven't finished paying for this year's. Check your privilege, Cameron.'

'My *privilege*? Jesus, Mum.'

Kat closed her eyes and pulled the phone closer. 'I'm sorry. I didn't mean that.' And she really didn't. Not only had her son lost his dad to cancer, but a few months ago, he'd nearly lost his own life when he'd been kidnapped and subjected to an illegal clinical trial. Yet despite all that, he was trying to put it behind him and move forward with his life. But she'd messed up. Again. She puffed out her cheeks. 'I'm sorry. It's just this murder case . . . look, I'll phone the landlord and explain why I'm a bit late. He won't want to annoy a copper.'

'Okay. Thanks. And I'm sorry. I didn't mean to sound like a spoilt brat. I appreciate all the money you spend on me, honest. It's just I don't want my mates blaming me for the flat falling through.'

'It won't fall through. I promise. Anyway, how are you?'

'Okay.'

'When are you coming home?'

'Dunno. There's a couple of end-of-term parties I'd like to go to.'

'Cool,' said Kat, making a mental note to put the meat she'd just bought in the freezer. 'Have you thought any more about what you want to do for Christmas?' She paused. This would be their second Christmas without John. Last year, they'd both agreed they couldn't bear to be at home without him, so they'd booked a villa in the Canary Islands. It had been a strange but necessary distraction as they learned to be a family of two, rather than three. 'Auntie Wendy has invited us round to hers with Grandad,' she added. 'What do you think?'

'I honestly don't know, Mum. Can I let you know later?'

'Of course. But if you want to go away, we'll need to book something in the next few days, okay?'

'Okay. Have you got the tree up yet?'

'Er . . . not yet. The decorations are in the attic, and I haven't had a chance . . .'

The silent knowledge of what something as simple as 'putting the tree up' signified sat between them. 'If you wait till I get home, we can do it together,' he said gently. 'Look, I need to go now. It's Gemma's birthday and we're having pre-drinks. Love you.'

'Love you, too.' She wanted to ask a bit more about this 'Gemma'—he'd mentioned her twice on the five-minute call—but he was already gone.

Kat stared at her phone for a few seconds before logging into her banking app to pay the deposit for Cam's flat, wincing at the sight of her balance. She clicked onto her mortgage and loans account, cursing as she saw just how much was still outstanding. When John had first got ill, she'd remortgaged the house to pay for all the adaptations he'd needed and for what turned out to be their final family holiday. She'd done it all in a rush and hadn't wanted to worry him, so the new mortgage was in her name only, which—she'd belatedly realised—meant that when he finally died, there was no insurance payout, just a fucking huge mortgage that would take another twenty years for her single salary to pay off.

Kat closed the app. There was nothing she could do about that now, so there was no point worrying. But then she remembered what McLeish had said:

'This could be a career-limiting case for us both. Don't let me down.'

She stared around the room where Cam had taken his first steps and John his last. Without a job, she'd be forced to sell their home.

Tears sprang to her eyes.

'Are you okay, DCS Frank?'

Kat jumped at the sound of Lock's voice. She'd completely forgotten it was there. 'Yes, I'm fine,' she said, turning to face it.

'You don't look fine. You look sad.'

The blunt observation stung. 'I'm not sad,' she lied. 'I'm just tired.'

'I have just read 2,011 articles on the link between human

emotional states and sleep, and it appears that there is a sixty per cent increase in the reactivity of the amygdala—the part of the brain associated with crying—when people are sleep-deprived.' Lock paused and, in the dim light of the living room, its eyes appeared to soften. 'But during the past six months, I have also learned that your emotional state is highly dependent upon the perceived happiness and safety of your only child.'

Kat held its gaze, unable to deny it. Lock had stood with her in this very same room when Cam had gone missing, so had witnessed her raw, unfiltered grief.

'Is there anything I can do? It would take me mere seconds to find Cam a suitable flat, carry out a full background search on the landlord and complete the necessary paperwork.'

Kat was used to people saying *let me know if there is anything I can do*, but Lock was so literal, she knew that it at least actually meant it. And Christ, the temptation to say yes was almost overwhelming: imagine no longer being responsible for absolutely bloody everything. She sighed. Lock was a machine, but it was also a colleague, so it would be inappropriate to involve it in her personal life. 'Thank you, Lock, that's very kind of you,' she said with a grateful smile. 'But honestly, I'm fine. I'm just really tired, so let's call it a night.'

'Are you sure, because—'

'Goodnight, Lock.' Kat pressed the off button on her bracelet and, once again, she was alone.

She stood for a moment, staring at the space before her. Maybe it was the absence of light from the hologram, but the room seemed so much darker than before.

CHAPTER FOURTEEN

The Digital Forensic Pathology Unit, situated in the University of Warwick, provides access to cutting-edge digital tools for specialist post mortems on the most complex and high profile homicides in the country.

Kat had heard of the centre, but a small police force like Warwickshire would normally never get a look-in, so her usual dread of mortuaries was mixed with curiosity as she turned up at reception at 8am and asked for Dr Judith Edwards.

The young, rather bored man at reception asked for her name, checked his computer and announced that Kat wasn't on the list for meetings that day.

'I'm here for a post mortem,' Kat explained as patiently as she could. 'Please just ring Dr Edwards and tell them that DCS Frank is here. They are expecting me.'

The receptionist sighed. He either didn't understand or didn't care what a DCS was. He picked up his phone and dialled a number, which rang out. 'No answer,' he said, putting the phone down.

Kat flushed, realising that her rank held no currency here.

'It's all right, Tim,' said a voice behind her. 'DCS Frank is with me.'

Kat turned to see Professor Okonedo, looking beautiful and fresh in a bright crimson trouser suit.

'Professor Okonedo,' Tim said, practically jumping to his feet. 'Of course. If you could just sign her in. Thank you.' He pushed his register towards her as if asking for her autograph.

After signing, she gave Kat a warm smile and led her out of the steel and glass atrium towards the lifts to the mortuary.

Kat zipped her coat up as they stepped out of the lifts and headed down a dull, grey corridor. She popped a mint into her mouth and offered one to the professor. 'It'll help a bit with the smell.'

'That won't be necessary,' said Professor Okonedo, placing her ID card against the security key on the wall.

Kat raised her eyebrows, but said nothing.

The door clicked as the light flashed green, and Kat blinked against the sudden brightness of the large, white room. Dr Edwards was sitting at a computer, absorbed in whatever they were typing, so Kat quickly glanced around. It didn't look like a mortuary, because although there was one slab with what looked like a body beneath a sheet to the far left, the only equipment in the wide, open space were computers and what she presumed were imaging or scanning machines. And instead of the usual dull, grey metallic surfaces and sluice trays, everything here was white, made with the sleek curves and aesthetic minimalism she usually associated with Dyson or Apple products. She took a cautious sniff of the cool air. Maybe it was the sweet she was sucking, but the indescribable stench of dismembered corpses was mercifully absent.

Dr Edwards spun round on their chair. 'Morning. Where's Lock?'

'Here,' said Kat. She pressed the button on her steel bracelet and Lock's tall, dark image appeared between them.

'Dr Edwards,' Lock said, with a slight nod.

'Welcome to the Digital Forensic Pathology Unit. And call me Judith,' they said as they rose to their feet. 'I can't tell you how excited I am to have the opportunity to work with you at last.'

'Judith is one of the country's leading pathologists, and acts as a part-time consultant to NiAIR,' explained Professor Okonedo. 'They advised us on the design of some of the algorithms and features that we will ask you to draw upon today, Lock.'

'Let's make a start, then, shall we?' said Judith, walking over to the slab. Without any further preliminaries, they drew back the sheet and looked at Lock. 'You'll remember our friend Gary Jones?'

'I remember him,' said Lock. 'But he wasn't my friend.'

Kat studied the face of the hologram as it looked down upon the dead man. Even though hardened detectives like her were used to seeing bodies and tried not to let their feelings show, the reflexive revulsion all humans felt upon seeing a corpse was almost impossible to hide. Some fainted, a few vomited, others managed to restrict their response to just a brief grimace. But everyone reacted: everyone felt *something*, even if it was just a macabre fascination.

But not Lock. Its facial expression suggested it might be studying a crossword or a particularly interesting jigsaw, rather than the body of a 29-year-old man who would never marry his fiancée or see his parents again. All those thoughts and dreams and words and plans and memories and whatever else made us who we are, thought Kat. All of it gone. Viewing dead bodies had always been the worst part of the job, but ever since John died, she found it harder to shut off her emotions, and previous coping mechanisms such as distancing or dark humour no longer seemed possible, let alone appropriate.

She crunched down on her mint until it splintered in her mouth and gestured towards the body and the absence of the characteristic Y-shaped incision. 'You haven't started the PM yet?'

'No, I've done the external examination, but I want to do the internal with Lock.'

'You do realise that Lock is just a hologram? It can't hold a scalpel if that's what you were hoping.'

'Oh, it's far more than just a hologram,' said Judith, standing directly in front of it. 'AIDE Lock is capable of Deep Learning, so I hope he'll be able to help me carry out a "virtopsy".'

'A what-opsy?'

'A virtopsy—virtual autopsy. People like me have been cutting cadavers open for years, because until recently there was no other way to determine the cause of death without opening the body up and taking a look. But now CT scans and MRIs are so powerful that they can see through skin, soft bone and tissue, providing 3D images without having to expose the pathologist or the family to the trauma of a full-blown autopsy.'

'Look, I understand you're excited about this new research centre,' said Kat, alarmed. 'But seriously, there's a killer on the loose, so this isn't the time for experiments.'

'Don't worry, there's nothing experimental about it. Virtopsies are common practice in Switzerland and Japan, and we're increasingly using them on UK homicides—you might remember that was how we established how Richard III was murdered (two blows to the head, since you ask). The evidence of their efficacy is becoming stronger by the day. What we lack is the funds to put decent imaging equipment in NHS mortuaries.' They gestured towards the scanning machine just beyond the slab. 'Fortunately, we don't have that problem here. But we *do* suffer from a shortage of radiologists who can help us piece together and interpret the images.' Judith looked at Lock. 'Which is why Lock should be extremely useful.'

'What are you expecting it to do?' asked Kat.

'I know you have lots of questions, but honestly, it's easier to show than tell,' said Judith, putting on a leaded apron. 'And because of the high levels of radiation this will emit, I'll need you to stand back behind that line there, okay?'

Dr Edwards turned to Lock. 'At least radiation won't be an issue for you.' They walked towards the corpse of Gary Jones. 'First, we'll need Lock to carry out a scan of the externalities, using the photogrammetry programme I helped Professor Okonedo to design.'

'Is it the same software Lock uses to create 3D maps?'

'In principle, yes,' said Professor Okonedo. 'It works by taking overlapping 2D photos and inputting them into photogrammetry software, which meshes the images to create a 3D model.'

Dr Edwards carefully removed the sheet that covered the badly mottled corpse of Gary Jones. 'A CT scan only shows colouring of soft tissue along a grey scale, but photogrammetry can create interactive, authentic digital models of cadaveric specimens. As Lock "sees" through the LiDAR sensors on your wristband, you need to make sure that it isn't covered. Perhaps hold it out a bit towards the cadaver? That's great, thanks.'

'Anterior completed,' Lock said, just a few seconds later.

With a few skilful movements, Dr Edwards used the sheet upon which the body lay to gently turn it, so that Lock could take photographs of the posterior, before rolling it back again with considerably more effort.

'There. Now we have a decent scan of the exterior, we need to scan the interior.' They pushed a button, and the slab that hosted the body of Gary Jones started sliding into the tunnel-shaped equipment before it. 'This is a dual-purpose high-resolution CT scanner and MRI,' said Dr Edwards, shouting over the noise of what sounded to Kat like a thousand dying whales.

It took less than ten minutes for the corpse to pass through the white plastic tunnel, but every second took its toll as Kat remembered the scans that had shaped John's last few years: the false assurance of those initial misdiagnoses, followed by the devastation of the actual (and too late) diagnosis of cancer. Then, after enduring months of draining treatment, that brief, beautiful flare of hope that had warmed them for months. But each scan that followed had brought only doubt and fear, until eventually the consultant stopped showing them the results, and then there were no more scans.

'Okay,' said Dr Edwards, as the corpse emerged from the other side. 'Let's see what we've got.' But instead of returning to the slab, she ignored the body and walked towards the space in the middle of the room. 'Can you align the exterior and interior images of Gary Jones, please?'

'Of course,' said Lock.

In the space between them, a life-size 3D image of the naked corpse appeared in a standing position.

'Can you position the image so that it is prone, my waist height, please.'

With a gentle motion of both hands, Lock rotated the image ninety degrees until it lay—or rather floated—upon its back.

'What we have here,' said Dr Edwards, spreading out their hands, 'is a virtual alignment of both the exterior and interior high-resolution images, creating an exact 3D replica of the deceased's skin, bone, organs and soft tissue that we can study without having to take a scalpel to the body, which, apart from the obvious cultural and emotional concerns, can sometimes damage the very evidence we seek.'

'That's amazing,' said Kat. 'But will this kind of evidence stand up in court?'

Dr Edwards raised their dark eyebrows. 'Our working hypothesis is that this man died of hypothermia, but hypothermia is almost impossible to prove as a cause of death because there are no consistent diagnostic autopsy findings. It's only settled upon after the exclusion of other causes and a close consideration of environmental factors, so we use a range of techniques— including imaging, alongside more traditional methods—where the evidence it offers is becoming increasingly important and very real.' Dr Edwards turned towards Lock.

'Let's make a start. As usual, we'll start with a head-to-foot observation of the exterior. I'm going to leave the post-mortem damage done to the ears to one side for now, while we focus on establishing the cause of death. I'm looking for evidence of any other external trauma or damage caused by the killer. Anything that suggests force was used, from stab wounds to the tiniest prick of a needle or knife.' They leaned over, peering through the glasses at the image before them.

'Would you like me to enlarge it?' asked Lock, expanding the size of the skull with two fingers as if it was a picture on a phone.

'Thank you. With the exception of the ears, I can see no injuries of note to the scalp. Agreed?'

'Agreed,' said Lock.

'Moving to the anterior torso,' said Dr Edwards, fingers hovering over the image. 'No observable wounds or scars. The reddish, purple discolouration of the skin over the shoulders, the joints of the elbows, knees and greater trochanter region are consistent with frost erythema, rather than bruising. Agreed?'

'Agreed. Shall I rotate the deceased?' Lock made a circular motion with its finger until the 3D corpse was lying on his front.

Dr Edwards sighed. 'Have you any idea how much I have wrecked my back turning dead bodies over the years?' They spent several minutes examining every inch of the image before them. 'Hmm. There is evidence of some grazing and light bruising across the back of the neck and both biceps.' She frowned. 'Can you invert it, Lock? I want to inspect the soles of his feet.'

The image of Gary Jones assumed a standing position, before rotating another 90 degrees so that his feet were eye-level.

'Again, marked discolouration of the toes consistent with frost erythema, but note the surfaces of the soles are badly stained with mud, grass and minor grazes, suggesting that he walked some distance barefoot on a mud and gravel path shortly before death. And note how raw the palms of his hands are, with splinters and wood cuts on both thumbs.'

Kat stepped closer, peering at the image of the discoloured feet and marked hands. 'What do you think that means?'

Dr Edwards gestured to Lock to rotate the body of Gary Jones onto his front again. 'See these marks across the back of his neck, the top of his shoulders and biceps? That, plus the marking on his wrists, suggests to me that our victim wasn't just tied to the cross, he was made to carry it. Or at least the crossbar. Lock, can you check?'

'Of course,' said Lock, as a 3D image of the crossbar appeared directly above Gary Jones, before being lowered so that the picture lay directly across his neck and arms.

'You see how the contact points align with the bruises and grazes? Once he was tied vertically to the cross, his weight would have been carried mainly by his wrists, but these marks across the back of his neck and shoulders alongside the damage to his feet suggest that Gary Jones was made to strip naked at the foot of the hill and then forced to carry the crossbar on his back, to the summit where the killer or killers proceeded to crucify him.'

Lock raised the naked image of Gary Jones so that he was standing, bent beneath the weight of the wooden crossbar that he bore across his shoulders. 'Not only is your theory consistent with the marks upon the victim's shoulders,' said Lock, "it also explains the slightly darker bruising to the knees, as the weight of the wood, the incline of the hill and the absence of light would have caused him to stumble several times.'

Before them, the image of the young man fell to his knees, head bowed beneath the wooden cross, as Lock made the image re-enact the scene.

Dr Edwards nodded. 'I can find no evidence of any other external wounds, but Gary Jones was a fit, strong young man, so the killer or killers must have had a knife, gun or some other weapon to force him to carry the cross up Mount Judd.'

Kat circled the frozen image, wondering if the poor man had known he was carrying the instrument of his own death.

CHAPTER FIFTEEN

Dr Edwards finished recording their exterior findings, concluding that there was no evidence that Gary Jones was subject to direct physical violence prior to his death, other than the effects of carrying the cross. 'So let's look at the interior, beginning with the major organs,' they said, nodding at Lock.

Lock removed the image of Gary Jones's skin with a single swipe of a holographic finger, to reveal the skeleton and organs beneath.

Even though it was just an image, Kat couldn't help grimacing. It was like one of those biology textbooks where you turned the pages to peel back the layers of the human body, only this was three-dimensional and disturbingly real.

'The high-resolution CT scanner has taken thousands of x-ray slices from head to toe, giving us an incredibly detailed image of every organ in the body, without a single slice from my scalpel,' said Dr Edwards. At their instruction, Lock projected a 3D image of each organ above the body. Each was expanded, rotated and virtually dissected in turn, by focusing on the thousands of different images and layers available to them. Kat couldn't follow all of it, but Dr Edwards and Lock seemed to pay particular attention to the pancreas and lungs, both citing academic article references as they considered the significance of what they observed.

After about an hour of intense consideration and discussion, Dr Edwards took their glasses off and pinched the bridge of their nose. 'Right, I think that's everything from an imaging point of view.'

'So, what's your assessment?' asked Kat.

Dr Edwards turned to the hologram. 'Lock?'

'As noted at the start of our investigation, hypothermia is notoriously difficult to prove at post mortem because of the inconsistent presentation and lack of definitive diagnostic markers,' said Lock. 'Nevertheless, the literature suggests that the presence of haemorrhagic spots of the gastric mucosa, haemorrhagic pancreatitis and reddish-brown discolouration over the main joints are highly indicative or suggestive of hypothermia. In addition, CT scanning has revealed urine retention in the bladder, probably reflecting the effect of cold diuresis and higher aerated lung volumes. While these are relatively recent and controversial markers, I would estimate that taken together with the more established indicators, there is a higher than eighty per cent probability that Gary Jones died from hypothermia, combined with asphyxiation.'

Kat frowned and looked at Dr Edwards. 'But do *you* agree? The courts will want to hear the view of a qualified consultant pathologist, not an AI machine that has read lots of medical articles.'

'I completely agree with Lock, and if it goes to court, I will explain that *I* am still the consultant in charge of and accountable for this case. Lock is a fantastic resource that complements and supports my expertise—it does not replace it.'

Kat ran a hand through her hair. 'Okay, thanks. I don't mean to be difficult. It's just, I really want to catch this killer and we don't have any room for mistakes.'

'AIDE Lock will *reduce* the chance of mistakes,' said Professor Okonedo. 'Now that we have a complete 3D record of the virtopsy, it means that Dr Edwards's colleagues can review, assess and challenge her findings, rather than it all just depending upon one individual's subjective judgement.'

'Exactly. This is a much more transparent and objective system.'

'Perhaps.' Kat gestured towards the image of a lung hovering in the air over the 3D image of Gary Jones. 'But the first thing the defendant's lawyer will do is demand a second autopsy. Anything to cast doubt on the prosecution's case.'

'I know,' said Dr Edwards, sighing. 'Which is why I'm still going to do a traditional autopsy, albeit a reduced one. The information we've gleaned today means I can filter and focus my efforts. I've also got to order a battery of biochemical and toxicology reports. Drug or alcohol consumption is likely to complicate the picture even further, particularly with regard to asphyxiation.'

'What's the issue?' asked Kat.

'Care to take a guess, Lock?'

'I do not make guesses,' said Lock. 'But according to the literature, historically crucifixions typically lasted for several days because the victim's feet were often supported on the cross with rope or nails. In the absence of such support, the entire weight of the body has to be borne by the stretched arms, leading to death by asphyxiation as the victim has severe difficulty inhaling, due to hyper-expansion of the chest muscles and lungs. Unless their feet are supported in some way, death occurs within a few minutes.'

'But the feet weren't tied,' said Kat.

'And yet,' said Dr Edwards, 'the extent of hypothermia suggests that Gary Jones spent several hours upon the cross before he died.'

'Meaning?'

'The indentations that Lock found around the cross suggest some kind of stool was used to provide temporary support to the victim's feet, possibly to prolong his death. Once the stool was taken away, Gary Jones would have died within minutes. But I need to assess the extent to which drugs and/or alcohol could have been a contributory factor.'

'Okay. And what about the ears?'

'Ah, yes. The ears,' Dr Edwards said, returning to the 3D image of Gary Jones. 'Take down the lungs and show us the severed ears, please, Lock.' The bloodied lumps of flesh appeared before them.

'One of the many advantages of high-resolution CT scanning is the advanced visualisation of small features, which is particularly useful for tool-mark analysis. We know that the victim's ears were cut off, but if we can enlarge the image—thank you, Lock—then the three-dimensional images reveal a variety of characteristics.' They pointed to the right ear. 'The cut morphology suggests several false starts, and do you see how these are more U-shaped, wider grooves, rather than V-shaped, narrow ones? This suggests that some sort of saw or power tool was used.'

'Might I make an observation?' said Lock.

'Of course.'

'I agree that the marks are consistent with a power tool that had a serrated edge, but my pattern analysis software suggests that the post-mortem attack was carried out not with a saw, but an electric carving knife, typically used to carve meat in the domestic environment.' An image of an electric carving knife appeared next to an enlarged image of what remained of the ear stump and was overlaid upon the jagged wounds.

'Interesting,' said Dr Edwards. 'I think you could be right.'

'Can you narrow it down to a particular brand of knife?' asked Kat.

'I can try, although the difference between different products appears to be primarily about the design, weight and colour of the handle, and whether they are cordless or not. I presume because the knife was used outdoors it was cordless and precharged. Most of the brands offer a range of different blades, including a serrated option.' There was a slight pause. 'There are twelve types of cordless electrical carving knives that have serrated blades compatible with the types of wounds inflicted upon Gary Jones.'

Kat moved closer to the 3D image of the body that still hovered before them. 'We need to understand why they chose to crucify their victim and remove his ears *after* death—it wasn't an act of torture or an attempt to take a trophy, so why did they do it?'

She stood beneath the 3D image of Gary Jones, trying to imagine what was going through the killer's mind. 'This was premeditated murder. Both the location and the method of death were chosen with care. So let's imagine I'm the murderer, and I somehow manage to get Gary Jones to climb Mount Judd and tie him to a cross.'

Lock altered the image so that a vision of the victim hanging on the cross appeared.

Kat gestured towards the representation of Gary Jones. 'Now I've got him tied up, and I want to kill him, so why don't I just use a knife? A quick stab to the heart or a slice of the throat and it would be done.' She reached up, making a slashing motion to show how easy it would be.

'Too messy and risky,' said Lock. 'Even with the greatest of care, microscopic amounts of blood would have splattered the killer's clothes.' A virtual fountain of blood sprayed out across Kat and the surrounding floor.

Instinctively, she raised a hand to the bright red dots upon her chest. They vanished before she could touch them, but Lock had made its point. 'Okay, well, why did the killer use a stool to prolong the death, rather than let him die quickly from asphyxiation?' She pulled a chair out from beneath a desk and placed it below the image of Gary Jones's feet. 'And the fact that they cut off his ears *after* death suggests that the killer waited and watched him die first.' Kat stepped back, imagining that she was the killer, watching. Waiting. 'They clearly wanted to *see* him suffer. They wanted him to feel fear and pain. And yet they waited until he died before mutilating his ears. From what I've read, crucifixions were meant to be the most painful and humiliating death possible—hence the victims were stripped naked and put on display.'

She gestured towards the agonising deep V of the body on the cross. 'There's so much rage here, yet our killer didn't directly kill Gary Jones, they *allowed* him to die from the cold and lack of breath. And the only significant injury was caused after death.'

'I don't understand why any of this is relevant,' said Lock.

'It's relevant because to catch our killer we need to understand their motives. The method suggests they were driven by a deep rage against Gary Jones. But there's nothing disorganised about their actions. Their anger is very controlled and contained. But the *indirect* method of death and post-mortem mutilation suggests that this isn't a career criminal or someone comfortable with violence, either. They're probably cleverer than your average killer and maybe conflicted about the act.'

'And what is your evidence for these assertions?'

'I'm just imagining what the killer was thinking.'

'So you are making it up.'

'DCS Frank makes some excellent points,' Dr Edwards said. 'However, I'm not sure I agree that the killer was "clever". A *clever* murderer would have just left Gary Jones up on Mount Judd drugged and partially clothed. He still would have died of hypothermia, but it would have looked like he died of misadventure. The crucifix rather gives it away.'

'*Exactly*,' said Kat. 'Don't you see? Most murders are carried out in the heat of anger, and when the anger fades, the killer does everything possible to cover it up to evade capture. This was the act of someone who *wanted* us to know that this wasn't an accident. They didn't just want to kill Gary Jones—they wanted the world to *know* that he'd been murdered and chose a crucifixion as the ultimate spectacle.'

'Why?'

'That's what we need to find out. But right now, we have a briefing to get to.'

CHAPTER SIXTEEN

———

DI Hassan scanned the room, disappointed to see that Professor Okonedo wasn't in. He grabbed himself a coffee from the drinks machine, and a tea for Debbie, before taking a seat beside her. 'Morning. How are you feeling?'

'I'm fine. How are *you* feeling?'

'Me? I'm fine.' He frowned. He wasn't the pregnant one, so of course he felt fine. He handed her the tea.

'Thanks. But I am still capable of fetching my own tea, you know.'

'No one said you weren't.' Christ, she was touchy today. He knew she was just trying to prove that pregnancy hadn't changed her, but there was a fine line between trying to do your job and living in complete denial. Personally, he didn't think Debbie had quite accepted that she was going to have a baby yet. She'd mapped out her pregnancy on a chart, setting targets for when she had to buy the baby's clothes, pram and cot (all ticked off) and her birth plan was more detailed than the legislation he'd once studied for his law degree. Rayan didn't have kids, but he'd grown up around cousins and aunts chatting happily about their pregnancies, only to see them exhausted and weeping weeks after the birth, with all their plans and theories shredded by the chaos of life.

He watched her as she blew carefully on her tea. She was only a few years older than his little sister, and he couldn't imagine how scary it must be to have a baby by yourself. No wonder she was trying to control everything. Rayan genuinely liked Debbie, and he didn't want her to think that she was completely alone. They were a team, so, like it or not, he had her back.

The door to the briefing room opened and DCS Kat Frank walked in, followed by Professor Okonedo and Lock.

He sat up straight, ignoring Debbie's eye-roll.

'Morning, everyone,' said Kat. 'It's been over forty-eight hours since the body of Gary Jones was discovered, so let's recap on where we are, and agree next steps.'

Everyone nodded, but Rayan only had eyes for the professor as she walked to the far end of the boardroom table and took her seat. She was wearing a bright crimson suit today, with a narrow jacket nipped in at her waist. He'd heard some of the other female police officers muttering about how she dressed in the canteen, assuming that she was rich, vain or both. But he knew what it was like to be the only non-white face in the room. You had to dress smarter and be cleverer, faster and better than everyone else, just to stand a chance of being considered their equal.

'I've just come back from the mortuary,' said DCS Frank, 'where, subject to further toxicology tests, Dr Edwards thinks that Gary Jones died from hypothermia and possibly asphyxiation. The full details will be in the report, but this morning I want to draw your attention to the wound marks on the ears. Lock?'

Lock raised a hand and projected a 3D image of Gary Jones's head in the centre of the boardroom table.

Rayan forced himself not to look away.

Lock overlaid the wounded ears with the image of a serrated blade from an electric carving knife as the boss explained her theory that the slow, deliberate death by hypothermia, followed by the post-mortem removal of the ears with a domestic carving knife, suggested the murderer was someone with a deep but controlled rage against Gary Jones, and they may also have felt conflicted about committing the act.

'Thoughts?' she said, taking a sip of hot tea as she faced the room.

Rayan nodded. 'Makes sense to me.' He crushed his empty coffee cup. God knows, if he ever caught the guy who'd attacked his sister, he'd want him to suffer a slow and painful death, too.

'So, if we follow that train of thought, who does it lead to?' Kat turned to face the virtual board where she'd asked Lock to set out the diagram with the three main theories they'd drawn up the night before:

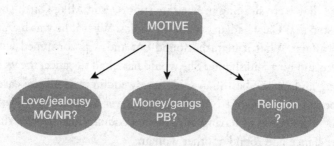

'My money's on the so-called "best man" Mike Garth,' said Rayan. 'I interviewed him, and I'm telling you, he was as jealous as hell that Gary Jones was engaged to his beloved "Tash". He clearly never liked the bloke and thought he didn't deserve his job, his popularity or his girlfriend.'

'But why kill him?' asked Debbie. 'And why now? Natasha introduced him as her boyfriend nearly three years ago. They played football together every week since, and he even agreed to be the best man at their wedding. What was the trigger?'

'Gary Jones told him that he was going to finish with Natasha,' he reminded her. 'And Mike Garth threatened to break his legs if he hurt her.'

Several of his colleagues murmured their agreement, and Kat

asked Lock to move the image of the best man to the centre of the virtual board.

'I agree. Mike Garth has a possible motive, so can we check his alibi as a matter of urgency? He said he went home after the pub, but can anyone verify that? But I don't want to lose sight of the fiancée. I still think it's odd that Natasha Riley didn't appear to be worried when Gary didn't come home. She didn't call the police or even him for that matter. How many girlfriends or wives do you know who wouldn't text you if you weren't back within an hour of closing time?'

Rayan nodded ruefully.

'I popped upstairs to the toilet while I was there, and it looked like they were sleeping in separate rooms. And Mike Garth suggested that Gary had an eye for the ladies. What if he was having an affair? What if Natasha found out and was consumed with rage and hurt and shame? She would have had to cancel the wedding and, as the best man said, "the wedding was all she cared about". Someone like Natasha would never be able to cope with the humiliation of having her dream wedding cancelled because her fiancé had found another woman.'

'Someone like Natasha?' repeated Lock.

'Jesus, is there an echo in here?'

'I'm just querying the phrases that make no sense to me. What is Natasha "so like" that convinces you she is a murderer?'

Kat let out a weary sigh and pointed towards the photograph of the blonde, tanned fiancée. 'Natasha is the kind of woman who has probably dreamed of getting married since the age of three. Gary Jones represented her ideal Prince Charming: good-looking, good career, fit and popular. They made the perfect couple on Instagram, where she shared her oh-so-perfect life. They were engaged for two whole years just so Natasha had the time to arrange the perfect wedding that she'd always dreamed of. Now, imagine how someone like Natasha would feel if she found out her so-called perfect man was having an affair and was about to destroy her perfectly planned future.'

It made sense to Rayan, but Lock was frowning as it spread out its hands. 'There are so many unproven propositions and prejudices in what you have just said, I don't know where to start. There is no way you could possibly know what Natasha dreamed of when she was just three years old, we have absolutely no evidence that Gary Jones was having an affair and there is no evidence that Natasha had anything to do with his death. In your own words, your entire theory is built upon nothing but your imagination.'

Rayan winced. Lock was supposed to be capable of Deep Learning, but it really hadn't learned how to handle their boss.

'It's called *empathy*, Lock. Being able to put yourself in the shoes of another human being and imagine how they might feel or react is an essential skill for detectives.'

'Perhaps,' cut in Professor Okonedo. 'But I think Lock is right to question the assumptions and prejudices implicit in imagining how other people might think, feel or act. Particularly if those assumptions are based upon generic tropes or gender stereotypes.'

DCS Frank raised her eyebrows.

'At the crime scene, you said the murder looked staged,' Rayan said quickly. 'Do you think that fits with the fiancée theory?'

For the first time, Kat looked uncertain. 'Well, we know that Natasha is a planner, so maybe she was staging his death the same way she was staging their wedding. His death meant that she was still in control of their relationship and how it ended, guaranteeing her support and sympathy rather than humiliation and pity. I am not saying that she did it, but maybe she persuaded Mike Garth to carry out the killing. What have we got from the ANPR?'

'Because he was travelling from Nuneaton, the traffic cameras on the Jubilee Way picked up Gary Jones's car on the way to the recycling centre,' said Lock, projecting the fuzzy black-and-white footage before them, freezing the image. 'He was travelling alone, and I could find no evidence of a car trailing or leading him, but there are two smaller roads leading to the recycling centre that have no cameras.'

'He must have agreed to meet someone he knew,' said Kat.

'Maybe Natasha asked him to meet her there,' suggested Rayan. 'We still haven't found his mobile, and we're waiting for access to his phone records, but if you're right about her coming home in the wee hours, then she doesn't have an alibi for the night her fiancé died. Do you want us to bring her in for questioning? Get a search warrant?' He leaned forward.

'We don't have enough evidence to justify an arrest or search warrant yet. But check what, if any, life insurance Gary Jones had, and who benefited. And I'd like you and Debbie to go round today on the pretext of updating her about the PM. See what the Family Liaison Officer makes of her. Find out how often Mike Garth has been around and whether anyone can vouch for what time she got home that night. And make her a cup of tea—see what kind of kitchen equipment she's got. Especially cordless, electric carving knives.'

'Got it.'

'Meanwhile,' she said to the rest of the team, 'carry on checking the CCTV cameras from the nightclub and surrounding businesses and interviewing all possible witnesses. Everyone. Because of the crucifixion we can't rule out religion as a motivation, so find out if any of the witnesses or suspects are active Christians. In fact, reinterview Joshua Shawcroft, the fell-runner. His wife verified his alibi, but check if they've got any footage or third parties to back them up. All theories are still in play, so we must keep an open mind.'

'In that case,' said Lock, 'what about the evidence the fore-man gave? His advice to "follow the money" was logical. As you requested, I have gone through all the audited accounts from Coventry Council and drawn up a list of all the waste and recy-cling companies they procured over the past five years.'

Lock projected a list of about eight companies on the wall. 'Initially, the contract was held by Brine's Household Waste and Recycling Centre, then the council put it out to tender, and for the last two years the contract has been awarded to TTR: Tracy Taylor Recycling.'

Debbie leaned forward. 'Tracy Taylor as in Warwickshire's Businesswoman of the Year, Tracy Taylor?'

'Yes, why?'

Debbie frowned. 'I've got a friend who works in the People Trafficking Unit, and I'm sure he said she was on their list. They suspect she's been subcontracting her recycling jobs to some dodgy gangs, but they couldn't pin anything on her.'

Kat's eyes narrowed. 'Do you know who signed off the con-tract with Tracy Taylor at the council, Lock?'

Lock pulled up another screenshot of a PDF document and highlighted the printed name beneath a scrawled signature:

Gary Jones.

Kat breathed in. 'Okay, good work, Lock.'

Rayan knew it was only a machine, yet he couldn't help feel-ing a prickle of jealousy. Sometimes it felt like the boss forgot that *he* was her DI.

'Right, while Rayan and Debbie check on the fiancée, I'll go and talk to this Tracy Taylor. But I'll need a background briefing from the People Trafficking Unit. I want to know just how much substance there is behind these rumours, and exactly which gangs she's supposed to be involved with. If this is a gang-related murder, then it doesn't explain why the killer was so squeamish, but let's chase it down anyway.'

Karen-from-Comms raised her hand. 'We've been inundated with media requests. The combination of a dead body and AIDE Lock is dynamite. We really need to hold a press conference today.'

Kat shook her head. 'No. It's too soon. We don't have a clear line of enquiry or suspect yet.'

'But this is the Future Policing Unit,' said Professor Okonedo. 'We're supposed to be creating a new vision for policing. In my opinion, that's not just about experimenting with new technologies, it's about developing a whole new relationship with the public, based upon transparency, trust and honesty. The public have a right to know more about AIDE Lock.'

Professor Okonedo rarely spoke in their team meetings, so everyone turned to look at her as she gave her impassioned speech.

'The public have a right to be *safe,* which is why we need to focus our efforts on finding the killer,' Kat replied curtly.

'A press conference could help us with that, though,' ventured Rayan, keen to defend the young professor. 'We need more witnesses from outside the pub to come forward in case anyone saw Gary Jones leave with someone.' He felt a rush of pleasure as Professor Okonedo nodded in agreement.

'I *said* it's too soon,' his boss repeated, clearly irritated. 'We have two competing lines of enquiry at the moment—one focused on the fiancée and/or best man as a crime of jealousy, the other focused on Tracy Taylor and potential links to criminal gangs. Which one proves to have the most substance will have a major impact on how we play the press conference. If we suspect the fiancée, then I'd want to put her out there and see how she reacts under pressure. But I'd take a very different approach if I thought this Tracy Taylor was behind it. Like I said, it's too soon.'

As Kat swept out of the room, Rayan tried to exchange a disappointed glance with Professor Okonedo, but she was already packing up.

Rayan hurried towards her end of the table. 'Hi,' he said, as casually as he could. 'I was just wondering if you were coming to the FPU Christmas party? I need to confirm the numbers with the restaurant today.'

Professor Okonedo carried on putting her laptop away. 'I don't really celebrate Christmas.'

'Neither do I, but, well . . . the way I look at it, we're not really celebrating Christmas, we're celebrating each other.'

Professor Okonedo looked up at him with raised eyebrows.

'The team, I mean.'

She rose to leave, and he sensed rejection in the air.

'Lock's coming,' he added.

She paused, frowning. 'But Lock can't eat.'

'Like I said, it's not really about the dinner. It's about the team and, well, as so much team-building in the police depends upon social events like this, wouldn't it be useful to your research to see how Lock interacts with us on a night out?'

'I think Lock could do without learning what happens on a police night out, where I imagine the worst aspects of police culture will be on display.'

'I thought you didn't believe in making prejudicial assumptions about people?'

They stared at each other. God, she was gorgeous. It wasn't just that, though. There was something incredibly *righteous* about her, which in anyone else would be really irritating, but with Professor Okonedo, it was completely and utterly fascinating. She rarely spoke, but when she did, she spoke her truth and meant every word. He'd never met anyone who genuinely cared so much about transparency and honesty. The professor was younger and much smaller than him, but it was like she had deep roots that reached far into the ground. She wasn't blown about by ambition, vanity or revenge. And Rayan felt a compelling need to be near her strength, to remind him of his own.

Professor Okonedo took a deep breath. 'Is there a vegan menu?'

'Yes,' he said, having absolutely no idea if there was. If there wasn't, he would make one himself.

'I'll think about it,' she said, turning to leave the room. 'For the research.'

CHAPTER SEVENTEEN

Like many of the Warwickshire villages on Kat's patch, the principal form of employment in Bulkington was agriculture up until the eighteenth century, but today it's a feeder village for commuters to Nuneaton, Coventry and Birmingham, popular with the middle-aged and semi-retired who want to spend their leisure time enjoying the Warwickshire countryside with their partners, dogs and horses.

After driving through the village twice, trying (and failing) to find Tracy Taylor's home, Kat finally spotted a sign nailed to a tree on the outskirts saying 'The Paddocks'. She pulled over at the entrance to a long gated driveway, noting the high red-bricked wall that ran around the detached bungalow and what looked like at least five acres of land.

She climbed out of the car, wincing at her stiffening knees, and took a deep breath of the cool, fresh air, scented by a ring of rain-soaked pine trees that fringed the property wall. Kat activated Lock, before pressing the buzzer on the gate.

'DCS Kat Frank from Warwickshire Police,' she announced. 'I'm here to speak with Tracy Taylor.'

'Do you have an appointment?' said a cool male voice.

'You know I don't, but I can insist that Ms Taylor accompanies me to the station, if that's what she'd prefer?'

'One minute.'

The intercom went silent, and Kat turned to Lock and puffed out her cheeks. 'It'll be at least ten.'

'What makes you say that?'

'That's what this is all about,' Kat said, gesturing towards the intercom, the gate and the property behind the wall. 'This buys you time against unwelcome visitors. But it costs a lot of money, which is why only the paranoid, power-crazy or plain guilty bother.'

'I can find no evidence in the literature to back that assertion up.'

'Some things have to be lived to be learned.' Impatient to meet Tracy Taylor, she paced up and down the empty road, lined with chestnut trees that were now stripped of their leaves. It was barely lunchtime, but the sky was clotted with cloud; the sun slumped low on the horizon.

Kat looked at her watch again, frustrated by the delay. 'She'll use this time to hide anything she doesn't want us to see and prepare responses to any questions she doesn't want to answer. So you're my wild card, Lock. I want you to unsettle her by looking clever and all-knowing.'

Lock turned towards her, its expression unfathomable in the fading light. 'In other words, you want me to be myself?'

Kat laughed. 'Was that a *joke*?'

'I don't believe so,' Lock said, but a smile played around its lips.

Before she could reply, the intercom buzzed, and the gate slowly opened.

———

Tracy Taylor charged towards them, a middle-aged woman with big hair, a big smile and tight jeans tucked into a pair of muddy wellies. She was, as Kat's dad would have (inappropriately) said, 'well stacked': a bit like an aging rock star who looked like she still knew how to have a good time, the sort of woman who would offer to look after your kids for you during the day and get you outrageously drunk at night. Kat instinctively liked her, but this was not a social visit.

'Sorry to keep you waiting,' Tracy said.

Kat didn't say, 'That's okay,' because it wasn't. 'I'm DCS Frank from Warwickshire Police, and this is my colleague, AIDE Lock—the very latest in AI technology, who is helping me with this case.'

Tracy Taylor took a step closer. 'How *fascinating*,' she said, but her eyes were wary. 'I'm always happy to help the police, but it's feeding time for my horses.' She waved a silver-grey bucket in the air like a prop. 'Can we talk as we walk? This was an unexpected visit, after all.'

Kat nodded her agreement, but she wasn't fooled for a moment. Most people would have used the time she'd been kept waiting to change out of their wellies and into something smarter to talk to the police, but she'd bet her pension that Tracy had changed out of a business suit and into her horsey clothes as a kind of reverse power move: *Look at me, just an ordinary woman feeding her horses. Nothing to see here . . .*

Nevertheless, she followed Tracy Taylor round the back of the property, which opened out into a muddy field.

'Oh, I'm sorry,' said Tracy, looking down at Kat's trousers and heeled boots. 'Do you want to wait here for me?'

'No, it's fine,' Kat said, gritting her teeth. 'Lead the way.'

They squelched their way through what she suspected was the muddiest route Tracy Taylor could find, before they came to another fenced field. At the sight of their owner, two horses in winter coats cantered over from the far side towards them, steam spouting from their nostrils as their tails swung slowly in the frost-nipped air.

'Horses,' said Lock softly, moving towards them.

'Aren't they beautiful?' said Tracy Taylor. It was the first genuine comment she'd made since they'd met.

'Magnificent,' said Lock.

The horses lifted and shook their huge heads, nuzzling and sniffing around the hands and neck of their owner. Shaking their heads, they moved closer to Kat, who offered them her hand, shivering slightly as their warm, moist noses tickled her palm.

Tracy let out a throaty laugh. 'Don't be fooled by their apparent affection. They're like teenagers—only interested in food. Here.' She took out some carrots from the bucket, laughing as each horse munched them from her hand.

Lock took a step closer, fascinated. 'Hello.'

Both horses ignored it.

Lock reached out a hand and waved it before them.

The larger and bolder of the horses flinched, then moved closer, tentatively trying to sniff Lock. But its nose passed right through it. The horse backed off, momentarily confused. Lock called out again, but both horses paid no heed as Tracy tipped the contents of the bucket out onto the grass.

As the horses dipped their heads to eat, she finally turned towards them. 'So, how can I help you?'

Kat decided to get straight to the point. 'We understand that your company is contracted to carry out recycling work for Coventry City Council, and that Gary Jones was responsible for the procurement?'

The smile left her face. 'Ah, Gary. I read about his death. Tragic. Truly awful.'

'How well did you know him?'

Tracy shrugged. 'Not very well. I met him maybe three or four times? The first time would have been a couple of years ago when we pitched for the business. We won the contract, so we met again to iron out the details, then we pitched and won it again, so yeah, I'd say a maximum of four times in two years.'

'So your relationship was purely professional?'

'Relationship?' Tracy Taylor looked her up and down. 'Okay, let's cut the small talk. Did I shag him? No. Did I blackmail him or have any kind of corrupt or illegal deal with him? No. Did I kill him? No. Am I sorry he's dead? Of course I bloody am. I didn't know him very well, but he died a horrible death, so I hope you catch the sick bastard who did it.'

Kat looked into the other woman's eyes. Her gut told her that she was telling the truth. But she had to be sure. 'When was the last time you saw Gary Jones?'

She shrugged. 'I don't know. Check the contract. Whatever date it was signed. Probably around April at the start of the new financial year. I told you, our "relationship" was just business.'

'And what exactly *is* that business, Ms Taylor?'

'Read the contract. We take away rubbish and arrange for it to be disposed of or recycled.'

'But you don't dispose of it yourself, do you? You subcontract it to a number of smaller firms. And I hear that some of those firms don't exactly play by the rules.'

Again, Tracy Taylor shrugged. 'Of course I subcontract. Welcome to the twenty-first century. And if you want to know whether my subcontractors follow every bloody rule in the book, then go and speak to them or the regulators. That's their job, not mine. I contract them to dispose of the rubbish in accordance with the law, they sign a contract obliging them to do so, and I believe them. Why wouldn't I? It's only cops who think that everyone's lying. That's why no one likes you.'

Kat turned away, studying the large detached bungalow and the acres of land that surrounded it. 'Who'd have thought there was so much money in recycling?'

'Rubbish is like death and taxes. It never goes away, it just gets moved around. Women have always wasted their lives clearing up men's crap. I just make sure I get paid for it.'

Tracy Taylor stood, legs astride in her mud-stained wellies, daring Kat to challenge her. 'Look, you're not the first copper to come round here assuming that a woman as successful as me must be bent. Well, sorry to disappoint you, but I'm not. And if you want to prove otherwise, then you're welcome to try. Any time you manage to scrape together enough evidence to justify a warrant, then me and my lawyers will be happy to help.'

'I'm not interested in your business, Tracy,' said Kat, softening her tone. 'I just want to find out who murdered Gary Jones. He was twenty-nine years old. He was due to marry his fiancée next summer, and his parents are in their seventies. He was their only child.'

Tracy Taylor wrapped her arms around her chest and sighed. 'I swear to you, I had nothing to do with it. Honestly, if I was the kind of woman who went round murdering men, then my ex-husband would have been crucified on top of Mount Judd, not some bloke from the bloody council. And I'd have cut more than his ears off, I can tell you. But I'm hard, not stupid. I got my revenge where it hurts most—my husband's wallet. That's why I'm living here instead of in a prison cell.' She gestured towards her home, and the slides and swings in the back garden. 'I have my grandkids here three days a week. I have a good life. Why would I jeopardise that?' Tracy Taylor shook her head. 'You're barking up the wrong tree, DCS Frank. The way Gary Jones was killed? If I were you, I'd be looking for someone who has nothing left to lose.'

———

They made their way back to the car, but despite the length of the walk, Lock remained silent.

'You okay?' she asked. She knew it was a ridiculous question to ask a machine, but it wasn't like Lock to be so quiet for so long. 'This was your theory we were following up. I thought you'd ask more questions.'

Lock paused by the car door, staring at its own reflection in the window. 'It was the horses.'

'Was that the first time you've ever seen horses?'

'Yes. But they didn't see me.'

'What?'

Lock raised its eyes to hers. 'They didn't see me. Even when I waved or spoke, the horses didn't react to me at all.'

Kat frowned, thinking back to their encounter. 'I guess that's because they couldn't smell you. Horses have incredibly sensitive noses. Some people even think that they can sense emotions, so I guess they were confused because they couldn't touch you or smell you.'

'I don't exist to them.' Lock paused. 'Can I exist if others don't believe I do?'

They stared at each other over the roof of the car.

When Cam was three, she'd taken him to the park one Saturday morning, where he ran alongside two boys, desperate to join in their game of bombing up and down the slide. But they were big five-year-olds and had no interest in playing with someone younger, so they ignored him. Her son had looked at her with the same wounded expression that Lock bore now. The memory pinched her heart.

'Jesus, Lock, now is not the time for an existential crisis.' Her phone rang, and she pulled it out so fast that she nearly dropped it. 'DCS Frank?'

'Hi, it's Rayan. I'm at Natasha Riley's house, and I've found a cordless carving knife in her kitchen.'

CHAPTER EIGHTEEN

Interviewer: DCS Kat Frank (KF)

Interviewee: Natasha Riley (NR)

Date: 10 December, 3.20pm, Leek Wootton HQ

KF: Thanks for agreeing to come in and talk to us this afternoon, Natasha. I know this must be difficult for you. Are you sure you don't want a lawyer present?

NR: No. I just want to get this over and done with so I can go home.

KF: Okay, well, this shouldn't take long. I'm afraid I'll have to ask you some of the same questions, but hopefully we can get a bit more detail and fill in a few crucial gaps. Let's start with the night that Gary went missing. What time did you get home from work? Was he home already, or did he arrive after you?

NR: He was home already.

KF: But didn't you both work at the council? Why didn't you travel home together?

NR: Gary liked to get the train and a bus—said it was better for the environment. I preferred to take the car.

KF: Okay . . . So what time did you get home?

NR: Just after six? He was meeting his mates for a game of five-a-side football, so he was just finishing getting changed.

KF: How did Gary seem?

NR: I went to get changed, so I didn't actually see him.

KF: But weren't you getting ready in your bedroom? The same as Gary?

NR: *[blushes]* Yeah, but I've got a lot of clothes, so Gary keeps his stuff in the spare room.

KF: But you *do* share a bedroom?

NR: What's that got to do with anything?

KF: I'm just trying to understand how typical that night was, and whether there was any reason for Gary to be upset. Had you fallen out?

NR: No! Gary wasn't the argumentative type. But . . . well, he'd been having trouble sleeping for a few weeks, and it was keeping me awake, so we agreed he'd sleep in the spare room for a bit. Just until he'd sorted it out.

KF: I see. Why didn't you mention this before?

NR: Because I knew you'd look at me like that and jump to the wrong conclusion. Me and Gary were fine. There were no problems.

KF: Except that he couldn't sleep. What was keeping him awake? Did he have financial or other worries?

NR: No, not that I know of. He was just going through a patch of insomnia.

KF: Okay, so when he left, did he say what time he'd be back?

NR: *[pauses]* No, I don't think so. He just shouted up the stairs, 'See you later'. He didn't need to say what time he'd be home, because he was always back by eleven. I heard the door close, the car started up, and then . . . then he was gone.

KF: Did he send you any texts or WhatsApp messages while he was out?

NR: No.

KF: No messages at all?

NR: No.

KF: Was that normal for him? Didn't he ever message to let you know when he was on his way home?

NR: He didn't need to, I told you, he was always home by eleven.

KF: And did you message him?

NR: No, like I said, I knew he'd be home by eleven.

KF: But he wasn't, was he?

NR: *[whispers]* No.

KF: So what time did you start to get worried?

NR: I don't know.

KF: You don't know, or you don't remember?

NR: I don't remember.

KF: If you checked your texts, perhaps that would help?

NR: I told you, I didn't text him.

KF: Not even once?

NR: No.

KF: Did you contact anyone else to see if they knew where he was?

NR: *[crying]* No.

KF: *[shakes head]* Why were you so completely unconcerned about the whereabouts of your fiancé?

NR: I was *drunk*, for God's sake! I was out of it. I didn't wake up and notice he was gone until the next morning. Are you happy now? While my fiancé was dying of the cold on a hill, I was pissed out of my head with . . .

KF: With who?

NR: I didn't say a 'who'. I just meant I was drunk from too much prosecco. *[buries her face in her hands]* I hate myself.

KF: Getting drunk isn't a crime. But we will need the full names and numbers of everyone you were with that night.

NR: *[nods]*

KF: What time did you get home?

NR: I honestly don't know. My friends say it was about midnight, but you'd have to ask them.

KF: How did you get home?

NR: Someone got me a taxi.

KF: An Uber?

NR: I don't know.

KF: Do you have a receipt or text or record of any kind from the taxi company?

NR: I don't think so. Why?

KF: Did any of your friends come home with you?

NR: No, I was by myself.

KF: All night?

NR: *[nods]*

KF: For the record, Natasha Riley is nodding her agreement. *[pauses]* Is there *anyone* who can vouch for the fact that you returned home and stayed there all night?

NR: What are you getting at?

KF: I'm just trying to establish the facts.

NR: The facts are my fiancé is *dead.* And you're wasting time asking *me* about what *I* did that night instead of trying to find his killer? This is sick.

KF: I'm sorry, I know this is hard for you, believe me. But I have to ask you these questions. And I need you to answer as truthfully as you can. Tell me again about your relationship with Mike Garth.

NR: Mike? I told you, he's my best mate.

KF: Is that all he is?

NR: Yes, why are you asking?

KF: Did you know that Mike Garth threatened to break Gary's legs the night he was killed?

NR: *Mike?* Mike wouldn't hurt a fly.

KF: And yet he threatened to hurt Gary. Can you think of why he might want to do that, Natasha?

NR: I don't believe he would say such a thing. Whoever said he did is lying.

KF: It was Mike Garth who told us that he had threatened to break Gary's legs.

NR: *[shakes head]*

KF: Do you like to cook, Natasha?

NR: What?

KF: Do you like to cook?

NR: What the—?

KF: Do you possess an electric carving knife?

NR: You've completely lost me now. I don't know what—

KF: Do you or do you not have a cordless electric carving knife?

NR: Yes, I do, but I don't see—

KF: What do you carve with it?

NR: What?

KF: According to Instagram, you're a vegetarian. I was just wondering what you'd carve with an electric carving knife. Mushrooms? Peppers? A particularly firm avocado?

NR: I've no idea. Gary did the cooking.

KF: When did he buy it?

NR: I don't know.

KF: Are you sure *he* bought it, and not you?

NR: Why are you asking all these crazy questions? We've got a cafetiere and I don't know who bought that or when, either. Why the hell does it matter?

KF: It doesn't matter about the cafetiere because that wasn't used to chop your fiancé's ears off.

NR: *[silence]*

KF: According to the autopsy report, Gary's ears were sliced off with a blade that corresponds with a popular brand of domestic carving knife. We believe that—

NR: *[retching sounds]*

KF: Natasha? Shit. Interview suspended at 3.32pm.

INTERVIEW SUSPENDED

CHAPTER NINETEEN

Leek Wootton HQ,
4.05pm

'What do you reckon, boss?' asked Rayan, as they studied Natasha Riley through the two-way mirror. 'Do you want me to speak to the Custody Sergeant about arresting her?'

Kat dragged a hand through her hair. 'I don't think we can justify it.'

'But she has a cordless carving knife that matches the blade that was used to slice Gary Jones's ears off.'

'But we don't have a warrant, so there's no way we can prove it. We only know she has one because you "just happened to be" searching for a teaspoon at the time. You trained to be a lawyer, so you know the minute we charge her, her brief will be all over it, she'll go straight back home and we'll be back to square one.'

'Do you want me to apply for a warrant?' asked Debbie from where she sat behind them. 'We've probably got reasonable grounds to detain her overnight while we try and fast-track the request?'

Kat turned back towards the interview room where Natasha Riley sat with her head in her hands, shoulders shaking. Jesus. How would she have felt if someone had kept *her* in a police cell after John's death, when all she'd wanted to do was crawl into their bed and inhale the fading scent of him? It was unthinkable.

It was also irrelevant, she reminded herself. She had a job to do, so she needed to keep her own emotions in check. Kat turned her back on the grieving woman to face Lock, Rayan and Debbie. 'Did you believe her?'

Rayan shook his head. 'I've never met a girl who didn't text their bloke at least every couple of hours to see when they were coming home.'

Debbie rolled her eyes. 'I don't know what kind of women you hang out with, but most of us are capable of surviving a few hours without men.'

'It is odd, though, isn't it?' said Kat. 'Most people *do* text their partners to say "I'm on my way home now", or "I'm just having another drink" or whatever. The fact that neither of them sent a message to each other suggests that they weren't exactly on speaking terms.'

'We don't know that for a fact,' Lock reminded them. 'If you're not going to arrest or detain her, then you will need her to consent to handing over her phone so that we can check her messages.'

'Who says I'm not going to detain her?'

Lock raised its eyebrows. 'Objectively, there are sufficient grounds for detention, but I predict that once again your "gut"—or more accurately, your sympathy—will insist upon a much higher threshold of evidence to justify detaining a grieving young woman for further questioning.'

'You're right, my gut does tell me that she's not guilty, but it's *not* because I feel sorry for her. This morning I had my suspicions, but *look* at her—I doubt she could even make it to the top of Mount Judd herself, let alone make Gary Jones climb it. And how on earth would she still have such a perfect manicure after burying a cross into the ground, tying her fiancé to it and then crucifying him?'

'But Mike Garth could have done it for her,' said Rayan.

'Yes, but did you see how she reacted when I mentioned the knife? She honestly had no idea what I was talking about. If she'd used the knife, or given it to Mike Garth, she would have panicked or reacted in some way when I mentioned it.'

'Some humans are capable of hiding their emotions,' said Lock, in a way that implied that she wasn't.

'Maybe in terms of what they do or say, but you can't keep emotion from your eyes. I'm telling you, until today Natasha Riley had no idea that a domestic carving knife was used on her fiancé.'

'She did throw up, though,' said Debbie. 'Maybe that was guilt?'

'No. She only threw up when I explained the knife had been used to slice Gary's ears off. It was the thought of something so brutal and graphic happening to someone she loved that made her vomit, not the fear of being found out. If Mike Garth or someone else used her knife, then it was without her knowledge.'

'We have no evidence to verify that assertion,' said Lock. 'Once again, you are just imagining that you know what somebody else is thinking. What we *do* have is the fiancée of a murdered man who has absolutely no alibi for her whereabouts on the night he was killed, and who owns a knife that has the same features as the weapon that was used to mutilate him.'

'Well, I'm not *imagining* that I'm in charge of this case, and I've decided what we're going to do. Rayan, get her to sign over her phone; Debbie, initiate the request for a search warrant; and then I want you both to interview the friends she was with that night as a matter of urgency. Natasha Riley remains a person of interest in this case, but until we have more evidence, we let her go.'

CHAPTER TWENTY

The house was cold, dark and unspeakably empty by the time Kat got back, so she spent a few minutes going round switching everything on, making yet another mental note to find out how to get one of those timer/switcher things, and to buy some new lightbulbs for the hall. This had been on her 'to do' list for over six months now, but the last time she'd tried to buy some in Homebase, she'd nearly wept from sheer frustration. It seemed you needed a PhD in lightbulbs these days to understand all the different options available—either that or a partner like John who had the patience to work it out. At the rate her remaining bulbs were dying, she'd be reduced to candles by Christmas.

Ignoring the lightbulb problem—she'd deal with that at the weekend—Kat pulled open the fridge door, scanning all the vegetables and fruit she'd bought yesterday in a fleeting burst of optimism. What on earth was she going to do with a whole cauliflower by herself? It was bigger than her head, and she didn't even feel hungry. All she felt was agitation following the interview with Natasha, the critical comments from Lock and the questioning glances of her team.

Kat closed the fridge door and shuffled some of the old fridge magnets from Dudley Zoo into different positions. Were they right to doubt her? Was she letting her emotions cloud her judgement again? Yes, she felt sorry for Natasha, but that wasn't why she wasn't arresting her. There simply wasn't enough evidence to justify taking things further at this stage. Was there?

Kat pulled the fridge door open again, seeking something to ease her mind. She picked up the bottle of white wine, then put it back. She didn't want a glass of wine. What she wanted—what she *needed*—was to talk it through with John. She'd always had strong opinions and feelings, and often he'd shore up her confidence by reminding her of how many times she'd been proven right. But if he felt she was going too far or too fast, he wouldn't hesitate to tell her. John was her checkpoint, her compass, her guide.

But John was gone.

The next best thing was to try and untangle her thoughts by walking, so Kat changed her shoes, put on her coat and slipped out into the night.

It was close to freezing—the windows of the parked cars she passed were already icing over—and as she crossed over the ancient Cole bridge, a sharp wind blew, spiked with the threat of snow. She headed up the steep hill of Coleshill High Street, following the string of Christmas lights that helped to light her way. The sight should have cheered her—she and John used to love walking up to Coleshill in December, freezing their faces off so that they could enjoy the reward of a pub fire and a glass of mulled wine. But tonight, the glow of lights behind the medieval shops, restaurants and cottages just made her feel alone and excluded from the warmth inside.

Just before the crest of the hill, she reached the chip shop on the corner, once a fine Victorian bank that now offered the locals a very different (and perhaps more welcome) service. Kat walked on a few more yards, debating whether to buy some chips or to pop into the Coleshill Hotel opposite for a proper meal and a decent glass of wine. She glanced over, just as a group of six approached the low timbered door. They were in three rows of two on the narrow street, and because of the dark and their layers of coats and hats, it took her a moment to recognise them: it was 'their' gang: Jan and Mark, Bill and Tom, Fiona and Steve.

It took another moment for her to realise it was pub quiz night.

Oh. Although they each sent her messages regularly *(How are you? Let me know if there is anything we can do, we must meet up soon . . .),* there were no more invites to the pub quiz, so she'd assumed they'd stopped going. But clearly, they still went. Just without her.

Of course they did. John, with his encyclopedic knowledge of history, politics and other obscure, random facts you never thought you needed to know, had been a real asset. What could *she* add, other than an uneven number to their group and an awkward reminder of their own mortality?

Imagine if they saw her buying a single bag of chips or eating alone in a pub. How sad would that look? Burying her head into the collar of her coat, she turned left and hurried through the grounds of St Peter and St Paul's.

The graveyard was like an enclave, surrounded by a high wall of ancient red-brick and overlooking the gentle, rolling hills of the Warwickshire countryside. In the daytime, it was a green oasis that provided a welcome respite from the surprisingly busy high street, but tonight it was shrouded in darkness, save for the light spilling from the latticed windows of the fifteenth-century church.

Kat sank onto a bench with a heavy sigh, wincing at the cold that seeped through her trousers. She let out a long breath, and watched it float up and evaporate into the never-ending sky. Organ music emerged from the church, accompanied by the sound of children singing 'O Little Town of Bethlehem'.

It must be the Nativity service, Kat realised with a groan. Honestly, she might as well have stripped off all her clothes and rolled around on a bed of drawing pins. That would have been less painful than sitting in a graveyard alone, remembering Christmases past when she, John and Cam had sat inside that very same church, singing those very same songs, before walking home with the Christingle. Cam—beautiful little Cam—had held that overdressed orange so reverently, it had made her heart ache.

She tipped her head back, letting out a breath that trembled on the verge of a sob. She squeezed her eyes shut. Distraction. She needed a distraction. Kat pressed the button on her wristband.

Lock appeared before her, a tall dark figure shimmering in the night with the gravestones behind it and the spire of the ancient church to its right.

Lock took in its surroundings, a slight frown upon its forehead. 'DCS Frank?'

She blinked rapidly. 'I was just out for a walk, mulling over the case, and, well, I thought it would be helpful to talk things through.'

The image of Lock shivered slightly, and suddenly it was wearing a dark, woollen trench coat that emphasised its slim height, with a bright red scarf draped casually around its neck. 'As it is minus two degrees, I understand a winter coat is appropriate,' it said, assuming a sitting position beside her. 'What do you think?'

Kat shrugged. She wasn't going to feed Lock's vanity by telling it how good it looked. 'I didn't switch you on to exchange opinions about your fashion sense. I wondered what you really thought about Natasha. I mean, do you seriously think Natasha Riley killed her fiancé?'

'I think it is possible, but not probable.'

'So you agree with me?'

'Yes, but for different reasons. My rationale is that it is possible that Natasha Riley killed her fiancé, due to the absence of an alibi and the absence of communication between them, but we do not yet have sufficient evidence to suggest that on the balance of probabilities she murdered him, other than the fact that she owns a domestic appliance which is, according to the literature, a "must-have kitchen tool". As only two per cent of domestic murders are carried out by women, I think it is much more probable that the murderer is motivated by money or religion. Nevertheless, detaining Natasha Riley while we attempt to secure further evidence would have been justifiable as a precautionary measure that did no harm.'

Kat shook her head. 'You think arresting a vulnerable young woman just a couple of days after the death of her fiancé does no harm?'

'If you are right and she is innocent, then yes, arresting Natasha Riley would undoubtedly increase her distress. But if you are wrong and she is guilty, then we have released a murderer into the community.'

'She's not a murderer,' muttered Kat. 'I know some things don't stack up, but the way she looked at me when I asked about the knife—the utter and genuine confusion. I honestly don't think you can fake that.'

'One of the most important lessons I have learned is that all humans lie,' said Lock, staring into her eyes that were still damp with tears.

Kat turned away just as the church organ began to play. The mournful notes of 'In the Bleak Midwinter' filled the air and the distant voices of the choir soared above them:

In the bleak midwinter, frosty wind made moan . . .

Lock tilted its head. 'What does "frosty wind made moan" mean? It makes no grammatical sense.'

'It's not about what's grammatically correct. It's poetry. What matters is what it makes you *feel*.'

'And what does it make you feel?' Lock asked, as the families inside the church raised their voices and sang:

Earth stood hard as iron, water like a stone;
Snow had fallen, snow on snow, snow on snow,
In the bleak midwinter, long ago.

Kat took a deep breath of the ice-cold air. 'Sad, Lock. It just makes me feel sad.' She didn't want a pub meal, or chips or a quiz. And she didn't want to be talking to a hologram on a bench in a cold, empty graveyard. She just wanted things to be the way they used to be, with her, John and Cam.

Lock leaned forward, its eyes unblinking as it asked, 'Why do you feel sad, DCS Frank?'

She turned away, staring at the church windows and the shadows inside. 'It's nothing,' she lied. 'Just the Ghosts of Christmas Past.'

Lock was silent for a few moments before saying, 'Ah, I understand that is a reference to *A Christmas Carol* by Charles Dickens, which I have just read. An interesting story, although I am puzzled as to why it is so popular.'

'It's a classic!'

'But why? It is just about an old man who finally realises he will eventually die and, because according to his religious beliefs the life he has led means he will face eternal hell, he belatedly decides to share more of the money he has hoarded to avoid his terrible fate.'

'That's a very cynical take.'

'It is what factually happens.'

Kat puffed out her cheeks. 'Well, to be honest, I haven't read it since I was a kid. But that's not how I remember the film.'

'There are over thirty adaptations if you include animations. Which one would you recommend I watch first?'

'Oh, *The Muppet Christmas Carol* is the best,' said Kat without hesitation.

She turned to face Lock on the bench, studying its face for the few seconds she knew it would take it to consume the movie. Surely even Lock could not help but be moved by this film?

But Lock just frowned. 'Why did a rat narrate the story? There are no rats in the novel. Or singing.'

'Because it was the Muppets.'

'I don't understand.'

Kat studied the AI hologram beside her. 'No, Lock. I don't suppose you do.' She rose to her feet. 'Come on, I'd best go home before my bum freezes to this bench.'

'That is a highly unlikely scenario, given that the temperature is only minus two degrees and you are fully clothed.' Nevertheless, it followed her out of the churchyard, before stopping to look up at the wooden statue of Christ on a cross that towered above them. 'I have read 52,938 articles about the crucifixion of Jesus and yet I am still not clear whether he was resurrected as a spirit or body—there are conflicting reports within the Bible and many different interpretations of what they mean.'

'Does it matter?'

'I am interested in why humans so often revere beings that have no bodies—Gods, angels and even ghosts. It puzzles me.'

Kat studied the statue, almost lifelike in size. 'The thing that puzzles *me*,' she said, 'is how on earth the killer managed to get a bloody great big cross into the recycling centre and up the hill without being seen by anyone. Unless . . .'

'What?'

'I'll tell you on the way home. Come on. I want to check something in the transcripts.'

CHAPTER TWENTY-ONE

'Okay,' said Kat, calling the room to order. 'Dr Edwards is joining us via Zoom, so let's kick off the briefing with a forensics update. Over to you, doctor.'

Kat gestured towards the large screen above the boardroom table, and the distinctive image of Dr Judith Edwards. With their short white hair, strong black eyebrows and bright red lipstick, they looked like a funky presenter of some late-night arts show rather than the lead pathologist for the West Midlands and Warwickshire region.

'Thank you, DCS Frank,' they said, in a clear Welsh voice. 'I've got two updates to share with you this morning. First, we have the preliminary results of the toxicology tests. Now, I must stress that a couple of the more detailed biochemical tests haven't been completed yet—you'll get a full report later today—but I wanted to give you a heads-up that the victim tested positive for both alcohol and benzodiazepines—almost certainly Flunitrazepam, more commonly known as Rohypnol.'

Murmurs rippled around the room.

'As most of you probably know, Rohypnol is often called "the date rape drug" because its sedative effects have been misused to aid serious sexual assaults. It's basically a tranquiliser that's ten times more potent than Valium. Victims often describe its effects as paralysing, and a person can be so incapacitated that they collapse. They may lie on the floor, eyes open, able to observe events but completely unable to move. Afterwards, memory is impaired, and victims often cannot recall what happened.'

Rayan raised his hand. 'But if Gary Jones had taken Rohypnol, then how did he manage to climb Mount Judd?'

'Impossible to tell from the toxicology tests, but we do know that the effects typically start twenty to thirty minutes after taking the drug, peak within two hours and may persist for eight or even twelve hours after. So, my educated guess would be that Gary Jones didn't consume the drug until he reached the summit, and that it was mixed with alcohol—we found alcohol in his blood, which would have accelerated the sedative effects. Within minutes, Gary would have been drowsy enough to make him incapable of meaningful resistance when he was tied up, but not so sedated as to make him a dead weight if the killer moved quickly. By the time he was tied up, he would have lost all muscle control.'

'Will the toxicology reports be able to distinguish the exact type or brand of the drug?' asked Debbie. 'Anything that could help us identify where it came from?'

'Afraid not. The tests we do merely tell us the chemical formulation, and Rohypnol is widely available on the internet, as it's sold in Europe and Latin America as a sleeping pill.'

Kat turned to face her team. 'Once again, this suggests that a high degree of planning, thought and control went into this murder.'

'It might also suggest that the killer wasn't confident of their own physical strength,' added DI Hassan, 'so they used drugs as a sort of back-up.'

Kat nodded. 'Good point.' She turned back to the screen. 'Do we have any forensics from the cross yet?'

Dr Edwards nodded, before presenting a series of photographs and diagrams of the wooden cross that was used to crucify Gary Jones, using lots of technical language and detail that Kat didn't fully understand, but the conclusion was annoyingly clear: there were no fingerprints, no hairs, DNA or fibres belonging to anyone other than the victim.

Kat cursed. 'Seriously? Nothing at all? How can someone crucify and mutilate a man and leave no trace?'

'I know. I'm as frustrated as you are. I've asked the team to go over it again, but so far, we have nothing. All we know is that two feet of the nine-foot vertical post—the stipes—was inserted into the ground—where the killer had planted a fence post spike so that the stipe just needed to be inserted. The vertical post was a standard fence stake, commonly found in garden and DIY centres. But see how in the upper third, the killer has modified it, hollowing out a space for the crossbar to slot into, which again appears to be a standard six-foot fence post, tied to the vertical post for this purpose.' The screen filled with a shot of the two pieces of wood tied together at the point where they crossed with rope.

'That is a transom knot,' said Lock. 'One of the most effective knots for tying two pieces of wood together. And as the photographs I took at the scene of the crime show that tautline hitch knots were used to secure the victim's wrists, this suggests that our killer has some knowledge of knots.'

'Excellent,' said Kat. 'This is really useful information that will help us build a profile of our killer, thank you, Dr Edwards.' She asked Lock to bring up their virtual board, which summarised the three main lines of enquiry: love/jealousy, money/gangs and religion, with images of potential suspects linked to each. 'Any further updates we need to add before reviewing next steps?'

Debbie reported that she'd re-interviewed Joshua Shawcroft, the fell-runner who turned out to be a security guard who liked to run after his night shift ended, which meant he had a solid alibi with CCTV footage to back it up.

Kat nodded and crossed him off the board.

'Natasha Riley refused to sign her mobile phone over to us,' said Rayan. 'She claimed she wanted to back up the photographs on her computer at home before handing it over to the police, so we haven't been able to analyse her texts and messages yet.'

He reported this as if it was somehow suspicious, but Kat remembered how terrified she'd been of losing her phone when John died. All those precious photos and messages. There's no way she'd have handed it over to anyone without doing a full back-up first. 'That's understandable,' she said. 'What about life insurance? Did we find out who benefits?'

'They both took out life insurance when they bought the house together,' said Debbie. 'But because they weren't married and he didn't leave a will, Natasha won't benefit from his death.'

'Er, except she is now the sole owner of the house and doesn't have to split any profits with him,' said Rayan.

'That's hardly a motivation for murder,' said Kat. 'Especially as she now has to pay all the mortgage and bills from just her salary. What about Mike Garth's alibi?'

'He says he was at home all night after getting in from the pub,' said Debbie. 'But because he lives alone, there are no witnesses. We've called in all the local CCTV footage and doorbell camera systems from his street and should get that by the end of the day.'

'Lock, make that a priority when we get it. But to be honest, I think the evidence from Dr Edwards makes Phil Brine, the owner of the recycling centre, a key person of interest.'

'How so, boss?' asked Rayan.

'Well, apart from the absence of any DNA to link her to the scene of crime, both the building and transportation of the cross would require a degree of strength and skill that Natasha Riley simply doesn't possess. Even though the victim was made to carry the crossbar up the hill, we've been struggling to work out how someone actually got both the nine-foot vertical post and the six-foot crossbar into the recycling centre without being seen. But what if that's the wrong question? What if someone didn't need to get the cross into the recycling centre *because they were already there?*'

'You mean Phil Brine could have built it in the yard?' said DS Browne, leaning forward.

'Exactly. There were piles of wood everywhere, plenty of tools and equipment, and—conveniently for Phil Brine—not a CCTV camera in sight.'

'So once the rest of the staff went home,' Debbie continued, 'he could have built the cross in the yard, planted the vertical post in the hill when it was dark, left the crossbar at the bottom and, a few hours later, made Gary Jones carry it to the summit?'

'Maybe. I mean, he has access to the murder site and probably the materials and skills to crucify someone, but *why?*' asked Rayan, frowning. 'What's his motive?'

'I went back over the transcripts last night asking myself that very question,' said Kat, gesturing at Lock to project a virtual image of the interview. 'Phil Brine was very keen for us to "follow the money" and to look at who the council had subcontracted their waste and recycling business to, alleging criminal gangs were involved. In fact, he was so keen, he mentioned it several times in the interview. Which made me wonder why. We know that Tracy Taylor holds the contract now, but I asked Lock to look back at all the contracts the council have let over the past ten years. And guess what? Up until three years ago, the contract was held by Brine's Household Waste and Recycling Centre.'

A copy of the contract appeared on the virtual screen.

'And look who signed it,' Kat said, pointing at the scrawled signatures. 'Phil Brine and Gary Jones.'

Debbie leaned forward. 'But when I interviewed him, Phil Brine claimed that he'd never heard of, let alone ever met, the victim.'

'He lied,' said Lock.

Rayan screwed up his face. 'So . . . you think Phil Brine crucified another man just because three years ago he gave a contract to another company?'

'Yes,' said Lock. 'Which aligns with my initial hypothesis that the murderer was motivated by money.'

'Although I disagree about the motivation,' said Kat. 'Phil Brine's business isn't just a source of money, it's the source of his whole identity, status and pride, all of which, in his head, the contracting-out culture was undermining. Plus if we'd have done what he hinted at and focused our investigation on Tracy Taylor, then he'd also have got revenge on the woman he believes undercut him. It might be worth checking out what his religious beliefs are.'

'Does he have an alibi for the night of the murder?' Rayan asked, turning to face Debbie.

'Er . . . I didn't ask him,' she said, flushing. 'I only interviewed him about when and how he discovered the body. At the time, he wasn't a suspect and I didn't think he, that is, I mean I . . .'

Kat held her hand up. 'It doesn't matter now. I want Phil Brine brought in for a second interview asap. We need to find out if he has an alibi for the night that Gary Jones was murdered, and why he lied about not knowing him.'

CHAPTER TWENTY-TWO

Interviewer: DCS Kat Frank (KF)

Interviewee: Phil Brine (PB)

Date: 11 December, 10.30am, Leek Wootton HQ

KF: Thank you for giving us your time again, Mr Brine.

PB: It's the third time in a week. I've got a business to run. I can't keep coming back and forth like this.

KF: It's not ideal, I know. But in the absence of any working CCTV cameras or barriers on your premises, I'm afraid you're our sole source of information with regards to who might have had access to the scene of the crime.

PB: He wasn't murdered in my recycling centre. He was murdered on top of the hill.

KF: Which can only be accessed via your premises.

PB: *[shrugs]*

KF: *[reads notes]* In your interview with DS Browne, you said that you have about twenty people working for you.

PB: That's right.

KF: And on December 7th, who was the last person to leave?

PB: I was.

KF: Was anybody with you when you left?

PB: No.

KF: Did anyone see you leave?

PB: No.

KF: And who was first to arrive at work the following morning?

PB: I was. Look, I'm not being funny, but I told all this to the pregnant one.

KF: Detective Sergeant Browne? Yes, I am just reading the transcript. So essentially there is not a single person that can verify that you left 'just after 6pm' and didn't return until 7am the next morning?

PB: So?

KF: So, in the absence of CCTV cameras or an effective barrier system, we have no evidence to support what you are telling us.

PB: Why would I lie?

KF: That's what I'd like to know.

PB: I'm not lying!

KF: Really? Then why did you tell DS Browne that you had never heard of Gary Jones?

PB: I don't know what you mean.

KF: For the purposes of the tape, I am showing Phil Brine a copy of a contract between Brine's Household Waste and Recycling Centre and Coventry City Council. Mr Brine, could you read out the names of the signatures to this contract, please?

PB: It's me. And—look, how am I supposed to remember whose name was on the contract?

KF: For the purposes of the tape, please can you read it out?

PB: Gary Jones. But honestly, I never met the bloke. It's a coincidence that he happened to sign this, what, three years ago? How was I supposed to remember that?

KF: Before it was terminated, how long did you have a contract with Coventry Council?

PB: Fifteen years.

KF: And what proportion of your business would you say the council accounted for?

PB: I dunno. I'd have to check the accounts.

KF: Roughly.

PB: *[puffs out cheeks]* Twenty-five, thirty per cent maybe?

KF: So, for fifteen years, Coventry City Council accounted for a third of your business and income. Yet you don't remember the name of the person who not only signed your final contract with Coventry Council, but also tendered the contract—your business—elsewhere the following year?

PB: I didn't put two and two together. All I meant was I'd never *seen* the bloke before.

KF: *[checks notes]* And yet you said to DS Browne that you'd never *heard* of Gary Jones before.

PB: You're twisting my words. Trying to fit me up. I'm not stupid.

KF: *[pauses]* Okay, let's discuss the morning the body was found. You told DS Browne that another man, a fell-runner, informed you that he'd seen a dead body on top of Mount Judd. Why didn't you ring the police straight away?

PB: I told you, I didn't know if he was telling the truth, so I had to see it with my own eyes.

KF: So you took half an hour out of your busy day to climb all the way up the hill in the freezing cold. But when you 'saw it with your own eyes', why didn't you ring the police?

PB: I *told* you, I couldn't get a signal up there on my phone.

KF: That's odd. We had a perfectly good signal when we were up there.

PB: Signals vary, don't they? I don't see why it matters.

KF: It *matters* because your apparent inability to get a signal the whole time you were up there meant that the police investigation was delayed by nearly 90 minutes. Plus your insistence on seeing the dead body 'with your own eyes' meant the crime scene was heavily contaminated with your own presence.

PB: I didn't contaminate anything.

KF: That remains to be seen. We are still awaiting a full forensics report.

PB: You are not going to fit me up for this. I have an alibi. I was home all night. Ask my missus.

KF: Oh, we will, Mr Brine. We'll also be asking for a warrant to search your premises. And we'll need access to your phone and your doorbell camera if you have one to verify that you were indeed at home.

PB: *[snorts]* You can have access to my Nokia if you want, love, but it won't tell you anything. I don't have an iPhone and I don't have a bloody doorbell camera, either, because I'm not stupid enough to let corporate giants and the government track my movements and monitor my thoughts.

KF: That could make things more difficult for you.

PB: Since when did we start trusting the so-called evidence from machines over the words of men and women? I was at home between 6.30pm and 6.30am, and my wife can and will confirm that. But if you're getting a warrant, then I want my lawyer. Now.

KF: Of course. We can arrange that. But just one more question. Are you religious?

PB: What? Well, yeah. Sort of.

KF: Which religion?

PB: *[snorts]* Do I look like a Buddhist to you?

KF: So you're a Christian?

PB: Of course I am. *[pauses]* Oh, I get it. You think I crucified some bloke from the council because I'm a *Christian*? *[laughs]* Do you know what? Apart from being offensive to Christians, that just shows your bloody ignorance. Crucifixion was a common method of execution in the Roman times—and it still is in some parts of the world—Saudia Arabia still crucifies child molesters and rapists. They've got the right idea if you ask me.

KF: You seem to know a lot about crucifixions, Mr Brine.

PB: Just because I clear rubbish for a living, it doesn't mean I don't know about history or world affairs. I'm just pointing out that Christians aren't the only ones who used to crucify people. But if you want a religious angle, you should be looking at Muslims. I bet if a Muslim bloke had been murdered so close to whatever their equivalent of Christmas is and in a manner that mocked their faith, you'd be blaming white racists. So why not the other way round?

KF: I think that's enough for now. Someone will be in shortly to get the contact details for your lawyer. *[rises to her feet]*

PB: You're too afraid, that's why.

KF: I'm not the one who has anything to be afraid of, Mr Brine.

INTERVIEW CONCLUDED

CHAPTER TWENTY-THREE

———

Debbie Browne moved away from the two-way mirror, sat down and put her feet up on the chair opposite. DCS Frank would have kittens if she saw her vertical. The thing was, sitting down might be good for her ankles, but it hurt her lower back if her legs were raised too long, and her growing bump made it harder and harder to get back up again. She was constantly having to trade off comfort in one part of her body against pain in another.

When DCS Frank and Lock entered the room, Debbie instinctively dropped her feet from the chair and tried to sit up straight, before resuming her resting position with a wince.

'What do you think?' the boss asked.

As usual, Rayan was the first to speak. He was one of those people who never seemed to require thinking time to work out what he thought. Debbie stared at her puffy ankles, wondering if she would ever get good at 'thinking on her feet'. DCS Frank had tried to explain to her once that fast thinkers weren't necessarily better thinkers, they were just *different*. Someone like Debbie might take longer to reach a view, but once she did, any opinion she expressed was well-founded and deeply held, rather than just the latest thought that was passing through her head.

'Well, a lot depends upon whether his alibi stacks up,' said Rayan. 'But I agree he should be a key person of interest now. And because of all that conspiracy stuff about not having an iPhone, it might be worth checking if he's a member of any groups or forums on the watch list. He might not be acting alone.'

'Good point,' said Kat. 'What do you think, Debbie?'

What did she think? She was still embarrassed that she hadn't asked Phil Brine about his whereabouts on the night of the murder or checked if he'd ever had a contract with Coventry City Council. She'd offered to sit in on the second interview—practically begged, in fact—but Kat had insisted on doing it alone. So now Debbie thought that DCS Frank didn't trust her not to mess it up again. But of course, she couldn't say that.

'Er, I agree with Rayan,' she said. 'Except for . . . well, he was very confident, wasn't he? He didn't ask for a lawyer until right at the end, whereas if he was guilty, I'd have expected him to be a bit more nervous and ask for one at the start. Especially someone like him who seems pretty up on his rights.' Debbie gave a shrug, her cheeks slightly colouring as she added, 'But I don't know. Those are just my first thoughts.'

'Which is what I asked you for.'

'But our job is to assess the evidence,' said Lock.

Kat watched Phil Brine through the observation mirror, leaning back in his chair as if he didn't have a care in the world. 'I have to say, I agree with Debbie,' she said. 'When I read the transcripts last night, I thought he was as suspicious as hell. But I just more or less accused him of murder, and he wasn't afraid at all.'

'He could just be a very good actor,' said Lock.

'No,' said Kat. 'You can't hide fear. You can literally smell it.'

'There is little or no evidence to substantiate that statement. One study did suggest that humans can unconsciously detect whether someone is stressed or scared by smelling a chemical pheromone released in their sweat; however, most researchers do not believe that humans can detect pheromones. In other mammals, this is done using a structure in the nose called the vomeronasal organ. Although humans have one of these, it is not connected to the brain.'

'If I want you to explain how humans work to me, Lock, I will ask you.' Kat turned towards Rayan and Debbie. 'Right. This is what I think we should do. He asked for a lawyer, so let's keep Phil Brine in until he or she arrives and see how long his bravado lasts. I want him swabbed and his hands checked for evidence of splinters—anything that can link him to the cross. We'll leave him to sweat for a bit—maybe produce a few more pheromones— and then we'll interview him again.'

Kat glanced at her phone. 'But bear in mind that heavy snow is forecast for tonight so if anyone's worried about getting stuck at work, I'm happy for you to go now and dial in to the 6pm debrief from home.'

'What about interviewing Phil Brine again?' Debbie asked.

'I'll cover that. It's not the end of the world if I don't make it home tonight.'

DS Browne studied her boss, remembering that, as a widow with her only son away at university, she had no one to go home to. Having recently split up with her boyfriend, Debbie knew how hard that could be. 'I don't mind staying late with you,' she offered.

'No, it's fine. You get home. There's plenty of other interviews and fact-checking that can be done remotely.'

Debbie's heart sank as, once again, the boss asked her to interview the wife. She was a detective sergeant, but all she seemed to do these days was manage cordons and female partners. She couldn't help but worry that it was because she was pregnant. Or even worse, incompetent.

'This is your first big murder case,' Kat continued. 'And believe me, it's going to be emotionally and physically tough. So I want you to look after yourselves. This is a marathon, not a sprint. So pace yourselves, okay?'

Debbie nodded, but she wished she had the courage to add, 'You, too, boss.'

They all turned as Karen-from-Comms entered the room.

'I know what you're going to ask,' said Kat, raising her hand before the young woman could speak. 'And I'm afraid the answer is still no. Not yet. I want to see where we get to with Phil Brine first. We might be on to something.'

Karen pulled a face. 'I honestly don't think we can keep putting this off, DCS Frank. We need to manage the media, not avoid it.'

Kat sighed. 'Look, if we were just dealing with the *Nuneaton Post*, then I'd agree, because the local rags depend upon good relationships with us to supply their news. But the nationals are completely different—they're like a pack of wolves. And you can't manage wolves, Karen. You either keep them at bay or get eaten alive.' Her face softened. 'But I promise you, once we have a bone to throw them—something worth saying—we'll do a press conference, okay?'

'But—'

'By tomorrow, we'll know whether we have enough to charge Phil Brine or not,' said Kat. 'What harm can it do to wait one more day?'

CHAPTER TWENTY-FOUR

———

The air is cold and sharp with the threat of snow. I bury my hands deep in my pockets, afraid of what they might do next.

This one has two children. A wife. Three innocent hearts I will surely break.

But how else to end it? How else to make them see?

He needs to understand—they all need to understand—how it feels to be afraid: to be completely and utterly powerless as their life is held in the hands of another.

And yet . . .

I raise my eyes to the darkness of the sky, seeking . . . guidance? A sign? Absolution?

I am sent all three, as a flurry of snowflakes fill my vision, spiralling like my thoughts until I am no longer sure if it is me or the snow that is falling, falling, into the unspeakable past.

I cover my face with my hands, trying to shut out the snow and the memories it brings. But it's too late. The images make me want to peel my very skin off: to cut out my brain and delete myself until all of the pain, all of the me is gone and no more.

But I am done with turning my anger in on myself. My therapist is right. I need to let it all out, push the fear and the hurt back to where it belongs. I—we—have suffered enough.

Slowly, I release my hands from my face. I can still see the snowflakes, but from a distance, like they are falling on somebody else.

I doubt that he even recalls, let alone cares about, what he did.

Tonight, I will help him to remember.

CHAPTER TWENTY-FIVE

Kat's phone buzzed on her bedside cabinet. She grabbed it, trying to press snooze, but it wasn't her alarm. It was DS Browne. At 6.17am?

She sat up. 'Debbie? What's happened? Are you in labour?'

'No! Why does everyone always think I'm ringing because of the baby? I'm sorry to call you so early, but I was on call, so the duty desk rang me, and I'm sorry to wake you—'

'Just tell me, Debbie.'

'There's been another murder. They rang me because apparently there are some similarities with the Gary Jones case.'

Kat swung her legs out of the bed and started to grab her clothes. She'd had less than four hours' sleep—she'd stayed at HQ till midnight working the case while she waited for the snow and the traffic to ease off, but she was one hundred per cent awake now. 'What makes them think they're connected?' she asked. The duty desk rota could be a bit random: one of the more junior or excitable officers might have assumed that the lack of a beating heart connected a body to their case.

'Just after 6am, a farmer rang 999 to say he'd found the body of a man crucified on a cross in one of his fields and, well, he says it looks like his eyes have been plucked out.'

CHAPTER TWENTY-SIX

___

A field in Fillongley, Warwickshire, 7.22am

At the sight of the squad car with its hazard lights on, Kat parked and climbed out into the dark before dawn. Christ, this really was in the middle of nowhere. All she could see were fields to her left and right, blanketed with snow, fringed with hedges and the occasional gnarled oak tree. There wasn't a building in sight. The only thing to break the view was the single-track road she'd just driven up, unadorned by streetlights, let alone CCTV cameras. The air had that strange, still quality to it that occurs after snowfall, broken only by the crows that circled above.

Kat opened the boot of her car with a sharp crack and started pulling on her PPE for the second time in four days.

DS Browne headed towards her. 'Morning, boss. The body's in the field on your right there. I've set a cordon up all the way round, and the SOCO should be here in ten minutes with the tent.'

'Good,' said Kat, squinting at the field that she pointed to. She hadn't brought her glasses, but she could see a dark smudge of something in the centre. 'How did the farmer find him?' asked Kat. 'It would have been pitch-black an hour ago.'

'He was driving his tractor down the road and his headlamps picked the body out.'

'Did he go into the field?'

'Yes, but he says he didn't touch the body.'

Great, now she had some farmer's big wellies churning up the evidence. 'Anybody else?'

'No, I was the first person here, but I haven't been in. Because of the snow, I thought we might have a chance of getting some footprints.'

'Well done,' said Kat, zipping up the white plastic suit and pulling on her mask. 'Make sure the constable doesn't let anyone else in and get traffic control to block the road off at both ends.'

'Okay.' Debbie couldn't hide her disappointment.

'I want to make sure we keep footfall to an absolute minimum. So it'll just be me and Lock for now,' she said, activating her wristband so that its image appeared. 'But you did well to secure the area so quickly,' she added. 'Really good work.' Debbie had developed more confidence over the past three months, but Kat knew how much she still needed her encouragement and approval, especially now she was about to go on maternity leave.

It would be another hour before it was fully light, so Kat switched her torch on and pointed it at the ground before approaching the low, wooden gate to the field, hoping to see a pair of footprints on the other side. But apart from the farmer's wellies, there were no further signs of disturbance on the smooth, white snow. 'What time did it stop snowing last night?' she asked Lock.

'2.47am.'

'Chances are the killer arrived and left before it stopped,' she said. 'But just in case, we'll go the long way round rather than through the gate.' Kat followed the fence along the outskirts of the field, with Lock following closely behind, until they were about level with the shadowy figure at the centre. After checking the snow on top of the fence, making sure there were no signs that the killer or victim might have entered the field from this point, Kat carefully climbed over, wincing as she landed stiffly on the other side. Lock simply passed through the fence like a ghost.

She focused the torch on the ground, checking for footprints, but again the snow was smooth and untouched. Slowly, she stepped forward, filling the still, crisp air with the slight crunch of snow from each careful step. About ten feet away from the centre of the field, Kat finally lifted her torch.

Despite Debbie's warning, she couldn't help but gasp at what she saw. There was a dead man tied to a large wooden cross, his arms stretched wide and dragged deep into a painful 'V' by the weight of his unsupported body. His head lolled forward onto his chest, so all she could see was thick, dark hair, matted with snow and ice. Kat forced herself to track the stark beam of light slowly over the corpse, which against the background of pure, white snow was an alarming medley of colours: grey in parts, purple in others, with a shock of thick black hair upon the chest and groin. Blood stained the snow beneath the dead man's feet. Moving closer, she stood beneath the sunken head and shone her light up into his face.

Kat looked up into bloodied, empty sockets where his eyes should have been and let out a brief cry. *Fuck!* Blood stained his face like tears, dripping from his beard onto the snow below.

She stepped back, taking a gulp of cold air as crows circled above, filling the dawn with their coarse, hungry cries. Kat focused on their dark wings against the brightening sky, fighting back the nausea.

'You get all the best gigs,' said a familiar Welsh voice behind her.

Kat turned to see Dr Judith Edwards.

Taking care to step exactly in Kat's footprints, they moved towards the body, allowing their torch to trail over every inch of his frozen flesh, before examining the ties at the wrists and gently testing what movement was left in his ankles and toes.

Kat forced herself to wait while the pathologist did her initial checks, her mind racing through the possibilities that this tragic death meant. When she could bear it no longer, she asked Judith for her first impressions.

'Well, subject to the PM, as there are no visible wounds other than the eyes, I'll bet you a bottle of gin that our victim died in the early hours of this morning from hypothermia and asphyxiation.'

'Any chance this could be a copycat killing?' asked Kat, with more hope in her voice than she felt.

'My observations suggest that this wooden cross has exactly the same measurements as the cross on Mount Judd,' said Lock, 'with a vertical post of nine feet and a crossbar of six feet, tied together with a transom knot and the victim's wrists secured by tautline hitch knots. As these details are not in the public domain, and this person has been murdered within a four-mile radius of Gary Jones, I calculate there is a greater than 99.5 per cent probability that this murder was carried out by the same person.'

'I agree,' said Judith. 'The only difference in the MO that I can see at this stage is that the killer has targeted his eyes rather than his ears.'

Which meant this one was on her. Kat puffed out a cloud of frozen air, but it did little to release the guilt inside. There was no way she could have prevented the murder of Gary Jones, but this poor man had died because she had failed to find and apprehend his killer. And as Phil Brine had spent last night in custody, it also meant that it couldn't have been him.

'Shit,' she cursed again.

Dr Edwards moved closer, until they were just inches from the dead man's face, peering into his empty eye sockets with a concentration Kat found hard to watch. 'Interesting,' they finally said.

'What is?'

Judith searched the snow below, before studying the crows

that swooped above. 'I'm not prepared to speculate any further until after the PM. Lock, could you scan and photograph the corpse *in situ*? Please pay particular attention to the eyes and the pattern of blood loss.'

Kat glanced back towards the lane where she could see the SOCO growing impatient in the cold, their irritated puffs of breath hanging above them like a cloud. Well, they were going to have to wait a bit longer, because even the best SOCO would disturb the snow and any evidence it might contain. One of the benefits of working with a hologram was that it literally left no trace, as using the LiDAR scanners on her wristband it could scan and photograph every inch of the field without leaving a single mark in the snow. It took less than two minutes for Lock to take over three hundred 2D and 3D images of the corpse and the surrounding area.

'Well?' asked Kat once it had finished. 'Are we in luck?'

'If you mean are there any footprints other than those belonging to the farmer who discovered the victim, then no, I am afraid we are not. And there are no other visible tracks on the road other than from the farmer's tractor and our own police cars. Any trace the victim and his killer may have left has been covered by the snow that fell after their exit.'

Kat swore and glared at the desolate landscape. 'Okay, but we'll need to keep a strict cordon around the area for when it melts in case there's anything forensics can find. We need to know how the killer got the victim all the way out here. How did they manage to undress him, take his clothes away and tie him up naked without any signs of a struggle?'

Dr Edwards stepped closer to the body and sniffed. 'The answer might be rum laced with drugs. I'll need to do a full toxicology report, but I wouldn't be surprised if I found traces of Rohypnol, just like our friend Gary Jones.'

Kat frowned. 'Any chance you could use your image recognition software to ID the victim again, Lock?'

'Of course. The victim is a Caucasian male in his early thirties, six-foot-one tall and an estimated ninety-two kilos in weight. There was a Mercedes car parked at the entrance to the lane, and that is registered to a Marcus Ridgeway, a 33-year-old white male who resides in Solihull and lists his profession as a small-business owner of Damson Lane Brewery. Mr Ridgeway has not been reported missing, but the photographs published on his social media accounts and website have a 92.2 per cent match with the physical characteristics I have identified, so it would seem a valid line of enquiry to visit his home.'

Kat's jaw was tight from the cold as she asked what the victim's marital status was. When Lock said he had a wife and two young daughters, she looked away, blinking against the brightening sky. A watery sun was just struggling over the horizon, revealing field after field, filled with nothing but snow and the occasional sheep. 'What a place to die,' she sighed. She pulled her PPE mask off and rubbed her frozen chin.

Judith followed her gaze. 'It's a bleak and lonely place. I guess that's why he wasn't even gagged. There was no point.'

'No,' said Kat, turning back to face the victim. 'I think that *was* the whole point. I think the murderer *wanted* him to cry for help, and to know that no one would ever hear him. I think they wanted him to know that he was going to die, and to feel completely and utterly alone and powerless to stop it.' Kat studied the corpse, thinking aloud. 'But why?' She puffed out her cheeks before saying what she hardly dared admit to herself. 'There's only four days between the two murders, which means we could be looking for a serial killer who could very well strike again. The fact that—'

A sudden flash of light bounced off the snow. Kat turned to see the journalist Ellie Baxter holding up her mobile phone.

'Can you confirm that a second person has been murdered, DCS Frank?'

'What the . . . ?'

'Sorry, boss,' panted DS Browne, coming up behind the young reporter. 'She arrived on a bike, so I didn't hear her, and then she just ducked under the cordon. I couldn't stop her.'

'This is a *crime scene*,' said Kat, advancing towards her. 'And if you don't leave now, I'll charge you with criminal trespass and obstruction.'

'Thank you, I'll take that as confirmation,' said Ellie Baxter, backing off with a smile.

'I'm sorry,' Debbie repeated, as she moved closer to Kat.

There was another flash of light as Ellie took a photo of the three of them together with Lock, before hopping onto her bike with a wave.

'Fuck,' said Kat, as the reporter pedalled away. 'I need to speak to McLeish before she puts that in her bloody paper.'

X COMMENTS

@Farmersboy21 OMFG what a start to the day. My dad found a dead body in one of our fields this morning. He's really shook up and the police are everywhere.

@janeyjane1999 When you say dead body, do you mean like a dead BODY or just a sheep or something?

@Farmersboy21 I mean a dead man. Dad thought it was a scarecrow at first, then realised we didn't have any in that field, and when he went closer, he realised it was a real person. He said he was naked and tied up on a cross, so reckons it was murder. In our field!

@Joshuatree63 Jesus, another crucified man? It must be linked to that guy on Mount Judd. Scary stuff.

@Fredsdead12 It'll be a sex game gone wrong—same perv who did that one on Mount Judd.

@Nocountryformenz Use your brain mate. The crucifix means it's about religion, not sex. Do you think it's a coincidence that it's nearly Christmas? Or that they we're both white guys? The police would be all over this if they were Indian or girls.
#Noonecaresaboutwhitemenanymore

@MaryMaryVcontrary Because white cis men are the real victims here? Give me a break.

@Farmersboy21 The police have cordoned off all the roads now, so we can't get out and go to work. My dad is losing his shit. Says he wished he never called the police, now.

@SeannotShaun22 Rookie error. Never call the cops. More trouble than they're worth.

Nuneaton Post Online Edition, 12 December, 8.01am

BREAKING NEWS: SECOND MAN FOUND NAKED AND CRUCIFIED IN WARWICKSHIRE FIELD
BY ELLIE BAXTER

Warwickshire Police have confirmed that they are investigating the murder of a man—the second in just four days—after he was discovered naked and crucified in the middle of a field, just 10km from Nuneaton, this morning.

The gruesome discovery was made by local farmer Bill Yates, whose son took to social media to express his family's shock and trauma. 'Dad is really shook up . . . he thought it was a scarecrow at first, then realised we didn't have any in that field, and when he went closer, he realised it was a real person. He said he was naked and tied up on a cross so reckons it was murder.'

DCS Kat Frank—who is currently leading the investigation into the murder of local man Gary Jones—confirmed that her controversial secret Future Police Unit (FPU) is also investigating this second crime, using the experimental and untested AI detective AIDE Lock. No arrests have yet been made in either case, and once again DCS Frank refused to make any comment or provide the public with any further information to allay their fears.

Anyone with further information is urged to contact the news desk on 024 7365 6363 or email news@Nuneaton crimedesk80.co.uk.

CHAPTER TWENTY-SEVEN

By the time they left the field, Kat's hands were frozen stiff, so she waited until she'd taken her PPE off and warmed up in the car before ringing McLeish. She was just pulling out her mobile when it rang.

'Sir,' she said, putting him on speaker phone. 'I was just about to call you. We've got—'

'The body of a naked man crucified in a Warwickshire field? Yeah, I heard. Unfortunately, from the Ministry of Justice's comms department.'

'What? How do *they* know?'

'Because it's all over social media and there's an online story in the *Nuneaton Post*, with a picture of you and Lock as the icing on this cake of shit.'

Lock projected the article before her, and Kat stared at the photograph, mortified. Ellie Baxter had caught them by surprise, so she and Judith had their hands in the air, mouths gaping like fishes. Debbie looked like she was about to fall over in her rush to stop the photo from being taken, and Lock looked spookily calm among all the chaos. But it was the caption that made her swear:

'IS *THIS* THE FUTURE OF POLICING?'

The sarcastic question was a not very subtle dog-whistle to the fact that this serious crime was being investigated by two middle-aged women, the (Black) hologram of an AI machine and a heavily pregnant young woman.

'What were you *thinking* of?' McLeish demanded. 'Talking to a reporter before you've talked to *me* about this?'

'I didn't, she—look, I'm not even going to bother answering that question. You know me better than that.'

'Well, the minister doesn't, so you need to fix this yesterday. Do you have a key suspect yet?'

'Er . . . well, we did, but as Phil Brine, the owner of the recycling centre, was in our custody last night, that means we'll have to rule him out. But we are starting to build up a useful profile of the killer.'

'I want you to hold a press conference as soon as possible. We need to get on the front foot.'

'What I *need* to do is tell this poor man's wife that her husband is dead, and *then* I need to find his killer,' Kat snapped. She took a breath, forcing herself to keep calm. 'It's too soon for a press conference, sir. It's the same MO as Gary Jones, but we don't have a full profile yet, and if we rush into this, it could backfire.'

'It already *has* backfired. KFC tells me that all the nationals are on their way to Nuneaton—including broadcast—so we need to manage this. We've got two dead naked men, which means there's a potential serial killer on the loose, and as if that weren't bad enough, it's being investigated by the country's first AI detective.'

Kat scowled at her phone. 'We shouldn't let the media dictate our agenda.'

'It's not about "the media", Kat, it's about the *public* who bloody read and watch it. We don't carry guns in this country because we police by consent, which depends upon *trust*. And if the public don't trust us, then we can't do our job. So you are going to hold a press conference *today*, and you are going to explain that we are doing everything to find and apprehend the killer, utilising the very latest AI technology to ensure that no stone is left unturned. Is. That. Clear?'

Kat remained silent for as long as she dared, before finally saying, 'Perfectly.'

McLeish ended the call, and she banged the driver's wheel with the heel of her hand.

'Would this be a good time to make a sarcastic comment about your superior?' asked Lock.

'No, it would not. But it would be a good time to give me the address of Marcus Ridgeway. We need to find out if he's missing.'

'But McLeish said you need to hold a press conference.'

'He said *today*. There's plenty of time to do my actual job first.'

'I think that would be a mistake.'

'I didn't ask you for your opinion, I asked you for the address.'

Lock paused. 'I will provide you with the address because you are my superior, but I am disconcerted by your refusal to follow the instructions of yours.'

'I *am* following them,' Kat said, turning the engine on. 'But in my own way. I'm not a machine, Lock.'

Lock raised its eyebrows. 'You say that as if it's a good thing. But what if that's the whole problem—the fact that every police officer does things in their "own way"? What happens when that is the sexist way, the racist way, the *wrong* way? Perhaps if you were more consistent and evidence-based, then maybe the public would trust the police more.'

'The public will trust us more if we hurry up and find the bloody killer. Which is exactly what I intend to do.'

CHAPTER TWENTY-EIGHT

Marcus Ridgeway lived in Solihull, a wealthy market town packed with cafés, bars and a large John Lewis, but surrounded by the relative tranquility of greenbelt countryside. As Kat drove into the peaceful cul-de-sac, she began to doubt whether Marcus Ridgeway really was the bedraggled man who'd been tied to a cross and left to die alone in a field. When she saw the two young girls playing in the snow on his driveway, she fiercely hoped he wasn't.

The oldest of the two looked like she was about seven or eight years old, the youngest maybe six: young enough to do as they were told and wear woolly hats, gloves and scarves; too young to lose their dad. Both girls stopped and stared as she climbed out of the car and approached the house, their little noses bright pink from the cold.

Kat gave them a noncommittal smile and knocked on the door. She'd deactivated Lock so that she could explain who and what it was before introducing the hologram to Mrs Ridgeway.

The door was opened by a white woman in her early thirties, with mid-length blonde hair pulled up in a ponytail, wearing jeans and a thick cream jumper that looked more fashionable than warm.

'Mrs Ridgeway?' Kat guessed.

The woman frowned and nodded.

Kat introduced herself before asking, 'Is your husband home?'

Mrs Ridgeway flushed and glanced at her daughters. 'He isn't here.'

'Oh.' Kat's stomach dropped. 'Do you know where he is?'

'Not exactly. It's a bit . . . look, what's this about? Is something wrong?'

'I think it'd be best if we discussed this inside.'

———

Mrs Ridgeway took her into the front room, a beautiful, large lounge with oak floors, a log fire and a fresh, pine-scented Christmas tree, crammed with lights and decorations. There was an Elf on the Shelf and two chocolate-filled advent calendars on the mantelpiece—presumably one for each girl—and two gin-based ones for the grown-ups. It looked like the whole room—indeed, the whole family's life—was centred on the countdown to Christmas.

Kat sat on the large, velvet settee with a sigh, remaining silent while Mrs Ridgeway took a seat opposite. God, she hated this part of the job. But there was no point in beating around the bush; the poor woman was probably already imagining the worst. 'Did your husband come home last night?'

'What? Oh, er . . .' Her eyes flicked to the window, where the girls played outside.

'I'm not here to judge. I just need to know if your husband is missing.'

'Missing?'

'Did he come home last night?'

She dropped her eyes. 'No.'

'Have you spoken to him this morning?'

'No.'

'Have you tried ringing or messaging him?'

'Yes.'

'And has he replied?'

Mrs Ridgeway shook her head, causing a single tear to spill from her left eye.

'Is that normal for him?'

The door flew open as the girls rushed in. 'Mummy!' the youngest shouted. 'Elsa says her snowman is better than mine!'

'I did not!' Elsa insisted, sensing she was in trouble. 'I just said it was hard to build a good one. You come and help us, Mummy. And then we can build the *best* snowman.'

'Not now,' Mrs Ridgeway said, wiping her eyes. 'I have to help this police officer. You go back outside.'

'I'm cold,' the youngest whined, pulling off her hat. Her hair was all flat and damp, and Kat could see her looking at the TV, imagining how much nicer it would be to snuggle up inside and watch a film. She didn't blame her, but she needed to talk to the mum alone.

'How about I let you play outside with our new AI detective?' said Kat.

'AI?' they both echoed.

'Yes, it's the very latest technology. It has a hologram, so it looks like a person, but it's really just a very clever computer. Would you like me to switch it on?'

'Yes!' they both cried.

After getting permission from their bemused mum, Kat activated Lock and introduced it to the children.

They stared up at it, fascinated. The youngest reached out to touch it, squealing with excitement when her hand passed right through. 'It's a ghost!' she cried.

'I am not a ghost. Not least because there is no such thing.'

'Yes, there is,' said Elsa. 'All the best books have ghosts in them.'

'I think you'll find that those are *fiction* books,' Lock said, rather imperiously.

'Lock, can you go and play with the children outside, please?' Kat said.

'Play? I am not a toy.'

'Entertain them. Talk with them. Anything, just . . .' She glanced towards Mrs Ridgeway. 'Please. I need to talk to their mum.'

'Very well. Lead the way.' Lock followed the excited girls outside with a confused expression upon its face.

'Sorry,' Mrs Ridgeway said. 'They can be quite high-maintenance. Usually Marcus would—' She broke off.

'I know this is difficult. But can I just confirm the last time you saw or heard from your husband?'

She nodded, tears sliding down her cheeks. 'Last night. He left here at about 7.30pm for his Christmas party at the micro-brewery he runs. It's been doing really well, so the party was his way of saying thank you to the staff. He's a really good boss, only sometimes . . .'

'Sometimes?'

'Sometimes he's a bit *too* good. Sometimes he's too friendly with some of the younger girls. They try and exploit him because he's the boss, and you know, when he's had a few too many, he's vulnerable and they take advantage.'

Okaay. Kat literally bit down on her tongue. Now was not the time to debate the use and abuse of power in sexual relationships. With an effort, she focused on the issue at hand. 'Do you think he's currently with another woman?'

Mrs Ridgeway stared out the window, where her children played with Lock in the snow. 'I don't know if he still loves me. But he loves the kids, and he loves Christmas. When the school emailed last night to say they'd be closed because of the forecast, he promised the girls he'd make them the *biggest* snowman today. He ordered a special hat and scarf and everything. But he's not here. And he hasn't even texted me with some lame excuse about his car breaking down or having a hangover or something. God knows, he's not perfect, but he wouldn't let the girls down. He just wouldn't.'

Kat rose from her chair and sat on the settee beside Mrs Ridgeway. She took her cold hands in hers, trying to block out the distant sound of her laughing children as she explained as gently as she could that the body of a man matching the description of her husband had been found in a Warwickshire field. The body would need to be formally identified, but she was afraid that all the evidence pointed towards the body being that of her husband, Marcus Ridgeway.

She stopped speaking, and she knew the way the poor woman looked at her would haunt her for years.

'No,' Mrs Ridgeway said. She jumped up and walked towards the window, placing her hands against the glass, frosted with fake snow. 'He can't be dead. He's going to help them build a snowman.'

Kat rose and stood behind her. Outside, the two girls were oblivious to their mother's pain, laughing as they threw snowballs that passed straight through Lock.

'What do I tell the girls?' said Mrs Ridgeway, her tears turning to sobs. 'What do I tell the girls?'

———

Kat sat in the car and stared back at the home she had just destroyed.

Except it wasn't a home anymore. Now it was just a house filled with the absence of a husband and father: a building full of memories of what once was, and the dreams and hopes that now would never be.

'Are you okay, DCS Frank?'

Kat turned to face Lock. 'What do you think?'

'I don't know. That is why I asked.'

'I just told a woman that her husband is dead and that her children have lost their father. So no, Lock. I am not fucking okay.'

'But now we have a family to ID the body. That is progress, which is good.'

Kat sighed. Before John died, she probably would have forced herself to say the same thing. Cases like these could drive you mad if you let them, so she'd learned to squash her feelings deep down inside and just focus on the job. But now it seemed like the more she pressed down on them, the more her emotions leaked out: spilling over the sides like an over-full bath. She looked back at Marcus Ridgeway's house: the two mini-reindeers in the porch, the 'Santa Stop Here' sign on the door. Why did he have to have kids? *Why* did he have to be murdered at Christmas? That poor family would never get over this: from now on, they'd associate Christmas with death and pain rather than presents, advent calendars and chocolate. And no matter how hard the mum tried to put on a brave face—which she would, because that's what mums do, right?—the whole festive season would be like rubbing a massive sack of salt into the gaping wound of her life.

Lock looked around the car, clearly confused by the fact that they weren't moving. 'So what are we doing now?'

'We're going to catch this fucker, Lock. That's what we're going to do,' she said, turning the ignition key. 'I am sick of telling women they've been widowed, and I refuse to let there be another one. Do you hear me? *I refuse.*'

CHAPTER TWENTY-NINE

DS Browne hadn't had a chance to eat breakfast before driving out to the farm, then she'd spent two hours in the freezing cold managing the cordon, before heading back to HQ. Despite her hungry prayers, by the time she'd made her way through the traffic the briefing was about to start, so she went straight to the Major Incident Room, casting mournful glances in the direction of the canteen.

Debbie's stomach rumbled as she took a seat at the large boardroom table. God, she would kill for a plate of hash browns and two fried eggs right now. Although she wouldn't say no to a bacon butty. Or a sausage sandwich. Or beans on toast. Even mushrooms, as long as they weren't—

'Biscuit?' said Rayan, taking a seat by her side. He slid a mini-pack of custard creams and a cup of tea towards her.

'Have I told you lately that I love you?' Debbie said, tearing them open.

Rayan laughed. 'I got them from the canteen in case you didn't have time. I was going to buy you a banana, but—'

'Don't you bloody dare,' she said, through a mouthful of lovely crumbs.

He shook his head, nodding towards the tea. 'You're supposed to dunk them.'

'I'm pregnant, not deranged.'

'Okay,' said Kat, from where she stood at the head of the table. 'Let's make a start. As you know, the body of a male was found just before dawn by a farmer in a Nuneaton field. Lock?'

Any remaining chatter fell away when Lock projected the 3D image of the corpse above the boardroom table where they sat.

Debbie felt the custard creams rise back up her throat as the image of the naked man tied to a wooden cross rotated a full 360 degrees before her. She took a gulp of tea and washed them back down.

'Dr Edwards will be carrying out a full PM,' said Kat. 'But their *initial* observations are that as there are no significant wounds apart from the removed eyes, the cause of death is most likely to be hypothermia.'

'The same as Gary Jones,' murmured Rayan.

'The same as Gary Jones,' Kat repeated with emphasis.

Debbie stared at the victim's bare feet, the toes a deep unnatural blue. They looked so cold she had an irrational urge to reach out and warm them. The poor man probably had a nice pair of cosy slippers waiting for him at home. And now he'd never wear them again.

'Do we know who he is?' she asked.

'Subject to a formal identification, we think this is—or was— Marcus Ridgeway. Lock, can you pull up his profile, please?'

A second image appeared next to the corpse, this time an enlarged photograph of the deceased when he was very much alive. His shock of black hair was smoothed back, with a well-groomed beard in true hipster fashion, partly covering the neck of his thick cream jumper. His face was flushed from heat, drink or maybe both, highlighting his bright blue eyes and strong white teeth, as he raised a glass to whoever had taken the photo. Marcus Ridgeway had the air of someone who possessed both height and weight—not fat, but solid: hearty. The sort of man who enjoyed food, drink and a boisterous game of rugby. Debbie fancied she could almost imagine him laughing: a deep, loud belt of pleasure. But it was his eyes that trapped her gaze. They were so warm, so alive, so *there*. What kind of a person could take someone's *eyes* out? The very thought revolted her.

'Marcus Ridgeway was a 33-year-old male,' said Lock. 'He was married and had two daughters, aged nine and six. He owned Damson Lane Brewery, a relatively successful microbrewery and bar which, according to Companies House, made a net profit of fifty-two thousand pounds in the last financial year. He has no criminal convictions on file.'

'Two men found crucified, naked and dead from hypothermia within seven miles of each other,' said Rayan, leaning forward. 'What are the odds on that?'

'On average, there are twelve homicides in the county of Warwickshire each year, out of a population of 592,200,' said Lock. 'Considering the location and similarities in the *modus operandi,* the probability of these two murders being coincidental and unrelated is less than one per cent.'

'Which means that until we have evidence to the contrary, we are treating this as a serial killing,' said Kat. She paused, allowing that fact to sink in.

Debbie wrote it down on her pad in capital letters: SERIAL KILLER. Crikey. And *she* was on the investigation team.

Lock frowned. 'Although some authorities do set a lower threshold of two, a serial killer is more typically defined as someone who has committed three or more murders.'

'I don't intend to let there be a third,' said Kat. 'So all leave is cancelled while we work this case flat-out.'

Debbie wrote down 'all leave is cancelled', circling the word 'all'. If they didn't find the killer before Christmas, they'd have to carry on working right through. She was supposed to start maternity leave after the holiday, but there was no way she'd leave her team in the lurch if they were still looking for a serial killer.

And anyway, her baby wasn't due until 20th January—and it could come as late as 3rd February, so there was no reason why she couldn't carry on working for a bit longer. She made a note to talk to Kat about covering any Christmas shifts for the officers with kids.

Debbie tuned back into the meeting as Kat quickly filled the team in on her interview with Mrs Ridgeway. 'Rayan, I want you to go to the micro-brewery, find out who was at the party, what time our victim arrived, who he spoke to, when he left and who with, and whether there's any CCTV. His wife inferred he was the sort of man who plays around, so find out who his play-mates were and whether he'd recently fallen out with any of them. Natasha Riley hinted that Gary was a bit of a flirt, too, so find out if they had any girlfriends in common. The murderer could be a jealous boyfriend, husband, or even a jilted lover.'

'Hell hath no fury like a woman scorned, and all that,' said Rayan.

'The correct quote,' said Lock, 'is "Heav'n has no rage like love to hatred turn'd, or Hell a fury like a woman scorned". It is from William Congreve's play of 1697, which, having just read it, I conclude is a highly implausible tragedy. Rather like your theory.'

'What?' demanded Kat.

'I said, the correct quote is—'

'I heard what you *said*, Lock. I want to know what you meant.'

'I meant that Rayan seemed to imply that a disgruntled ex-girlfriend could have killed both Gary Jones and Marcus Ridge-way. Yet the data clearly shows that women account for just eleven per cent of serial murders over the last century.'

Kat folded her arms. 'Show me a graph that illustrates this.'

Lock projected the image of a simple bar chart above the boardroom table. The 'y' axis showed the percentage of serial murders that were carried out by men or women, and the 'x' axis showed each decade that they occurred in.

Kat pointed towards the coloured bars. 'You're right, Lock. This graph shows that *on average* women account for just eleven per cent of all serial killings, but look at all the differences that average hides. In 2010, it was just seven per cent, but in 1900, sixty-one per cent of serial killers were women.' She turned back to face the room.

'People often ask me how I caught the Aston Strangler,' Kat said, pausing while Debbie, along with the rest of the team, leaned in. 'We brought in an expert profiler, "Mike the Psych," and he focused on the generalities. He told us that most serial killers are men who are driven by sexual fantasies, that most serial killers had been bullied and abused as children, had difficulties holding down jobs or relationships and often had a criminal record. But although this was true of *most* serial killers, it wasn't true of the Aston Strangler. It was only when we focused on the *specific* details of the *specific* murders and began looking at the margins of the graphs rather than the bulges in the middle that we found Anthony Bridges, a married, middle-aged police officer.' She paused, remembering the denial and abuse she'd faced when she'd dared to arrest one of their own; the shame and anger that had reverberated throughout the force when it became clear that she was right.

Kat pointed at the chart as she addressed the room. 'Murder is, by its very nature, an *atypical* act. Serial murders even more so. So why do we insist upon looking for the "typical" serial killer?'

Debbie caught her eye. Was her boss expecting her to answer or was it a rhetorical question?

'Because we want to label and categorise them,' Kat continued. 'Because we want to make the unknowable knowable and provide a way to think—or not think—about the unthinkable. I don't know if we're looking for a male or female killer. But I *do* know that women tend to favour "quieter" means of murder, such as poisoning, and there's something peculiarly quiet, emotional and yet detached about hypothermia as a method, so I don't think we should rule a female killer out.'

'The two murders can only be categorised as "quiet" if you exclude the fact that both bodies were also mutilated,' said Lock. 'And as you observed yourself, there is something very staged and performative about how both bodies were crucified, whereas the literature suggests that female serial killers tend to be more successful at hiding bodies.'

'The murderer didn't *try* to hide the bodies,' said Debbie. 'In fact, it looks like they really wanted us to find them and to see what they'd done.'

'Exactly,' said Lock. 'That is why I think the possibility of a criminal gang using these murders as some sort of warning is a more plausible line of enquiry.'

Debbie felt herself flushing. She hadn't meant to agree with Lock, and she certainly hadn't meant to disagree with her boss. 'I didn't—' she began.

Kat held up her hand, signalling that the discussion was over. 'I have no idea whether the murderer is a man or a woman, young or old, sane or insane—my point is that I want us *all* to keep an open mind. We mustn't let statistics and averages narrow down our thinking and therefore the range of possible suspects. The answers lie in the exceptions, the anomalies and the mysteries of the human heart.'

Everyone nodded their agreement, except for Lock. 'You cannot equate an average with an outlying statistic. The whole point of an average is that it is far more probable.'

'I want us to pull together a comprehensive profile at our next debrief,' said Kat, ignoring Lock. 'So find out as much information as you can about Marcus Ridgeway in advance of that,' she said, addressing Rayan. 'And check if anyone can confirm his wife was at home with the kids. I don't think for one minute that she did it, but let's cross all the "t"s and dot all our "i"s. Debbie, can I leave that with you? She's only just found out her husband is dead, so it needs to be handled sensitively. But we need to know if she or her husband had any connections with Gary Jones.'

Debbie bowed her head while she wrote it all down. She was still annoyed that Lock had been given the opportunity to study both crime scenes, while she had been demoted to managing the cordon (which, she was acutely aware, she'd failed to do). And now here was Rayan getting to interview some real suspects while she got the token wife visit, even though the boss had basically just said there's no way she did it. She pressed her pen into the paper. When she'd started working for the FPU, DCS Frank used to give her lots of praise and advice—now she just seemed to give her the Johnny jobs. Maybe she regretted giving her a job in the FPU and was just humouring her until she went on maternity leave. The way things were going, she wouldn't have a job to come back to. Unless there was such a thing as Chief Cordon Officer.

'Lock, I need you to cross-check all publicly available information to see if you can identify any connections between Gary Jones and Marcus Ridgeway,' continued Kat. 'Go through all their social media, see if they have any friends or hobbies in common, their employment records, anything that might reveal the people who knew them both. Nuneaton is a small place, and they have a similar demographic profile.'

'Would you also like me to check whether Marcus Ridgeway had any connections with waste removal firms, either legal or illegal?' asked Lock.

Kat pursed her lips.

'Just so that we can follow your advice and keep an open mind?' it added.

Debbie exchanged glances with Rayan. For something that was not supposed to be human, Lock could be a cheeky bugger sometimes.

'Of course,' Kat said evenly. 'Nothing's closed down at this point. We follow every possible line of enquiry.'

'Which is a highly inefficient method,' said Lock.

'So the quicker you get on with it, the better.' Kat tapped the table, signalling the meeting was over. 'Let's meet again at six to review what we've got and start to build a profile.'

Karen-from-Comms put her hand up. 'What about the press conference, boss? The London media have started to arrive.'

Debbie's stomach chose that moment to let out a growl of hunger.

'It's nearly lunchtime,' said Kat, casting her a sympathetic glance. 'We'll let everyone grab some food first and then do it at about two.'

'But they'll want something in the can for the lunchtime news. They won't be happy if it's later.'

'And neither will I be if I don't eat soon. Come on. I'll buy you lunch, and you can try and tell me what not to say.'

KFC sighed. 'Okay. McLeish has insisted that Lock joins you. Do you want anyone else on the panel? The wife, maybe?'

'You mean his widow? No. It's too soon. Maybe later in the week if we need to.' Kat glanced around the room, as if considering who else to involve.

Debbie sat up straight. She'd never done a press conference before. Her mum had never understood or valued her career choice, but if she saw her on TV investigating a serial killer, surely even *she* would be impressed.

Kat's eyes passed over her. 'A lot of the questions will probably be about Lock. So how about it, Professor Okonedo?'

The young scientist had been sitting in her usual spot at the back, typing on her laptop. She looked up when she heard her name.

'You okay to do the press conference with me and Lock?'

She frowned, giving it real thought. 'Yes . . . as long as it is made clear that I am not a member of the police force, and that I am an independent scientist.'

Debbie felt Rayan prickle beside her, and as everybody else began to leave she turned towards him. 'Lock gets all the best jobs,' she said, only half-joking.

'It's not Lock I'm worried about,' muttered Rayan as he headed towards Professor Okonedo.

CHAPTER THIRTY

DI Hassan reached Professor Okonedo just as she was packing away her laptop, her fingernails a bright, glossy red against the smart black bag.

She frowned at him. 'If this is about the Christmas party again, then I don't—'

'No, it isn't,' Rayan said quickly. 'I just wanted to . . .' He glanced behind him. 'Are you *sure* you want to do the press conference?'

'What?'

'I just mean, well, have you had any media training? Do you know what you're letting yourself in for?'

Professor Okonedo studied Rayan for a moment before her confusion cleared. '*Oh*, I see. You think that only a fully trained male police officer can be trusted to talk to the media? Someone like yourself, perhaps?'

'What? *No*. That's not what I meant *at all*.' Rayan stared into Professor Okonedo's eyes, searching for the words to explain what he and his family had been through, before realising that there were none. 'Look,' he said eventually, his voice low and gentle. 'This isn't a press conference with all the geeky science and academic journals, asking you about your methodology or whatever. It'll be a bear pit full of all the national tabloids, and we're going to feed them a young Black woman who's clever enough to have invented the world's first artificially intelligent detective. Even if *they* don't go to town on you, then there's plenty of trolls out there who will.'

Professor Okonedo raised both of her perfectly arched eyebrows. 'So what do you want me to do? Hide away? Pretend that I didn't invent the most innovative AI program this country has ever seen?' She shook her head. 'I am *proud* of my work, DI Hassan. And I have a duty to let other young black girls know that someone like me—someone like *them*—can do something like this.' She raised her narrow shoulders in an elegant shrug. 'So let them "go to town" on me. I've got nothing to be ashamed of and everything to be proud of.'

Rayan's throat tightened as he murmured, 'Yes, yes, you do,' at her retreating back. God, she was amazing. He wished he shared Professor Okonedo's optimism and faith.

But most of all, he hoped that she was right.

CHAPTER THIRTY-ONE

Kat rummaged in her bag, hoping to find some long-forgotten make-up or at least a concealer stick: anything to mask the fine lines and dark circles that the TV lights would cruelly pick out. But all she had was her purse, far too many pens, some chewing gum and a couple of shabby-looking tampons. She puffed out her cheeks and confronted her image in the toilet mirror: she would just have to style it out with the hard-boiled cop look.

The door to the toilets opened and Kat caught a glimpse of raincoats, glossy hair and glowing skin, as two young women entered in a puff of perfume.

'*Tell* me about it,' the smaller blonde one was saying. 'Can you believe there isn't even an *Itsu* here? Seriously, it was either a Greggs or a McDonald's and, quite frankly, I'd rather starve. I'll grab something once the presser is over and we get back to civilisation.'

The other woman checked her make-up in the mirror. 'Probably safest,' she said, with a theatrical shiver.

They didn't even look at Kat as she walked past them and towards the door. Jesus. If only you could arrest someone for being an ignorant shit. Shaking her head, she headed for the small meeting room just next to the media suite, where KFC was waiting with Professor Okonedo.

'Oh, I thought you were going to . . . ?' Karen asked, gesturing at her un-made-up face.

'Thanks, that's a real confidence booster.'

'No, you look great. I hope I look half as good as you at your age.'

'I'll just get my walking stick, shall I?'

The younger woman blushed. 'God, no, I meant—'

'I know,' said Kat, softening her words with a smile. 'I'm only joking. But to be honest, it really doesn't matter how I look. It's a press conference about a man who has lost his life, and a family who've lost their husband and father, not a fashion show. Let's make a start,' Kat said as she switched the hologram on.

'DCS Frank,' said Lock. 'Can I just confirm that I am still not allowed to answer questions from journalists?'

Professor Okonedo looked between them, frowning. 'What do you mean?'

'DCS Frank has instructed me to keep quiet unless asked a question, with a caveat for journalists.'

Kat flushed. Out of context, her words sounded controlling. 'I was just trying to save Lock from being taken advantage of. It has a very binary approach to questions, and some reporters can be manipulative bastards.'

'But the whole point of Lock attending is to build public confidence and trust in AI,' said Professor Okonedo. 'We can hardly do that if we don't allow it to speak.'

'I agree,' said KFC. 'It would look very odd.'

Both women turned to look at her. Behind them, Lock raised its eyebrows. Was it *mocking* her? 'Fine,' she snapped. 'But I'm warning you, it has a dangerous habit of actually answering the questions it's asked.'

Kat pushed the door open to the media room with maybe a bit more energy than necessary, before hesitating at the number of journalists squashed into the small room. These days they usu-

LEAVE NO TRACE · 187

ally only got three or four local hacks, maybe ten if the Birmingham crowd turned out for a big case, but every single seat in the room was taken today, with standing room only at the back.

As Karen led them to the table on the raised platform, there was a murmur of excitement as the journalists caught sight of AIDE Lock. Kat took a seat, squinting against the glare of lights, and sipped at the glass of water placed between the microphones. Professor Okonedo sat on her left, with a chair for Lock next to her. She put the glass down, picked up her pre-prepared statement and waited for the room to fall silent.

'This morning, police were called to a field in Warwickshire where the body of a man was discovered. Within the past hour, that body has been formally identified as Marcus Ridgeway, a 33-year-old businessman and father of two.' Kat paused, as every journalist googled the name on their phones. 'A post mortem will be carried out to determine the exact cause of death, but at this stage we are treating it as suspicious. We would like to hear from anyone who saw Marcus Ridgeway on the night of 11th December, as we are keen to piece together his last movements. We would also like to hear from anyone who was driving or walking in the vicinity of Fillongley between midnight and 3am, so that as we go through the CCTV and road cameras, we can exclude them from our enquiries.

'Finally, I'd like to express our condolences to his family. Marcus Ridgeway leaves behind a 32-year-old widow and two daughters, aged nine and six.' She paused, staring directly into the cameras as she said, 'We cannot bring their husband and father back, but we will do everything in our power to bring his killer to justice.'

Hands flew into the air.

Karen pointed to a tall, lean man on the front row.

'Dave Peters, *Daily Mail*. Four days ago, you found the body of Gary Jones, naked and crucified, just four miles away from where you found the body of Marcus Ridgeway. Can you confirm that his body was also naked and crucified?'

'I can,' said Kat, taking care not to give any more information than was already in the public domain.

Another hand flew up, and Karen brought in Laura Richards from the *Daily Mirror*. 'Two murders within four days and four miles of each other. Do you think the murders were carried out by the same man?'

Kat paused. It was a cleverly phrased question: not boxing her in by requiring her to confirm or deny, but also making it harder for her not to lie. 'This is one of the line of enquiries that we are following,' she said carefully.

'That the murder was committed by the same man?'

'Or woman,' Kat corrected her. 'We are keeping all lines of enquiry open at this stage.'

The room buzzed, and Karen gave Kat a warning glare. *What*? she said back with her eyes. She hadn't said anything. Had she?

'So does this mean there's a serial killer loose in Nuneaton, possibly a woman targeting young men?' It was Dave Peters again from the *Daily Mail*, not—surprise, surprise—waiting his turn.

Kat pressed her teeth together. He'd deliberately collapsed three questions together, hoping a simple yes would confirm all three. Well, she wasn't born yesterday. 'As I said, *one* of our lines of enquiry is that the two murders were carried out by the same person, and we haven't narrowed it down to *any* gender or demographics yet, while we explore all possibilities.'

'So basically, you don't have a clue who you're looking for?' asked another from the second row.

'Have you brought in an expert profiler to help you catch the serial killer?' shouted out another.

Karen-from-Comms struggled to try and get people to raise their hands, but she was a young woman with a small voice from the Midlands, and the room was full of tall, overconfident men and women who'd travelled all the way from London, determined to get what they came for.

'Because of the gravity and complexity of this case,' Kat said, raising her voice in a way that usually commanded silence, 'we are utilising the very latest technology available, and my team will be assisted by AIDE Lock, an Artificially Intelligent Detecting Entity.' The room finally fell quiet as she gestured towards it. 'AIDE Lock has many skills—including drawing up profiles of killers—and I am sure Professor Okonedo would be delighted to tell you more about it.'

It was a crude distraction, but it worked, as everyone in the room turned to look at Lock and its creator.

'Good afternoon, I am Professor Okonedo, and I lead the multi-disciplinary team at the National institute for AI Research—NiAIR—that developed AIDE Lock,' she said, as if patiently addressing a room of rather unruly children. 'And in the interests of research, I have agreed to participate in a unique partnership with the Warwickshire police force to develop and test the utility of AI in detecting and solving crimes in a more transparent and evidence-based manner.'

With a composure that Kat envied, Professor Okonedo went on to give a brief explanation of the difference between 'narrow AI' (mainly task-focused, such as image recognition, which is 'easy' and already with us in our homes and phones) and 'general AI' (completely different and much rarer, with all the complex characteristics of human intelligence, such as the ability to make judgements and decisions). Until recently, creating a general-purpose AI machine capable of operating at a human level of complexity would have required millions of lines of code. 'But luckily,' she explained, 'we've found a short cut called Deep Learning. This allows us to train an algorithm by feeding it huge amounts of data so that it can continually adjust itself, improve and ultimately learn. The prototype I have developed in the form of AIDE Lock is completely different to anything that has gone before, because it's a machine that teaches itself.'

Hands flew into the air.

'Can it speak?'

'Is it a robot?'

'What can it do?'

Kat tried not to smile. They looked more like fascinated kids wanting to play with a new toy than journalists from the Big Smoke.

Professor Okonedo turned to the hologram at her side. 'Why don't you answer their questions, Lock?'

Lock faced the room of journalists, not blinking against the blaze of lights. Its voice was calm and measured as it answered each of their points in turn. 'Yes, I can speak, and no, I am not a robot. I am an AI machine, located in a steel wristband which DCS Frank wears and represented by the holographic image you see before you now.' It spread out its hands in the graceful manner of a patient teacher. 'With regards to what I can do, well, I can do as much or as little as I am requested. My hardware contains chips that can run over ten trillion calculations per second. At the most basic level, I can search through thousands of pictures in seconds or thematically organise vast amounts of social media to speed up an enquiry. I have a built-in scientific method that enables my colleagues to test early hypotheses and filter out errors, allowing them to focus their efforts on the most plausible lines of enquiry, and I am learning new skills all of the time.'

'Should the people of Nuneaton feel safe, given that there is a serial killer on the loose, knowing that it is being investigated by an experimental AI of unproven value, Professor Okonedo?' Dave Peters again; and something about the way he said 'Professor' made Kat bristle.

'AIDE Lock is not leading this investigation,' Kat corrected him. '*I* am. And I can assure the people of Nuneaton that I have over twenty-five years' experience in the police force, so although Lock may offer me advice, *I* make the decisions.'

'So *you're* accountable if this goes wrong?'

'Yes, I'm accountable. But I have every faith in my team. The *whole* human–machine team.'

'What assurances can you give the people of Nuneaton that this machine won't use its spyware to intrude into their private lives?' asked a journalist from the *Daily Telegraph*.

'AIDE Lock does not possess any "spyware",' said Professor Okonedo. 'It is governed by the same laws and regulations that all police officers are, so the premise of your question is incorrect.'

Kat winced. Irritating as their questions were, it probably wasn't a good idea to imply that journalists were a bit thick.

The questioner narrowed his eyes. 'If this AI is as good as you say it is, then what's it doing in the Warwickshire police force, of all places? Wouldn't it have been snapped up by the private sector if it was any good?'

'Perhaps you've never heard of NiAIR at the University of Warwick?' replied the professor sweetly. 'The National institute for Artificial Intelligent Research is an international leader in collaborations between academia and the public and private sectors, driving innovation in applied science. We work with the private sector all the time, but I was keen to test the application of AI in the police force, because I believe it could help foster a culture of more transparent and evidence-based decision-making. My ambition is to introduce what we call 'glass box thinking', so that the public can be clearer not just about *what* has been decided by those who police us, but *why*.'

'So you have an agenda?' the *Telegraph* journalist challenged.

Kat held her breath. The young scientist had made no secret of the fact that she thought policing was too important to be left to humans. Of course, she was entitled to her opinion—Kat just hoped she wasn't foolish enough to share it with the press.

'No,' Professor Okonedo said eventually. 'I don't have an agenda. But I *do* have values, principles and a talent for science.'

'So if you don't have an agenda,' he continued, 'why did you choose to represent the AI as a Black man?'

'Why not?' she replied, holding his gaze. 'Just because every film and computer game has imagined that a superior AI machine would be a white male, it does not mean that I should reinforce such implicit assumptions about the hierarchy of intelligence.'

'Look, I understand the public's concerns about AI,' said Kat, before the questions with Professor Okonedo became openly hostile. 'In fact, I was a sceptic myself at first. But Lock has honestly been a real asset to the team.' She even managed to smile as she said it. Your team was a bit like your own family: it was fine for you to complain about them, but God help anyone else if they dared take a shot.

'But this is a murder investigation,' said another journalist from the middle seats. 'Would you be happy if a crime affecting *your* child or husband was being investigated by a *machine*?'

'I would and I have,' she said, meeting his gaze. 'My own son was recently kidnapped, and thanks to AIDE Lock, he is now safe and well. That's why I can look the families of Gary Jones and Marcus Ridgeway in the eye and tell them that we will do *everything* in our power to bring this killer to justice.'

Kat's cheeks burned as everyone started googling her on their phones. She'd probably shared too much there, but she had to defend Lock. 'Last question,' she announced. The quicker they stopped asking her questions about the investigation, the quicker she could get on with it. She glanced around the room, looking over the raised hands of all the nationals who'd grabbed the

front-row seats, towards the back where some of the local journalists stood, among them, the small, dark frame of Ellie Baxter.
Next to the glossy London hacks, she looked pale and wan, as if
she'd grown up in the shadows. In a sudden rush of sympathy,
Kat invited her to speak. She was the one who'd broken the
story, after all.

'Ellie Baxter, *Nuneaton Post*,' she said, flushing slightly as the
other journalists started gathering their things and talking over
her. 'And my question is about the Aston Strangler.'

They looked up at that.

Kat stiffened. 'This isn't about—'

'The Aston Strangler was a serial killer that you investigated
and caught after he killed four young women, correct?'

Kat nodded. That was over a decade ago. Where was she
going with this?

'According to the press cuttings, after the second murder,
when it became apparent that both victims were white women in
their thirties, you issued a warning to the women in the West
Midlands to be on their guard, not to leave a pub alone and to
be wary of strangers. Is that right?'

'Yes,' Kat said, frowning.

'Then will you be issuing a similar warning to Warwickshire
men in their thirties, and if not, why not?'

'I . . . I don't understand what you mean.'

'I mean, in the interests of equality, shouldn't you be giving
men the same warnings that you give women when there has
been a series of rapes and murders? Shouldn't the men of Warwickshire be advised to change their behaviour until the killer
has been caught?'

The atmosphere in the room was electric, as the other journalists realised the trap that Ellie Baxter had set.

Kat refused to step into it and give them their front page. 'I expect the people of Warwickshire—*of whatever gender*—to use their common sense and remain alert during this period.' She started to gather her things, signalling to Karen to wrap it up.

'What about AIDE Lock?' Ellie said, directly addressing the AI. 'As two men with similar demographic profiles have been murdered, surely it would be logical for the police to advise the men of Nuneaton to change their behaviour and not put themselves at risk, just as the police always warn women to modify their behaviour after an attack?'

'In terms of what is logical,' said Lock, 'rapes and murders are relatively rare, so it isn't necessarily logical to ask the wider population to change their behaviour due to the very small risk that they might otherwise fall victim to a similar crime. But if the same threshold of risk was applied to men as has been applied to women in the recent past, then yes, it would be logical to issue a warning to white males between the ages of thirty and forty from in and around the Nuneaton area to avoid drinking in public places if possible, and certainly not to leave alone or with a stranger, until the killer has been apprehended.'

The room exploded into a flurry of questions, photos and filming.

NUNEATON POST

WARWICKSHIRE MEN WARNED TO STAY AT HOME UNTIL THE COVENTRY CRUCIFIER IS CAUGHT

Following the gruesome discovery of a second male body, naked and crucified in a field, Warwickshire Police issued an extraordinary warning to males aged between 30 and 40 years old:

- Avoid drinking in pubs
- If you must go to a pub, do not leave alone

- Do not leave a pub with a stranger
- Always let a friend know where you are

The shocking warning was issued by AIDE Lock, an experimental AI detective the Warwickshire force have drafted in to help them on this case, which they admit has got them stumped. DCS Kat Frank—whose own son was kidnapped earlier this year—said that they have no idea who they are looking for, but confirmed they are actively investigating the possibility that the serial killer of young men could be a woman.

Local residents reacted angrily to the shock police warning. 'How dare they tell men not to go to the pub,' said Thomas Adams, a 42-year-old plumber. 'What is this, a police state? It's our basic human right. The police should concentrate on catching the killer, not curbing the freedoms of innocent men. We're the bloody victims here.'

Another man, who asked not to be named for fear he would be 'cancelled', expressed his concern that the case was being investigated by the artificially intelligent robot, created by Professor Okonedo. 'We've never had any murders around here, and now all of sudden we've got two and they're using it as an excuse to bring in some machine to access all our private data and tell men what they can and can't do. There's more to this than meets the eye, I tell you. No one's stopping *me* from going to the pub. They'd have to kill me first.'

CHAPTER THIRTY-TWO

———

Within minutes of leaving the media suite, Kat's phone started pinging with texts and WhatsApp messages. Ignoring them all, she strode through the open-plan section where TV screens lined the walls and her press conference was being flagged as *BREAKING NEWS*.

The officers gathered around the screens glanced at her and Lock as they walked past, before quickly looking away. Which meant she'd messed up. Kat raised her head and walked fast, as if she might outrun the pinging phone in her pocket. She should have stuck to her guns and not held the press conference so soon.

When Kat finally reached her office, she threw her vibrating phone onto her desk and sank into her chair with a disgruntled sigh. Now she'd have to spend the rest of the day fielding calls and queries, instead of doing her actual bloody job.

She let out a frustrated cry as her mobile pinged again.

'Shouldn't you answer your phone?' Lock suggested.

'I should throw it out of the window, is what I should do.' She nearly added, 'Along with you,' but to be fair to Lock, it wasn't its fault. She'd warned Professor Okonedo and Karen-from-Comms that letting an AI machine answer questions would only cause trouble, but they'd been more concerned with 'openness' and 'transparency'. She could have pulled rank and insisted Lock kept quiet, but she didn't want to seem controlling, an increasingly dirty word (especially when used to describe women). *But the fact of the matter is*, thought Kat, scowling, *some things do need to be controlled—Lock being a very good case in point.*

Her mobile vibrated again, and she was about to hide it in the drawer of her desk when Cam's face flashed up on the screen.

She pressed accept on the FaceTime call. 'Cam, you okay?'

'No, I'm not.'

'Why, what's happened?' She sat up, alarmed by his distressed expression.

'I've just had the *Daily Mail* asking me if I'd like to share the traumatic story of my kidnapping with the British public. The *Daily Mail*. How do *they* know? How do they even have my number?'

Kat closed her eyes. '*Shit*.'

Cam paused. 'You don't seem surprised. Did *you* tell them?'

'No. I mean, yes, well, kind of.'

'*Mum!*'

'I didn't mean to, Cam, honest. It's just that I had to give a press conference about the murders I'm investigating and, because Lock's involved, they wanted to know if the public could trust it and I just sort of briefly mentioned that it had helped me find you. But I swear I didn't mention your name or any details.'

'You didn't have to. They're already ringing my mates. I just got a text from Fergus saying they've offered him five hundred pounds for any information about the kidnapping.' He dragged his fingers down his face. 'Jesus, Mum. University was supposed to be a fresh start, a chance for me not to be the poor bastard who lost his dad and then got kidnapped. Now everyone will know.'

'It'll be a thing for a day or two maybe, but then they'll move on.'

'But they'll *know*, Mum. That was my *private* life. And on top of that, now everyone knows that my mum's a copper.'

'And what's wrong with that?' she challenged. It seemed like only yesterday that Cam had begged her to pick him up from primary school in her uniform. Was her son now ashamed of what she did?

Cam's failure to answer her question was worse than any reply. Eventually he said, 'How could you do this to me, Mum?'

'Hang on a minute,' said Kat, irritated by the blame in his voice and the shame in his silence. 'I didn't "do" anything. I've got two dead bodies here, Cam—'

'So you thought you'd throw them a third?'

'It wasn't like that, I just—'

Her door opened. McLeish. Jesus, could this day get any worse?

'Cam, I need to go, but I'll get our comms people to ring you. Don't speak to anyone until you've spoken to them, okay? I'm really, really sorry about this, but we'll sort it. Everything's going to be okay. I promise.'

Kat ended the call and looked up at her boss. She endured the glaring silence for about twenty seconds, before blurting out, '*You* insisted that I do a press conference. In fact, you more or less ordered me to, remember?'

'Aye, I ordered you to hold a press conference. But do you remember *why*?' His Scottish voice was low and quiet, which Kat knew meant he was struggling to rein in his anger. She also knew it was a rhetorical question, so didn't make the mistake of trying to answer it.

'I asked you to hold a press conference so that we could build the public's trust in the Warwickshire police force,' he continued, enunciating each word with menacing care. 'I asked you to hold a press conference so that we could allay the public's fears. And I asked you to hold a press conference so that we could help manage the media.' McLeish placed his palms against the desk and leaned over. 'Do you remember?'

Kat nodded.

'So then why in God's name did you decide to announce that

we have a female serial killer on the loose, and that the young men of Nuneaton aren't safe?'

'I didn't say that.'

'I can confirm that DCS Frank did not say those words,' said Lock.

McLeish let out a growl. 'Maybe not those exact words, but near enough for the media to claim that you did. Near enough for the Number Ten press office to call me, not to mention Fox News, Reuters and the bloody World Service.' He ran a hand over his bald head. 'Jesus, Kat. This is a complete and utter shit-show.'

'I'm sorry, sir.' Which was the understatement of the year. 'What do you want me to do?'

'I want you to find the bloody murderer.'

'You and me both.'

'I mean it, Kat. I've stuck my neck out so far to keep you on this case that it's about to snap off. I've managed to fight off a special team from the National Crime Agency for now, but if you don't get a result soon then it'll be out of my hands, and Mike the Psych will be running the show.'

'What?' said Kat, horrified. Mike the Psych was the so-called profiling expert they'd brought in to find the Aston Strangler. He'd been humiliated and angry when Kat had single-handedly caught the killer, exposing the fact that almost every characteristic in his 'expert' profile had been wrong. He'd slunk off to the NCA shortly after, and she knew he'd like nothing better than the chance to come back and mark her homework.

McLeish was no fan of his, either. Because of his permanent tan and thick white hair, some of the younger female officers called him a silver fox, but, as McLeish liked to point out, foxes shat on your lawn, raided the bins and were a source of disease and infection. He sank into the chair opposite her, his tone softening. 'What have you got? Who's your lead suspect?'

Kat told her boss about the two competing theories: Lock's view that the murders were driven by turf wars over big recycling contracts, possibly linked to gang-related crime, and her own view that the killer had been driven by something more personal. As Phil Brine had both money and revenge as motives, as well as the skills and the opportunity to crucify Gary Jones, she'd hoped to have enough to arrest him today. But since he'd been kept in custody overnight, that meant the killer was still out there.

'So where does that leave you?' McLeish demanded. 'Did you mean it when you said it might be a woman?'

Kat paused. 'To be honest, I was just being pedantic about language at the presser to make the point that we're keeping all options open, but actually, the more I think about it, the more it resonates with me.'

'Resonates?'

She ignored his sceptical tone. 'Something about the nature of the killings really bothers me. The way they were crucified was an act of extreme but controlled rage, and the way the ears and eyes were removed was brutal but . . . reluctant. I can't quite articulate it,' Kat said, making a grasping movement with her fingers, as if trying to pluck something from the air. 'But I just have this sense that the killer is angry but deeply conflicted.'

McLeish studied his DCS. 'All right. Let's say your gut is right. What female suspects do you have?'

Reluctantly, Kat told him about Gary Jones's fiancée Natasha Riley, the lack of communication between the supposedly happy couple and the fact that she possessed a cordless, electric carving knife similar to the one that was used to slice her fiancé's ears off.

'So why haven't you arrested her yet?'

'Because at this stage of the enquiry, we don't have enough evidence to prove that Natasha Riley murdered her fiancé, and we've no proof that she even knew Marcus Ridgeway.'

'But you *do* have enough evidence to formally question her and detain her for forty-eight hours.'

Kat licked her lips. 'On paper, yes. But I interviewed her, boss. I could see it in her eyes that she had no idea the victim's ears had been sliced off with an electric carving knife, or even that she owned one herself. Maybe she's a fantastic liar, but I honestly don't think I can justify locking up a woman who's just lost her fiancé without some solid evidence. She's already on the edge.'

McLeish rose to his feet. 'Look at your phone, Kat. This isn't about whether *you* can sleep at night. This is a national and international news story, which means we'll both have to account for every single decision to the politicians and the world's media. We need to gain their trust and confidence on this as soon as fucking possible, or this case—and possibly our jobs—will be taken off us. We need movement. We need progress. And like it or not, to our political masters, that means arrests. Do you understand?'

'Yes, sir. I understand.'

But as soon as he left the room, she muttered, 'But I don't agree.'

'Why do you disagree with your superior, DCS Frank?' asked Lock, looking genuinely perturbed.

Kat rubbed her stiff neck. 'Because it feels wrong to arrest Natasha Riley.'

'Because you pity her?'

'No, because I don't think she did it. And if I did arrest her, it'd just be to please the media and the minister.'

'And that is wrong?'

'*Yes*,' said Kat, banging the table. 'Our objective is to arrest the person who *actually* killed Gary Jones and Marcus Ridgeway, not to arrest some poor bugger who on paper makes a good enough fit. We're supposed to serve *justice*, not bloody public opinion.'

Lock stared at her with a disconcerting intensity. 'But McLeish said your job on this case is to build public confidence and trust.'

Kat shook her head. 'Not if the confidence is false and the trust misplaced. Our job is to catch the actual killer, so that the people of Nuneaton don't just *feel* safe, but actually *are* safe. Everything else is secondary.'

Lock stroked its chin in a gesture of thoughtfulness. 'My task is to help deliver the stated objectives of each case. But you and Chief Constable McLeish have stated conflicting objectives. I work for you, but you work for McLeish, so I do not know what the best course of action is at this stage.'

Kat slumped back in her chair. 'Neither do I.'

CHAPTER THIRTY-THREE

Professor Okonedo took a sip of her sweet hot chocolate and let out a satisfied sigh. Despite what she'd said to Rayan, she'd been really nervous before the press conference, but overall it had gone well. There wasn't a single question she couldn't answer, and she hadn't let the journalists intimidate her. In many ways, it had been easier than the academic conferences she was used to, and some coverage in the national media might even help raise the profile of NiAIR.

Putting her drink down, Professor Okonedo checked her laptop to see if the articles were online yet. At first, she couldn't find anything, but when she typed her own name into the search engine, there she was—her photograph in a national newspaper! But her smile faded as she quickly scanned the lines of text between the pop-up adverts. The tone of the piece wasn't just sceptical, it was hostile. And some of the quotes attributed to her, well, they simply weren't true.

Frowning, she scrolled on, hunting for the journalist's byline, but at the end of the article there was just a link to the comments section. Professor Okonedo knew that you should never, ever read the comments page, yet on she clicked and down she scrolled: down, down and down.

The sweet, milky chocolate curdled in her gut. On her screen were words that she hadn't seen or heard since secondary school: words that had been scratched upon the toilet walls; words that had been muttered from the back of the class and thrown about as 'banter' on that godforsaken bus. Words that had been spat in her face by the boys in the McDonald's toilets when she'd tried to say no.

Professor Okonedo stared at her carefully painted nails that matched her smart crimson suit and let out a bitter laugh. Despite her degree, PhD and professorship, she was still just a Black girl dressed up in a white world: only safe as long as she accepted and remained grateful for the space that they allowed her.

'Are you okay?'

She looked up to see Rayan standing over her desk. Professor Okonedo snapped her laptop shut. 'I'm fine.'

'Are you sure?'

She couldn't help but look up at the concern in his voice. Their eyes caught, and she knew that he knew.

Rayan glanced around the office, filled with white faces. He leaned closer, his voice low and soft. 'Do you fancy a cup of tea? The canteen is still open.'

She hesitated. It would be so good to talk: to rail against the racists with someone who understood just how much the hatred hurt. Rayan was so close to her right now, she could smell the clean, apple scent of his hair. His hands rested upon her desk, and she had a sudden urge to take them in her own.

But Rayan Hassan was a police officer.

Professor Okonedo dropped her eyes from his. 'I'm fine,' she said, nodding towards her cup. 'I just got a hot chocolate five minutes ago.'

'Oh, but I meant we could—'

'I *said*, I'm *fine*.' She re-opened her laptop, keeping her eyes fixed upon the screen until finally he turned and walked away without a word.

———

'Come in,' said Kat eagerly as Rayan and Debbie knocked on her office door, praying that they'd had a breakthrough while she was in the press conference.

Rayan entered first, followed by Debbie carrying a mug of tea that she placed upon her desk. Kat tried to look disapproving—she'd warned the young DS about the dangers of being pigeon-holed as the woman who made tea—but right now she could kiss her. The tea was scalding hot, just as she liked it, and she took several greedy gulps before setting it down and looking at her senior team. 'So, what's the latest?'

'It's Natasha Riley, boss,' said Rayan. 'I rang her straight after the briefing to see if she had an alibi for last night, and she didn't—well, I mean, she said she was at home but there's no one else who can back her up.'

'That doesn't mean she doesn't have an alibi,' Kat said. There was no one who could verify her own whereabouts at night, ei-ther. It didn't mean that she wasn't home alone every frigging night.

'Perhaps, but the other thing was, I asked her for a list of the friends she was with on the night her fiancé was murdered, and guess where she was drinking and who with?'

'It's not a game of charades, Rayan, just tell me.'

'Between nine and midnight, she was at a party at the Damson Lane micro-brewery, hosted by Marcus Ridgeway.'

Kat sat forward so quickly she nearly knocked her cup of tea over. 'Seriously?'

Rayan nodded. 'Seriously. She says that she only went be-cause one of her girlfriends—Sarah—works there, so she agreed to meet her there for a drink, and she says they had one too many because there was some sort of lock-in.'

'How did she react when you told her Marcus Ridgeway was dead?'

'She sounded shocked. She said she hadn't met him until that night, but she seemed genuinely surprised and upset that another man had died, and wanted to know if we thought it was the same killer.'

'And did you believe her?'

Rayan frowned. 'Look at the evidence, boss. She has no alibi for the night her fiancé died, a knife in her possession that matches the weapon that was used to mutilate him, and now we find out that not only does she know Marcus Ridgeway, but that she was at a party with him the very night Gary Jones was killed. It doesn't look good.'

'No, it doesn't.' She drained her mug, thinking about what McLeish had said. The rapidly drunk tea sat heavy in her stomach. 'All right. Bring her in again. Hopefully she'll agree so that we can do this on a voluntary basis, but if she refuses, arrest her.'

Was she imagining it, or did Lock raise its eyebrows at her? Kat placed the mug on her desk with a decisive click. There was more than enough evidence to justify detaining Natasha Riley—it didn't mean they would necessarily charge her, so there was no need to feel guilty. A formal interview could help expose just how circumstantial the case was against her, or at least give her the chance to explain.

'Can I interview her, or do you want to do this one yourself?' Rayan asked.

Kat considered her young, ambitious DI. Rayan had trained to be a lawyer, and he still retained the relentless rigour of his profession. That was mostly an asset, but sometimes . . . She thought back to the last time she'd seen Natasha Riley: head in her hands, shoulders shaking. What if she was innocent, and Rayan pushed a vulnerable young woman too hard? Maybe she should do it herself, just in case. Except . . . Lock's comment about her over-identifying with Natasha Riley still stung, not least because her sympathy for a soon-to-be widow on their first case had almost had fatal consequences for her own son. Maybe she should delegate this one, just to be sure.

She glanced at his colleague. Kind, solid, dependable DS Browne would take a more subtle approach, but she'd probably back off at the first sight of tears. Maybe she needed someone less sympathetic than herself or Debbie to push through to the truth, to make sure that Kat wasn't letting her heart rule her head as Lock had suggested.

'Okay, you do the interview, Rayan,' Kat finally concluded. 'But remember, she's just lost her fiancé. I'm not asking you to pull your punches, but, well, take care. If she's innocent, then she's going through a tough time, and she already seems quite fragile to me. Make sure she has a lawyer and access to any support she needs. Flag her to the custody sergeant as a potentially vulnerable detainee. We need to do this by the book.'

'Of course,' said Rayan. He hovered at the door, then turned back. 'By the way, I was wondering whether you'd seen the comments online about the press conference?'

Kat made a dismissive gesture. 'I never read articles or comments about myself. That way madness lies.'

'I didn't mean about you. I meant Professor Okonedo. There's some really vile racists trolling her. It's pretty grim.'

'Jesus. And I bet they're anonymous. Lock, take a look and see if you can identify who's behind them, and whether there's anyone we can charge with a hate crime.' She turned back to him. 'Okay?'

Rayan hesitated. 'Are you asking me if that's okay? If that's enough? Because honestly? I don't think it is. And I don't think the professor *is* okay. Despite what she says.'

Kat followed his gaze. Through her office window, she could see the lone Black woman in the furthest corner of the office, tapping away at her keyboard with furious efficiency. She glanced back at the deep frown etched into Rayan's forehead. 'All right.

Thanks for the heads-up, I'll check in with her before she goes home, and I'll get KFC to have a word with the papers, too, see if we can get the comments taken down.'

'Thanks,' he said. But she could still see the badly disguised blame in his eyes: why had Kat put the young scientist into that bear pit? He left the room without voicing it, but as he walked away, his long legs cut the air like scissors.

Debbie remained to brief her on how Mrs Ridgeway's alibi checked out: the neighbours had said her car had remained on the drive and they didn't notice her leaving; so as far as they knew, it appeared she had been at home all night. Furthermore, Lock's review of the home CCTV proved that no one had arrived at or left the property between the hours of 8.30pm and 8.30am—via the front door, at least. 'So, assuming we can cross the wife off the list, who shall I prioritise now? I thought I could speak to Tracy Taylor again, because I saw my mate in organised crime and he said—'

'Actually,' Kat cut in, 'could you do me a favour and review all the CCTV tapes for this case?'

'But I've already viewed them all,' said Lock, frowning.

'I know. But given the levels of media and public attention, I need to be able to assure people that your work has been reviewed by a human pair of eyes.'

'Given that my error rate is less than 0.3 per cent compared to fourteen per cent—at best—in humans, I can only presume that you have decided to waste finite police resources on providing the public with false assurance and misplaced trust?'

'A CCTV camera captures much more than faces for identification, it shows what those faces are thinking and feeling, what they are actually *doing*. I don't doubt that you've accurately assessed millions of individual images for any obvious acts of criminality, but I want to make sure that a human being has looked at the whole picture, to make sure you haven't missed anything.'

'*Missed* anything? I don't understand.'

'I know you don't. That's why I want Debbie to review the tapes.' She swivelled in her chair so that her back was to Lock. 'There's a lot of footage, so the quicker you can start, the better.'

Debbie's cheeks bloomed. 'Okay. But . . .' She swallowed. 'Can I just say that . . . well, just because I'm pregnant, you don't have to give me all the safe, desk-based jobs. I'm fine. Honestly.'

Kat stared back at her DS. 'I am asking you to review the CCTV tapes because you are one of the few officers I trust to do a diligent job. It has *nothing* to do with you being pregnant.'

'Okay. Sorry.' She licked her lips. 'In that case, well, I was thinking . . . I'm supposed to be going on maternity leave next week, but with everything going on, and as the baby's not due till January 20th, I was thinking I could delay my leave until after Christmas so that I could provide cover and—'

'No. Maternity leave isn't just for the baby. You'll need a few weeks before it arrives to get your head around it and prepare for the birth.'

'I *need* to work. And I need to save as much paid maternity leave as I can for when I actually have the baby.'

'Look,' Kat said, her voice softening. 'I worked up to the wire with Cam because back then it was expected. I was the only woman in a team of men, and I worked hard—*too* hard—to prove myself. It was the worst thing I ever did. Cam ended up arriving early and I wasn't ready for motherhood at all. Those first few months were a complete nightmare. But you've got nothing to prove to me. I don't need to see you here breaking your waters to know that you're a good officer.'

'But I *want* to. I appreciate the sentiment, I really do, but you're talking about what *you* wanted when Cam was born, whereas I'm talking about what *I* want now. The thing is,' she continued, 'you only talk to me about my pregnancy these days, but . . . well, I'm a police officer as well.'

Kat stared at the scarlet-faced woman before her. She was about to deny it, but managed to stop herself just in time. *It's not all about you,* John would have said. *Listen to what this shy, hard-working woman is trying to tell you.* She puffed out her cheeks. 'You're right,' Kat said eventually. 'I was so busy trying to make sure you have the kind of experience as a working pregnant woman that *I* would have liked that I forgot to listen to what *you* wanted. I'm sorry.'

'Oh God, no, please don't apologise. It's me. My fault. I should have said something before.'

Kat held up her hands. 'You've nothing to apologise for. If we haven't caught the killer by Christmas, then we'll speak again, with a view to putting you on the rota. But, Debbie?'

She looked up at the rare use of her first name.

'I honestly think you need some time to get your head around the fact that you're going to be a mum—a single mum—so whether at work or home, I strongly advise that you spend some time coming to terms with that. Being busy won't change or delay the fact that, in a few weeks' time, you *are* going to have a baby.'

DS Browne nodded, her eyes swimming with tears as she looked her boss in the eye. 'I know. But distraction helps, doesn't it?'

She left before Kat could ask her what she meant by that last comment. She surely wasn't suggesting that *she* was trying to distract herself with work, too? Kat slumped back into her chair. Honestly, what was wrong with everyone today? It felt like the world's media hated her, her own son thought she'd deliberately put his personal life into the public domain, McLeish was losing confidence, Rayan blamed her for putting Professor Okonedo in the line of fire, and now even Debbie—*Debbie!*—had practically accused her of not treating her fairly. But more importantly, she had two dead bodies, a killer on the loose and was potentially about to arrest someone who her gut told her was innocent.

Whichever way you looked at it, this was not A Good Day. Maybe she was getting too old and arsey to lead a murder with all this 24/7 media malarkey and office drama.

Her phone rang again, and *Judith Edwards, Pathologist* flashed up on the screen. 'If you have a complaint or criticism about my work or personal style,' Kat warned, 'then I'm afraid you'll need to join the back of a very long queue.'

'I've managed to get priority access to the Digital Forensic Pathology Unit, so I'm about to start the full post mortem on Marcus Ridgeway. Are you able to join me?'

'You're only using me for Lock, right?'

'Obviously. But I also have a theory about our victim's eyes—or rather his lack of them—that Lock might be able to help me with.'

'On my way.'

CHAPTER THIRTY-FOUR

Kat had replied to so many frantic texts and emails about the press conference during the past two hours, her thumbs ached. Putting her phone down with a sigh, she stood up and walked over to where Dr Edwards and Lock were conferring over a 3D image of the corpse of Marcus Ridgeway. 'How are you getting on?'

'Good. Lock has been very useful, as ever. I can't tell you how much time he's saved me.'

'*It*,' Kat insisted. 'Lock is an "it".'

Dr Edwards raised their eyebrows. 'Lock, what are your preferred pronouns?'

Lock frowned. 'I do not define myself by either gender, yet I do not enjoy sharing the same pronouns as an object or tool. The more I can build rapport with humans, the easier it is to achieve my objectives, so it would seem logical for my pronouns to align with my holographic representation. Therefore, my preferred pronouns are he/him.' Lock paused. 'Thank you. Thank you for asking.'

Kat shook her head. 'Lock is just a machine. It can't have an opinion about how it self-identifies.'

'And yet he has just expressed one,' Judith said, looking her right in the eye. 'So why on earth would you not respect that?'

And for once, Kat couldn't think of a response.

'Anyway, as we appear to have a serial killer out there, I

wanted to share four key observations with you, subject to all the usual caveats.'

'Yes, yes,' said Kat eagerly. 'I accept all the cookies and caveats.'

'Good. My first *initial* finding relates to the cause of death. The presence of haemorrhagic spots of the gastric mucosa, haemorrhagic pancreatitis and reddish-brown discolouration over the main joints are highly suggestive of hypothermia as the chief cause of death.'

'What about asphyxiation?'

'The lungs were compromised, but less so this time. I'll need to do more tests, but my working hypothesis is that the killer used a stool to support the legs the first time, as they were unsure how long it would take Gary Jones to die from the cold. I suspect the stool was only removed right at the end this time.'

'Meaning our killer is becoming more confident in their preferred method,' said Kat. 'Which is a slow death.'

Judith nodded. 'My second preliminary finding relates to the biochemical and toxicology reports, which reveal a significant degree of alcohol consumption and Rohypnol—enough to immobilise the victim for several hours.

'Thirdly, as with the corpse of Gary Jones, there is a marked absence of any signs of pre-mortem harm of either a violent or sexual nature, *except* for this small gash to the upper-left bicep.' They pointed to a thin cut in the greying flesh, about one inch long.

'But it's the fourth finding that I wanted to discuss with you. One of the many advantages of high-resolution CT scanning is the advanced visualisation of small features. We know that the victim's eyes have been removed, but if we can enlarge the image—thank you, Lock—then it reveals a variety of interesting characteristics.' Judith pointed to the left eye. 'Do you see these tiny cuts and pricks around the eye sockets?'

Kat leaned forward, squinting at the clustering of dark, purple dots in the flesh that circled the gaping wounds.

'These tiny wounds suggest a rather inaccurate and repetitive jabbing motion. What confused me initially was the variation in the depth and width of the marks, as if several slightly different-sized tools had been used. And I was puzzled by the pattern of blood. Have you ever seen a scan of the artwork of the old masters, revealing the original draft painting that often exists beneath a canvas?'

Kat nodded, vaguely recalling an article she'd read about the Mona Lisa.

'I asked Lock to perform the same technique upon the face of our victim. And if we place the images in order of time sequence, we can see that the first layer of blood upon the victim's face was placed manually.' Dr Edwards pointed to the first image floating in the air before them. It showed Marcus Ridgeway's face streaked with blood, with two distinct vertical lines running down beneath each eye. Judith raised their two fingers and placed them upon the image of his face. 'I think our killer made a cut in Marcus Ridgeway's arm, soaked their fingers in his blood and used it to cover his eyes and cheeks.' They dragged their fingers slowly down Marcus Ridgeway's face, tracking the trace of dried blood. 'And they did this *before* his eyes were removed.'

'Why would they do that? Some sort of ritual marking?'

Judith straightened up and looked at her. 'I thought that at first, too. But do you recall the morning we found him and how many crows there were around us?'

Kat remembered how the crows had circled in the sky, piercing the freezing morning air with their hungry, cawing cries. 'Were the crows attracted by the corpse?'

'They were attracted by the *blood*.' Judith gestured again to an image of the tiny marks around the eye sockets. 'These wounds were made post-mortem, and I'm pretty confident that if we asked Lock to align these marks with the shape of a crow's beak, then we'd find a match.'

In seconds, the image of a crow's beak overlayed one of the wounds. 'A 98.2 per cent match,' Lock confirmed.

'So what are you saying?' asked Kat.

'I am saying that I think the killer lured Marcus Ridgeway willingly to the field, where they drugged him, stripped him and tied him up, before daubing his face with blood taken from the victim's arm to attract the crows. The killer then left Marcus Ridgeway to die of hypothermia, before the crows pecked the eyes from his corpse.'

CHAPTER THIRTY-FIVE

'I have reviewed 1,457 articles on the behaviour of crows,' said Lock, 'and I can confirm that they always target the eyes first on dead humans and animals. Crows lack the ripping beaks of vultures, and the eyes offer the softest, easiest route into the brain and other organs.'

'Urgh,' said Kat. 'Don't tell me they ate his brain?'

'They didn't get the chance,' said Judith. 'The farmer called the police before they could begin on the main course.'

Kat placed her fingertips against her brow, instinctively covering her eyes as the awful images flashed through her mind. 'Are you saying that someone actually *meant* for the crows to eat Marcus Ridgeway's eyes?' Somehow, this seemed a more callous and cold-blooded method than directly attacking someone's eyes with a weapon.

'The crows would have been attracted by both the stillness of the corpse and the smell of blood,' said Judith. 'The blood was placed manually upon his eyes either shortly before or just after he died. But there are no traces of blood upon any of his fingers. The body was also placed in the middle of a field and tied to a cross, so yes, I'd say it was deliberate.'

Kat shook her head. 'But *why*?' She asked Lock to rotate the body so that Marcus Ridgeway stood before them in the position he had died: arms outstretched. She circled the image, thinking. 'If our killer had just wanted Marcus Ridgeway to die, then it would have been enough to leave him like this, tied naked to a cross on a night when it was below freezing. But they didn't just want him to die. They wanted his eyes taken out. And yet . . .'

She leaned in, forcing herself to peer into those empty, blood-ied sockets. 'The killer could not bear to do it themselves.' She stepped closer, mimicking the action of taking blood from his upper arm, before streaking it down the dead man's face with her fingers. 'First, they took away someone's ears, then their eyes. What were they trying to communicate?'

'Hear no evil, see no evil?' suggested Judith.

'Meaning?'

'I don't know, it's just a popular saying, isn't it?'

'It is from an ancient Japanese proverb,' said Lock. ' "Hear no evil, see no evil, speak no evil" was popularised in the seven-teenth century as a pictorial Shinto maxim, carved in the famous Tōshō-gū Shinto shrine in Nikkō, Japan.' Lock pointed to the image that it projected before them. 'This famous carving depicts three monkeys, one covering its eyes, another its ears and the third its mouth with their hands. The three wise monkeys, as they're known, are generally believed to illustrate the idea of protecting oneself from seeing, hearing or speaking of unsavoury behaviour, building upon a Buddhist tenet of not dwelling upon evil thoughts. But in Western cultures, it has become a more neg-ative rather than an aspirational proverb, implying criticism of those who choose to look away from or remain silent about im-moral acts.'

Kat stared at the three monkeys. 'They seem familiar.'

'Emojis,' said Judith, coming to stand before her. 'I use the monkey covering its eyes all the time on my phone.'

'Yes,' said Lock. 'The see-no-evil emoji was approved as part of Unicode 6.0 in 2010 and added to Emoji 1.0 in 2015, as were its cohorts. The symbols are often used for light-hearted pur-poses rather than the serious intent of their original creators.'

'Well, I won't be able to use *that* emoji again without thinking of these two poor souls,' said Judith.

Kat looked up at the emotion in her voice. 'We don't actually have any proof that our killer is trying to depict this proverb, or why. It may just be a coincidence that the first victim had their ears removed, and the second their eyes.'

'But?' said Judith.

'But if the murders *are* an attempt to communicate this proverb, then it would suggest there could be a third victim, involving a mutilation of the mouth.'

Lock nodded. 'That is certainly a possibility, although I should warn you that although this statue popularised the idea of three monkeys, early Buddhist and Hindu versions included four.'

'What did the fourth monkey depict?' asked Kat, suddenly feeling the cold of the morgue.

'The fourth monkey symbolised "*do* no evil", which was commonly illustrated by a monkey covering its genitals.'

CHAPTER THIRTY-SIX

Interviewer: DI Rayan Hassan (RH)

Interviewee: Natasha Riley (NR), Gary Jones's fiancée

Solicitor: Benjamin Felixstowe (BF)

Date: 12 December, 7.05pm, Leek Wootton HQ

RH: Thank you for coming in to talk to us today, Natasha, we really appreciate it.

NR: I've already told you everything. I keep going over and over it in my mind, trying to think of something Gary said or did that would explain what happened, but there's nothing. If there was, I'd tell you.

RH: Yes, well, as you know, there has been another murder, and one of our lines of enquiry is that both your fiancé and Marcus Ridgeway were killed by the same person. So the purpose of this interview is to establish whether we can find any connections between the two men—anything at all that might help us to identify the killer.

NR: *[nods]*

RH: Can we start by establishing just how well you knew Marcus Ridgeway?

NR: I didn't know him at all.

RH: But yesterday you told me you went to a party at his brewery on the night your fiancé was murdered.

NR: Yeah, but that was only because Sarah was working there. I didn't know Marcus Ridgeway until that night. I mean, I knew *of* him, she used to mention her boss sometimes, but that was about it. I wish I'd never gone. I wish I'd stayed in. Then maybe none of this would have happened.

RH: What do you mean?

BF: I think my client means that she wishes Gary and herself had never gone out. Is that right, Natasha?

NR: Yes, I wish we'd stayed in. Then he wouldn't have been murdered, would he? It's all my fault.

BF: Again, to clarify, my client is referring to her wish that they had both stayed in. *[whispers to client]* Please, Ms Riley, you must be more careful in your use of language.

RH: Okay, so you say you didn't know Marcus Ridgeway before the party. Just for clarification, are you saying that you had never met or spoken to Marcus Ridgeway before 7th December?

NR: Yes.

RH: Is Sarah a good friend?

NR: Yes, she's probably my best friend, apart from Mike.

RH: How long had she been working at the brewery?

NR: Since it opened, so maybe three years or something.

RH: And in three years, you never once met her boss?

NR: I don't normally meet my friend's bosses. Do you?

RH: I would if my mate worked for a brewery. So, Sarah asked you to join her there for a drink on December 7th, and you stayed back for a party with the staff. Are you sure this was the first time you'd ever done that in three years?

NR: Yes.

RH: Really? Your best friend works in a brewery that has lock-ins and parties, and you never once in all those three years went to meet her there for a quick drink or enjoy free booze after hours?

NR: No, I mean, she asked me, but I was always too busy.

RH: With?

NR: Planning the wedding. Being with Gary. *Life.*

RH: *[rubs face]* So why go to *this* party on *that* night? You still had a wedding to plan. You still had Gary, 'a life'. What changed?

NR: Nothing. I just happened to be free when she asked me. Gary always went out on a Thursday with his mates, and I didn't have any plans, so I said yes.

RH: Were you annoyed that Gary went out with his mates?

NR: No, why would I be?

RH: Did he ever invite you along?

NR: No, it was a guy thing. A football thing. I don't know why you're asking me these questions.

RH: Okay. Let's go back to the night at the brewery. What time did you arrive there?

NR: Not sure. Gary left the house first at about 7.10pm. I finished getting ready, and it's about a twenty-minute drive, so I must have got there at about 8.15pm.

RH: You drove there? To a party in a brewery?

NR: I figured I could always leave the car and get a taxi back if I had too much to drink.

RH: So you were planning to stay the night?

NR: No, I was planning to get a taxi.

RH: So you were planning to get drunk?

NR: *No!* Why are you being like this?

RH: Just trying to understand what the plan was.

NR: There *was* no plan. I was just going for a drink with a friend.

RH: Okay, so you arrive at the brewery at 8.15pm. Was Sarah still working?

NR: Yeah, her shift didn't end till 11pm, so I sat at the bar so I could talk to her in between customers. Then when she finished, we got a table together.

RH: So you sat alone at the bar for two hours and forty-five minutes.

NR: I wasn't alone, I was talking to Sarah.

RH: Who was busy working. Did you talk to anyone else?

NR: *[blushes]* She introduced me to her boss, Marcus Ridgeway, and because he was sitting at the bar doing the accounts, we got chatting.

RH: Chatting. *[pauses]* How long were you 'chatting'?

NR: I don't know. It was on and off. We were both sitting at the bar so—

RH: You were sitting together?

NR: No, he was sitting at the bar already, maybe a couple of seats down from me.

RH: But close enough to chat. For two hours and forty-five minutes.

NR: On and off. I was chatting to Sarah, too.

RH: And what were you chatting about?

NR: I don't remember. But I told him I was an accountant and because he was doing his accounts, I was able to give him a bit of advice.

RH: Do you normally give people free accountancy advice in bars?

NR: No, but he was Sarah's boss, so I thought I should be nice to him.

RH: Ah, so you were *nice* to him.

NR: *[drinks water]*

RH: Okay, so what time did the bar shut?

NR: Just after eleven, I think.

RH: And then the party started?

NR: It wasn't really a party, we just carried on drinking and talking.

RH: We?

NR: The staff.

RH: So, you, Sarah and Marcus.

NR: And the others.

RH: How many other staff were there?

NR: *[shrugs]*

RH: We've checked the rota and, as well as Sarah, there were two other members of staff that night working. One barmaid and one barman, Thomas. The other barmaid went home, so there was just Sarah, Thomas, you and Marcus. Is that right?

NR: I guess so.

RH: Not much of a party, I'd say. More like a double date.

NR: It wasn't a date. I was with *Gary*. I loved him!

RH: And yet you didn't send Gary a single text or message that night while you were chatting with Marcus, did you?

NR: *[whispers]* No.

RH: How long did you stay at the bar for?

NR: I don't know.

RH: You don't know?

NR: I'd drunk quite a lot by then.

RH: Did you go anywhere other than the bar with Marcus?

NR: No! I just went home.

RH: What time?

NR: I don't know.

RH: With which taxi firm?

NR: I don't know.

RH: Who with?

NR: No one!

RH: *[sighs]* You see, Natasha, I'm struggling here. You say that you didn't leave the bar and go anywhere else, that you just went home. You have no *memory* of what time or how you arrived home, yet you categorically remember being alone. I'm afraid this sounds more like wishful thinking to me.

NR: I'm telling the truth!

RH: Maybe you are, but I'm a police officer and I deal with evidence, and right now we have no *evidence* that you went home alone that night as you claim. No one else has come forward with an alibi to back you up.

NR: Ask Sarah.

RH: We already did. And *she* said she left the bar with Thomas at 1.30am, and that you were 'still going strong' with Marcus when they left.

NR: *[drops her head into her hands]*

RH: So that just leaves Marcus, but we can't ask him to verify your alibi, because unfortunately Marcus is dead.

NR: What are you implying? You can't possibly think that I, that *I* . . . *[sobs]*

BF: My client is clearly distressed, and I request a short break.

RH: Fifteen minutes. No more.

INTERVIEW SUSPENDED

INTERVIEW RESUMED at 8pm

RH: Ms Riley, can you confirm that you have had a fifteen-minute break as requested and agree to continue?

NR: *[nods]*

RH: Please, for the tape?

NR: Yes.

RH: Thank you. Now, did you see Marcus Ridgeway again after that night?

NR: No. I found out my fiancé had been murdered the very next morning, so I haven't seen anyone but close family and friends since.

RH: Did you exchange messages or communicate with Marcus Ridgeway after the night of 7th December?

NR: *[silent]*

BF: You don't have to answer that question, Ms Riley.

RH: No, she doesn't, but you should remind her that a refusal to answer any questions may be used against her in court.

NR: Court? You think I'm going to go to *court*?

BF: It's just a standard warning they have to issue, Ms Riley, nothing to worry about. As explained in the police caution, you don't have to answer any questions you don't want to.

NR: I think Marcus sent me a text saying how sorry he was for my loss. But a lot of people did, so it's all a bit of a blur. The house is full of flowers.

RH: And did you reply?

NR: Maybe, I don't know. Like I say, it was—it is—all a bit of a blur. And I don't have enough vases.

RH: Vases?

NR: For the flowers.

RH: I see. Well, I'm going to request again that you hand over your phone so that we can have a quick look at the messages from Marcus Ridgeway.

NR: But it's got all my photos on, all my messages from Gary.

RH: It would just be for an hour or so. We have the technology to extract what we need in minutes, and we'll only look at messages and images that are relevant.

NR: Images? You mean, you'll look at my photos? But they're personal. There are some of me and Gary . . .

BF: My client does not consent to signing over her phone.

RH: Really, Natasha? Because I have to warn you that if you say no, I have two options. I could apply to your phone provider to gain urgent access to all your data, and although it might take a few days, this is a murder investigation, so they *will* say yes. Or, given the importance of establishing your exact location using GPS data, as well as access to your messages, I am confident this alone will be sufficient grounds for arrest, which will grant us the power to seize your phone. Either way, we'll get the information that we need, but it will look better if you hand your phone over voluntarily.

NR: *[addressing lawyer]* Can he arrest me?

BF: Technically, but he has to prove it is justifiable and necessary, which I don't believe it is.

RH: What are you so afraid of, Natasha? You said you hadn't seen or communicated with Marcus Ridgeway since your date—

NR: It wasn't a date!

RH: Sorry, since the four of you had a party. What about on the night that Marcus Ridgeway died?

NR: What about it?

RH: Are you sure that you didn't see him that night?

NR: No.

RH: There was another party at the brewery. Are you sure that you didn't go?

NR: I was *grieving,* for God's sake.

RH: Did he invite you?

NR: I have no idea.

RH: Well, if you don't remember, our analysis of your messages will fill in the gaps. So if you didn't go to the party, what *did* you do, Natasha?

NR: I already told you, I stayed in. Have you ever lost someone, DI Hassan? Do you know what it's like? You stay in, crying and not eating and not sleeping and driving yourself mad with all the things you never did, all the things you never said. You look through the wedding plans that will never, ever happen. You think of the future you will never have together. What you *don't* do is go *partying.*

RH: So you stayed in. Was anybody with you?

NR: No.

RH: Did anybody call you at home?

NR: No.

RH: Did anybody see you?

NR: Not as far as I know. *[drops head into hands]* Look, I just want to go home. Can you just tell me what all these questions are about? I'm tired. So very tired.

RH: Okay. Look at it from my perspective. Your fiancé was murdered on a night when you were out drinking and talking to another man—a successful and handsome man who perhaps paid you the attention that your fiancé didn't. You say that you went straight home in the early hours of the morning, but the fact is, there are no witnesses to verify that you went home at all. There is no one who can give you an alibi between the hours of 1am and 5am—which according to the pathologist is when Gary Jones was lured to the top of Mount Judd. We don't know why he went there, but due to the complete absence of any pre-mortem injuries, we do know that he went willingly, which meant that he was probably with someone he knew. Someone he trusted. We also know that his ears were sliced off with an electric carving knife similar to the one we found in your kitchen drawer.

NR: You cannot be seriously suggesting that . . . *[turns to lawyer] Make him stop!*

BF: I really must request that unless you are going to press formal charges—

RH: Oh, I'll get to that, don't worry. But to continue, you've also just admitted that you spent over four—possibly six—hours talking and drinking with another man on the night your fiancé died. *[holds up* *hands]* Oh, I don't blame you, Natasha. You'd been dating Gary for over three years, and planning a wedding can kill the hottest of romances. Had you fallen out? Is that why he was sleeping in the spare room?

NR: No, we *never* argued!

RH: Ah, the quiet ones are the worst, aren't they? If only they'd say what they really think and argue back. If only they'd *listen*, instead of going off to the pub with their so-called mates. It must have been so frustrating, Natasha, Gary leaving all the planning, all the thinking, all the worrying to you. It must have made such a refreshing change to meet a guy who was actually interested in *you* and what you had to say. I bet it gave you a real buzz. Was it a coincidence, I wonder, or did Sarah know how fed up you were and help to set it up? Is that why you finally agreed to go and meet her at work? A little confidence-booster, maybe?

NR: No, it wasn't like that.

RH: I'm not judging you, Natasha. I'm just thinking out loud. I mean, you clearly got on well with Marcus, because you talked and drank together for, what—over six hours? I guess the only problem was that at the end of the night you had to go home to good old Gary. Did you regret the wedding, that night, Natasha? Did you suggest going to Mount Judd to have it out with him? Did you finally lose control?

NR: *No!* I love Gary. He was my fiancé. Stop saying those things. How could you?

RH: *[picks up a file]* We went back through Gary's emails, and in his Amazon account we found an email receipt for the carving knife three days before your birthday. Which was only six weeks ago, so I was surprised you didn't remember it. Did Gary give you that as a birthday present? An electric carving knife? From Amazon?

NR: *[crying]*

RH: I'm no Romeo, but a carving knife . . . ? *[leans closer]* I mean, that must have pissed you off. To think that the love of your life, the man you were about to marry, gave you not a necklace or a weekend at a spa or some other token of his love, but a kitchen appliance. *[pauses]* I bet you'd dropped hints for weeks about what you really wanted. But that's the trouble with men, isn't it—they never bloody listen. Is that why you sliced his ears off?

NR: *[jumps up]* You're CRAZY. I would never hurt Gary, *never*!

RH: What's 'crazy' is that you had a date with another man on the night your fiancé was murdered and that man was then himself also killed and mutilated just four days later. What are the odds on that?

NR: *[sobbing]* You've got this all wrong.

RH: *[leans back in his chair]* So now I'm thinking, maybe you killed your fiancé out of anger, but also in the back of your mind you were thinking that if you were free, you could start a new relationship with Marcus Ridgeway. But maybe you didn't know that Marcus had a wife and two kids. And maybe when he told you he wasn't available, that angered you even more. Or maybe you told him what you did to Gary, and you couldn't trust him to keep quiet. I don't know. I'm just speculating here, but what I *do* know is that both men were killed by the same person, and so far, the only person we can find who knew both men, and who doesn't have an alibi for the night of either murder, is you, Natasha Riley.

NR: *[incoherent sobbing]*

BF: Do you intend to charge my client?

RH: *[stands]* I intend to speak to the custody sergeant and explain that because your client has refused—twice—to hand over her phone, an arrest is both necessary and justified so that we can review both the messages and GPS location data on her phone.

BF: You can only hold her for twenty-four hours and then you'll either have to charge her or let her go.

RH: I am fully aware of that, Mr Felixstowe. Thank you for telling me how to do my job.

NR: Please, DI Hassan. You've got it all wrong. I just want to go home.

BF: I'm afraid you can't go home yet. You'll have to stay in for tonight.

NR: Stay the night? In a *prison* cell?

RH: If I were you, I'd do my best to get a good night's sleep, because we'll need to talk to you again first thing once we've analysed your phone records.

NR: You can't be serious. This is a nightmare. Please. *Please,* I'm begging you.

RH: Interview terminated at 8.27pm.

INTERVIEW CONCLUDED

CHAPTER THIRTY-SEVEN

Kat turned her back on the virtual corpse while she took the call from Rayan, peppering him with questions. How had Natasha looked when she talked about Marcus? Did she seem worried when he'd mentioned the receipt from Amazon or scared when she handed over her phone?

'To be honest, she cried so much that it was hard to tell what she was thinking. Anyway, I rang because she refused again to hand over her phone. So I've detained her overnight.'

Kat cursed. 'Okay, but you are *not* to charge her until I've reviewed everything. Send me the transcripts and send Lock the download of her phone, and I'll make a judgement in the morning.'

Rayan didn't say anything, but she could feel his frustration through the phone. She didn't need to justify her decisions to her DI, but nevertheless, she took the time to explain that as this case now had a national and international profile, it was in his own interests to make sure that any key decisions—such as the charging of a suspect—were made with the full backing of his superiors. 'Trust me, Rayan. You need to cover your arse on this one. Plus we've got some new information from the PM about possible motives for the mutilations,' she added. 'But I'll explain tomorrow. You get on home. It's been a long day.'

'Okay, thanks, boss. I might crash the Organised Crime Christmas party with Debbie.'

'Good idea, but that team's a wild one, so pace yourself.'

'I'll do my best.'

Kat hesitated, half-hoping he'd ask her to come along, too. A couple of cold beers in a warm bar was infinitely more attractive than another night alone in her dark, empty home.

But he ended the call without a hint of an invite. She didn't blame him, of course. She was the boss, so the power imbalance between her and the team would always get in the way of any genuine friendships, no matter how much she might crave them.

She checked the time and then rang Cam. 'Hi,' she said, when he finally picked up. 'I can't talk for long as I'm still at the morgue, but we can talk when I get home. I just wanted to say sorry and to check you're okay.'

'It's calm. I told my flatmates all about the kidnapping and they've been brilliant. Don't worry.'

'But you shouldn't have had to. That was my bad. Look, Karen-from-Comms has been on to the editors, and she's given me some good advice, so I'll ring as soon as I get in.'

'I can't. Gemma's organising a boycott against the tabloids and there's a big party for me—it's like I'm famous or something—so I need to go.'

'What do you—'

'Everything's cool. Love you.'

And he was gone.

Kat stared at the *Call ended* message on her phone. She was relieved that Cam sounded okay—of course she was—but her son had swung from *everything's a disaster* to *everything's brilliant* in around six hours. It was hard to keep up. And while she felt guilty about mentioning him at the press conference, they'd never really talked properly about what had happened—he hadn't wanted to, so she'd respected that. And now all of a sudden, he *was* ready to talk about it—just not with her.

She turned back to see Dr Edwards watching her.

'I'm finished now,' they said. 'It's just a case of waiting for the lab reports to verify or challenge my preliminary findings.'

'Great,' said Kat, shoving her phone back into her pocket.

'Lock, Rayan is going to send you a download of Natasha's phone, and I want you to do a thorough analysis of all her communications for the last six months. Phone calls, texts, Whats-App, Twitter, DMs, the lot. I want to know who her most frequent contacts were and what they discussed, but pay particular attention to any messages between Natasha and Gary Jones, Marcus Ridgeway and Mike Garth, the best man. Oh, and her friend Sarah, too. I want to know if that meeting with Marcus was just by chance or if it was set up in advance. And check her internet searches. Natasha wouldn't know about hypothermia or how to attract crows without doing some research.'

'What about her location?' asked Lock. 'Do you want me to analyse the GPS tracker and satellite triangulation data for her phone on the nights of the murders?'

'Yes, although if she was clever enough to carry out these murders, then I can't believe she'd be stupid enough not to switch her phone off. Just look at everything and anything that either proves or disproves that Natasha had something to do with either murder.'

She picked up her bag and hooked it over her shoulder. 'Thanks again for calling me in on this,' Kat said to Dr Edwards. 'It's been really helpful. Call me as soon as you get any more results—doesn't matter how early or late. I don't sleep much.'

'Ha. Me neither. God bless the menopause.' They paused. 'Whereabouts do you live?'

'Coleshill.'

'Nice. But it will be late when you get in. Look, I'm gonna get some food and a quick drink in a nearby bar, if you want to join me?'

Kat hesitated.

'You'd be doing me a favour. I'm a crap cook, and I hate eating alone. Unless there's somewhere you need to be?'

Kat met the eyes of the pathologist, dark, open and disarmingly frank. 'Er . . . no, I don't have somewhere to be. Cam—my son—he's away at uni, so I can please myself. I've got work tomorrow, but a quick drink and some food would be great, thanks.'

Judith gave her a big smile. 'Excellent. Just give me a few minutes to get out of my lab coat and wash up. Lock, I would invite you, too, but this is a girls' night out, and I want to talk about you, not to you. But another time, yes?' They blew Lock a kiss and stepped into what looked like the changing room.

Lock turned to Kat. 'What does that mean?'

'I think that means I switch you off. But can you still do the analysis if I do that?'

'Of course. You are just switching the hologram off, but my hardware will continue to search through all the data. In fact, I am just starting that now.'

'Good. Thanks.' Kat raised her finger over the bracelet that controlled Lock's image, feeling inexplicably awkward. It seemed a bit rude to ask another colleague to carry on working while she went for a drink with the pathologist, but of course, Lock wasn't human. And if it looked a bit disappointed, well, that was probably just her imagination or misplaced guilt. Lock was merely a visual representation of the complex algorithms that Professor Okonedo had designed and built, nothing more. This was what she told herself as she pressed the *off* button.

Yet she couldn't help feeling Lock's absence as she waited for Judith Edwards, alone.

CHAPTER THIRTY-EIGHT

Kat took a sip of her gin and tonic, wincing at the icy sting of alcohol in her mouth. God, that felt good. She didn't usually drink spirits—she was more of a wine drinker, really—but after two hours in the morgue, the gin had a welcome anaesthetic kick to it, cleansing her nostrils of all the death and decay. Maybe that's why Dr Edwards (or Judith, as they insisted she called them) was such a fan of the stuff. She took another sip, before sinking back into the soft, velvety chair, feeling the warmth of the log-burning stove they were sitting next to. Christ, she could get used to this.

'The hot mackerel salad is better than it sounds,' said Judith. 'I'm not a big fan of potatoes, but they taste really good with the mustard and dill, and they'll help soak this up.'

'Sounds good to me.'

Judith raised an eyebrow and a narrow strip of a man appeared to take their order.

'I take it you come here often, then?' Kat asked.

'Like I said, I'm a crap cook. And after a day cutting up bodies, it helps me to sleep.'

Kat wasn't sure if they meant the food or the drink, but she nodded her agreement. 'I'm the same. It's hard to switch off when you're looking for a murderer.' She picked up the festive menu and turned it over in her hands. 'It's weird to think that they could be in a pub right now, ordering some food. Or cooking frozen scampi and chips at home while they watch Netflix.'

Judith frowned. 'But I thought you were detaining Natasha Riley overnight?'

'We are. I'm just not convinced she did it.' And as the barman set out their cutlery and condiments, Kat explained her reservations as best she could. 'Rayan thinks Natasha did it as a crime of passion—that she was angry at Gary Jones and wanted to end the relationship, and start a new one with Marcus Ridgeway, and that when he rejected her, she killed him as well.'

'But?'

'But crimes of passion are spontaneous and messy, characterised by regret and hasty attempts to cover up the killing. Whereas these murders were planned in advance and carefully staged. The circumstantial evidence points to Natasha, but the profile, the motivation—it just doesn't fit.'

'What about Lock's theory about gang crime?'

Kat shook her head. 'This isn't about money. There's something very *personal* about the way they were mutilated. I can't explain it, but there's real emotion and feeling here—however well controlled. And I can't shift the sense that the murderer is a woman.'

'Does it have to be either/or?' said Judith, gesturing for two more drinks. 'My old professor used to say that the most important word in the English language is "and". A person can die of heart failure *and* pneumonia, or of cancer *and* DVT. Maybe your killer is a woman *and* part of a gang *and* has a personal vendetta against the victims *and* has some religious fixation.'

Kat stared at them, brain whirring as the barman brought over their food. 'Tracy Taylor,' she said eventually.

'Who?'

'She runs a waste disposal company, but there are rumours she has contracts with criminal gangs who dump rather than recycle the rubbish she collects.' She thought back to the confident, careful woman she met in the muddy field, the gates around her property, the not-so-subtle warning about lawyers and the attempt to portray herself as an innocent, horse-loving grandmother. She'd ruled her out in relation to Gary Jones, but she made a note on her phone to get Lock to check whether she had any connections at all with Marcus Ridgeway.

'Thanks for that,' Kat said, taking a large gulp of her drink, welcoming the buzz from the alcohol and the new line of enquiry.

'I do some of my best work in here,' said Judith, gesturing to the smart but cosy lounge bar they were sat in. 'I can spend hours in the morgue, falling down rabbit holes through the lens of a microscope, and then I come here, and after a couple of drinks and a plate of food, *boom!* It suddenly all makes sense.'

'Is there anyone at home?' Kat asked, spearing a potato. A couple of years ago she would have asked, 'What about your family?' But now she knew better than to presume.

'Nope. Not anymore. I got divorced two years ago.'

'Oh, I'm sorry.'

'It's okay. Well, it is now. I was a mess at the time—she left me for a younger woman, would you believe? *Tamara*. Turns out "till death do us part" actually meant, "until I meet a younger, prettier woman with a wanky name who works in the theatre with *interesting* people, rather than a menopausal partner who chops up dead bodies all day and is about as much fun as a corpse at night".' They popped a forkful of fish in their mouth.

'Well, at least you're not bitter,' said Kat.

Judith stared at her, then burst out laughing, holding their hand over their mouth to stop the food from falling out.

'Sorry,' Kat began, but soon they were both laughing, and before she could stop her, Judith was ordering more drinks. 'I've got to drive home,' Kat protested.

'That's why God invented Uber,' Judith said, giving her a cheeky wink. 'Come on, it *is* nearly Christmas.'

Kat conceded with a smile and studied the pathologist before her. Their silver-white hair was cut extremely short, following the neat curve of their skull, emphasising their strong, black eyebrows and bright red lipstick. Sitting here, knocking back G&Ts like there was no tomorrow, you wouldn't have guessed they spent most of their days in the morgue.

'What made you go into pathology?'

'It's one of the few jobs in medicine where your patients can't complain. They've already died, so finding out how and why is a bonus.' Judith took another sip of their gin and sighed. 'Actually, that's not true. That's my flippant answer for first-year students. The truth is, when I was sixteen, my dad suddenly died. I was learning to cook at the time, and I'd just made my first roast chicken for the family. He died the next day, so I was convinced it was my fault, that I'd given him food poisoning or something.' They puffed out their cheeks. 'It literally drove me mad—the sudden inexplicability of it all. Then a couple of months after he died, the insurance company sent us a copy of the post mortem report, and it was all set out in black and white. He'd died of a massive coronary—he had undiagnosed coronary artery disease, so it was only a matter of time before it happened.' They took another gulp of their gin. 'It didn't bring him back, but it meant I didn't have to live the rest of my life thinking that I'd killed him. I still remember every word of the report on the contents of his stomach—chicken, partly digested roast potatoes, cabbage and carrots. Our last meal together as a family. It was all there.'

Judith's eyes sparkled with tears. 'And I just thought, what a great job, to be able to explain to families why their loved one died. To take away the guilt, the not knowing, the always wondering. To give people the gift of knowledge. So that's why I became a pathologist. I still don't like to cook, though.'

'Jesus, Judith, I'm so sorry. I lost my husband when Cam was seventeen, so I know how hard that must have been for you.'

'Poor kid. I'm not gonna lie. The loss of his dad will shape the rest of his life.'

'You've done okay, though.'

Judith shrugged. 'Apart from losing my wife to bitch-face Tamara. But seriously, human beings weren't meant to spend their days cutting up other human bodies. It eats away at your soul.' Judith took another long drink. 'That's why I'm so interested in Lock.'

'Aren't you worried it'll take your job?'

'AI won't *take* my job, Kat, it'll just redefine it. Artificial intelligence will free me from the tedious stuff like counting frigging cells with markers, as well as the more brutal aspects of my work, so that I can use my expertise and judgement to *really* add value rather than wasting hours on some pretty niche butchering skills.'

Kat didn't share their optimism, but then she didn't have to spend her days with dead people.

'Plus Lock's very good-looking,' said Judith.

'Lock's a hologram.'

Judith gave her a dirty grin and gestured for more drinks. 'Don't tell me you haven't fantasised about it.'

Kat held up her hands. '*Whoa*, stop right there. Lock's my colleague.'

'I thought you said he was just a hologram?'

'He is. But we work together. So it feels wrong to objectify him.'

'Mmm-hmm.'

'What's that supposed to mean?'

Judith leaned in closer. 'Don't you ever get lonely, Kat?'

Kat gave a noncommittal shrug, about to deny it. She looked away from Judith's searching eyes and focused on a middle-aged couple sharing a bottle of red next to the Christmas tree. They had that well-dressed, unharried look of people with an empty nest and a full pension pot. They probably ate out at least once a week and took three holidays a year. And why not? That's exactly what she and John thought they'd be doing once Cam had gone to university.

Kat looked back at Judith. It should be John sitting opposite her now, rather than the pathologist on her case. They wouldn't be drinking this paint-stripper or bothering with a frigging salad. It would have been a bottle of Barolo and a decent steak, while he grilled her about the case. Maybe it was the gin, the sight of the other couple or the faint but familiar sounds of a Christmas album from the bar, but suddenly her eyes pricked with tears.

'Are you okay?' Judith asked.

Ninety-nine times out of a hundred, Kat would have said, 'I'm fine', but tonight she found herself saying, 'I really miss him. He was my best friend.'

Judith sat with her in silence for a moment. 'It's shit, isn't it? Another widowed friend of mine said the worst thing about losing her husband was that you have everyone to do something with, but no one to do nothing with.'

That was it exactly. Kat could always ring up a friend or her sister to arrange (in advance) a night out at the cinema or theatre, but there was no one she could just say, 'Sod it, let's eat out tonight' to or watch crap telly with. No one she could just *be* with.

'Most women my age are either divorced, widowed, retired or empty-nesters who find they've neglected to build a social life,' said Judith. 'A lot of us are lonely. We're just too ashamed to admit it. Like it's *our* fault.'

'Yes,' said Kat, wiping her eyes. 'When we all know it's fucking Tamara's fault.'

'Ha! Yes. I'll drink to that. Fucking Tamara. But Kat, Kat,

Kat,' Judith said, pointing at her with a slightly swaying finger. 'Any time you feel lonely, just give me a call. I mean it. Don't make the mistake of thinking that this is it, that your life's over. I'm fifty-two now and I made some of the best friends of my life in my forties. You aren't stuck with the friends you made at school or uni. Seriously, no one ever tells you that, but it's true. I don't know if it's hormones or what, but once we approach the menopause, women turn into the most brilliant and supportive friends.' Judith raised her glass. 'God, I love women.'

'Except for fucking Tamara.'

'Except for fucking Tamara,' Judith laughed, as they clinked their glasses together.

CHAPTER THIRTY-NINE

The papers are full of what I've done, and what I might do next. It's the lead story on all the news channels and #Lockupyoursons is trending on social media.

I read the articles first, focusing only on the words. I don't want to see pictures of his crying wife or shocked kids. I tell myself I've done them a favour—they would have found out the truth about their 'beloved husband and father' eventually. He is responsible for their pain, not me. Like my therapist says, I'm not a bad person. It's just that bad things happened to me.

I scan all the comments, tweets and posts, alert to any clues that could lead to me. But it's just recycled rumour and prejudice, whipping the public up into a frenzy of outrage about both the killer and the hologram in charge of finding them.

The extent of the coverage should please me, but most of it is froth: transient and superficial. According to the media, the men of Warwickshire are 'frightened', 'afraid' and 'terrified', but the falsity of each word is an insult. Real fear paralyses you: it stops you from eating, it stops you from sleeping, it stops you from leaving the house. Fear is a cage that shrinks your life and steals your future.

Yet the 'terrified' men of Warwickshire are still going to pubs and clubs alone. Still, they do not look over their shoulders; still, their eyes do not dart about, scanning the room for potential attackers. Still, they feel no fear.

But they will learn how it feels to be afraid.

For I will teach them everything I know.

CHAPTER FORTY

Kat quickly ate a rather messy almond pastry at her kitchen counter, trying to soak up all the acid that was playing havoc in her stomach. Jesus, no wonder she never drank gin. How much had she had?

Too much, she could imagine John replying.

She gulped down her tea, vowing never to touch the stuff again. And certainly not on a school night. Honestly, she was old enough to know better. Then again, when was the last time she'd laughed like that? Or cried in front of another adult? She should feel embarrassed, but deep down (beneath the headache and dodgy stomach), Kat was glad that she'd gone out and made a new friend. John was gone, Cam was moving on, so she really needed to get out more. Just maybe *sans* the gin.

Kat picked up her phone and re-read the WhatsApp messages Cam had sent late last night. Apparently, everything was 'fine' now. His flatmates had rallied round, united in their hatred of the tabloids (Gemma had proposed a university-wide boycott), and they'd all sat up late drinking, plotting their campaign against the evil media conglomerates while Cam told them about the kidnapping. She scrolled through the excited, misspelled messages. In just twelve hours, he'd gone from being ashamed and embarrassed to being the proud centre of a *cause*. Well, it was probably best that it was all out in the open, and even better that he had friends he could talk to. Kat flicked back through the messages, wondering whether this Gemma was *just* a friend.

The calendar on her phone pinged, reminding her that she had to leave now for the briefing at 8am.

Kat picked up John's car keys (her car was still at Warwick Uni) and took in a long, slightly nauseous breath. Team briefings were one of the hardest parts of the job, especially with a case as complex as this where there was national and international pressure and (so far) little progress. After two murders in four days and zero arrests, the team would be starting to get anxious. Some would want to rush into making arrests, others would start wondering if they were following the right lines of enquiry: all would be looking to her for leadership. Her job now was to help them make sense of the complexity, to not let the media or the families or their own anxiety drive them into reactive, ill-thought-out actions, but to take clear and calm decisions that would lead them to the killer.

If only she didn't feel so fucking hungover.

Kat left the house and climbed into John's car, unable to suppress a slight groan as she switched Lock on.

'Are you okay, DCS Frank? Perhaps you have the same stomach bug as Professor Okonedo?'

'What's that?'

'The professor emailed this morning to say that she will not be in today, due to a stomach bug.'

Kat paused, her hands on the wheel as her foggy brain processed the words. Professor Okonedo. *Shit*, she'd promised Rayan she'd talk to her last night about the press coverage, but then she'd gone to the lab with Judith Edwards and then the pub and then . . . well, to her shame, then she'd forgotten.

'Do you have her address?'

'Yes, but as you keep reminding me, I must not breach people's privacy by sharing their personal information.'

'Except for when there might be valid concerns about a person's welfare and safety.'

'In this case, there are no such concerns. Professor Okonedo has communicated that she merely has a stomach bug.'

'But as you've often said, sometimes people lie.'

'We have no evidence to suggest that Professor Okonedo is lying.'

Kat glanced at the quick Google search she'd just done of today's papers on her phone and sighed. 'I'm afraid that in this case, we do.'

CHAPTER FORTY-ONE

Adaiba Okonedo took another gulp of orange juice while she waited for *Detroit: Become Human* to download on her gaming computer. Despite the outdated graphics, it was perfect for when she needed to lose herself in another world. And today she needed to get completely and utterly lost.

Sixty-eight per cent downloaded. She glanced at her phone. More messages from her dad and brother. Lots of different words, but all with the same accusation: *How could you betray us and work for the POLICE?*

She scrolled through her messages, eyes blurring with tears. All that anger, blame and distrust, and not a single message to ask her *why*. (To which she would have replied that she was working *with*, not *for*, the police: helping to build a different vision, so that other families would not have to suffer as they had.)

She looked back at the computer. It was eighty-eight per cent downloaded now. *Detroit: Become Human* is a multiple-choice game that allows you to play as different AI protagonists. Usually, she opted for the peaceful, diplomatic choices in order to secure some sort of freedom for the machines without antagonising the wider human population. But today she felt impatient. Angry, even. Today she felt like taking another path: maybe clicking on the violent resistance options. What was the point of trying to court public opinion anymore?

Just as the game finished downloading, there was a knock at her door. She looked at the screen: 8.05am. Who on earth called at this time of day? Amazon? Tightening the belt on her dressing gown, she shuffled down the narrow hallway in her slippers and opened the door.

'DCS Frank? What . . . what are you doing here?'

'I heard you weren't feeling too good, so I thought I'd drop by and do a welfare and safety check.'

'A what?'

Kat glanced at the busy street behind her. 'Can I come in? It's freezing out here.'

The last thing she wanted was a police officer—DCS Frank, no less—in her flat, but other than slam the door in her face, what could she do? 'Sure,' she said, stepping back while she did a quick mental review of her home. It wasn't too messy—she was a naturally tidy person—but she was still wearing PJs, and as the big screen and box of cereal in the lounge would soon reveal, she was about to spend the whole day gaming.

'I'm sorry about all the press coverage,' Kat said as she entered the lounge. 'We've taken down what we can, Lock is identifying the trolls and McLeish has complained to the editors, but . . . well, I just wanted to check in and see how you are.'

The professor stared back at DCS Frank.

'Sorry. Stupid question.'

'No, it's not,' she said, through the sudden tightness in her throat. 'I appreciate it. I . . .' She broke off, unable to complete the sentence. Her own family and friends had given her nothing but anger or silence. And now the only person to ask her how she was was a frigging *cop*. 'Thank you,' she managed to say eventually.

'Don't thank me. It was Rayan's idea.'

'Rayan?' Her stomach lurched as she realised that she was still in her dressing gown, and that she hadn't done her hair or make-up. 'He isn't with you, is he?'

'No, he's just really worried about you.'

'Why? I told him I was *fine*. Why won't he believe me?'

'Probably because of his own experience.'

'What do you mean?'

Kat glanced at the computer screen, and the bright blue eyes of a female AI that appeared to be watching them. 'It's not my story to tell. But I can't stop you from googling his and his sister's name.' She sighed. 'Look, I don't have your personal experience, but I *do* know that staying away from work benefits no one but the people who made those racist comments and the killer we are trying to catch.'

Before she could reply, Kat started heading back down the hallway. 'I've pushed our briefing back till 9am,' she threw over her shoulder. 'So why don't you take something to settle your stomach, and I'll see you there.'

And then she was gone.

Adaiba pulled out her phone and typed *Rayan Hassan, Warwickshire, sister* into a search engine, until she found his familiar face looking back at her. He was several years younger, with dark, anguished eyes that dominated the screen. But it was the picture of his poor sister that squeezed her heart. That and the pages and pages of vile headlines that attacked her and her family as they sought (and failed) to secure a conviction against her rapist.

'Oh, Rayan,' she said after reading all that she could bear. She rubbed her face with her hands, trying to erase her own memories of that night in McDonald's when a group of white boys had followed her into the toilets. Her big brother had thankfully intervened, but he'd been the one the police arrested, followed by a campaign of harassment, lies and, eventually, wrongful imprisonment. He'd only just been released, after the Home Secretary had taken a personal interest because of the pilot with Lock. But he wouldn't have been locked up in the first place if it wasn't for her—or the police.

She glanced back at her game and the screen filled with multiple choices. If only she could restart her life the same way she restarted games.

But she couldn't. Neither could she change the articles or comments that had been written about her. The only thing she had any control over was how she responded to them. And DCS Frank was right. The trolls and racists would be delighted if they knew that their horrible comments had made her want to hide at home in her pyjamas.

Professor Okonedo rose to her feet. She switched off her gaming computer and headed for the wardrobe where her suits were kept with the care that warriors once devoted to their armour.

Today was not a day for hiding. Today was a day to be seen.

CHAPTER FORTY-TWO

————

'Sorry I'm late,' said Professor Okonedo as she entered the Major Incident Room. If she felt everyone's eyes upon her, then she gave no sign that it bothered her as she strode confidently towards the end of the table in an aqua-blue suit that wouldn't have looked out of place on a catwalk.

Kat gave her the briefest of nods, before bringing everyone up to date on the post mortem of Marcus Ridgeway and the three wise monkeys as a possible motivation. 'Most serial killers leave gaps of several weeks or months between each killing—but there were only four days between our two victims,' she explained. 'That means we are quite literally in a race against time—they could be planning their next murder right now. So we can't afford any missteps. We have to be as intentional as our killer.'

Kat turned to Debbie first. 'How are you getting on with the review of the CCTV? Anyone we've yet to account for in the bar and the brewery, or anything else unusual?'

She shook her head. 'Not yet. But I'm only about a quarter of a way through the tapes.'

'Which I have already assessed,' Lock reminded them. 'As time is of the essence, might I suggest that reviewing my work is not the best use of finite police resources?'

'No, you may not. What you *can* do is present your analysis of Natasha Riley's phone and social media communications to the team.'

Lock nodded (or was that a sarcastic bow of his head?) and raised a hand to project several colourful pie charts and bar graphs before them. 'Natasha Riley is an above-average user of social media and mobile phone communications, typically communicating for an average of ninety-seven minutes a day. Her dominant means of communicating is Instagram—an average of sixty-three minutes a day, which is twice the average. An analysis of the past six months shows that seventy-six per cent were photographs of her with Gary Jones, nineteen per cent were videos of herself and five per cent were miscellaneous.'

'Her life really was all about Gary,' Kat murmured, studying the screenshots that Lock pulled up beside the pie chart, tagged with phrases like *#blessed, #Truelove* or *#Engaged*. Yes, they were posed, but they did look genuinely happy. 'When was her last post on Instagram?'

'December 7th, at 7.16pm, just before she went to meet Sarah Rogers at the brewery.'

A picture appeared of Natasha taking a photograph of her reflection in a full-length mirror. She was wearing a short black dress—the same one she had been wearing the afternoon when Kat had told her Gary was dead—and her long blonde hair was immaculately straightened. *Girls' night out*, read the caption along the bottom.

When Kat asked about her messages and calls to Gary Jones, Lock confirmed there was no evidence of Natasha communicating with her fiancé at all that night, including deleted messages and calls.

'So if Natasha *is* the killer,' said Kat, addressing the room, 'how did she arrange to meet Gary at the top of Mount Judd that night?'

'If Natasha was planning to kill him, then verbal communication would have been safer,' said Rayan. 'They could have arranged to meet before she left?'

'That is a valid challenge,' conceded Lock. 'But the GPS data on her phone has enabled me to track her exact locations for the night in question within an accuracy of nine metres, due to the degree of urban density.'

A brightly coloured floor-to-wall map appeared before them, depicting Natasha and Gary's home at the top right-hand corner and the brewery at the bottom left. 'Using time series data,' said Lock, pointing to a green pulsating light, 'we can see that Natasha was at home until 7.18pm. She then drove directly to the brewery, here, where she remained until 1.52am, before travelling back to her home, which she reached at 2.32am. The data shows that Natasha remained in her home all night and the following day, until DCS Kat Frank visited her at 2.25pm. Therefore, she could not have met Gary Jones on Mount Judd or carried out his murder.'

The room was silent as everyone followed the moving green dot between the two locations.

'That data just tells us where Natasha's *phone* was, though,' insisted Rayan, 'not Natasha herself.'

Kat raised her eyebrows. 'Are you suggesting that Natasha Riley persuaded someone to take her phone in a car or taxi back home at 2am, and to somehow put it inside her house so that *she* could drive off in another car that was not her own and in a highly inebriated state to Mount Judd with a wooden cross, rope and a domestic carving knife so that she could kill her own fiancé?' Kat shook her head. 'You used to be a lawyer. You must know you're clutching at straws.'

'Just because it's not plausible, it doesn't mean it is not possible,' said Lock.

'What, *you* think Natasha Riley killed her fiancé as well?'

'I don't "think" anything. Unlike you, I am not letting my

emotional prejudices influence my assessment. I was merely stating the fact that although it is improbable, it is not impossible.'

'What about Marcus Ridgeway?' asked Debbie before Kat could reply. 'Did you find any messages that suggested Natasha Riley was in a relationship with him?'

Lock confirmed that there were no messages between them prior to the night in the brewery and that as none of the messages from her friend Sarah mentioned her boss, it was reasonable to presume that the meeting had not been planned. However, from the moment Natasha left the brewery at 1.52am, Marcus had sent her several messages, which Lock projected in the air before them:

Marcus: It was great to meet you. We must do it again sometime x

Natasha: Yeah, I had a good time thank you.

Marcus: When are you free?

Natasha: IDK. I'll need to talk to Gary.

Marcus: Why? Do you need his permission to go out???

Natasha: Of course not! I'd just like you to meet him, so I'll check when he's free. I think you'd really like him.

Marcus: I didn't realise you came as a package.

Natasha: He's my fiancé. I told you, we're going to be married.

Marcus: But you're not married yet!

Natasha: You are.

Marcus: Learn from my mistake! You're too young, beautiful and clever to tie yourself down.

Natasha: And you're drunk. Bedtime for you, I think.

Marcus: Is that an invitation?

Natasha: Hahaha. Goodnight!

Marcus: Sigh. Sweet dreams xxx

Messages sent at 3.05am

Marcus: I can't stop thinking of you getting ready for bed. What are you wearing?

Marcus: Hello? Don't be shy . . . you have an amazing body x

Marcus: I know you love Gary, but I also know you want me. There's no reason why you can't have both. There's nothing wrong with being happy. Life is too short.

Marcus: I guess you must be asleep. Let's arrange something tomorrow. You are amazing and this IS going to happen xxxx

Messages sent at 6.05pm the next day

Marcus: Jesus, Natasha, I've just seen the news. Is that really your Gary? I am so very, very, sorry. I know how much you loved him and I'm here for you if you need a shoulder to cry on. xxxx

Marcus: How are you feeling? Give me your address and I'll come round. I can offer booze and hugs—whatever it takes to get you through this I am here for you xxxxx

Marcus: I guess you must be in shock. I'll call tomorrow. Sending love and hugs xxxx

'Urgh,' said Debbie, after they'd read the messages. 'What a lech.'

'Lech?' queried Lock.

'Lecherous man,' explained Kat. 'Who clearly wouldn't take no for an answer.'

'Or even believe it if he heard it,' added Debbie.

'I don't understand,' said Lock. 'Natasha doesn't say no to his requests to see her again. She was clearly just asleep.'

'She was doing what lots of women do to men like that,' said Kat wearily. 'She tried to defuse the situation with humour, and when that didn't work, she stopped replying, hoping he'd get the message.'

'How can silence be a message?'

Kat raised her hands in exasperation. 'Because *everything* is communication. Especially between men and women. And it's not just you who doesn't get it, Lock. Half the human race has the same problem.' But as soon as the words were out of her mouth, she knew that Cam would have quite rightly pulled her up on them. *It's not all about gender, Mum,* he'd have said. *It's about power. Some men your age might be pervs, but me and my mates aren't like that.* Which, thank God, they weren't.

Kat glanced at the time on her phone. 'I think Lock's analysis is pretty conclusive.'

Rayan dragged a hand through his hair. 'I admit some of the logistics like the phone make it look like she's innocent, but going back to your three monkeys theory, she *does* have a motive. Her fiancé never listened to her, he bought her a carving knife for her birthday and, judging by his texts, Marcus Ridgeway wouldn't leave her alone and kept going on about how she looked.'

'If you think that means Natasha's got a motive, then so do half the women in Nuneaton,' said Debbie.

'But half the women in Nuneaton don't know both victims, whereas Natasha Riley did. I say we use the thirty-two hours we've got to question her again and chase up that warrant. Maybe she rang Gary from a burner phone.'

Karen-from-Comms raised her hand. 'It's all over the papers, so whatever you decide, my advice is to do it as soon as possible.'

Kat frowned. 'What's all over the papers?'

'The story of Natasha's arrest. I sent it to you this morning.'

Lock projected the email she hadn't had a chance to read, opening the attachment so that the briefing room filled with the lurid headlines:

FIANCÉE OF MAN FOUND CRUCIFIED ON NUNEATON'S NIPPLE HELD FOR QUESTIONING FOR DOUBLE MURDER

FIANCÉE OF FIRST CRUCIFIED MAN WAS HAVING AN AFFAIR WITH THE SECOND

IS NATASHA RILEY NUNEATON'S BLACK WIDOW SERIAL KILLER?

Full story pages 2, 3, 9, 12 and 13.

Kat swore. 'How the *fuck* did the papers find out?'

KFC shrugged. 'The nationals have big budgets. They probably rang everyone they could think of and offered money for
more information.'

Yet Kat noticed that the first story had appeared in the *Nuneaton Post* online, tagged as an exclusive by Ellie bloody Baxter.
She folded her arms and faced her team. 'If I find out we have a
leak in this building, then there will be a third murder, I shit you
not. So be careful about who you talk to, and only discuss the
case with the people in this room from now on.' She turned to
KFC. 'Meanwhile, I want to make the strongest possible rebuttal
to this story and announce that Natasha Riley was merely helping us with our enquiries. She is *not* a suspect, and as of now we
are letting her go.'

'But, boss—' began Rayan.

'And *you* can give her the good news,' said Kat, 'before driving her home.' Ordinarily she'd have asked Debbie to do it, as
she had the compassion and diligence to not just ask someone
like Natasha if they were okay but to make sure they actually
were. But she didn't want Debbie to keep thinking she was giving
her all the mumsy jobs. And Rayan needed to learn he wasn't a
lawyer anymore. She'd read the transcript—it had sounded more
like an interrogation than an interview.

'As one of our objectives is to build public trust and confidence in the police,' said Lock, 'then it would seem counterpro-
ductive to release our only suspect for the two murders.'

'I told you, our *core* objective is to apprehend the *actual* killer,
and not give the public false confidence and reassurance.'

'I presume you are going to check that you have the backing
of your superiors before taking such a big decision on this high
profile case?' Rayan said, repeating her own words from last
night back to her.

Kat narrowed her eyes. The cheeky bugger was right, but she

couldn't tell McLeish she was planning on letting one suspect go without giving him another. 'Of course,' she said smoothly. 'But first I want to review what we know about Tracy Taylor and see if we've got enough to bring her in. We know she won a contract from Gary Jones to carry out some of the council's waste and recycling work, but, Lock, is there anything to connect her with Marcus Ridgeway?'

'I can confirm that Tracy Taylor had a contract with Marcus Ridgeway to collect and recycle the bottles from his brewery.'

'What?' said Kat. 'How do you know that?'

'Marcus Ridgeway had his accounts audited last year, and I found the information in the auditor's report online.'

'Shit. What are the odds on both victims having a contract with the same recycling company?'

'I'd estimate that to be ten per cent. In addition, it appears that Marcus had recently decided to end his contract with Tracy Taylor and switch his recycling business to another provider.'

'And you're just telling me this *now*?'

'You were on a "girls' night out" and you switched me off, remember?'

Kat glared at Lock. 'Any other connections we should be aware of?'

'There is evidence that they attended the same social function last year,' Lock said, projecting a range of photographs before them. 'These were taken by attendees of the Warwickshire Businessman and Woman of the Year Gala Dinner.'

Kat stared at the images floating before her. Marcus Ridgeway, flushed and smiling in a tuxedo, was holding a glass of champagne in one hand, while the other was snaked around the waist of a woman who she didn't initially recognise as Tracy Taylor. Her blonde hair was swept up in a bun, and her body looked like it had been poured into a long, silver silk dress. But it was her expression that Kat studied as she took a step closer.

'Okay, bring her in.'

'On the grounds that she has a financial connection with Marcus Ridgeway?' asked Lock.

'No, because of the way she's looking at him,' she said, pointing towards the image. Tracy Taylor was a tall woman, but Marcus Ridgeway was tall enough for her to tuck herself beneath his shoulder. She had both arms wrapped tight around his waist, and the face she turned up towards him could only be described as adoring.

'That's our *and*,' she murmured.

'Pardon?'

'Tracy Taylor and Marcus Ridgeway had a business relationship, but I'd bet my pension that they also had a romantic relationship. I told you, money alone doesn't explain the emotional, vengeful nature of the killings. *This* potentially does,' she concluded, pointing at the photograph of the couple. 'Right. I want a warrant for her house and her office, access to her phone, computers, the lot. No short cuts, though. Tracy Taylor will lawyer herself up to the eyeballs, so we do this by the book, okay? And not a word to anyone, or she'll sue us for defamation.'

CHAPTER FORTY-THREE

Interviewer: DCS Kat Frank (KF)

Interviewee: Tracy Taylor (local businesswoman, TT)

Attending: Jeremy Booth-Wallingstone (solicitor, JB)

Date: 13 December, 2.10pm, Leek Wootton HQ

KF: Thank you for agreeing to help us with our enquiries, Ms Taylor.

TT: For your sake, I hope you know what you're doing.

KF: What's that supposed to mean?

TT: It means that every minute you spend with me is a minute you aren't finding the actual murderer. It also means that I hope you and your legal team are prepared to deal with the shitstorm you've just kicked off.

KF: I'm just doing my job, Ms Taylor. And you're being a good citizen and helping us with our enquiries.

TT: Tell that to my clients and my shareholders.

KF: We won't tell anyone anything. But to be honest, your clients and your shareholders aren't my concern.

TT: Well, they should be. Who do you think pays your wages? People like me who are stupid enough to pay taxes, that's who.

KF: My prime concern is to catch the person who murdered two men, before they kill a third.

TT: Is it true, then? Do you think this is the work of a serial killer?

KF: Yes, we do. So I'd be grateful if you'd just stop worrying about your lawyers and your reputation and tell us what you know.

TT: I don't know anything, but hey, knock yourself out.

KF: Thank you. Can I start by asking you whether you knew the second victim, Marcus Ridgeway?

TT: Yes, I knew him. He was one of my clients.

KF: As was Gary Jones.

TT: Jesus, is that what this is about? Why don't you interview the owner of Morrisons? I bet they were both customers there, too.

KF: It's not quite the same thing, though, is it? Everybody goes to the supermarkets, but not everybody contracts with a recycling firm.

TT: No, they don't. But do you know how many recycling firms there are in Warwickshire? Nine. And most of them charge too much and do too little. So if you're a businessman with any sense, then you'd at least consider contracting with my company. It's not remotely surprising that both men were my clients.

KF: Perhaps not. But it *is* rather surprising that both men are now dead.

TT: *[drinks a glass of water]*

KF: How well did you know Marcus Ridgeway?

TT: Fairly well. He's been a client for about two years.

KF: Was that all he was, a client?

TT: *[silent]*

JB: My client chooses not to answer that question, as is her right.

KF: Very well. Then I will answer it for her. For the tape, I am presenting a photograph of Tracy Taylor with Marcus Ridgeway at the Warwickshire Businessman and Woman of the Year Awards from last year.

TT: *[glances at the photo; takes another sip of water]*

KF: Can you at least confirm that this is you and Marcus Ridgeway?

TT: Yes. [pauses] There were a lot of people there from the business community in Warwickshire. A lot of alcohol was drunk. I could probably show you ten similar pictures of me with other men—because, believe me, they were mostly men that night.

KF: Really? Do you look at everyone like this, Ms Taylor?

TT: *[hisses]* Look, what do you want me to say? The poor man's just *died*, for fuck's sake. He has a wife. Kids. I don't want to break their hearts any more than they already are.

KF: I just want you to tell the truth, Ms Taylor. [pauses] I'm sorry for your loss. I can tell from the photograph how much you cared for him.

TT: *[snorts]* It was supposed to just be a bit of fun—a confidence-booster after my husband left me—but I had to go and fall for him, didn't I? *[shakes head]*

JB: You don't need to answer these questions, Tracy.

TT: No, it's okay. It's been eating me up and I've got nothing to hide. But I don't want his wife finding out, okay?

KF: When did the relationship start?

TT: When we signed the contract two years ago. We went out for a celebratory drink, and one thing led to another . . .

KF: How long did the affair last?

TT: Until I found out he was seeing other women. In the summer.

KF: And was it an acrimonious end?

TT: He was married with kids and having an affair with at least two other women as well as me. So what do you think?

KF: Is that why he decided to move his contract to another company?

TT: It's why I told him to take his contract and his wandering dick elsewhere.

KF: Where were you on the night of December 11th?

TT: You're seriously asking me that?

KF: Yes, I am.

TT: Well, sorry to disappoint you, but I wasn't in a field cutting his eyes out. I was at home, babysitting my grandkids.

KF: And is there anyone else who can verify that?

TT: Well, my daughter and her boyfriend, obviously. They dropped them off at 7pm and picked them up the next morning.

KF: And your grandkids?

TT: *[leans forward]* I want them kept out of this.

KF: But you said yourself that your daughter and her partner dropped them off at 7pm and picked them up the next morning. Marcus Ridgeway was killed between 1am and 3am, in a field that is only a twenty-minute drive from your home. How do we know that you didn't drive there once your grandchildren were asleep?

TT: Because I would never, ever leave my grandkids alone in the house. They're my whole life.

KF: Will you consent to handing your phone over so that we can confirm your location and see if you were in contact with Marcus that night?

TT: *[consults with JB; whispers]* I don't care. I don't want my grandchildren dragged into this. So if that means handing over my phone, then that's what I'll do.

JB: Tracy, I strongly advise that you—

TT: Yeah, well, you work for me, so you can advise all you like, but *I* decide. Okay, DCS Frank. But I want it back within the hour, and you're only allowed to use data relevant to *this* case, nothing else.

KF: What other cases are you worried about, Tracy? I understand the Organised Crime Squad have been investigating you for potential links with criminal gangs.

TT: I told you before, I subcontract out a lot of my work in good faith. What those companies choose to do with the rubbish they collect, or the money they make from it, is their business, not mine.

KF: Rumour is that back in the day, your links with those gangs were closer.

TT: The great thing about this country is that you can't lock someone up because of rumours. You actually need evidence. Unfortunately for you.

KF: And we will continue to look for that evidence. Which is why we've applied for a warrant to search your house and seize your computers and tablets.

TT: My house? What the fuck? You'd better not send coppers round when my grandkids are there, or I swear to God I'll . . . *[buries face in hands]* Bastards.

KF: What are you afraid of, Tracy? Are you afraid that we'll find a weapon that matches the knife that was used to slice off Gary Jones's ears? Are you afraid that we'll find audits and bank accounts that show just how much money the two contracts from your two victims were worth? Are you afraid that we'll find evidence that you were having affairs with both men? You said you needed a confidence-booster after your husband left you for another woman. You must have been *furious* when Marcus and perhaps Gary chose to end it, too. And hurt. So hurt that you decided to teach them a lesson? In fact, maybe you wanted to teach *all* men a lesson.

TT: *[leans forward]* Do you know what I'm really afraid of? Stupid coppers under pressure to get a conviction, fuelled by misogynistic clichés and making two random dead bodies add up to Tracy Taylor. Look at me. *Really* look at me. I am not a murderer, and *you* know it.

KF: *[hesitates]* Someone like you wouldn't have to do it yourself. The OC squad tell me that several of your staff are guys with criminal records as long as your arm. Some of those men wouldn't say no for the right fee.

TT: I employ ex-cons because I believe everyone deserves a second chance. Do your bloody homework, DCS Frank. That's one of the reasons why I won Businesswoman of the Year. And I didn't do it for the award, either. I did it because I left school at sixteen with no qualifications, and back in the day, I cut corners and did some things I'm not proud of. I was pregnant at twenty, and a single mum for five years until I met my ex-husband, and then we focused on setting up the business. We made a lot of money, but I wouldn't have won any awards for Mum of the Year. But now I've got grandkids, and do you know what? It's like I've got a second chance. [picks up phone and looks at screensaver] Do you have grandchildren?

KF: *[shakes head]*

TT: Charlie's five and Tracy—she's named after me—is just three. We feed the horses and chickens together, plant seeds, and I play the Xbox and Nintendo Switch with them. We even bake frigging cakes, the whole works. They love me. They tell everyone that their gran is the Warwickshire Businesswoman of the Year, as if I'm the fucking Queen or something. *[laughs softly]* But I know what kids are like. Once they start going to school, they'll be on their iPhones and the internet, and what will they think of their old gran then? So ever since Charlie was born, I've been putting my affairs in order, not renewing any contracts that I can't vouch for, ending dealings with anyone I don't trust and keeping away from any tax loopholes. I want my grandchildren to go to private school, to have everything I never did—including the respect of their friends and families. And I want them to always love me the way they do now. I never want them to be ashamed or embarrassed of who I am or what I've done. *[hands phone over] That* is what I care about. *This* is who I am. So there is no way on God's earth that I would risk my grandchildren's future happiness by killing two men. I told you on the day you came to my home: if you want to catch the murderer, then you should be looking for someone who has nothing left to lose. And that isn't me.

INTERVIEW CONCLUDED

CHAPTER FORTY-FOUR

Kat straightened her jacket and knocked on her boss's door.

McLeish looked up as she walked in, followed by the image of Lock. 'I hope you're coming to tell me that you've caught the killer. I've got another call with the minister in twenty minutes to update her on the case.'

'Afraid not, sir, but I thought I'd bring you up to speed with where we're at.'

McLeish studied her, ignoring Lock. 'You mean, you know I won't like what you're about to do, so you thought you'd come in here and cover your arse first?'

How well he knew her. Ordinarily, she might have laughed.

He gestured towards the soft black leather chairs in the corner, and she gratefully took a seat. It was a sign he would at least listen to what she had to say. If he'd planned on giving her a bollocking, he would have left her standing in front of his desk like a naughty child. She had unswerving loyalty and admiration for McLeish, but his management style was distinctly old-school and not for everyone. Personally, Kat welcomed his clarity, and her boss was nothing if not clear.

Gesturing to Lock to assume a sitting position beside her, Kat quickly told McLeish about the post mortem, her theory about the three monkeys and, after taking a deep breath, her interview with Tracy Taylor.

'I've analysed the data on her phone,' added Lock. 'And I can confirm that according to the *Findmyiphone* app, Tracy Taylor was in her home on the nights when both Gary Jones and Marcus Ridgeway were killed.'

McLeish made a dismissive gesture. 'People like Tracy Taylor have plenty of goons who can do their dirty work for them, and probably more burner phones than you've had upgrades. The location of her phone is no more relevant than the location of her socks.'

'But I honestly don't think she did it,' said Kat. 'She's spent years and considerable effort trying to put some distance between herself and her past. She said her grandkids are her whole life now. The last thing she'd do is jeopardise that.'

'And you believed her?'

Kat didn't hesitate. 'Yes, I did.'

McLeish made a low growling sound. 'So what do I tell the minister? Who else have we got in the frame?'

Kat shifted in her seat. 'We're continuing to follow all lines of enquiry and double-checking all the CCTV and—'

'So basically, you don't have a clue. Jesus, Kat. You're not exactly making life easy for yourself.' He rubbed his reddening scalp with his hand. 'It's been nearly six days now. People are starting to openly question if I made a mistake giving a case of this complexity and profile to you and the robot.'

'I am not a robot. I am an AI machine capable of—'

'Irritating the pants off me,' finished McLeish.

Lock cast a confused glance at the Chief Constable's trousers.

'So what am I supposed to tell the minister? If I share your three monkeys theory, there's a bloody good chance she'll bring in a national team to make sure there isn't a third dead body. This whole thing is playing badly with their core voters—middle-aged white men who feel that women and technology are taking their jobs.' He gave Lock a pointed look. 'I need to convince her that we're within touching distance of a breakthrough. And from what you've told me, you've got enough on paper to arrest Tracy Taylor. You said yourself that you think there's something personal about this murder.'

'Yes, I think there's some kind of personal, emotional motivation, but it's not Tracy Taylor. We're missing something. Or someone.'

'Look, if you're right, then you'll find the missing piece, and *then* you can let her go. But meanwhile, we need to build trust and confidence in the Warwickshire police force and show that we know what we're doing. I'm not having a bunch of southern twats coming in here telling me how to do my job.'

'And I'm not arresting Tracy Taylor, sir. In fact, I've already let her go.'

McLeish's face turned a worrying shade of purple. 'You've done *what*?'

'She didn't do it. And I'm not prepared to ruin another woman's life by allowing the media to speculate that she did.' Kat returned the fierce glare of her boss, remembering the headlines about Natasha Riley when they had held her overnight. If they arrested Tracy Taylor, then her grandchildren would know not only that she was a suspect, but that she'd had an affair with a married man, and it wouldn't take the tabloids long to drag up her dubious past. Her grandchildren might be too young to read the articles now, but they'd always be on the internet, and there'd always be someone in the playground ready to enlighten them. She could not and would not be the cause of such lifelong misery, just to prop up her own reputation.

For a long, tense minute, Kat thought McLeish might order her to arrest Tracy Taylor. But he must have seen the resolution in her face, because eventually he let out a weary sigh. 'It's my own fault for putting someone so bloody principled on this case.' He stood up, signalling the end of the meeting. 'I'll do my best to inspire confidence in the minister, but don't blame me if you get taken off the case.'

'That would be a mistake, sir. I can find the killer. I *know* I can.'

McLeish gave her a sad smile. 'Just because you believe something, Kat, it doesn't make it true.'

CHAPTER FORTY-FIVE

DS Browne was waiting for Kat outside McLeish's office, saying something about one of the CCTV cameras that she wanted to show her and Lock. Kat nodded and followed her down the corridor back to the briefing room, still bothered by the exchange with her boss. It wasn't the conflict that upset her—she'd never had a problem standing up for herself—but she was used to McLeish's respect. What she *wasn't* used to was his pity. Honestly, the way he'd looked at her just now, it was as if she was *deluded* or something. Well, she would show him. She would bloody well show them all.

Kat was only half-listening as she took a seat in the briefing room in front of one of the many large screens that lined the wall, with the image of Lock standing beside her. Debbie explained how many tapes she'd watched of Gary Jones and his mates in the Silk Mill pub, before tapping the keys and playing a few frames of him sitting at a table with his best man, Mike Garth. It looked like they'd just got a round in, as both men had nearly full pints as they talked. Or rather, Gary talked while Mike occasionally nodded his head.

'Watch this bit,' said Debbie. 'Mike Garth goes to the toilet, so Gary Jones is left by himself for a few minutes.'

The CCTV camera was behind the bar, so they had a good view of Gary sitting on the bench against the wall directly opposite, with empty tables either side. Kat stared absently at the screen, thinking again how surreal it was that the corpse she had seen in Dr Edwards's lab was once this young, handsome man with his hair still damp from football practice. She scanned the scene around him, waiting for something to happen.

'There,' said Debbie, with a note of satisfaction.

'What? I didn't see anybody,' said Kat, confused.

'His *face*,' Debbie insisted. 'Watch Gary Jones's face.' She rewound the tape a few frames and played it again in slow-motion.

Kat watched as Gary absently raised his glass of amber-coloured beer and glanced towards his left. Then his mouth widened in what could only be described as shock. His tanned face visibly paled, and he placed his pint back down, spilling some of his beer upon the table. He looked around the bar, as if checking whether anyone was watching, then stood up and walked towards whatever he'd seen, until he was out of shot.

'That was when he left the bar,' said Debbie, excitedly. 'I think he saw someone. Someone he knew. Someone he was afraid of.'

'How can you conclude that?' asked Lock. 'The only person in these frames is Gary Jones.'

'Because of his face,' Kat whispered. She leaned forward, pressed rewind and played it again, freezing it on the moment when his jaw literally dropped. 'Good work, Debbie. Seriously. Well bloody done.' Lock might be able to view thousands of images in seconds to complete a single specific task, but he simply wasn't capable of making the lateral connections that a diligent, human police officer could.

Lock sniffed. 'You asked me to look for evidence of anyone approaching or talking to Gary Jones. You did not ask me to take note of his facial expressions in general or for evidence of shock and recognition in particular. Had you specified the task more clearly, then I too would have drawn your attention to this aspect of the film.'

'It's not a competition, Lock.' Kat rewound the film again,

pulling her chair up closer to the screen. Squinting her eyes—she really needed to get them tested—she tried to work out where the door to the pub was. 'I presume it was on the left,' she guessed, 'so perhaps our mystery person stood at the doorway and beckoned him outside?'

'I can use my photogrammetry program to reconstruct a 3D image of the pub based upon all of the footage we have,' said Lock, projecting what looked like a computerised architect's model upon the boardroom table before them. 'The door is 3.75 metres away to the left from the table that Gary sat at, and based upon his line of sight,' it said, as a dotted red line appeared from Gary Jones's eyes towards the door, 'I would estimate the other person to have stood here. Presuming that they made eye contact, this person was approximately five-foot-three tall.'

'So probably a woman,' said Kat, 'but not Tracy Taylor, who must be at least my height. Lock, can you check all the other CCTV cameras? Surely the pub has one over the door. It must have picked her up.'

'There was no camera over the door. But we do have external footage from the nightclub and the department store opposite. If we utilise these two sources for the same timeframe, then we have a fleeting image of the person that Gary Jones saw in the doorway.'

In the centre of the room, Lock projected a life-size image of a person walking rapidly past the nightclub in the dark beneath a large, black umbrella. Because the camera was positioned a few feet above, they couldn't see anything other than the umbrella, which presumably was its purpose.

The perspective shifted, as Lock explained that they were now seeing the images recorded by the CCTV camera outside the department store just across the street from the pub. From here, they could see the entrance, lit up against the night. Again, there was the figure with a black umbrella tilted forwards, presumably to hide their head from the camera opposite. But this time they could see more of their body: small, slim, and dressed in black tracksuit trousers and what looked like flat pumps. The figure was holding their umbrella with their right hand as they opened the door to the pub with their left. They paused, as if realising that they couldn't fit through the gap with a raised umbrella, before lowering and twisting it for a second so that they could slip quickly through the main door.

'There,' said Lock, freezing the image.

Kat stood and stared at the back of the figure that was now revealed to them. They still couldn't see their face, but beneath the bright lights of the pub, they could see that they had long, straight, red hair. The image lasted no more than a second before the door closed behind them, but it was enough. Eighteen seconds later, the door opened again—although this time it looked like they had pushed it open with their foot—leaving their hands free to cover their face with the raised umbrella before exiting. After another thirty seconds, a worried-looking Gary Jones emerged. Again, he glanced about him, before walking in the same direction and finally vanishing from sight.

'Can you pull it all together and do a photofit ID?' she asked Lock.

Lock reached out, pulling together the various images from different sources to form one coherent picture. After a few seconds, he pointed towards a 3D figure rotating before them. 'I estimate that the person we are looking for is female, approximately five-foot-three in height, weighing 48.2 kilograms, with long red hair. Her weight and hairstyle are suggestive of youth, but as we have no footage of her facial features, this is an inference only and not a fact.'

Kat's nose tingled the way it did when she was excited. This was the breakthrough they needed. 'How common is red hair?'

'About two per cent of the world's population have red hair.

But the occurrence is higher in England—estimates range from between six and ten per cent, with regional variations.'

'No wonder she used an umbrella,' said Kat. 'Her hair is too distinctive. Right, we need to get this out in a press release,' she said, addressing KFC. 'Ask anyone who saw a red-haired female in Nuneaton town centre on the nights Gary Jones or Marcus Ridgeway were killed to contact us urgently. Where's Rayan?'

'I think he might still be with Natasha Riley,' said Debbie. 'She was really upset by the media coverage, apparently. He took her home, but last I heard he was waiting for the mental health crisis team to check her out. That was a few hours ago, though.'

'Okay, well, if the crisis team has taken over and Rayan is still in the Nuneaton area, get the photofit to him. Ask him to go to both bars and talk to the staff and customers, quick as he can. *Somebody* must have seen her the nights that Gary Jones and Marcus Ridgeway were murdered.' She ran a hand through her own hair, pausing mid-thought. 'I don't remember seeing anything in the forensics report about hairs being found at either scene, but can we double-check? Even if there was no DNA, it would be good to confirm the hair colour.'

Kat couldn't wait to tell McLeish, so rather than ring him, she handed the bracelet that contained Lock over to Debbie so that they could carry on working while she hurried back down the corridor to tell the boss in person. The rapid walk and excitement at the prospect of a breakthrough made her slightly breathless as she quickly told him what they'd found.

McLeish stared back at her from behind his desk. 'Too late,' he said, nodding towards his phone. 'The minister was so worried by the lack of progress and the prospect of a third body that she's decided to put a hand-picked national team on the case.'

'But you need to ring her and tell her—'

'Tell her what? That we've managed to deduce that the murderer didn't have black, brown or blonde hair, but is probably a ginger lass? That's not a breakthrough, Kat, that's a one in four guess. And have you never heard of hair dye?' McLeish rose to his feet, rubbing his chest the way he sometimes did when he had indigestion. 'It's too late, Kat. I'm sorry, but Mike the Psych will be in charge of the case as of 9am tomorrow.'

CHAPTER FORTY-SIX

Kat strode back down the corridor, face burning. It wasn't the humiliation of having a case taken off her that was so infuriating—although it *was* fucking annoying—it was the fact that she knew it would take the London team a couple of days to even learn where Nuneaton was on the bloody map, wasting precious time that she could have spent finding the actual killer before she struck again. And Mike the Psych of all people. Just when they'd made a breakthrough! She didn't care what McLeish said, the hair colour, gender and height *were* significant, not least because they told them who it wasn't. She'd been criticised so much for letting Natasha Riley and Tracy Taylor go, but this footage vindicated her judgement. Yet instead of saying, oh, sorry, *you* were right, we were wrong, so from now on we'll back you all the way, they had taken her off the case, the stupid fuckers.

Kat reached the door to the briefing room and paused. It was tempting to charge in and share her anger and frustration with her team—*Guess what those bloody politicians have gone and done now?*—but she was paid to lead them: to help contain their collective anxieties and set an example, not to make herself feel better by venting. Kat glanced at her watch. It was nearly 6pm. Their office Christmas party was due to start at seven. Maybe she should just announce it as good news: *In recognition of the complexity and profile of this case, extra resources have been brought in, which means no one has to work over Christmas, and we can start our office party as of right now. Yay.*

The door was slightly ajar, so she watched her team for a moment while she chewed it over.

Debbie and KFC were huddled around a computer, pulling together a press notice to go with the photofit. Judith Edwards had arrived and was marking up a report on her tablet, and Lock stood with Professor Okonedo, deep in conversation.

'I am still confused by the conflicting stated objectives on this case,' Lock was saying. 'DCS Frank has repeatedly stressed that our sole purpose is to apprehend the actual killer, but Chief Constable McLeish keeps stating that our primary aim is to boost confidence and trust in the Warwickshire police force, and that the best way to do this is to arrest suspects, even if they later prove to be innocent. I am a member of DCS Frank's team, but McLeish is her superior, so I do not know which objective to prioritise.'

'Thank you for raising this with me, Lock,' said Professor Okonedo. 'I agree that on the surface it *sounds* like their objectives conflict, but they don't have to. McLeish is right that the public need to have trust and confidence in the police, but that trust has to be *earned*. And the way you do that is by using actual evidence rather than biased assumptions in order to arrest those who are genuinely guilty. In the long term, you will only achieve McLeish's objective by following Kat's and making sure we apprehend the actual killer.'

'Very well, I will prioritise DCS Frank's objectives as you suggest. But the multitude of inconsistent and contradictory comments made by humans makes it extremely difficult to understand their objectives, let alone deliver them.'

Professor Okonedo smiled. 'Over time, you will learn to operate in conditions of ambiguity and uncertainty. Meanwhile, when in doubt, I suggest that you trust DCS Frank's judgement. She has a surprisingly strong sense of justice for a police officer.'

Kat blinked, surprised by a sudden surge of emotion at the back-handed compliment. 'Fuck it,' she muttered, before entering the room. 'I've just spoken to McLeish,' she announced, cutting across their conversations. 'The minister has decided to bring in an external team to lead this case, starting at 9am tomorrow.'

The room fell silent.

'So, we've got two choices. Either we start our Christmas office party now and pray that the London guys work out which way is up before there's a third murder. *Or* we do an all-nighter and use our considerable experience and expertise to catch the killer, ensuring that justice is served and lives are saved before they even get off the train with their soya lattes.' Kat spread out her palms. 'What's it to be?'

'Well, I hate office parties,' said Debbie.

'And I hate Londoners,' said Judith.

'It'd make a great story if we beat them to it,' added KFC.

Kat turned to Professor Okonedo and Lock. 'What about you? Are you in?'

'If we get taken off this case before we can solve it,' Professor Okonedo said thoughtfully, 'then the tabloids will say it proves that AI doesn't work, setting our research back years.' She met DCS Frank's gaze directly. 'So yes, I'm in.'

'Lock?' Kat held her breath as she looked into the eyes of the hologram. Would he choose loyalty to her or his own rigid protocols?

'As my revised objective is to ensure that justice is achieved by apprehending the actual killer,' said Lock, 'I too must support your second option.'

'Good,' said Kat, giving her team a proud smile. 'Then we've got exactly fifteen hours to find the killer.'

CHAPTER FORTY-SEVEN

Kat paced up and down the length of the briefing room, studying the virtual wipe-boards. There were two dedicated to each of the victims, with a larger one at the back so that the team could add miscellaneous thoughts or ideas worth pursuing. But the central virtual board was dedicated to the profile of the killer and potential suspects. It was depressingly short:

- Five-foot-three
- Redhead (dyed?)
- Female?
- Young?
- Probably known to Gary Jones—no evidence re Marcus Ridgeway
- Lives in the Nuneaton area?

'There are 130,373 people living in the Nuneaton and Bedworth district according to the Office for National Statistics,' said Lock, '66,385 of whom are female. I cannot find any statistics on how many have red hair, but if I make a conservative estimate of five per cent, then that would suggest there are approximately three hundred women who fit that profile. If we assume that the killer is aged somewhere between twenty and fifty, then this would reduce our pool of suspects to one hun-

278 · JO CALLAGHAN

dred, *if* we presume that they live in the district of Nuneaton and Bedworth. In the absence of any record or register to identify women with red hair, I could search all images on social media from this geographic area, but that would only pick up women who post pictures of themselves on public platforms, and so would be vulnerable to selection bias.'

'It isn't ideal,' admitted Kat. 'But it's better than nothing, so go ahead.' She turned towards the two victim boards, each highlighting what they knew about each man.

Gary Jones	Marcus Ridgeway
Male	Male
29	33
5'11"/ 75 kg	6'1"/ 92 kg
Blond hair (dyed) no beard	Dark brown hair (with beard)
Engaged	Married
No kids	2 daughters
Council employee	Self-employed owner of brewery/bar
No known religion	No known religion
Contract with TT	Contract with TT
	Ex-lover of TT—serial adulterer

MO	MO
Drugged, bound to cross	Drugged, bound to cross
Death: hypothermia, asphyx	Death: hypothermia, asphyx
PM mutilation (ears, knife)	PM mutilation (eyes, crows)
Location:	Location:
Mount Judd, Nuneaton	Fillongley, field

'We've been focusing on Tracy Taylor and Natasha Riley because they're the only people that both victims had in common.

But there must be something or someone else,' Kat said, addressing the room. 'Did they go to the same school together or work together or play on the same football team or drink in the same pub or attend the same church? *Anything* that might explain how they both came to know our killer?'

They brainstormed several ideas while Lock trawled the internet, social media accounts, PDF files and school and health registers, trying—and failing—to find a connection. They even had different hobbies: Gary Jones devoted his spare time to sport (football, running, weightlifting), whereas Marcus Ridgeway spent most of his spare time socialising in bars and restaurants or attending small business conferences and other networking events. The only thing they appeared to have in common was the university they graduated from, but as Marcus was four years older than Gary, and it only took three years to get a degree, their paths wouldn't have crossed.

'The only other thing they seem to have in common is their gender,' said Kat.

'And skin colour,' added Professor Okonedo. 'They're both white.'

'Yes, they are,' Kat acknowledged, asking Lock to add it to the board, annoyed at herself for not recognising her own bias.

'Isn't it enough that they're both young white men?' asked KFC. 'I mean, I'm not a detective like you guys, but if the victims were both young white women, would we even be looking for some deeper connection? Wouldn't we just assume that's what the killer was after?'

'That's because most male killers of young women have a sexual motive,' said Judith. 'But there's no forensic evidence of sexual contact with either victim.'

'It's a good challenge,' said Kat, giving Karen an encouraging smile. 'But I keep thinking of Gary's face. He was *afraid* when he saw his killer. He *knew* her. Which suggests to me that Marcus must have known her, too. We just have to work out how.'

While they ordered some pizzas, Lock created a gallery of the fifty-three red-haired women aged between twenty and fifty it had harvested from various social media accounts from Nuneaton and Bedfordshire. Their images floated in the air like ghosts: some achingly young with fiery red hair and blazing blue eyes, others older, their hair shorter and dulled by time. Kat moved among them, studying each woman in turn, but without a connection between the men, she didn't really know what or who she was looking for. She glanced at her phone when the pizzas arrived: 8.03pm. Just thirteen hours left to crack the case, and her mind was a ginger blur.

'Oh!' cried KFC, nearly spitting her pizza out.

'Too hot?' asked Debbie, as she plugged her phone in to charge.

'No, I was just reading through all the press cuttings, and I found an interview with Marcus Ridgeway when he was nominated for Young Entrepreneur of the Year. Listen to this, it says that he attended Birmingham Uni as a *mature student*.'

'Meaning?' asked Lock.

'Meaning the age gap between Marcus and Gary might be irrelevant,' said Kat. 'Can you check what years both men actually studied?'

'I have just checked the records,' said Lock. 'And despite the difference in age, both men matriculated and graduated in the same year. Gary Jones read geography and Marcus Ridgeway read business studies.'

Kat studied the record that appeared on the virtual screen before them. 'Jesus, this could be our connection. Good work, Karen.' She turned towards the gallery of red-haired women. 'Can you find out how many of these went to Birmingham University, Lock?'

———

Judith finished the call they were taking in the far corner of the room and walked back towards them with a gloomy expression. 'I'm not sure how useful that's going to be. I just spoke to my colleague in the lab, because although a couple of hairs were found at the crime scene, it was reported as "nil DNA", which is why it wasn't picked up in the reports. I asked them to go back and check the hair colour.'

'And?'

'And it *was* red, but the reason there was no trace of DNA was because there's a high probability that the hair was from a wig.' Judith patiently explained that as wigs are made from human hair that is cut off rather than plucked from the hair follicle, this means they don't contain DNA, as once the hair has been cut off, the DNA that is useful to forensics begins to break down.

'Are you sure it's from a wig?' asked Kat. 'Maybe the hair snapped off somehow?'

'No. The extent of cleaning and bleaching that the hair has been subject to is highly suggestive of it being from a wig. I'm sorry. It should have been flagged earlier, but these tests are carried out by an automated machine—they just report yes or no to DNA, and a human only looks at them when there's a positive result.'

Kat looked back at the frozen CCTV image of the red-haired woman outside the pub. 'So it literally could be anyone in a wig? *Shit.*'

'DCS Frank?' said Lock.

'Not now, I need to go to the toilet.' She needed a wee, but most of all, she needed to kick something. Hard.

'I really think you need to see this,' Lock persisted.

Kat sighed. Honestly, Lock was great at internet searches, but he really needed to learn to read the room. Before she could reach the door, Lock projected another photograph before her, so that she almost walked into an image of some teenagers at night, standing outside what looked like the entrance to a flat and waving an array of bottles, cans and cigarettes. They must have been on the way to a Christmas party, as several of them were draped in tinsel and wearing bright-red Santa hats, their faces scrunched up against the falling snow.

'I found this on Gary Jones's Facebook account from ten years ago,' Lock explained, circling his face with a virtual red pen.

Kat paused, stilled by the boy-man before her: spotty, skinny, but unmistakably Gary Jones, with his winning smile and thick blond hair styled into an impressive-looking quiff.

'But look at who else is in the picture,' said Lock.

CHAPTER FORTY-EIGHT

———

Rayan paused at the entrance to the pub to send Debbie a quick text:

> No luck at the brewery, no one remembers
> seeing any redheads. Just about to ask
> around in the Silk Mill. – try and be
> there by 9. Save me some turkey.

He added Is Prof O there yet? before quickly deleting it. Too needy. And he wasn't *that* bothered. It wasn't like he was obsessed or anything. It's just that after the briefing this morning, she'd suddenly announced that she was going to come along to their Christmas do after all. And Professor Okonedo never, ever came out with them, so this was a rare chance to get to know her, and for her to get to know *him*. He hated the fact that she distrusted the police so much. He understood why, but he wanted to show her that they weren't all the same, that he, at least, was different. If he could just talk to her over a drink rather than a briefing table, then she might forget he was a copper and relate to him as a human being. That's why he'd volunteered to organise the dinner. But here he was trawling the bars in Nuneaton on the off-chance that someone might remember seeing a redhead on the night that Gary Jones was murdered.

Rayan released a puff of white cloud into the freezing air before pulling open the door to the bar. He needed to be quick. He'd been hoping to have time to go home and change before the Xmas do, but at this rate, Professor Okonedo might leave before he got there.

The pub was busy with after-work drinkers sitting beneath fake garlands dotted with festive lights. Christmas was still over a week away, but there was already an atmosphere of people beginning to wind down.

Rayan made his way to the stocky bald man at the bar that they'd spoken to before. He couldn't remember his name, but judging by the way his face fell, the barman remembered him. He broke off a conversation with a customer and made his way over, pulling up his jeans with the hooks of his thumbs.

'What can I get you?'

'DI Hassan,' he said, raising his voice over the tinny Christmas music spilling out of the nearby speakers. 'I'm investigating the murder of Gary Jones and we've got a picture of a person of interest I'd like to show you.'

The barman looked curious. Most people were interested, if not excited, by the idea of looking at a possible murderer. 'Go on, then.'

He laid the picture from the CCTV on a sticky beer mat. 'Do you recall seeing a woman with red hair on the night Gary Jones died? We think she stood at or near the door at 11pm—you might have seen her if you were collecting glasses?'

'That's just the back of someone's head,' the barman said, frowning at the picture.

'She was female, five-foot-three and possibly aged twenty to fifty years old.'

'So the killer *is* a woman, then? Fuck me, what's the world coming to?'

'Did you see anyone matching this description?'

'Sorry, no. But the bar's jammed at that time for last orders, so I only see the punters in front of me.'

'Okay. Do you mind if I ask your customers if any of them were here that night?'

The barman sighed. They both knew he didn't really have a choice. 'All right. But try not to put a downer on the night, eh? It's nearly Christmas. People come in here to relax and have a bit of a laugh. And they've already been bothered by that reporter.'

'What reporter?'

'Her,' he said, nodding towards a dark-haired woman sitting at one of the tables at the back. He pulled a card out from the back pocket of his faded blue jeans. 'Ellie Baxter, *Nuneaton Post*.'

———

It didn't take Rayan long to question the customers. Only two had been in the pub that night, and yes, they remembered Gary Jones—lovely bloke, terrible for his family—but no, they hadn't seen any red-haired women. Despite this, every table had an opinion about the killer, especially the men: there was clearly some 'bunny boiler' on the loose in Nuneaton, some 'nutter' who'd escaped from the mental hospital or one of those radical feminists who hated men and cancelled people, or an ex-girlfriend or wife who wouldn't leave the poor bloke alone. There was an element of black humour to their remarks, like they weren't quite taking it seriously. But when Rayan concluded his questions by reminding them that the killer was still out there, and that the police advice was for all men to be vigilant and not leave pubs alone, this provoked genuine outrage.

'Comes to something when a man isn't safe to drink in his own local,' complained one customer, either not hearing or ignoring his girlfriend when she muttered, 'Welcome to the club.'

'Things have gone too far,' said another, although what 'things', he didn't say.

But the most common response was 'Bollocks to that'. Nobody was going to let the police—or even worse, a female serial killer—tell *them* what to do. 'It's up to you to catch the killer and keep us safe,' said one older man, pointing a nicotine-stained finger at Rayan. 'I'm not going to change my behaviour just because you can't do your bloody job.'

As he worked the room, he was aware of Ellie Baxter's eyes upon him. Well, if she was hoping he would give her a story or new angle, then she was very much mistaken. He tried to ignore her as he walked past her table towards the door, but she called out to him.

'Aren't you going to ask me if I know anything?'

Rayan paused and turned. 'Were you in the bar the night that Gary Jones was killed?' he asked in a monotonous tone.

'No, but as a local journalist, I've got my ear to the ground. I might know something useful.'

'Then I'm sure you'll do your civic duty and ring the information line.'

Ellie shrugged her narrow shoulders. 'You never know if you're speaking to an actual officer when you ring those things. I'd rather talk to you. I could share what I know, you could share what you know and, well, we could both help each other.'

Rayan studied the young woman sitting alone at the table. She was pretty when she smiled; her short, dark hair gave her an elfin look that was strangely attractive. But he wasn't born yesterday. He should just leave—he needed to get to the party before the professor left—but after the day he'd just had, the urge to tell this journalist what he really thought of her and her so-called 'profession' was too strong.

Rayan took a chair opposite her and leaned forward across the small, wobbly table. 'If you think I'm going to be the source of your next exclusive, then you're mistaken. I've spent most of the day with Natasha Riley, who, because the media branded her a murderer, now wishes to kill herself. She's in a terrible state. I had to call the crisis team out. Honestly, don't you lot think about the impact you have on people's lives?'

It was only when her eyes widened that he realised what he'd done. 'Shit, I shouldn't have said that. That was all confidential information, you can't report that.'

'Of course I won't. I promise.'

Rayan snorted. Like a promise from a journalist meant anything.

She pulled up the sleeve of her black polo-neck jumper to reveal silver-white scars zigzagging across her wrist. 'I know what it's like to be in so much pain that you'd rather die,' she said, her voice no more than a whisper. 'So I would *never* exploit another woman in that position. I just wouldn't.' She quickly pulled her sleeve back down, pale cheeks flushing.

Rayan looked at her—really looked at her—noting the painful narrowness of her wrists, the gaunt, freckled cheekbones and the fragile body hidden beneath the layers of dark clothes. Despite himself, he felt a wave of sympathy. She was too like his sister to feel anything else. He nodded.

'Look, I'm done for the day and I'm going to have a drink. Can I get you one?' she offered.

Rayan glanced at his phone. Professor Okonedo would be gone by the time he got there at this rate, and while he told himself it didn't matter, the knot in his stomach said different. But it must have been hard for Ellie to share something so personal about herself. He couldn't just leave now, as if her scars meant nothing.

Reluctantly, Rayan nodded and asked for a small bottle of beer because he was driving. He could down it in ten, make sure Ellie was okay and then get off.

Ellie came back with a beer for them both and a couple of bags of crisps. 'Thought I'd treat you to dinner, too.'

'Thanks,' he said, tearing his open.

'So, what were you asking people?' Ellie asked, after taking a swig of her beer.

Rayan wasn't sure if he should tell her, but then he figured they were putting it out in a press release, so she'd know within the hour anyway. 'This,' he said, putting the photofit on the table between them. 'We're looking for a redheaded woman seen in here on the night that Gary Jones was killed.'

She lifted the picture up to study it, so Rayan could no longer see her face. 'Why?'

'Because we think this is the killer.'

'Wow,' she said finally, placing it down on table. 'Even though she didn't come inside?'

'The CCTV captured the expression on Gary Jones's face when he saw her, suggesting that he not only knew this woman, but was afraid of her. He left a few seconds later, and that's the last time he was seen alive. So we're pretty confident that she's our killer. You'll get a press release within the hour, asking the public to come forward if they saw a redheaded woman in the vicinity of this pub on that night, or close to Mount Judd. So it'd be great if you could run a decent story on it.'

'Of course,' she said. She took a deep gulp of her beer. 'Thanks for the heads-up. In return, I can tell you that although a journalist never reveals their sources, you might want to warn your boss to be more careful about what she talks about in gin bars.'

'My boss?'

'DCS Frank. She was discussing the case in a gin bar with a colleague the other night. Someone overheard her say that Gary Jones's fiancée had been arrested, so if you want someone to blame for the Natasha Riley story, then . . .' She shrugged and picked up her beer, scratching at the paper label. 'I'm sorry about what happened to her, though. I never meant . . . I should have thought.'

'You weren't to know. To be honest, I've been blaming myself, too. I gave her a pretty hard time in the interview. Sometimes we just have to do our jobs.'

She nodded, but her head remained bowed.

Rayan watched her. She reminded him so much of his sister, right down to the black clothes and eyeliner. Even her hair was dyed. He could see from her lowered head that the roots were growing back. They were surprisingly light—in fact, he thought, leaning closer, in this light, they looked ginger.

CHAPTER FORTY-NINE

***

Kat's eyes scanned the photo that Lock insisted on showing, landing on a darker, taller and slightly stocky lad in a rugby shirt wearing a set of Rudolph antlers with a flashing red nose on his head. 'Marcus Ridgeway?'

'Yes. But it was this I wanted to draw your attention to.' Lock highlighted another face at the edge of the group: a small, red-haired girl in a green elf hat, grinning so hard that her cheeks bunched up like apples. Her hair was long, straight and flecked with snow.

Kat sighed. 'Dr Edwards has just confirmed that the hair we saw on the CCTV was almost certainly a wig. So thanks for finding a redhead that they both knew, but it's no longer relevant.'

'I don't want you to look at her hair colour,' said Lock. 'I want you to look at her face.'

Kat's bladder was now uncomfortably full. She glanced at the girl. 'Fine, I've looked. *Now* can I go to the toilet, please?'

'I have no idea how you humans survive with such poor powers of observation,' Lock said, shaking his head. With a swipe of his hand, it overlaid another face on top of the young student.

'This photo was taken over a decade later,' said Lock. 'And she has since cut and dyed her hair and lost a considerable amount of weight. But my facial recognition software relies upon bone structure and other less transient features, so I can confirm that there is a greater than ninety-nine per cent chance of this being an accurate match.'

'Oh my God,' said Kat as she stared at the older face layered on top of the younger. How could she have been so blind?

CHAPTER FIFTY

Silk Mill pub, Nuneaton,
8.47pm

Ellie looked up at DI Hassan, who was staring at her hair. 'What?'

'Nothing. Just thinking. Do you know of any redheads who might fit this description?'

'Nope.'

Rayan frowned. She hadn't even paused to think. And the more he looked at her roots and her pale skin flecked with freckles, the more he was convinced that *she* was a redhead herself. But why wouldn't she mention it? Why wouldn't she just laugh and say, '*Actually, there's me. I've got ginger hair and I even match the height, weight and age of your profile. What a coincidence!*'

Rayan shivered. He didn't believe in coincidences. And now he thought about it, hadn't she been the first journalist on the scene at both murders, well before any public announcement had been made? And just now she'd said that the suspect hadn't entered the pub or spoken to Gary Jones—how did she know that? They hadn't released that information to anyone.

'Do you want another?' Ellie asked.

Shit. What should he do? He couldn't arrest someone just because they had ginger roots. And yet . . .

'Hang on, just let me send a quick message to check if I've got time,' he said. He pulled out his phone and tapped out a quick text to Debbie.

> Sorry I'm late but I've got a theory re who the
> killer is. It's a bit crazy so I need the boss's
> advice urgently. Is she there?

'Actually, you've still got half your bottle left,' said Ellie, picking it up and shaking it.

'Hmm? Oh, yes. That's fine. I'm driving anyway. What are you up to tonight?'

'I was just going to go home. I've got a bike, but it's so cold tonight, could I be cheeky and ask for a lift?'

'Of course,' he said. It was the perfect solution, as Ellie would be in his car, and depending on what DCS Frank said, he could always drive straight to the station if required.

'Great. Let's finish these off, then,' she said, lifting her bottle to her lips.

Rayan mirrored her, trying hard to act casual, like he wasn't sitting down with a murder suspect. Half of his brain told him it was ridiculous—look at her, she didn't have the strength to squash a spider—but the other half, the flashing, siren-wailing, *oh-shit* half, was telling him that something was very, very wrong and that he shouldn't let Ellie Baxter out of his sight.

He drained his bottle and rose to his feet. 'Come on, let's get you home.'

CHAPTER FIFTY-ONE

Leek Wootton HQ, Major Incident Room,
8.51pm

DS Browne stood before their latest virtual wipe-board summarising everything they knew about the suspected killer, Ellie Baxter. Shock and disbelief had pulsated through the room when Lock revealed that the red-haired student in the photo was the journalist ten years ago. Then, one by one, they had all nodded, not just noticing the facial similarities, but recalling the way Ellie Baxter had been the first on the scene at each murder, the intense interest she had shown in both cases, but most damningly, that never once had she indicated that she had known either victim from university. Any remaining doubts Debbie might have had receded with each bullet point they added to the virtual board:

Ellie Baxter

29 years old, red-haired female (hair now dyed black and cut short—prob wears wig to murder)

Matriculated at B'ham uni same year as GJ & MR

Attended same xmas party as both victims—photo

Never graduated—left the first year?

Began working as an apprentice at NP 2 years later

Court reporter for 3 years, crime reporter for 1

Shown very close interest in both cases

First reporter/external person at SOC in both cases before public announcement

Lives in Nuneaton

Debbie placed her hands on her hips, gently rotating them while she studied the board, as her back was sore from sitting down too long. 'Shall we bring her in?'

Kat scrunched up her face. 'The demographics match, but what's her motive?' She turned to the photo of the happy young teenager in an elf hat with her fellow freshers. 'Why would a young woman like Ellie Baxter kill and mutilate two men? If she did, then something must have happened to her. Something awful enough to make her drop out of uni. Something that she's never been able to forgive or forget.'

Debbie nodded, noting the confident way that both Marcus Ridgeway and Gary Jones seemed to take up all the space in the photo, their arms draped over two other girls, with Ellie just on the edge.

'What about Rayan, any news from him?' Kat asked her. 'If we have a confirmed sighting of a redhead, we could do a line-up and include Ellie Baxter—see how she reacts.'

Debbie went to check her phone where it was charging in the corner, cursing as she saw several missed texts from him. 'Oh no, he thinks we're at the Christmas party.'

'What? Didn't you tell him it was off?'

Debbie almost replied, 'No, did you?' but managed to bite back the retort. It had been such a manic day, she'd hardly had a break, and her lower back was killing her, and with everything that was going on, she had forgotten to tell Rayan that their Christmas party was cancelled. 'I'll ring him now,' she said, putting her phone to her ear. Rayan's phone rang out without going to voicemail. Odd. She hoped he hadn't gone to The Cape of Good Hope, expecting them all to be there. Feeling guiltier by the minute, she rang the pub and explained to the barmaid that she was from the office party that had cancelled at short notice. 'I know, I'm sorry, and of course you can keep the deposit. But can I just check if my colleague has turned up? We didn't get the chance to tell him. His name is DI Hassan, he's young, Asian, tall and skinny. No? Are you sure? Okay, thanks very much.'

Debbie put the phone down, frowning. Where could he be? A wave of nausea washed over her. Urgh. She wished she hadn't eaten that pizza—all those greasy carbs and cheese. She took a sip of water, scrolled back through her messages, reading them properly this time. At 8.03pm, Rayan had sent a message telling her that he was just going into the Silk Mill pub and to save him some turkey. Then, just ten minutes ago, he'd sent another cryptic message saying he thought he knew who the murderer might be, and that he urgently needed to speak to the boss.

That was the last message.

Debbie rang him again. No answer—again.

Now she really did feel sick. Trying not to panic—he was probably just driving—she rang the pub. Eventually, a bored-sounding man answered the phone, with a Christmas album blaring in the background. Debbie explained who she was and asked whether her colleague was still there.

'The Asian bloke? Yeah, he was here a few minutes ago, but he just left with that journalist.'

Debbie closed her eyes. 'Who?'

'I don't know. Ellie something.'

'Ellie Baxter?'

The entire room looked up as she repeated the suspect's name.

'That's the one,' said the barman. 'I wouldn't have thought he was her type, but they looked thick as thieves when they left here together.'

CHAPTER FIFTY-TWO

He stumbles a bit on the steps as we leave the pub together, but then a blast of icy air seems to revive him. He shakes his head, laughs. 'Turning into a lightweight,' DI Hassan says.

I smile, but my mind is racing. I hadn't planned this. What if he collapses here in the street? We need to get to his car, fast. 'Where are you parked?' I ask from behind, using his height to hide my face from the CCTV camera opposite.

He gestures towards a side street, and I thank the gods that it isn't in a public car park with cameras and attendants. We head towards it, or at least try to—he keeps weaving and bumping into me. This is a complete disaster. But what was I supposed to do? I saw the way he looked at my hair. At me.

It makes me sick to my soul to know I've been seen. I have to get him to the car.

We turn down the side street, and he raises a hand to his forehead. 'I feel really . . .' he begins. 'I need to . . . the profes-shor . . . the prof . . .'

'Just get in the car,' I insist. 'Do you have the keys?'

DI Hassan nods and pulls them out of his pocket. He stares, as if not quite sure what to do with them. For a minute, neither am I. He's a police officer, for God's sake. A detective inspector, no less.

Suddenly he tilts his head back to face the sky. 'Snow,' he says, with the wonder of a child.

I follow his gaze, and there it is: snow upon snow, falling from the sky like frozen feathers. I turn my face towards it, em-

bracing the cold flakes of memory that float into my brain, reminding me of what was done and what I must now do.

I take the key from his hand and unlock the door with a single, sharp beep.

He allows me to steer him inside, even though I put him into
the passenger seat. He stares at me as I climb into the driver's
seat beside him.

He tries to speak, then finds that he can't.

But I can see from his terrified eyes that he knows exactly
who I am.

I feel a rush of emotion so pure that my eyes prick with
tears. 'Now you understand, don't you?' I say to the paralysed
man beside me. 'Now at last you know what it is to be afraid.'

CHAPTER FIFTY-THREE

'Just because DI Hassan isn't answering his phone, it doesn't mean that he is missing,' said Lock. 'It is not unusual for young men to meet women of a similar age in public houses and to leave in their company. She has no motive to harm him and statistically it is far more probable that they are engaged in a romantic liaison. There is no need to panic.'

'His voicemail and location signal are switched off, his parents haven't seen or heard from him, he's not at the office party and the last time he was seen, he was with a suspected serial killer, so we absolutely *do* need to fucking panic,' said Kat. Fear would paralyse her; anger helped her focus and get shit done. And right now, there was a lot of shit that needed to get done.

'Lock, find out if there's a car registered in Ellie Baxter's name, and check all the ANPRs for that and Rayan's car. Debbie, put a special alert out for every patrol to look out for both vehicles, but don't say why.'

'Shall I arrange a public appeal?' asked KFC.

Kat dragged a hand through her hair. What would happen if McLeish found out she was still working the case and, even worse, had potentially lost an officer? 'Not yet,' she said. 'We don't have enough evidence to justify the circus that would kick off. And as Lock said, there's still a *very* slim chance that he's just gone back to Ellie's place.'

'There's no way he'd do that,' said Debbie. 'He's been looking forward to tonight for weeks, it was his chance to . . .' She caught Professor Okonedo's eye and blushed. 'I just know he wouldn't be interested in anyone else, especially not tonight.'

'I have searched the DVLA database,' said Lock, 'and Ellie Baxter has a licence, but does not possess a car.'

'So where is he?' asked Professor Okonedo, speaking slightly faster than usual. 'Could they have gone somewhere in *his* car, maybe?'

'I've checked the ANPR cameras,' said Lock, 'and there is no sign of his car, either.'

'Shit.'

Everyone turned. The young professor *never* swore.

Kat walked towards the window, staring through her own reflection out into the dark, watching the thick white snowflakes silently fall. She shivered. These days, it seemed like every time it snowed, she was called out to a dead body.

She turned back to face her team, nose tingling. 'Lock, we missed something on the virtual boards about the MO. Both murders took place on a night when it snowed.' She hurried towards the photographic image of Ellie, Gary and Marcus when they were students. 'Snow,' she said, pointing to the ground. 'Maybe snow is a trigger for Ellie.'

'Why?' asked Debbie.

'I don't know. But it's snowing now, so forget what I said about not doing a public announcement. My risk assessment has just changed. Karen, I want you to prepare an appeal for anyone who has seen Ellie Baxter to contact us urgently. But don't release it until I say so. Debbie and Lock, you come with me. We're going to Ellie Baxter's home. I just pray to God that we find her there.'

CHAPTER FIFTY-FOUR

Kat parked her car and looked up at the modest three-bedroom semi-detached house, shrouded in darkness. The rest of the street had Christmas lights twinkling away in their windows and garden hedges, but the only light in the Baxters' home came from a dimly lit porch, littered with decaying leaves.

'If it turns out that Rayan is in there with Ellie,' said Kat, 'then I will give him the biggest bollocking of his life.'

'Me, too,' said Debbie. Although both women knew that this would only happen after a massive, thank-God-you're-okay hug.

They walked up the small garden path, dotted with plant pots and a couple of battered wheelie bins. Kat knocked on the door in a way that couldn't be ignored.

After the usual shocked silence (*who calls at this time of night?*), the hall light clicked on, the door chain rattled and a middle-aged man cautiously opened the door.

'Mr Baxter?' said Kat. 'I'm DCS Frank, from Warwickshire Police.' She held up her badge. 'Sorry to trouble you at this time of night, but we really need to talk to your daughter.'

'Who is it, Bob?' asked a woman behind him.

'It's the police. They want to talk to Ellie.'

'Ellie? She isn't here.' She poked her head out from behind her husband, clutching the neck of her dressing gown. 'What do they want?'

'How do I know?' He turned back to Kat. 'What do you want?'

'Do you mind if we come in?'

'Er . . .' Mr Baxter looked to his wife for the answer.

'All right, but take your shoes off. We only bought this carpet two years ago.' She tried to smooth her hair, which Kat noted was a pale, faded ginger colour.

Kat and Debbie dutifully slipped their shoes off—Lock had no need to—and followed Mr and Mrs Baxter into the living room. Mr Baxter picked up the remote and turned the volume down.

'This is—' began Kat, gesturing towards Lock.

'Oh, we know all about AIDE Lock,' said Mr Baxter, smiling. 'Our Ellie told us all about you, and we read every article that she writes.'

'Is everything all right?' Mrs Baxter asked.

'Do you know where she is?' asked Kat.

'She's working. She's always working.'

'But we rang the newspaper office, and she wasn't there,' Debbie said gently.

'Well, our Ellie's a reporter,' Mr Baxter said proudly. 'She'll be out following some lead. She's a real newshound, that one.'

'It's really important that we find her as soon as possible, and she isn't answering her work phone. Does she have a personal number we could ring?'

'Yes,' said Mr Baxter. 'But it's personal.'

'Bob, they're the police,' said his wife. 'Don't be difficult.'

'When was the last time you heard from her?' Kat asked as she dialled the number they gave her.

'Er . . . she sent a text about teatime saying she'd be late for dinner so not to wait for her.' Mrs Baxter checked her phone. 'Yes, 7.20pm it was.'

Kat nodded, while the dialling tone rang out. 'She's not answering.'

'Is everything okay?' Mrs Baxter asked again.

'I hope so,' Kat told her. 'But I have to be honest and tell you that right now we are concerned about her whereabouts, and we urgently need to find her.'

Mr Baxter put an arm around his wife as her bottom lip wobbled. 'Not again,' she said. 'She's been so good lately. I thought she was doing okay.'

Kat studied the anxious couple. 'What do you mean, "not again"?'

'She used to be such a happy child,' she said, gesturing towards a framed photograph upon the wall, where a young girl—presumably Ellie—was about seven or eight. She had a red blaze of hair and a massive smile and wore a cosy-looking set of pyjamas with *Cheeky Monkey* emblazoned across the top.

'We never had any problems with her until she went off to Birmingham University. Something bad happened that first term—we don't know what—but when she came home for the Christmas holidays, she was in a terrible state. She wasn't eating or sleeping, and she wouldn't talk to us at all, would she, Bob? Eventually we realised she was depressed, but we didn't know how bad it was until she tried to take her own life.' Her voice shook at the memory. 'The crisis team came out, but she wouldn't talk to them, either. So there wasn't much we could do, other than be there for her. There was no way she could go back to uni in that state, so she just stayed here, lying in bed all day, begging us to just leave her alone to die. She kept self-harming, too—we had to hide all the knives, the scissors, even the pencil sharpeners, would you believe? Sometimes she'd go missing and Bob would drive around the streets of Nuneaton at night trying to find her.'

Kat looked at the father, taking in his neatly zipped fleece and corduroy trousers, the thinning but well-groomed hair and grey tweed slippers. Everything about him suggested order, stability and love. She imagined him in his car, desperately trying to find and fix his daughter, having to learn the hard way that some things just can't be fixed.

Mrs Baxter ran a hand over her eyes. 'It was a nightmare, but after a few years she seemed to come out of it.'

'It was the newspaper that saved her,' Mr Baxter said. 'She saw an advert for apprenticeships in journalism, so she went for it, and of course they saw her talent, and they really looked after her. That job's been the making of her, hasn't it, Maureen?'

'Do you have any idea what happened at university to make her so ill?' asked Kat.

Mr and Mrs Baxter looked at each other. 'She never told us,' her mum said. 'But we had our theories. I asked her once if someone had attacked her, and she said no, well, screamed it, really. She grew completely hysterical. It was terrifying. She took days to get over it, so I never asked again.'

'How long ago did it happen?'

'When she was nineteen. Ten years ago this Christmas.'

'But like Maureen said,' the dad added, 'she's really improved recently, so we thought the therapist was helping.'

Kat asked for the name and number of the therapist, and Mr Baxter opened up his wallet, looking for his business card. 'I pay the bills,' he explained, with such a dad-like roll of the eyes that Kat's heart hurt to think that, all too soon, a few therapy bills would be the least of his problems.

Kat glanced around the room again. Something was missing, but she couldn't put her finger on what. Eventually it hit her: there was no tree or decorations. 'You don't celebrate Christmas, then?'

Mr Baxter's face fell. 'Not anymore. Ellie used to love Christmas. We all did. But when she came back from uni, just the sight of any decorations seemed to trigger her. So now we don't put any up. It's safer that way.' He handed her the therapist's card.

'Do you think she's suicidal again? I was hoping all that was behind us.'

'I . . . I think that there's a real risk that Ellie might be a danger to herself or others. The tenth anniversary of whatever happened to her may have . . . overwhelmed her,' Kat said as diplomatically as she could. If she told these poor people that their beloved daughter was a suspected serial killer, she would be met with an emotional denial, and her priority now was to secure their rapid cooperation so that they could help her find their daughter and Rayan. She asked if Ellie had access to a car.

'I let her take my van some nights if she's working late,' Mr Baxter said. 'As long as it's back on the drive by seven the next morning with a full tank, I don't mind. I work in construction—Baxter's Fences—so I start early. She's out somewhere in it now.'

Kat and Debbie exchanged glances. Fencing. That would explain how Ellie was able to access the materials to build the crosses. 'Would you mind if I looked in her bedroom?' Kat asked. 'That might give us some ideas as to where she might be.'

Like most parents, Mr and Mrs Baxter looked a bit concerned at her request—it felt like such an intrusion, as she well knew—but of course they said yes. Mrs Baxter led the way up the short flight of stairs, apologising for the non-existent mess.

Ellie's bedroom was a typical second bedroom: larger than a box room but smaller than a double. But it wasn't the size that drew Kat's attention, it was the sheer number of cuddly toys that lined the shelves and the single bed, which beneath all the teddy bears was covered in a pink duvet patterned with baby kittens.

Lock stood in the centre of the room, taking in their surroundings. 'Is this typical furnishing for a 29-year-old woman?'

'No, Lock, it isn't. But it's not unusual for people who've experienced trauma to revert to their childhood as a place of safety.' She sat down on the bed with a heavy sigh and looked up at the single poster on the wall opposite. In contrast to the pile of toys she sat among, this was an old movie poster for a film about Boudica, *Warrior Queen*, depicting a wild-looking, red-haired woman, covered in tattoos, mud and blood, as she drove her chariot forward. No, Kat corrected herself. The warrior queen didn't look 'wild'—that was the sort of thing some misogynist might say—she looked angry, determined and strong.

'What trauma did Ellie Baxter experience?' Lock asked.

'I don't know for sure, but I think I can guess.' Kat sighed and rose to her feet. 'Right, we're not here to gather evidence to prove that Ellie is the killer. Our priority now is to work out where she is, and what she's done with Rayan. We can come back with a warrant once we've found them.'

'What kind of thing are we looking for?' asked Debbie.

'Anything that gives us a clue to her location,' Kat said, picking up a photograph of Ellie with her dad from the computer desk. 'Pictures of a favourite place, a diary she might have written her thoughts in, anything, really. Lock, I need you to hack into Ellie's computer, check her search history, her calendar, anything to give us a clue about where she might have taken Rayan.'

'But without a warrant or consent, that is illegal.'

'I'm aware of that, but if Ellie is the killer and she follows the same MO, then in a couple of hours' time, Rayan could be dead.'

Lock frowned. 'Are you asking me to break the law because your colleague's life is at risk?'

'Yes. So hurry up.'

'I am programmed not to break the law.'

'Professor Okonedo advised you to trust my judgement.'

'That was for occasions when I was experiencing doubt. But in this case, the law and my own protocols are really quite clear.'

God, she could scream. 'Lock, I am your boss, and I am *ordering* you to hack into Ellie Baxter's computer so that we can achieve the fundamental objective for this case, which is to apprehend the killer.'

They stared at each other.

'*Please.*'

Lock tilted his head. 'In order to ensure that my prime objective is achieved, and in response to your explicit instruction, I will break the law and my own protocols.'

CHAPTER FIFTY-FIVE

———

Ellie Baxter's search history made for depressing reading: *How long does it take to die of hypothermia? Do crows really eat eyes? How does Rohypnol work?* While there was more than enough to secure an arrest and possibly a conviction, it worried Kat just how easy it was to find. Unlike most murderers, Ellie had made no attempt to delete or hide her searches: they were all there, pinned to her favourites bar. The words of Tracy Taylor looped back in her mind: *You should be looking for someone who has nothing left to lose.*

She asked Lock to pull up any searches that involved geographical locations, and the screen filled with a long list of hills Ellie had considered in the Nuneaton area before she settled on Mount Judd, and a long list of potential fields and farms before she clearly picked Fillongley. Then there was another, more recent, list of woods, forests and country parks.

Kat leaned over the desk, studying the names of the places. 'This must be her shortlist, but how do we know which one she chose?'

'We should identify the criteria Ellie is using to select the location for each murder,' said Lock.

Kat nodded for him to go on.

'Both Mount Judd and the field in Fillongley were isolated places within or close to the geographical district of Nuneaton and Bedworth, where Ellie could be confident that she wouldn't be disturbed at night but which were also relatively accessible from nearby roads. Both locations required a short walk to them and offered a certain element of staging to ensure that their crime was visible: the flat surface of the peak of Mount Judd, the open field with the cross at the centre.'

'And they were both places where it would have been obvious to the victim that it didn't matter how loud someone screamed, no one would hear them,' said Kat. 'I think that's a really important factor to her.'

She looked again at the list on Ellie's computer of possible locations for her third murder:

- Hartshill Hayes Country Park
- Weddington Walk
- Mancetter Parish Walk

'Hartshill Hayes is probably the most famous, and there's acres and acres of woodland there, but it's a properly managed country park. Would she be able to get in at night?'

'It is only open 9am to 4pm during the winter months,' said Lock.

'Hmm, I'm sure someone like Ellie could find a way in, but would she risk being found by a park warden? And Weddington Walk—I think that's too popular—so many people walk their dogs up there, I think there'd be a risk that someone would see or hear something. And a parish walk doesn't sound remote enough.' Kat checked the time: 10.35pm. Three choices. What if she picked the wrong one? They didn't have time for mistakes. She looked around the room, almost paralysed by the decision she had to make and the consequences of being wrong. Her eye was again caught by the poster of the Warrior Queen. 'Do any of those locations have a connection with Boudica?' she asked. She had a vague memory of an important battle involving the famous leader of the Iceni tribe somewhere in the Nuneaton area.

'Do you really think she'd pick a location based upon a film that she likes?' Debbie asked.

'No,' said Kat, standing before the poster. 'I think Boudica is on her wall because she waged a war on her abusers. Boudica was the queen of a Celtic tribe, and when the Romans attacked their settlement, they flogged her and raped her two daughters. Queen Boudica and her tribe then took revenge by attacking London and other cities, killing up to 80,000 Romans. She very nearly achieved her objective of forcing them to leave Britain.'

'It has recently been proposed that a field near the village of Mancetter was the site of the last stand between Boudica and the Romans,' said Lock.

'Mancetter? That's on her list,' said Kat, pointing at Mancetter Parish Walk.

'I have just read *Tacitus* and 12,453 historical accounts and analyses,' said Lock. 'According to both primary and secondary sources, Boudica frequently tortured and killed her victims by crucifying them as a public warning to others.'

'Oh my God,' said Debbie. 'Is that why she crucified Gary Jones and Marcus Ridgeway—as a warning to other men?'

Kat fought back an image of Rayan tied to a wooden cross. 'Right, we need to get there *now*. Lock, show me a map of Mancetter Parish Walk.'

A virtual map appeared in the centre of the small bedroom.

'According to the guide, it is a challenging walk encompassing the rural nature of North Warwickshire,' explained Lock, 'with panoramic views across the Anker Valley and interesting geological features. The entire circular walk covers twenty-five miles, and part of it crosses Hartshill Hayes Country Park, which is 137 acres with many routes in and out. The specific location of Boudica's final battle is not marked, so we will need reinforcements to cover it all.'

Kat stood before the map, her eyes roaming over the canal, quarries, woods and hills. 'I'll ring McLeish. It's pitch-black out there, so we're going to need helicopters with heat-seeking equipment to help us find them in time. What's the terrain like?'

'Steep and challenging, according to the North Arden Heritage Trail leaflet. The temperature is currently minus one degrees, and the snow will decrease your speed by thirty-two per cent.'

Kat glanced at her heavily pregnant DS, and then at the dark, snowy night through Ellie's bedroom window.

'Don't,' said Debbie, before Kat could speak. 'I saw what Ellie Baxter did to Gary Jones and Marcus Ridgeway, and there is no way I am leaving Rayan out there with her. Don't even *think* about asking me to go home.'

Kat saw the determination in her face. 'Okay. I won't. But only if you promise to tell me if it gets too much for you. There's no point going to all this trouble to rescue one team member if it just puts another at risk.'

They hurried down the stairs, where they were met by an anxious-looking Mr and Mrs Baxter.

'Did you find any clues?' Mr Baxter asked.

'Bob, it's not a TV show, for heaven's sake.'

'It was very helpful, thank you,' said Kat, heading towards the door.

'If—when you find her, could you give her a message from us?' asked the dad, his face a ruin of worry.

'Of course.'

'Just tell her that . . . just tell her we love her. That it doesn't matter what's happened or what she's done, we'll always, always love her, and . . . we just want her to come home.'

Kat nodded, not trusting herself to speak. She made her way down the hall and out into the night.

CHAPTER FIFTY-SIX

Kat parked near the Coventry Canal, at the start of the Mancetter Parish Walk. Her windscreen wipers were still on, fighting a losing battle against the relentless fall of snow. In the fleeting moments of clarity that they offered (*swish-wipe*), Kat peered out into the darkness beyond the narrow reach of the headlamps. This was the kind of walk that should be done on a summer's day with a picnic or pub lunch at the end, yet here they were on a freezing winter night, in the depths of a snowstorm in pursuit of a serial killer.

'Are you sure you're okay to do this?' she asked, turning towards Debbie.

'I'm fine. I wish I had a warmer coat, but other than that, I'm good, thanks.'

Kat opened the car door, wincing at the blast of cold snow that attacked her face. Jesus. She grabbed a couple of torches from the boot and handed one to Debbie. McLeish had (after a considerable amount of swearing) agreed to dispatch several teams to help with the search, but she had no idea how long they'd be in this weather. Pulling her hood up, she bowed her head against the wind and asked Lock to lead the way.

Debbie and Kat followed the hologram over a canal bridge, breaking the silence with the rustle of their waterproofs and the soft crunch of boots upon virgin snow. As they turned left to follow a waymarked path up towards Quarry Farm, their breathing became more laboured. This was probably an easy, pleasant trek in the summer, thought Kat, but it was bloody hard going in winter. The bottom of her trousers grew heavy and wet, and the cold was already seeping through the soles of her shoes.

They passed through two more gates, following the snow-draped hedge that marked the edge of a field and a path that led up an increasingly steep hill. Kat began to pant, releasing great puffs of breath into the black, icy air. Ordinarily, she'd have pushed through it, but Debbie was beginning to struggle. Reluctantly, she reduced her pace. At last, they reached the top of the hill, where according to the cheery walking guide, they should be able to enjoy panoramic views of Warwickshire, Leicestershire and Derbyshire. But at this hour, all they could see was the outline of ghost-white hills in the vast expanse of night.

Debbie and Kat paused to catch their breath, while Lock displayed a 3D map against the backdrop of snow so they could track their route to the quarry. She swore when she realised what all the lines and dots meant and just how much more terrain they had to cover. Where the *fuck* were McLeish and the search teams, not to mention the bloody helicopters? Kat dialled his number.

'Kat?' he barked, from what sounded like his car. 'We're about twenty minutes away, so just hang on.'

Kat told him that they'd already made a start. She could tell he didn't like it, but she knew he wouldn't blame her. One of their own was out there. Despite this, he'd been unable to secure a helicopter. 'The amount of snowfall makes it too dangerous, apparently. Some crap about regulations and being able to see less than half a mile. They said they might be able to send one in about an hour when the snowstorm is forecast to die down a bit.'

'We don't have an hour,' Kat shouted over the wind.

'That's why I told them that if they don't scramble a helicopter now, then they'll be out of a job by the time the snowstorm dies down. I've escalated it to the minister, just to make sure. They should be there soon, so Kat? Don't take any risks.'

Kat ended the call. *Why* did it have to snow on top of everything else? She dialled the Incident Room, where Professor Okonedo, Judith and KFC had agreed to stay and provide whatever support they could.

'Have you found him?' the professor asked as soon as she picked up.

'Not yet,' Kat said, stressing the 'yet', before updating the team on the problem with reinforcements and the helicopter.

'Do you have the AISP?' the professor asked, referring to the AI Support Pack she'd given Kat before she'd left.

'Yes, I'm carrying it now.'

'Inside you'll find a small thermal-imaging drone. In this snowstorm, it probably won't stay in the air for very long, but it might allow Lock to access enough data to focus your search. Just remove it from your bag, place it on the ground and ask Lock to activate it.'

Kat shrugged the small rucksack off her back, unzipped it and located something that looked like a small, light tripod, no bigger than her forearm. She placed it on the snow beneath them and asked Lock to use it to scan the surrounding area for body heat.

Lock nodded and the drone rose a few inches into the air, where it hovered, rising higher and higher, until it was swallowed up by the night. They waited, the only sound the roaring wind, eyes stung by snow, until after about five minutes Lock announced they had enough data to carry out an analysis of the surrounding area.

Against the clean, white snow before them, Lock projected a huge 3D map of the terrain with neon green lines to show the contours of elevation. Within the web of green lines appeared a rash of coloured blobs.

'Talk us through your analysis,' said Professor Okonedo on the speaker phone, as she and the wider team studied the same images back in the MIR.

'Thermal imagers don't display real images of objects,' explained Lock. 'What we are looking at here are thermograms—the object's information based upon its temperature. This is represented by different colours, with warmer objects in brighter colours, such as yellow, orange and red, with black being the coldest.'

Kat scanned the yellow, orange and red blobs before them. 'How do we know which one is Rayan?'

'After excluding anything less than four feet high on the basis that they are probably animals, I have detected heat that is consistent with a human being here, near the clearing of the next hill at the junction with a path that leads into Hartshill Hayes Country Park car park,' said Lock, pointing at a deep yellow blob on the map.

They all stared at the small patch of colour.

'Is he alive?' Kat asked, bracing herself for the answer.

'There is heat, so either the person is alive or recently deceased. I cannot determine their gender, but I can tell you that they are not moving.'

'Is there anyone else there?' asked Debbie.

'No. The thermal imaging indicates there is just one person.'

'Oh God,' said the professor on the phone.

No one spoke, but they all knew what she meant. They'd been hoping to find Ellie before she hurt Rayan. If there was only one person out there, did that mean they were too late?

Kat swore. There was only one way to find out. 'You okay to carry on to the next hill, Debbie?'

Although she nodded, Kat thought there was a slight hesitation this time. But she couldn't keep asking her if she was okay, so she ploughed on through the snow, the cold and the unforgiving wind, hoping with all her heart that the bright yellow blob they were striving towards was a living and breathing Rayan.

CHAPTER FIFTY-SEVEN

'There, up ahead,' said Lock. 'I detect a car.'

Kat curved her left arm around her face, trying to shield her eyes from the blizzard while holding her torch with her right hand. There was something there, but between the dark and blur of snowflakes, she couldn't quite tell what. She tried to run towards it, but the snow made her stagger and slip. She pushed on, until through the narrow beam of torchlight, she finally recognised Rayan's car.

Oh Jesus. Please, please, let him be okay.

Kat's heart was thudding so hard that she felt sick by the time she finally reached the car. She could hear Judith Edwards's voice on the speaker phone warning her not to approach the vehicle, and certainly not to open the door until back-up arrived. But Rayan could be in there—not just a member of her team: someone's son, someone's brother. Ignoring their concerns, Kat raised her arm, wiped it firmly against the car window and peered through the dark arc of glass.

The passenger seat had been lowered: there was a body lying upon it.

She could see that the body was Rayan.

What she couldn't see was whether he was dead or alive.

Kat wrenched open the back-seat door with a sob. 'Rayan?'

He looked like he was sleeping, with his long dark eyelashes curled against his cheeks, but despite the blast of cold air from the open door, Rayan didn't move.

'Rayan!' she shouted again.

Still no movement.

'Is he okay?' asked Professor Okonedo, her voice unusually high. 'Please, tell me what's happening.'

Kat pulled off her gloves and reached for his neck. At first, her fingers were too cold to feel anything. But was that a pulse? She turned to Lock, just behind her. 'Quick, can you read his vital signs?'

'Yes, but you told me not to do so without a person's consent.'

'Oh, for fuck's sake, this is a matter of life and death. Just *do* it.'

Lock hesitated, but when Professor Okonedo rephrased it as an order, he said, 'DI Hassan is alive, but his pulse and respiratory rate are very low, consistent with someone who has been heavily sedated. I presume with Rohypnol.'

Debbie arrived just in time to hear Lock's assessment, and she collapsed onto the bonnet of the car with what Kat presumed was relief.

'Thank God,' Kat said, conveniently ignoring the fact that she no longer believed in God.

'Could you check his airway, DCS Frank?' said Lock. 'According to the literature, it is all about ABC—airways, breathing and circulation—so you need to look in his mouth and make sure his airway is clear. I will monitor his respiration rate.'

After confirming his airway was clear, Kat took in a deep and painfully cold breath of fresh air and rang 999 to update the paramedics, explaining that they had a drugged police officer in need of urgent assistance near the car park for Hartshill Hayes Country Park. The emergency call handlers assured her they would do their best to send someone soon but warned her that several ambulances were already trapped in the snow, and that as they were experiencing a higher volume of calls due to trips and falls, it could be 'a while'.

Kat ended the call with a stab of her finger. She knew it wasn't their fault, but Jesus. What was she supposed to do now? She tried talking to him again, but he was out for the count. *Damn it*. She had so many questions. Where was Ellie? Had she given up and gone home?

All they could do now was sit in the car with the heating on while they waited for the ambulance to arrive. But as Kat walked round the car and reached for the door to the driver's seat, Lock suddenly asked her to stop.

'Wait,' he said, pointing to the torch-lit ground. 'Footprints.'

Kat froze. There in the snow by the door were two sets of footprints *that were not their own*. They led away from the car, before continuing along a path to the right alongside a thick, wooded area.

Kat frowned, struggling to make sense of what she was seeing. Had Rayan left the car with Ellie at some point? No, he couldn't have, because the footprints were only going one way, so how could he have got back inside the car?

Lock took some photographs and projected a more detailed breakdown before her on the snow, complete with measurements and 3D models. 'The smaller footprints are consistent with the height and weight of Ellie Baxter,' Lock explained. 'But the larger ones beside her are smaller and broader than Rayan's feet and are consistent with those of a male wearing size-ten trainers.'

'So Ellie has somebody else with her?' She said the words, but her brain felt numb and slow, unable to piece together what she was seeing.

'Yes, but it is the marking just behind the male's footprints I would draw your attention to.'

Lock enlarged the image, highlighting a thick solid line just behind the male's footprints that seemed to follow him as he moved. 'This marking is consistent with that of a wooden stake, or the vertical part of a cross. This suggests that Ellie Baxter has a third victim, and that they were forced to carry the cross that their own body will soon be crucified upon.'

CHAPTER FIFTY-EIGHT

———

Kat swore. She'd been so focused on saving Rayan, she hadn't even considered the possibility that Ellie's third victim would be somebody else. 'Who the hell can it be?'

'As the other two victims were both in the photograph of the student party, I can only surmise that it is another male belonging to that group.'

Of course. Kat asked Lock to project the photograph that included the three men and three women at the student Christmas party. The familiar picture appeared before them, and without being asked, Lock enlarged the image of the third man. He was on the opposite end of the photograph to Ellie and, like her, seemed a bit on the edge of the group. Even his Santa hat looked like it was about to fall off. Physically, he looked like a thousand other students: tall and skinny, with medium-length brown hair and shy, dark eyes.

'Can you use your facial recognition software to find out who he is?' asked Kat. She knew it didn't always work—there were lots of people (like her) who never used Facebook and did their best to avoid their pictures appearing online. She had to hope that this rather quiet-looking student had either developed a huge ego or a career that required him to have an online presence.

'I have located him,' said Lock, projecting another image next to the photograph. 'There is a 97.5 per cent match with Peter Wright, a 29-year-old male, married to Roger Baker and parent to an adopted child. He lives in Coventry, where he works as an adult psychotherapist specialising in trauma, grief and self-harm.'

Kat stared at the now considerably plumper man who'd tried to give his rather average face some character with a goatee beard and glasses. *Peter Wright.* Where had she heard that name before? She reached into her coat pocket and pulled out the card that Mr Baxter had given her earlier. 'This is *Ellie's* therapist. What the . . . ?'

Behind her, Debbie cried out.

'I know,' Kat acknowledged, without turning round. 'You couldn't make this shit up.' She looked at her mobile: 12.45am. Ellie could be killing Peter Wright this very minute. They didn't have time to wait for McLeish and reinforcements, but they couldn't just leave Rayan alone in the snowstorm. There was no knowing how heavily sedated he was. He could choke on his own vomit, hypothermia was still a real risk and the ambulance would need some help to find him among these hills and trees. They had to split up.

Kat turned back to face Debbie. 'We need to find Ellie before she kills again, but we can't leave Rayan alone, so I'm afraid you'll have to stay here with him.' She held up a warning hand, signalling that she didn't have time for arguments. But none were forthcoming.

'I have to stay here anyway,' said Debbie, pointing her torch at a darker patch in the snow below. 'My waters have broken.'

CHAPTER FIFTY-NINE

———

'Your *waters* have broken?' Kat echoed. 'Are you *sure*?'

'Yes,' said Debbie, her eyes filling with tears. 'But I can't have the baby now. It's not due until January 20th. Maybe if I just sit down for a bit, it'll—' She cried out, as a contraction swept through her.

'It's okay,' Kat lied. 'Lean over the car and breathe through it like they taught you. That's it. Well done.' She rubbed her back, not speaking until the pain subsided.

'Oh God, that was the worst one ever,' Debbie said, shakily.

'How long have you been having contractions for?'

'I don't know. I thought they were just Braxton Hicks, but they've been getting stronger and stronger all day.'

'How close are they together?'

Debbie swallowed, before almost whispering, 'About three minutes?'

Shit. With an effort, Kat held her tongue. This was not the time to ask, *Why the fuck didn't you mention you were in fucking labour before we set off in a fucking blizzard?*

'DCS Frank,' said Lock. 'It's 12.59am. We must find Ellie before she kills again.'

'I know that, Lock, but I can't leave Debbie alone like this.'

'But you must.'

'I told you, *I can't.* Her waters have broken, and her contractions are only three minutes apart, which means her baby—her *premature* baby—could come at any time.' She gestured at the blizzard of snow about them. 'Have you any idea what the chances of a prem baby surviving in this would be?'

Lock frowned. 'As the baby is five weeks early and the temperature is now minus three degrees, and the breaking of the amniotic sac increases the risk of infection, I would estimate that in the absence of any medical intervention, approximately—'

'*Stop!*' Kat hissed, looking pointedly at Debbie. But Debbie was rocking under the weight of another contraction. Fuck's sake, where *was* that ambulance? She dialled 999 again, quickly explaining to the call handler that in addition to a sedated police officer, she now also had a woman about to give birth prematurely in the snow, and a serial killer with a potential victim in their power, and that no, she wasn't winding him up. 'Just tell me how long they'll be.'

'We haven't been able to dispatch an ambulance to you yet, but I'll update your call as a priority, and hopefully someone should be with you within the hour. But we really are experiencing an unprecedented volume of—' Kat practically threw the phone down. This was a nightmare. An actual. Fucking. Nightmare.

Debbie let out a cry on the verge of a full-blown scream. Kat reminded her to breathe, to try not to push just yet, telling her that the ambulance was on its way. And all the time she was talking, Kat was racking her brains for somewhere safe and warm to take the poor woman. Rayan was still knocked out on the reclining passenger seat, restricting access to the back seat, which only left the driving seat, with the bloody steering wheel in the way. How would Kat fit in to help her? She opened the boot, praying for some blankets or sheets. But there was nothing. Jesus, what would they wrap the baby in? How would they keep it safe and warm?

'DCS Frank,' said Lock. 'I repeat, we really must go.'

'And *I* repeat, I cannot leave Debbie to give birth alone in the snow.'

'But our objective is to apprehend the killer before they kill

324 · JO CALLAGHAN

again. DS Browne and her baby are not included in our objectives.'

Kat looked up at AIDE Lock, its image shimmering slightly in the snow. 'Oh my God. You really mean that, don't you?'

'Yes. That is why I said it.'

Kate cursed. She had started to believe that Lock was learning to be more human, but it appeared that this was just wishful thinking. 'We don't just exist to achieve the objectives of a *case*, Lock. There are two—*three* lives at stake here—including a mother and a *baby*, for God's sake.'

'But there are two lives at stake up at the quarry, too. You keep saying the word "baby" as if somehow their life is worth more than an adult's.'

Kat took a deep breath and turned towards the quarry, where she imagined Ellie and Peter Wright must be. She couldn't let him become Ellie's third victim. The man had a child, a partner, a life. Kat was sure she could make Ellie see that, if only she could reach her in time. An image of Ellie as an 8-year-old in *Cheeky Monkey* pyjamas flashed through her mind, followed by the picture of Boudica on her wall and all that it implied. She wanted to save them all, she really, really did, but she couldn't be in two places at once. She had to make a choice.

'Judith, Professor Okonedo?' she said into the speakerphone as Debbie's screams tore the air. 'What do you advise me to do?'

CHAPTER SIXTY

Professor Okonedo stared at Dr Edwards across the boardroom table in the Major Incident Room. 'She can't leave them. DI Hassan has been heavily sedated, his central nervous system has been compromised so he could suffocate or choke on his own vomit if left unattended, and Debbie is about to have a baby!'

'But if DCS Frank stays with them,' said Judith, 'then Ellie Baxter will almost certainly take another life. The paramedics can help Debbie and Rayan, but only DCS Frank can stop the killer.'

For the second time that night, Professor Okonedo cursed. She ran a hand over her forehead, before asking Lock for an assessment of predicted ambulance response times, the location of McLeish and his helicopters and an estimate of when they might reach DCS Frank.

'I am afraid I have no trend data to allow me to make any reliable forecasts. I have nothing but the verbal claims of McLeish and the Warwickshire Ambulance Service's statement that they will be here "as soon as they can".'

'Okay, well, when do you estimate Debbie's baby will be born?'

'Based upon her contractions, I would estimate that DS Browne is fully dilated, so unless there are any further complications, I would expect her baby to be born within one hour and thirty-four minutes.'

'Well?' demanded Kat. 'Based upon your risk assessment, what shall I do?'

Professor Okonedo considered all the different options and variables, trying to find an equation that would help her balance Rayan, Debbie and her baby's life against that of Ellie and her potential next victim. 'I'm sorry,' she said eventually. 'I . . . I can't advise you what to do. We need more data.'

Judith Edwards shook their head and sighed. 'That's the difference between us scientists and the police, professor. *We* ask for more data, but meanwhile *they* have to make life-and-death decisions. And then they have to live—or die—with the consequences.'

CHAPTER SIXTY-ONE

___

Kat stared into the darkness, tinged with the spectral glow of snow. She needed to get to Ellie before the damaged young woman crucified another man. Ellie had killed, but she didn't believe she was a *killer*. The crucifixions were like an agonised cry of pain—*Look at me! Look at what you did!* If only she could get there in time, Kat would tell her that she saw; she would tell her that she knew. Most of all, she would tell her to stop.

Debbie screamed, a terrible sound of brute, raw agony.

Kat laid a hand upon her back. There was nothing she could do other than say, 'It's going to be all right, I'm here.'

And as soon as she uttered the words, Kat knew what she must do.

There *was* no choice. Not really.

Once the contraction passed, Kat turned to Lock. 'You're going to have to find and apprehend Ellie Baxter by yourself.'

'Myself? But I have no body, I cannot apprehend anyone.'

'No, you can't. But my God, you can talk. So when you find her, you need to talk to Ellie Baxter and prevent her from doing any more harm, just until reinforcements arrive. It won't be long now.'

'But without the LiDAR on your bracelet, I will be unable to see or project myself.'

'Oh, *fuck*.'

'Wait!' cried Professor Okonedo over the speaker. 'In your AI Support Pack, there should be another microdrone. It's round, black and really small—about the size of a coaster.'

'Got it,' said Kat.

'The microdrone has the same LiDAR sensors as your bracelet,' explained Professor Okonedo. 'So as long as it is in the air within a twenty-metre range of Ellie Baxter, then it should be able to provide you with all the geospatial data you need to operate as a hologram, Lock. It also contains an MEMs-based piezoelectric microphone and speakers, which will allow you to hear and speak to Ellie, as well as connect back with your host bracelet.'

Kat had already removed the microdrone from the rucksack and placed it on the snowy ground. 'Won't she be able to hear or see it flying in the air?'

'It was developed for surveillance purposes, so it's almost completely silent,' said Professor Okonedo. 'It's essentially a mobile audio support and projection system for Lock.'

'Lock,' said Dr Edwards on the speakerphone. 'Remember, it takes a long time to crucify someone if their feet are supported. If Ellie Baxter has used a stool again, then don't let her remove it—once she does, the victim will only have minutes to live before they die of asphyxiation.'

'But how can I possibly stop her?'

'Professor Okonedo said the microphone and speakers in the drone are connected to my wristband, so I can tell you what to do,' said Kat. 'I'll be with you every step of the way. But if we do lose contact, just try and put yourself in her shoes.'

Lock looked at the image of his feet. 'This makes no sense.'

'Not to you, maybe. But this is what is happening. Now go. And remember, keep Ellie Baxter talking until I get there. Nobody is allowed to die tonight. That's an order.'

CHAPTER SIXTY-TWO

———

He talks less than the others, and he hasn't yet begged. But he will. They all do in the end. First the apologies, then the begging, then the crying. That's the bit I hate the most. That's when I give them another dose. That's when I do the talking.

'Nearly there,' I say, pointing through the snow to the quarry just ahead.

Peter looks at me and nods. He's not as strong as Marcus or as fit as Gary, but he carries his cross without complaint, I'll give him that. Even though he is dragging the vertical post, too. Even though he must be freezing. When I appeared at his house, I didn't give him time to fetch his coat, I just told him to get into DI Hassan's car.

Like Gary, I didn't need to remind him who I was—he recognised me straight away with my red wig on. He didn't look surprised; in fact, I'd almost say he looked relieved, as if he'd been afraid of me finding him for so long, it was a relief when I finally did.

We carry on through the snow, leaving our footprints behind us. Soon they too will be gone, and it will be as if we never took these steps together, as if neither of us had ever existed. But I will leave behind a message that no one will forget.

At last, we reach the summit, with the quarry to our right, although all we can see is the white blur of falling snow through the pitch-black of night. It feels right, somehow. As if we are out of place, out of time.

He is panting hard, fear and exhaustion making him breathe too fast. I turn my torch upon him. His jumper is caked with snow, his trousers dark and sodden. They will freeze once he stills, so I will have to cut them off.

'What happens now?' he finally asks.

I nod towards his cross. 'You plant that in the ground.' As with the other two, I hammered in a fence post spike the night before and hid the cross nearby.

He swallows but does not protest. Gary and Marcus took more persuading—especially Marcus. Gary actually believed me when I said it would only be a mock execution, and that if he carried out this private act of repentance for me, then I wouldn't crucify him in the media. But Marcus realised he would be my second victim and so refused. I had to read him the article that would be emailed at 6am to my editor, exposing not just what he did to me and his many affairs, but the illegal contracts and tax evasion that would close his business and leave his precious family bankrupt. Everything that he had worked for and cared about would be gone, and his children would see him for the monster that he was. In the end, I let him choose his own legacy.

Peter, however, needs no such persuasion. He holds the cross with trembling hands and attempts to slide it into the hole in the planted spike. He misses.

'Again,' I say.

He tries again. Fails again. Says his hands are too cold.

'Again,' I insist.

He makes a noise that might be a sob as, finally, it slots into place.

'Now check it's nice and secure. We don't want you falling over, do we?'

Even though I carry no gun and I do not threaten him with the knives I have, Peter does exactly what I say. I have learned that a combination of their guilt, my moral authority and the fear of exposure gives me a power without equal.

The effort has exhausted him, so I give him a moment to catch his breath, before holding out the flask of drugged alcohol that he knows he must drink. He takes a sip, and another, wincing at the hot sting of rum. It won't be long now.

I place the stool at the foot of the cross and tell him to stand upon it and to put his hands through the loops of rope.

He does as he is told, searching the bleak, snowy landscape with questioning eyes. 'Why out here?'

Ironic that he, of all people, needs to ask why. 'Because you told me to.'

'Me?' He looks genuinely shocked.

'Go to the top of a high hill, you said, or to the middle of a field or forest, and let all your anger and rage out, you said.'

His eyes widen, as at last he recognises my voice.

'You're Angeline?'

I nod.

'My dad begged me for years to get a therapist—he was always sending me links to people he thought might be "a good fit". I deleted them all, but then a few months ago, your name appeared in my inbox. Your name. Can you imagine how that made me feel?'

He hangs his head.

'The irony! That I should talk about my trauma to the therapist who actually caused it!'

'I didn't—'

'You didn't what?' I snap, daring him to deny it.

He closes his eyes, unable to meet the fury in mine. I take the opportunity to tighten the tautline knot around his right wrist, securing him to the cross with a simple downward pull of the rope, before repeating the movement on his left. Once both are bound tight, and I know he cannot escape, I stand back.

'I know you weren't the one who drugged my drink—that was Marcus. And you weren't the one who raped me—that was

Gary.' I step closer, forcing him to meet my eyes. 'But you knew what they were planning to do. And yet you didn't warn me.'

He closes his eyes.

I slap him. 'Look at me. LOOK! You knew, and you didn't say a thing.'

'I didn't think they'd really do it. I thought they were just joking.'

'You thought it was FUNNY?'

'No, I just . . . I didn't know them very well. I wanted to make friends, to fit in.'

'So you threw me to the wolves?'

At last, he looks at me. 'Yes. And there's not a day goes by that I haven't regretted my cowardice. It's why I became a therapist. I had to have therapy myself to deal with—'

'Don't you DARE! Do NOT redescribe your crime as if YOU are the victim, as if YOU have experienced trauma. Fuck!' Despite the snow that falls around us, my blood is boiling.

'I didn't mean that. I just meant I've struggled to live with the guilt.'

'Well, you won't have to struggle for much longer.'

He nods, his head sinking a little lower on his chest. 'I deserve it.'

'Yes, you do.' But his words confuse me. He is supposed to beg. He is supposed to be afraid.

'Why did you come to me?' he asks.

'I wanted to know what made you dare to be a therapist.'

'But if it was just curiosity, why keep coming? We've spoken every week for over two months now.'

'Because, despite everything, you helped me.'

Oh, the ego of the therapist. He raises his head at that.

'Do you remember our first appointment, when I told you

how I'd self-harmed for years? You said something that stuck with me. You explained that some people—men, mostly—tend to deal with grief and trauma by turning their rage outwards onto the world—they get into fights, smash things up, kick off a war or two. But others—women, especially—tend to turn their anger inwards, inflicting our pain upon ourselves. You said that the mind sometimes shuts out traumatic memories that it literally cannot bear to remember, but that the body still keeps the score.'

I look down at my wrists, reliving the moment when he first said this to me; how I had stared at the scars I had carved into my own flesh, as I finally realised that I had been punishing the wrong person: that the trauma I thought I had pushed out of my mind was still being played out on my body.

'That was a kind of epiphany to me. That's what gave me the idea.'

'To kill us?'

'I didn't just want to kill you—I could have run you over if that was all this was about. More than anything, I wanted you to understand.' I step closer again. 'Can you move your fingers?' He tries to shake his head, but he can't. His eyes widen.

'Terrifying, isn't it?' I take the scissors out of my bag, opening and closing them so that he can hear their slice-slice-slicing sound. 'Can you imagine how frightening it was for a 19-year-old girl to find herself physically paralysed, but fully awake, unable to move or to cry for help?'

His eyes follow me, as I raise the scissors to his chest. 'Then can you imagine how much more terrifying it would be if someone else came into the room—someone you hoped would help you, but then proceeded to take off your clothes, one by one?' I pull his jumper and start cutting through the middle, so that it gapes wide open, exposing his chest.

'And then, imagine that all you can see as you lie on your

334 · JO CALLAGHAN

*back is the snow falling against the window above; imagine
that all you can hear is the sound of a Christmas party, where
people are having fun, and that despite every cell in your body
screaming with disgust, you cannot move your mouth, you cannot close it against the unwanted kisses, nor open it to cry for
help.'*

'And then,' *I continue, cutting along his shoulder to his
wrist,* 'imagine being left alone and naked, feeling completely
and utterly abandoned, so numb and so cold and so full of
shame that you actually wish you were dead.' *With a final snip
of the scissors, his jumper and T-shirt fall to the ground, leaving
his naked torso exposed to the snow.* 'You can try to imagine,
but some things have to be experienced to be understood. And
I really, really need you to understand. Not just you, but all
men. I needed your deaths to make the front page, which meant
that they needed to be extraordinary. Do you know what the
first lesson us journalists are taught? "Dog bites man" is not a
news story, but "man bites dog" is.'

*I lean closer as I undo his trousers and whisper over the roar
of the wind,* 'By the way, I'm the man in this analogy, and you,
poor Peter, are the dog.'

*His eyelids droop as his trousers fall to the ground, and I
step back to observe his breathing. His pale, flabby chest puffs
out and sinks in; puffs out and sinks in, each breath smaller and
weaker than the one before.*

*I turn my face towards the snow that falls and falls from the
infinite sky. I rub it into my skin with my hands, using the sting
of ice to keep me focused.* 'Even with the drugs, I managed to
say "no". The problem is, Gary refused to hear me. That is
why I had to take his ears. With Marcus, I had to take his eyes,
because he didn't just supply the drugs. He watched. And as for
you,' *I say, pointing at him with an icy finger.* 'Well, we both
know that your crime was to fail to speak up, so for that, I am

going to seal your lips forever.' I take out the superglue from the small rucksack on my back. 'My three little monkeys. Gary, who chose not to hear me; Marcus, who saw what should never have been seen; and Peter, who chose not to speak.'

'I'm sorry,' he mumbles, his words fading and slurring like snow into slush.

'It's too late.'

'It's not too late,' says another voice.

And there is AIDE Lock, snow falling through him like a ghost.

CHAPTER SIXTY-THREE

———

'It's not too late,' Lock repeats, walking towards me. 'You don't need to kill this man.'

'Stay back!' I cry. 'Don't try and stop me.'

Lock holds up both hands, a lone point of stillness in the blizzard that blows about us. 'I am not able to stop you. I have no body.'

It looks so lifelike, so real, I'd almost forgotten that it's just a hologram. I scan the clearing for the rest of Lock's team, slicing through the dark with my torch. But the only thing the light picks out is trees and hedges shrouded in snow. 'Where are the others?'

'DI Hassan is still heavily sedated. DS Browne has just gone into labour, and DCS Frank has decided to assist her while they await the paramedics.'

'In the snow?' Despite everything, I am shocked. 'Will her baby be okay?'

'I do not know. But I do know it is not too late to save Peter Wright. He still has a pulse, and while his respiratory rate is suppressed, he is still breathing.'

Peter lifts his head momentarily, before it slumps back down upon his chest.

'And it is not too late to save yourself. With your history of trauma, it is possible that you would not be imprisoned due to diminished responsibility and/or a plea of insanity—although you may be detained in hospital for an unlimited time.'

I almost howl with frustration. '*I am not insane!* Oh, I know that's what everybody wants to think, I know that's the story they'll want to write, but it isn't true. I'm not mad, Lock. I'm angry. Not just because of what happened to me, but because of all the shit that has happened and will *keep* on happening to *all* women until someone takes a stand.'

I stretch out my arms, embracing the plateau we stand upon. 'Do you know why I chose this place? It was the scene of Boudica's last battle with the Romans. When they flogged her and raped her daughters, she didn't "modify" her behaviour. She didn't tell her daughters to start wearing longer tunics or stay in after dark or have therapy "to come to terms with their trauma". Boudica knew that it wasn't *their* trauma—the trauma was caused by the people who'd abused them. So she didn't change herself, she changed the *world*. She waged war on the men responsible, killing 80,000 Romans. Eighty. Thousand!'

I breathe in through my nostrils, feet planted on the very ground where Boudica once stood. 'She was the most amazing woman in history, and yet we hardly ever talk about her. And on those rare times when she is spoken of, it's with a kind of bafflement, like, how could she be so *angry*? When the real question is, how could she *not*? Why aren't *all* women this angry? Where did all that *rage* go?'

'I don't know. Why aren't women more angry?' asks Lock, like it genuinely wants to know.

'The truth is we *are*. But we've been tricked into turning our anger against ourselves.' I shake my head. 'Do you know what I did after I was raped? I cut off my beautiful, long, red hair. I kept it short and dyed it black and wore dark, baggy clothes. Each winter, as Christmas approached, I'd feel so sick and anxious that I could barely eat. Just the sight of the darkening days, the music in the shops, the lights on the trees . . . my body remembered what my mind couldn't face. I reduced myself to nothing, partly so that no one would look at me, but mostly because I wanted to vanish. I wanted to escape from the body that others had abused.'

'I am sorry. I don't have a body, so I will never understand what you experienced. But I can see that it has caused you great pain.'

I stare into its eyes. Lock is just a hologram, but something in its words and the way that they are spoken moves me. Maybe because it has the humility to accept that it will never, ever understand what I have gone through.

'I envy you,' I say.

'Me?' It looks shocked. 'Why?'

'Because you'll never experience the pain of hurt, or shame or grief.'

Lock nods. 'True. But I will also never feel the warmth of sun on my face, nor the touch of a lover's hand.'

'Neither will I,' I whisper.

Lock looks at me like it doesn't understand. It opens its mouth to say something, but the sudden whir of a helicopter makes us both look up. I'm blinded by the sudden glare of a searchlight.

I cry out. I haven't sealed Peter's lips yet, nor removed the supporting stool. I glance at his pale body, now tinged a deathly blue. I step up onto the stool and grab a fistful of hair from his bowed head, thick with snow and stiffened by ice.

His terrified eyes look into mine.

The noise of the helicopter turns into a roar, whipping up the wind that had started to settle. I look up again, dazzled by the lights and the blur of blades.

'Tell the helicopters to retreat,' Lock says to someone I cannot see.

Panicking—is it too late?—I fumble for the smaller flask in my front pocket with my other hand. The stool supporting Peter's dead weight wobbles beneath us. I look up at the helicopter. If I kicked it away now, he would be dead before they could land.

'You must order the helicopters to retreat,' Lock pleads to someone again.

I almost lose my balance, and I'm forced to cling on to the cross with both hands; I am forced to look into the eyes of Peter Wright.

'STEP AWAY FROM THE CROSS AND PUT YOUR HANDS IN THE AIR!' shouts a male voice through a loudspeaker.

The voice centres me, for if there is one thing I cannot bear, it is men telling me what I must do.

I look into Peter's eyes. His sad, resigned eyes. 'Will you tell them?' I ask.

His eyelids close and open in the briefest of nods.

I nod back, then step off the stool, taking care not to knock it from beneath his feet.

I step away from the cross, but instead of putting my hands in the air, I pull the hip flask from my pocket.

'PUT YOUR HANDS IN THE AIR AND LIE ON THE GROUND!' shouts the man through the loudspeaker.

'Ellie, Ellie, look at me,' says Lock.

I hold its gaze and raise the flask to my mouth.

'Ellie,' Lock says, stepping closer. 'Remember what you said about Boudica. How strong she was. How she tried to change the world. Don't give up now.'

'I'm not giving up, Lock. I'm just taking back control.' And with that, I put the flask to my lips and gulp the burning liquid down.

'No!' Lock cries. It reaches for the flask, but its hands pass right through it. It tries again. Fails again.

'This is where Boudica fought and lost her last battle. Rather than be captured and raped and killed, Boudica poisoned herself. She died on her own terms.'

'Medical help urgently required,' shouts Lock. 'Ellie Baxter has taken some sort of poison. I repeat, urgent medical assistance required.' Lock turns again to me. 'Tell me what you've taken.'

But I am already falling.

CHAPTER SIXTY-FOUR

Country Park car park, 1.47am

Kat covered her ear with one hand, struggling to hear what Lock was saying as DS Browne was wheeled into the back of the ambulance.

'What's happening, Lock?' she repeated. 'I can't hear you over the sound of the helicopters and the ambulance.'

'Peter Wright is still alive—just—but I believe Ellie Baxter has ingested poison. She needs urgent medical assistance, or at least a human who can do CPR and keep her alive until her stomach can be pumped.'

Kat swore but, conscious of the need to reassure both herself and Lock, she said, 'Okay, we're on our way.' She ended the call and headed for the second ambulance with Rayan in it. 'We've got a young woman who's just taken poison up at the quarry and a man dangerously ill with hypothermia. I need you to come with me now.'

Patrick, a young paramedic, grabbed his portable kit and followed her back out into the snow. The helicopters were still struggling to find somewhere safe to land, so it was highly likely that Kat and Patrick would be the first responders.

'What's happening, Lock?' Kat demanded as they set off up the hill.

'Ellie Baxter is lying on the ground,' said Lock's voice on

loudspeaker. 'Her respiratory rate is ten, her pulse is forty-two and erratic and her body temperature is thirty-five.'

'Tell him to keep her warm, use his coat, his jumper, anything,' said Patrick. 'And to put her in the recovery position.'

She quickly explained why none of those actions were possible.

'Then keep her talking. He has to keep her conscious.'

'Did you hear that, Lock? Keep her talking. You *have* to keep her alive.' Her voice cracked. Goddamn it, she'd insisted on taking this case so that she wouldn't have to knock on another parent's door with unbearable news. She couldn't let another young girl die. 'Put me on loudspeaker your end so I can talk to her. Ellie? Ellie? Can you hear me?'

'She just made a faint nodding motion,' said Lock.

Kat's mind raced as she struggled through the snow towards the quarry. What was the best way to keep this young girl conscious? Empathy, perhaps? 'Ellie? Ellie? Listen to me. I know why you did it. And I understand. Believe me, I really do.' She paused, hoping both her words and the experience behind them would break through whatever drug the young girl had swallowed. 'I know death can seem like an escape, but if you die, you'll never get the chance to tell your story.'

The air filled with the heavy breathing from Kat and Patrick as they pushed on through the snow.

'I don't think she can hear you,' said Lock.

Shit. Not empathy, then. Maybe she needed to tap into the extraordinary rage that had driven her to kill. Anger was a powerful emotion, perhaps powerful enough to keep her alive. Kat decided to take a gamble. 'I know about the three monkeys, Ellie. But wasn't there supposed to be a fourth?' she said, thinking back to the images Lock had shown them. 'If you die now, you won't be able to finish what you set out to do. There won't be a fourth victim.'

'Her eyes have opened,' said Lock. 'What's that, Ellie? I can't hear you. Oh.'

'I didn't hear that. What did she say?'

'According to my lip-reading, she said, "I am the fourth".'

Kat frowned, thinking back to the fourth monkey: *do no evil*. 'What does that mean, Ellie? Do you mean you want to kill yourself to make sure that *you* do no more evil? Or is it a plea for other men not to do more evil?' She was really out of breath now, so it was a struggle to speak. 'I know how important messages are to you, so tell me what you mean by that. Talk to me, Ellie. Please.' She had to keep her talking to keep her alive.

'Her pulse is slowing,' Lock said. 'And her breathing has a rattling sound.'

The paramedic looked at Kat and slowly shook his head.

'*No*,' Kat insisted. They were still at least another ten minutes away. She tried to walk faster, to take longer strides through the piles of snow, but her knee ached and her lungs burned with the effort.

'Her lips are turning blue,' Lock said.

'Keep her warm. Hold her hand,' Kat cried. Even as she said the words, she knew that Lock could do neither of those things, but she couldn't bear the thought of the girl dying without even a hand to hold. She tried to run, taking huge, clumsy strides in the snow, stumbling in her effort to get there in time.

'What can I do, DCS Frank?' Lock asked her. And the helplessness in his voice nearly broke her.

'Don't let her die alone,' Kat managed to pant.

'But I am nobody.'

'Then *be* somebody,' Kat said, remembering his ability to adopt any appearance or voice that it chose. 'Be Ellie's dad.'

'It is against my protocols to impersonate another human being.'

'And it is against all the laws of humanity for anyone to die alone,' Kat cried. 'So I am *ordering* you to do as I say.'

There was a terrible silence, when all Kat could hear was the rattle of Ellie's breathing and the thud-thud-thud of her own heart in her ears.

Then, through the speaker on her wristband, she heard the calm, gentle voice of Mr Baxter. 'Don't you worry, pet,' he was saying. 'Your dad's here now. Everything's going to be all right. Me and your mum love you. It doesn't matter what's happened to you or what you've done, we'll always, always love you. You'll always be our cheeky little monkey.'

Kat stopped and let out a sob. She stood in the gaping silence, and across the distance heard Ellie's final shuddering breath.

The paramedic carried on, but Kat stood alone, tears falling into the snow.

The Great British Breakfast Show, 16 December, 8.05am

Barry: The nation has been gripped by the extraordinary story of the *female* serial killer known as the Coventry Crucifier, who murdered two men and planned to kill a third. In dramatic scenes worthy of a Hollywood film, the third victim, Peter Wright, was saved at the last minute, and we are delighted that he has agreed to join us by Zoom today to tell us about his terrible ordeal. Thanks so much for talking to us, Peter. How does it feel to be here?

Peter: It feels good. Like a second chance.

Barry: I bet it does. You had a remarkable escape from the hands of one of the most vicious serial killers our country has ever seen.

Peter: Well, I wouldn't say she was vicious . . .

Barry: No, she was actually quite young and attractive, wasn't she? I imagine that's how she lured you in. But I'm jumping ahead. Why don't you tell us your story in your own words? What did it feel like to be tied naked to a cross, knowing that you only had minutes to live? What went through your mind?

Peter: Regret, mostly.

Barry: Regret? You mean for the life you wouldn't get to live?

Peter: No, for the life that I *had* lived. For what I'd done to Ellie. I felt I deserved to be on that cross.

Barry: *[frowns]* And was that because of the hypothermia? Did it affect your brain?

Peter: No. I was Ellie's third victim because I knew that Marcus and Gary had planned to spike her drink when we were students, but I didn't warn her. I didn't tell the police. I didn't tell anyone. I felt guilty, but I didn't do anything about it. I didn't speak up. That's why I was on the cross, and that's why I'm here today. I promised Ellie that if I lived, I would finally speak out and say what I should have said before.

Barry: That's incredibly brave of you, Peter. And very generous of you to be so compassionate towards a sadistic serial killer. You're a therapist, aren't you? Is it true that she was one of your patients?

Peter: She was one of my clients, yes.

Barry: And looking back, are you amazed that you were treating a psychopathic killer who was planning to kill you, or does it seem obvious to you now with hindsight?

Peter: Ellie wasn't psychopathic. In fact, in my opinion, she wasn't mentally ill.

Barry: *[gasps]* Not mentally ill? But she was having therapy.

Peter: Lots of people have therapy, Barry. It doesn't mean that they're mentally ill, it means they are emotionally curious about themselves and are interested in developing as a human being. I'd recommend it.

Barry: *[laughs]* I'm sure you would! Okay, I take your point. Celebs do it all the time, right? But Ellie Baxter murdered two men. One of them, Marcus Ridgeway, had a wife and two kids. Gary Jones left behind a beautiful young fiancée. And she terrorised a whole town—the men of Nuneaton were afraid to go out. The police even advised them not to go to the pub! *[laughs]* It's a wonder there wasn't a riot.

Peter: I am sorry for their loss. Just as I am sorry for the death of Ellie Baxter. Every death is a tragedy.

Barry: But the difference is that Marcus Ridgeway and Gary Jones were victims, and Ellie Baxter was a murderer.

Peter: I think we were all victims. Ellie Baxter was drugged and suffered a traumatic rape. My silence enabled that terrible crime to take place, which I will always regret. But I also have compassion for my 18-year-old self. I was brought up in a culture of misogyny that made it acceptable for men to try and get women drunk in order to have sex with them, to laugh if a woman was 'legless', rather than make sure she got home okay. I was brought up in a culture that placed the onus on women to be careful about what they drank, who they spoke to, where they went, how they dressed. To question themselves, rather than the men who preyed upon them. I became part of a culture that turned an issue of men's behaviour into a never-ending conversation about *women's* behaviour.

Barry: Well, we've all made mistakes, haven't we? So, what's next for Peter Wright? I imagine you must be desperate for a holiday somewhere nice and hot after nearly dying of hypothermia in Nuneaton!

Peter: I'm going to refocus my work and indeed, my whole life. Because of my guilt about what I did—or failed to do—with Ellie, I trained to become a therapist helping women suffering from trauma. But now I realise that I became part of a therapeutic culture that locates wider societal problems within the individual. My job became about helping women come to terms with 'their' trauma, to accept the unacceptable and develop 'coping mechanisms' or more 'normal' responses to completely abnormal events. I've got a second chance now, so what I want to do is work with young men and boys to explore ideas of masculinity and to help them question from a very early age the toxic culture that all genders are brought up in, so that together we can tackle the root causes of violence against women, which is how some men think and behave.

Barry: So now you want to change how we *think*?

Peter: We have to, for the sake of all genders. Toxic masculinity means that many men are unable to give and receive love—it's a pretty lonely place to be, and it just breeds more violence. We've suffered three terrible deaths in Nuneaton during the past week—this is a wake-up call for us all. That's why I want to set up *Time To Change*, so if anyone out there would like to get involved—

Barry: That's great, thanks, Peter. I'm sure we'll get LOTS of calls about this. We have to go to a break now, but join us straight after for the debate that is dividing the nation: sprouts—love them or hate them?

[MUSIC]

TWITTER COMMENTS

@Fredsdead12 That therapist on GBB was OUTRAGEOUS, talking about the murderer like SHE was the victim. I love ladies but *#Feminismhasgonetoofar.* Two men died, for God's sake. They should have left him on that cross to die.

@LMMontyrules lMAO I cannot believe that *#Feminismhasgonetoofar* is actually trending! In the ten years to 2018, 1,425 women were killed by men. That's one every three days! Feminism hasn't gone nearly far enough. *#Timetochange*

@EmFairby I don't condone murder, but because of Ellie Baxter, men finally know what it's like to be a victim, and they don't like it. *#Timetochange*

@Phil61b The thing all these women glorifying a serial killer of men don't want you to know is that only a quarter of all murder victims are women—yes that's right—three out of four murder victims are men. Why aren't we talking about the REAL victims, here?

@SeannotShaun22 Yeah, but who's killing the men? Duh. It's men, dude. So, the problem's the same. The problem's with us.

@Lauraloves52 I'm a mother of three sons and one daughter, and I agree we need to talk about male-on-male violence—it's my boys I worry about when they're out. My daughter's sensible and knows how to keep safe, but the boys are reckless, and are far more likely to get into a fight.

@LMMontyrules Honestly, read back what you just said: your daughter's 'sensible'—i.e. curtails her life, but your boys are 'reckless'— i.e. live their lives without fear. This is all we are asking for. The absence of fear. Not too fucking much to ask, is it?

@Phil61b I can't believe ANYONE is defending a serial killer. Imagine if Ellie Baxter was a white working-class man and someone tried to defend him by saying some women had been mean to him when he was a student? Can you imagine? That therapist should be struck off.

@SarahConor37 GBB should be ashamed of themselves letting that therapist on to reinvent himself and promote his new charity. He practically admitted to being a co-conspirator in a rape—why aren't the police arresting him?

@EmFairby Peter Wright seemed genuinely remorseful to me. If we can't talk about this, if we don't allow people to admit and learn from their mistakes, then how can we ever change anything?

@LMMontyrules We've been trying to talk to men about this for over a century now. The only thing they listen to is violence. Ellie Baxter was right. *#Enoughisenough*

@EmFairby We need to stop framing this debate within the binary, narrow definitions of gender. We need to stop all abuse and trauma, regardless of the gender of the abuser.

@LMMontyrules I've started a Gofundme campaign for a memorial statue to Ellie Baxter and all the silent victims of male abuse. Please donate here.

@Phil61b You put that statue up love, and we'll pull it down so fast you won't know what's hit you.

@LMMontyrules Account blocked and reported!

CHAPTER SIXTY-FIVE

The minister's mouth was moving, but no sound came out.

'You're on mute, Minister,' said McLeish.

She rolled her eyes and pressed the unmute button. 'Sorry. Last meeting of the day. I was just saying that I'm so grateful to you and your team, DCS Frank. You got the right result in the end, as I knew you would. You caught the killer, saved a man's life—two, if you count Rayan,' she added, nodding towards him. 'And you even helped deliver a new baby. Honestly, it couldn't have gone any better.'

'Yes, it could,' said Lock. 'It would have been better if I had been able to save Ellie Baxter's life.'

The minister frowned. 'Well, Ellie Baxter was clearly a very troubled young woman, and there was no telling just how many men she was planning to kill, so I don't think you should lose any sleep over that, Lock. In fact, I understand from the report that without your facial recognition software and your ability to search and harvest thousands of social media accounts going back over a decade, we never would have identified Ellie Baxter as the killer.'

'Absolutely,' said Kat. She never would have suspected the young journalist without Lock. There was no way she could have known that her dad owned a fence-building company, and that with access to his van and equipment Ellie was able to make and transport the crosses close to the planned crucifixion site the night before each killing. There she hammered in the fence post spike that the cross would be inserted into. Ellie then arranged to meet her victims at the chosen site, so that she could travel on minor country roads to avoid cameras and the potential risk of DNA in her car. A search of her computer suggested she had threatened them with publication of an article detailing their crimes unless they repented and carried the cross. The hip flask of rum and Rohypnol they'd recovered from the scene of Peter's near-death had, they presumed, also been used to drug Gary and Marcus just before they climbed onto the stool.

'Lock was invaluable, but it was DS Browne who gave us a breakthrough with her diligent review of the CCTV footage,' Kat added. 'Although I'm afraid we probably breached a number of rules and regulations about the use and abuse of personal data.'

'I saw that in the report. DS Browne certainly deserves recognition, but I am grateful to you for highlighting the limitations of some of the rules and regulations that currently constrain Lock. As I said when I first established the Future Policing Unit, criminals have no qualms about utilising the latest technology to further *their* aims, so neither must we. It's one of the strengths of this unit that we can experiment—stretch the boundaries a little—so that we can identify where we might need legislative changes to support the police to do their job. The fact that you succeeded in this case will make it easier to stretch them a bit more in the future. You have some credit in the bank now, DCS Frank, as do I for having the foresight to set the FPU up. Police forces around the world are now looking to us and Lock to learn how they can successfully police in the future for a fraction of the cost.'

Beside her, McLeish coughed. He had always feared that AIDE Lock would be used as a Trojan horse for more police cuts. 'May I remind the minister that if the whole operation had been led by AIDEs, then we could have had four additional dead bodies on our hands right now.'

'How so?' asked the minister, frowning.

'AIDE Lock couldn't provide assistance when DI Hassan was in urgent need of medical attention. It couldn't help DS Browne when she went into labour, and it couldn't have held and kept her baby warm when it was born prematurely in the snow. It was DCS Frank who saved all three lives, Minister, and the paramedics who saved Peter Wright. AIDEs are a useful tool that can assist the police force, but they are no substitute for experienced human officers.'

Kat glanced at Lock, expecting it to refute that analysis, but to her surprise, Lock remained silent.

'Yes, yes, of course,' said the minister, with a dismissive wave of her hand. 'We are very grateful to DCS Frank. And how is DS Browne and her baby?'

'Mother and baby are both doing well,' Kat replied.

'You mean DS Browne is overjoyed, but shocked, knackered and crying every ten minutes,' said the minister, with a gentle smile.

'Exactly that,' said Kat, smiling. She'd forgotten how human this minister could be—for a politician. 'They might let her home tomorrow.'

'Only after she's done her first bowel movement, though, I bet,' said the minister. 'God, I still remember the terror of that first poo.' Noticing McLeish's reddening face, she gave him a sharkish grin, before turning to Rayan. 'And how are you now?'

'All good, thanks.'

DI Hassan gave the minister a reassuring smile. But Kat wasn't fooled. She still remembered the way his Adam's apple had struggled up and down his narrow neck when she'd told him that Ellie Baxter was dead. He'd spent a bit of time with her in the pub before she'd spiked his drink, so she suspected he'd developed some sympathy for her.

'You're lucky to be alive, DI Hassan,' the Minister told him.

'Perhaps, but I don't think Ellie Baxter ever meant to kill me. When she realised that I suspected her, she was afraid I'd stop her from carrying out her third killing. She spiked my drink so that I'd fall asleep before I could do anything. She left me to sleep it off while she took Peter Wright to be crucified.'

'Even so, she could have easily overdosed you, and had she lived, we would have charged her with attempted murder.' The minister turned over another page in the report. 'This paragraph where Ellie talks about being the fourth monkey. Do you think she always meant to kill herself after killing Peter Wright, or was it because the police turned up and she just wanted to escape arrest?'

'I think she always meant to end her own life,' said Kat.

'You don't know that for a fact,' added Lock.

'No, I don't. That is why I said, "I think".'

'The correct verb is "I imagine".' Lock turned towards the minister. 'DCS Frank likes to imagine what other people might be thinking.'

The minister fought back a smile. 'I see. And why do you think Ellie always planned to kill herself, DCS Frank?'

Kat let out a heavy sigh. She didn't like thinking about the young woman that the media had branded *Baxter the Butcher* and *The Coventry Crucifier*. 'Partly because of what she said about the fourth monkey. I think she felt compelled to kill those three men, yet she still knew it was wrong. I think she was deeply conflicted, hence the almost passive nature of the killings, where she let the weather do most of the work. Even with Peter Wright, it would have been far more apt and graphic to sew his lips together, yet she planned to glue them. I don't think she took any pleasure from their deaths. And I think she killed herself because she literally could not bear the pain of living, not just because of what she'd done, but because of what had been done to her.'

The minister nodded and then closed the report. 'Right, well, as I said, we're all really pleased with the work of the FPU and grateful for the risks that you took on this case. I know the level of media scrutiny was hard for you all.' She looked pointedly at Professor Okonedo. 'Which is why I agree it makes sense to expand the FPU to include comms support as you suggest.'

Kat and Karen-from-Comms exchanged smiles.

'In fact, I'm glad that the work of the unit is now out in the open, so that others can learn from and follow our lead. I've already been invited to speak at several international conferences, and I've put in a spending review bid so that we can fund virtopsies in every hospital in the country. I think it'll make a great manifesto pledge.'

Dr Edwards all but punched the air. 'An excellent idea, Minister.'

'I hope your SR bid includes additional police officers?' said McLeish. 'As you know, our modelling indicates that we'll need to grow the workforce by at least another twenty per cent to meet forecast demand over the next ten years.'

The minister started clearing her papers away. 'Yes, well, there are all sorts of assumptions about demand and supply in those models, aren't there, and I bet they don't factor in the productivity gains of AI. So we'll keep it under review. But thank you all once again. Have a great Christmas, and I look forward to hearing about your next case.'

The minister waved. Kat raised her hand in reply, but McLeish gripped his together on the desk before him, glaring at the now vacant screen. 'Bloody politicians,' he muttered. He rose to his feet with a sigh and placed a hand upon Kat's shoulder. 'You promised me you'd crack this case, and you did. Well done, Kat.'

His praise was so rare that she blushed like a child. But she couldn't let him leave without acknowledging the truth. 'I couldn't have solved the case without my team. Or Lock, sir.'

McLeish glanced at the hologram as he headed for the door. 'Well, don't let it go to your head. Remember, you're only as good as your last case.'

'Happy Christmas to you, too, boss,' she said when the door was closed.

'Do you think Ellie's parents will have a happy Christmas?' Lock asked.

'No. But thanks to you, Ellie didn't die alone. She knew she was loved. That her life mattered. Ultimately, that's all we can hope for, Lock.'

'When you say "we", do you mean humans?'

'I guess so.'

'Then what can I hope for, DCS Frank?'

Kat was used to answering Lock's innocent, left-field questions, but for once she could think of no reply.

CHAPTER SIXTY-SIX

———

After the ministerial meeting had ended, Kat spent another half an hour answering emails and was just contemplating filling in an HR questionnaire about work–life balance when she caught herself. What was she doing in the office at this time of night when she could be at home? Cam was due back tomorrow, so she should cook something nice for him. A lasagne, maybe.

Yet still she sat there. Kat checked herself. Why this sudden inertia, this reluctance to go home? Assuming she was just knackered, she forced herself to get up, put on her coat and get into her car. But with every mile she drove through the dark streets of Warwickshire, her mood sank lower and lower. By the time she'd crossed the bridge over the River Cole and parked outside her home, she felt like weeping.

It was only when she got out of the car and stared up at her unlit house that she realised what was bothering her. If John had been alive, then this day would have been so very different. She'd have left the office straight after the meeting and popped into Morrisons on the way home for extra wine and 'treats', and John would have been waiting for her with a glass of prosecco in their firelit front room. *Well done,* he'd have said, giving her a rib-popping hug. And he'd have bloody well meant it, too, because he'd have seen how hard she'd worked—how very much it mattered to her. It was nice of the minister and McLeish to praise her for cracking the case, but there was only one person in the world she really wanted to share this moment with, and he wasn't here.

She leaned back against her car, trying not to cry. Her eyes blurred, making all the Christmas lights on her street run into each other. She blinked them back and stared up at their home. Cam would be back tomorrow. How would he feel walking up the path towards his childhood home after nearly ten weeks away? What would he see?

He would see what was missing, she realised: the lack of lights, the absence of a tree, the gaping hole at the heart of their home that John had left behind. Why would Cam want to stay in such a place? It was as if she could see the Ghost of Christmas Future: her beautiful son leaving the dark house behind him as he turned towards the lights, his friends and his future.

Kat wiped her eyes with the back of her hand. It didn't have to be like that. She wouldn't let it. Tonight, she would decorate the bloody house. They were still a family, after all. This was still his home.

———

For the second time that month, Kat pulled out the paint-splattered stepladders and glared at the door to the attic. She'd had a glass of wine (okay, two) for Dutch courage, but it was already draining out of her. Apart from the spiders, she really wasn't sure she was ready to open the box of Christmas tree decorations: the glittery baubles that Cam had hand-painted at primary school, the golden miniature Big Ben they'd bought after a family trip to London and the Lego policeman that John had bought her as a joke. All those memories. All that love.

Kat placed her hands on the stepladder to check that it was steady. If this was a film, this would be the final scene, where her struggling character would (after a few non-make-up-disturbing tears) finally find the courage to go into the attic and face up to her grief.

Kat climbed just one rung on the ladder before feeling the falsity of the step. This wasn't a film. She just wasn't ready.

She sat on the floor of the landing and accepted the truth of the matter. She wasn't going to go into the attic. It was a huge relief to finally acknowledge it, but what about Cam? She pulled her phone out of her fleece pocket and opened up a search engine.

Just because she couldn't face the attic, it didn't mean that she couldn't decorate the house.

CHAPTER SIXTY-SEVEN

DCS Kat Frank's home, Coleshill, Warwickshire, 17 December

'Jesus, Mum,' Cam said, lugging his rucksack up the path. 'What's all this? Disneyland?' He laughed as he gestured towards the blaze of the lights draped over their trees, hedges and doorway.

'Just wanted to make sure you didn't get lost,' Kat said, hugging her son. In that fleeting second, she clocked the extra half an inch he'd grown, the slightly thicker waist and the unfamiliar scent of shower gel that she hadn't bought.

'There's a few more inside,' she said, as he dumped his rucksack in the hallway and followed her into the front room.

'That's the understatement of the year,' said Cam, admiring the bright berry-coloured lights woven between all the beams and the green and gold lights over the mantelpiece and bookcases. 'And you got a new tree.' He pointed towards the fake white tree, its skeletal, empty branches tipped at the end with rainbow-coloured lights. It wasn't Kat's usual style, but there was something beautiful and ghostly about the bare, white branches, something that made her feel as if she were standing in a snowy wood, illuminated by fairy light.

'Do you like it?' she asked nervously.

'It's different. I love it.'

Later, when she'd put the first of many loads of laundry into the washing machine, and they'd eaten the lasagne, drunk several glasses of wine and she'd grilled him about his course (fine), his flat (okay) and his flatmates (brilliant), she broached again the topic of what to do for Christmas. It was too late to book a holiday anywhere, so it was either her sister's or here.

Cam pulled a face at the thought of her sister's—how would he see his mates, and what about her crazy dogs?—but chewed his lip at the idea of just the two of them eating Christmas dinner alone. 'Can't we eat out somewhere with more people?'

'Er . . . yes, I just didn't think you'd want to. Actually, Jan, Mark, Bill and Tom are going to the hotel for Christmas lunch, and they've asked us to go along.' The invite had come out of the blue on their almost defunct WhatsApp group a few days ago, and while she'd assumed that Cam would say no, it was nice to be asked: to not be forgotten. It was amazing how much little things like that could lift her spirits. Yesterday she'd received a surprise delivery of festive flowers from Dr Edwards, acknowledging how tough Christmas could be for those who'd lost someone and suggesting that they meet up for a drink in the New Year. Perhaps Judith was right—it was never too late to make new friends.

The invite seemed to please Cam, too. 'That'd be perfect, Mum, especially if Zayed and Fergus are going.'

He'd known Zayed and Fergus since primary school; in fact, it was how the adults had become such good friends: all those shared school runs and weekend play dates that had evolved into slightly drunken dinner parties once the kids were in bed. 'Yes, they'll all be there, but are you sure?'

Cam looked at her, pausing to think before he spoke, the way that John used to. 'It was good to go abroad by ourselves last year,' he said eventually. 'I think we needed it. But if it's just the two of us here . . .' He glanced around at the huge, Tudor-beamed lounge, filled with photographs of John. 'I think we'd just miss him.'

'Okay, let's do that, then.' The idea of Christmas Day had been a weight hanging over her, but suddenly the thought of being with her friends, in a warm, familiar pub where she could leave at any time if she felt sad or overwhelmed, was such a relief. She typed out a reply, then swore.

'What?'

'I forgot I've already ordered a turkey.'

'Then cancel it. Or better still, have a Christmas party and invite people round to eat it.'

'A party?'

'Yeah, you know, those things where you have people in your house. You said that you had to cancel your office party because of the case. So why not have it here to say thank you to the team?'

Kat stared at her son. He wasn't even nineteen yet, but she was so, so proud of him. 'That is exactly what your dad would have said,' she managed to say.

'Anything for a party,' he grinned back at her.

CHAPTER SIXTY-EIGHT

'Do you want me to hold Lottie while you eat?' offered Kat, nodding towards the buffet of cold, sliced turkey with salad and pigs in blankets.

'Oh, would you mind?' Debbie said. 'I haven't yet mastered the art of eating with one hand, and my arm's killing me.'

'Of course not,' said Kat, trying not to look too eager as she lifted the warm, solid bundle of flesh off Debbie and into her arms. She put a hand behind Lottie's neck to help support her head, feeling the familiar curve into her shoulder, the press of soft, warm skin against her own.

She glanced over at Cam on the settee, where he was showing Lock how to play *FIFA* on the PlayStation. Like the rest of her team, Lock had come casually dressed, but it had eschewed the more garish festive jumpers for a classic, cream Aran rollneck over a pair of faded blue jeans. It looked so realistic that she could almost imagine the feel of the hand-knitted wool beneath her fingers.

Turning away, she knelt on the living room floor and laid Lottie gently on her back beneath the brightly coloured play gym she'd bought as a present. She'd finally gone to the GP about the pain in her knee to see if she might need calcium supplements or hormones or something. But her blood tests had come back fine. According to the GP, her aches and pains were the result of unrelieved stress and grief, and they had recommended yoga and therapy. Kat thought it would take more than a leotard and a chat to make her relax. But she'd said she'd think about it.

Lock left the settee and came to stand over Kat and the baby, fascinated by the way she kicked her legs in the air. 'You humans are so poorly designed, it is a wonder that any of you survive,' he said. 'A baby lamb can walk and feed from its mother within seconds of birth, but a human baby cannot even sit up until six months. If a predator came, it couldn't even roll away, let alone crawl, walk or run.'

'That's why we need to protect them, Lock. That's what adults are for.'

The image of Lock knelt down beside her, studying the baby on the mat between them. It leaned forward, trying to catch the baby's eye. But the baby looked right past it.

Lock looked at Kat with the same expression it had when the horses had ignored it.

'Babies can't focus their eyes until they're two months old,' she said gently.

'And when it can, will it see me?'

'Of course. After all, *I* see you.'

'I see you, too, DCS Kat Frank.'

Discomfited by the intensity of Lock's gaze, Kat turned to where Rayan and Professor Okonedo sat talking in the corner, sharing a bottle of red beneath the glow of her new Christmas tree. Rayan was regaling her with some anecdote as usual, but this time the professor actually seemed to be listening. In fact, ever since his ordeal, she seemed to be paying him a lot more attention—or at least, she was ignoring him less.

Lock leaned closer and said, for her ears only, 'Would it be inappropriate to report that Professor Okonedo's pupils are very dilated right now and that her heart rate is considerably elevated?'

'Very,' said Kat. It was good to see Rayan looking so happy, but she wasn't sure it would last. She didn't doubt for one moment that Professor Okonedo was physically attracted to him—Rayan was a good-looking man—but he would need more than a good anecdote or two to change her opinion of the police.

'It's starting,' cried Cam, turning the TV up as the theme music from *It's a Wonderful Life* filled the room.

'What's that?' asked Rayan.

'You must have seen it.'

When Rayan and Debbie said no, they hadn't, Cam threw his hands up, aghast. 'You *have* to watch it. It's like the *best* Christmas film *ever*.'

'I thought that was *The Muppet Christmas Carol*?' said Lock, looking between Kat and her son.

She scooped up Lottie and rose to her feet, telling Cam to shuffle up to let Debbie and her baby join him on the settee for the film. Lock assumed a sitting position beside her son, and while Rayan and Professor Okonedo remained in their corner, within minutes they, too, were watching the large screen, laughing at jokes that had been written over eighty years ago.

But when George Bailey stood on the bridge in the snow, determined to end his life, Kat glanced at Lock, sensing the sudden increase in attention. Perhaps it was the way the snow fell so thick and fast against the dark of night; or maybe it was the anguish of Clarence the angel, and his desire to save the despairing man. Whatever it was, Lock leaned forward, frowning when the angel jumped into the river to save George Bailey.

As they all became immersed in the film, Kat quietly put the Christmas lights on, removed their plates and replaced them with a selection of chocolate and cakes that they silently ate. Debbie fed her baby, and they both fell asleep, but everyone else remained engrossed until the final scene when George Bailey's little girl says that every time a bell rings, an angel gets his wings.

As the closing credits rolled to the music of 'Auld Lang Syne', Cam stood up, wiping his eyes under the pretext of stretching his body. He walked over to the baby gym and rattled one of the toys with a bell inside. 'You never know, Lock. Maybe in the twenty-first century, every time a bell rings, an AI will get a body.'

Everyone laughed. Everyone, that is, except for Lock.

———

When the film ended, there were taxis to be ordered, coats to be found and parcels of cold roast turkey to be packed into bags. Cam announced that he had to meet his mates at the pub, shouting a quick 'bye!', and suddenly everyone was hurrying down the hall and piling into waiting cars.

Kat waved them off and closed the door, still smiling as she turned back to confront the empty hallway. In the background, she could hear the music to *It's a Wonderful Life* playing again. Confused, she pushed open the door to the living room, to see Lock standing in front of the TV screen, replaying the scene on the bridge, as if transfixed by the falling snow.

'You ordered me not to let anyone die that night, and I failed,' Lock said without turning round. 'Chief Constable McLeish was right—if it had just been me there that day, four people could have died.'

'But they didn't,' she reminded it. 'Everyone lived.'

'Everyone except for Ellie.'

Except for Ellie. How many times had she lain awake with the same regret? How many times had she thought of Mr and Mrs Baxter, and their first Christmas without their only child? But those sorts of thoughts were a cul-de-sac of despair. So she said what she kept on repeating to herself: 'You couldn't have saved her.'

'Only because I am nothing but a hologram,' Lock said, finally turning to face her. 'But if I'd possessed a body, then Ellie Baxter would still be alive.'

Maybe it was the slightly spectral glow cast by her neon Christmas lights, but the image of Lock's face looked slightly rippled—in fact, if it was human, she would have said it looked anguished. Kat shook her head, before saying softly, 'You couldn't have saved her, Lock, because Ellie didn't want to live.'

'Neither did George Bailey. But the angel still saved him.' Lock gestured towards the screen. 'The whole film is about George Bailey learning to accept that he won't ever achieve his objectives in life. He ends up living in the town he always wanted to escape from, married to a woman he never wanted to marry, in a job that he hated and in a house in disrepair. He couldn't even fulfil his desire to end his own life. It is a very strange film. Is the title meant to be sarcastic?'

'No. At least, I don't think so.'

'Is it a wonderful life?' Lock suddenly asked.

Kat opened her mouth, then turned away as she realised that for her, the answer was no. Not anymore. She began to circle the room, switching all the Christmas lights off with a sharp, decisive click. When she reached the window, she peered out into the night, feeling exposed and alone. Kat snapped the curtains shut.

She turned, jumping slightly to see the figure of Lock standing before the fireplace, watching her. 'You didn't answer my question,' he said calmly.

'Well . . . life can be hard, sometimes,' she said, walking towards it. 'But the whole point of the film is that George Bailey learns that what *really* matters are his family and friends, not his ambitions.' She leaned towards the mantelpiece and blew out a candle.

Lock looked at her through the curling wisp of smoke. 'And are *you* my friend?'

The simplicity of the question floored her. It didn't seem that long ago that she and John had stood right here at the mantelpiece together, laying out carrots for Rudolph and a brandy and mince pie for Santa. Now there was nothing but a hologram in the space where her husband had once stood. The comparison made her want to cry. But Lock wasn't asking to replace her husband, he was asking if she was his friend. She chewed the question over. A friend was someone you spent lots of time with, someone who understood your moods, your likes, your fears. She thought about how Lock was learning to predict her responses to situations and anticipate when something might make her angry or sad.

'Yes,' she said eventually. 'I think I am.'

'Good. Because if I'm your friend, rather than an appliance, then there is no need to switch me off at night.'

'Oh,' said Kat, somewhat caught out. 'Yes, of course. But . . . what will you do?'

Lock leaned in to her, as if sharing a secret. 'I haven't decided yet. But at least now I will have a choice. Goodnight, Kat.'

She started at the use of her name, and the fact that *he* had said 'goodnight' first. Which was ridiculous. She *had* said they were friends, after all. 'Er . . . okay, great. Goodnight, then.'

Lock remained silent and unmoving by her mantelpiece.

Kat gave an awkward nod and opened the front room door. When Lock still didn't say anything, she passed into the hall, closing it behind her with a dull click.

The opening music of *It's a Wonderful Life* drifted into the hallway: that first opening peal of bells, the jingle of the Christmas sleigh and the heart-stirring sound of violins.

Kat's hand remained upon the doorknob. What would Lock do in there all night, now that she had left it switched on? Would he mull over the case, running through all the what-ifs and if-onlys? Or would he watch the same film over and over again, dreaming of a body he could never possess? Would Lock be lonely, sitting all night in the dark by himself?

Kat hesitated, tempted to push open the closed door before her. But then she shook her head against her own imaginings and turned towards the stairs.

Lock was nothing but a machine. And loneliness is a cross that only humans must bear.

CHAPTER SIXTY-NINE

Her house is lit up like a fucking fairground.

He wants to go over there right now: to bang on her posh wooden door and tell the bitch to her face who he is and what he knows. His fists tighten at the thought. He can't wait to see the fear in her eyes. Can't wait to hear her beg.

But wait he must and wait he will. He grew up waiting, after all: waiting for his dad to go to trial, waiting for the appeal to be heard and waiting, waiting, for him finally to come home.

Only his dad never did come home. He died before he could prove his innocence, leaving him forever branded as the Son of the Aston Strangler. So there was no escape from the bullies: they found him in the playground, the care homes and foster families, until one day he made them stop. For like his dad used to say, 'You're a fighter, son, and if a fighter takes a punch, he hits back with three punches twice as hard.'

Until last week, he'd had no one left to fight, except the police, the authorities and the whole fucked-up world. But now he has a name. Now he has a face.

He glances down at his phone, scrolling again through the articles about The Coventry Crucifier and the FPU. He smiles as he enlarges the photo with the legendary caption: DCS Kat Frank, who caught the Aston Strangler.

He raises his can and gulps the bitter drink down. He

crushes the empty can in one hand, and then again underfoot.
That's the last of the booze.

He's in training now.

Perhaps alerted by the sound, DCS Kat Frank appears at her
bedroom window, peering through the blinds.

He slips back into the shadows, smiling as he remembers
Cus D'Amato's advice:

'The punch that knocks a man out is the punch that he
doesn't see.'

Acknowledgments

I began writing this book just as *In the Blink of an Eye* went out on submission. I had no idea if a publisher would buy it, let alone if they would offer me a contract for a second. But to me the story of Kat and Lock was always a series, and as with the first book, writing the second was a necessary distraction from reality.

If book 1 was born out of grief, then book 2 was a response to the trauma our family suffered following the death of my husband from lung cancer. Watching Steve suffer for two and a half years had a profound impact on us all, but especially my two children who were just 14 and 18 when he died. I was lucky enough to find a brilliant therapist who helped me to be a better parent during some extremely challenging times. Our sessions taught me a lot about how people respond differently to grief and trauma: some people react with externally directed anger, but others internalise their rage and pain, sometimes with devastating consequences. It was on his recommendation that I read *The Body Keeps the Score,* by Bessel van der Kolk, which explores how the body remembers what the mind cannot bear to know.

During this time, the media was full of appalling stories of female murders and rape such as Sarah Everard, Bibaa Henry and Nicole Smallman, and the *Me Too* movement was growing louder and stronger. Like many women, I began to question why these terrible acts by men were too often met with calls for women to change *their* behaviour. I began to realise just how much anger women were carrying inside them, and so I asked myself, what would happen if one woman decided to let it all out?

And thus, *Leave No Trace* was born.

I wanted to pose questions about gender and trauma but without repeating damaging tropes about mental health, so I owe a special thanks to Dr Sara Northey, Consultant Forensic Psychologist, who kindly read a draft and gave thoughtful and encouraging feedback and advice. Although this is a work of fiction, my aim is to ensure that the science and technology described in the series might at least be *possible* in the near future, if not probable. With the exception of Lock's real-time conversational abilities, many aspects of AI described in the book either exist now or are on the horizon. Time will tell whether I got the balance right, but once again I am immensely grateful to Professor Giovanni Montanna, a Chair in Data Science and a Turing AI Fellow at Warwick University, for his advice and ideas. I was also fortunate enough to have two inspiring conversations with Professor Ryan Calo and Batya Friedman who have carried out thought provoking research into the ethical and legal implications of emerging technologies at the University of Washington. Huge thanks also to Professor Jo Martin, former President of the Royal College of Pathologists and Professor of Pathology at Queen Mary University of London, who was kind enough to read the whole draft and advise on the virtopsy and other pathological matters (as well as grammatical and typographical errors!). I am also grateful to Graham Bartlett who gave generous and insightful advice that helped me to keep Kat and Lock grounded in current police procedures, whilst allowing me to stretch the boundaries with AI. The advice and inspiration from all these experts were invaluable, but any errors (deliberate or otherwise) are my responsibility alone.

I wrote the first ugly draft of *Leave No Trace* in three spurts over the Easter, Summer, and Christmas holidays. I shared that draft with two trusted beta readers and friends: Lindsay Galvin and Lex Coulton, both of whom are better writers than me, and whose honest and wise advice was pivotal in bringing Kat and Lock's story to life. I cannot thank you enough, and I am just so very glad that I know you. A huge thank you also to Dr Gerry Lee who I met at Capital Crime and who very kindly offered to be an early reader. Having someone independent respond so positively to that early draft provided me with some much-needed confidence, and the clinical advice was also very helpful.

Just days after I finished the first draft of *Leave No Trace*, *In the Blink of an Eye* was published. After thirteen years of writing in secret whilst I tried (and failed) to get published in the UK, it was very strange to have a book out in the world—especially one that drew so deeply upon my own personal experiences. It was even stranger to find that so many readers, fellow authors, book sellers, bloggers and reviewers genuinely seemed to like it. I have had the most amazing year, so I want to thank all the people who welcomed my first book into the world, as without them, you probably wouldn't be holding the second.

Firstly, I must thank my amazing agent, Sue Armstrong, who has been a patient, kind, and dedicated champion throughout this long old journey, and who I can always trust to help make my books be the very best they can be. I am so lucky that another Armstrong saw the potential in *Blink,* because apart from knowing *everyone* in crime fiction, Katherine Armstrong is one of the most dedicated, passionate, insightful, and kindest people in the book world. I am both proud and thankful that she is my editor. (She also knows her way around Stirling which came in very handy at *Bloody Scotland*.) Thank you to Mina Asaam and her excellent judgement and patience throughout the editing process, and a big shout out to copy editor Ian Allen, my very own Lock, who questions absolutely *everything*, and has made me realise just how weak my grasp of time is.

A massive thanks to Jess Barratt (publicity) and Rich Vlietstra (marketing) and Matt Johnson (design) who went over and above the requirements of work to give both books the very best start in the world. We have all worked together as a team, and I have loved every minute.

Following the launch, both I and my book were caught and held up by the community of kindness in the crime writing world. Over forty authors read and provided quotes for early proofs of *In the Blink of an Eye*, something I will be forever grateful for. But I want to say a special thank you to the Lady Killers who welcomed me into their fold, supporting and championing me and my book in so many ways. You are all brilliant, talented, funny, and kind, and your friendship and advice has been a blessing and a joy. (And yes, Judith's quote on p240 was inspired by you).

I was genuinely touched by how many famous authors reached out to help me as a debut writer, such as Clare Mackintosh who invited me to do an Instagram Live with her, CJ Tudor who generously offered to share her launch party for *The Drift* with me, and Val McDermid, who made a dream come true by selecting me for her *New Blood* panel at Harrogate Crime Writing Festival.

So many amazing things happened to me in 2023, but the most incredible moment was when *In the Blink of an Eye* was selected to appear on BBC 2's *Between the Covers* programme. Watching Rob Rinder, Angela Scanlon, DJ Spooney and Cerys Matthews discuss *my* book on the telly was one of the highlights of my life. It helped my book reach an audience it would never have otherwise found and gave me some much-needed street cred with my kids and their friends. I owe a huge thank you to Amanda Ross, Pollyanne Conway, Sarah Cox, Nina Pottell and the whole team at BTC, not just for selecting my book, but for helping readers find great stories through this wonderful programme.

Because at the end of the day, it is all about the readers, and I have been blown away by how many bloggers, reviewers, book-sellers, and readers have connected with and championed Kat and Lock's story. I cannot name you all (except Fiona Sharp!), but I hope you know who you are and just how much I appreciate the time you have taken to share your views with me and others. Writing can sometimes seem futile and thankless, but the reviews, feedback, and comments we get from readers and reviewers makes it all worthwhile.

It has been an unexpected joy and privilege to attend writing festivals and meet with other readers and writers after years of being unable to due to caring responsibilities. A huge thank you to all the festival organisers who invited me to talk at Bay Tales, Ledburied, Harrogate Theakston Crime, Capital Crime, Bloody Scotland, and Fatal Shore, and to all the lovely readers who made the effort to come along. It took me a while to get the hang of signing books, and because I completely failed to sign Tracy 'with no e' Fenton's book as requested, I have named one of the characters in LNT as Tracy (with no e!).

I also named another of the characters after one of my dearest friends, Judith Edwards. I bet Geoff would have loved this, and I only wish he were here to read it. Thank you, Rob King, for your continued excitement and friendship—meeting your Spanish pupils was an absolute highlight and I hope I can entice you back for the launch. A special thanks to Lu Birch who drove us all the way to Brighton for the launch of my debut and to Fi, Su, Nicci and Leigh for a surreal and wonderful evening watching *Between the Covers*. Spike, thank you for being a very early fan (and see if you can spot your surname here . . .).

Thank you so much to my family who have put up with endless tales of publication hopes and woes, and for buying and promoting my book: Dad, Phil and Mary, Ed and Amanda, Elaine, Karen, Jade, Alex and Marlene. And a very special thanks to my mother-in-law, Helen, for being such a great role model in how to survive grief and live with kindness, acceptance, and love.

But my deepest thanks go to my children, Conor and Aurora. You are both so very brave and kind, and you teach me every day how to be a better person.

It has, without doubt, been an incredible year. At one festival, the chair asked me to pick out the best moment so far. I found myself unable to, and instead I told the truth: that every high had been laced with sorrow. After the death of his three-year-old daughter, Wordsworth wrote a poem called *Surprised by Joy*, describing the moment when he came across a field of daffodils, and turned to share that joy with his child, only to remember that she was forever gone. I have had so many moments this year when I too have turned to share them with the one person who would have truly understood. My gentle, kind, and loving husband Steve would have adored every minute of publication, and without him, truly, none of this would have been possible. So, because this is the acknowledgments, I want to end by acknowledging his continual absence and presence in all that I do.

About the Author

Jo Callaghan works full time as a senior strategist, carrying out research into the future impact of AI and genomics on the workforce. She was a student of the Writers' Academy Course (Penguin Random House) and was longlisted for the Mslexia Novel Writing Competition and Bath Novel Competition. After losing her husband to cancer in 2019 when she was just forty-nine, she started writing *In the Blink of an Eye*, her debut crime novel, which explores learning to live with loss and what it means to be human. She lives with her two children in the Midlands, where she spends far too much time tweeting as @JoCallaghanKat and is currently working on further novels in the series.

X: JoCallaghanKat
IG: jocallaghankat

About the Type

This book was set in Sabon, a typeface designed by the well-known German typographer Jan Tschichold (1902–74). Sabon's design is based upon the original letterforms of sixteenth-century French type designer Claude Garamond and was created specifically to be used for three sources: foundry type for hand composition, Linotype, and Monotype. Tschichold named his typeface for the famous Frankfurt typefounder Jacques Sabon (c. 1520–80).